THE
MIDWIFE'S
TOUCH

THE MIDWIFE'S TOUCH

a novel

SUE HARRISON

INTEGRATED MEDIA
NEW YORK

ISBN: 978-1-5040-7625-8

Published in 2023 by Shanty Cove Books/Open Road Integrated Media, Inc.
180 Maiden Lane
New York, NY 10038
www.openroadmedia.com

SHANTY COVE
BOOKS

As always for my husband Neil, for his wisdom and courage

AND

For these strong, wise women who gave me hope during hopeless times and supported me from the beginning of my writing career

Rhoda Ackerson Weyr (1938-2021)

Loretta A. Barrett (1940-2014)

Maggie Crawford

✳

In memory of my mother

Patricia Sawyer McHaney (1928–2015)
For her love, kindness, and strength

A PLEA FOR UNDERSTANDING

Dear Reader,

Within this narrative, I abandon Secrecy and claim Truth as my most potent ally, not only for me but for anyone who possesses strange abilities or misunderstood talents.

To place my story into context, please consider three remarkable women of the ancient past—the Queen of Sheba, Eleanor of Aquitaine, and Joan of Arc. The Queen of Sheba so mesmerized King Solomon that their liaison forever changed the future of northeast Africa. Eleanor of Aquitaine became the queen consort of France and then of England at a time when the two nations were bitter enemies. Joan of Arc, an uneducated peasant girl, led French soldiers to victory against the most powerful armies of Europe.

Did charisma place these women in positions of great influence? Was it intellect or beauty? I believe we must ponder another gift. Name it as you will—blessing or curse—I also possess this odd power.

I will never be a grand lady or a saint, but a cast pebble creates wide ripples.

As you read these pages, please open your mind to unexpected realities. Faith is not a feeling. It is a persistent and hard-won decision.

—China Deliverance Creed

THE
MIDWIFE'S
TOUCH

PART I

HOME

From Ma Mère's Song:

Something you covet deep to the bone.

CHAPTER ONE

TANEY COUNTY, THE SOUTHWEST MISSOURI OZARKS
DECEMBER 23, 1851—AS TOLD TO ME BY MRS. JESSE SETTLE

Milksnake Hollow glides lithe as a cottonmouth between Grit's Hill and Prophet's Mountain, following the course of Deer Lick Creek. The nearest town of notable size–Springfield— lies north, a gateway to those lands where wealth is more than a cankered wish. Within that Hollow, in an old four-square cabin, Yvette Creed writhes upon the bed, delivering her firstborn, a child of prodigious lungs and a tight grip.

Yvette's husband, Parnell Haddeus Creed, planned to celebrate the birth with a jug of moonshine, but on that day, whether due to poor planning or lack of moderation, he was down to the last sip in his last jug.

When the midwife came from the bedroom, Parnell was sitting in a kitchen chair, a chaw of tobacco tucked inside his lower lip. The midwife was Cherokee, dark as river clay. Folks called her Miz Settle. Her Christian name was Jesse.

"Your wife's good, Mr. Creed, and you got a healthy daughter."

"A daughter? Sheeit."

Miz Settle washed her hands in the basin atop the dry sink then turned and fixed him with a hard stare.

"What?"

"Midwives get paid, Mr. Creed."

"You deliver me a daughter and still expect money? And here I am, trying to make a living upon a rock acreage, half of it vertical."

"Where you live ain't my problem," said Jesse Settle. "Keeping my body and soul together, that's my prime concern."

Parnell rubbed his forehead. "How about a chicken? Yvette's got a red-feathered hen. Lays good."

The midwife sat down in the other kitchen chair. "All right. Fair deal."

Parnell went into the bedroom to see his wife. A small woman, she lay in the center of their bed, her dark curls damp with sweat, her eyes a deep glimmering black.

She tried to smile. "I lived through it."

"You done a lot of hollerin'."

Her face turned red. "It hurt."

"And for all that you birthed a girl."

"She's beautiful, Parnell."

The baby, wrapped tight in swaddling, was lying in the cradle Parnell had made from green hickory, no mean feat, hickory being an ornery wood, hard as iron. Likely to him, all babies looked the same. Maybe that's why he startled when he saw the child for the first time. She had dark eyes like her mother, but her hair shone pale, nearly white. Parnell reached into the cradle and picked her up.

"She's got my hair," he said.

"She does."

He kissed the baby's forehead and swayed back and forth. "You know I expected a boy."

"It's not her fault she's a girl.

"True. Anyway, she's pretty as a china plate. Never seen a better baby. For a girl, I mean."

Yvette held out her arms. "Give her here, Parnell."

He turned his back on his wife and went out to the front room. "Right pretty, ain't she?" he said to the midwife.

"She is."

He tucked the baby into the crook of his arm and walked over to the pie safe where they kept their crockery and tins. He took out a small Spode plate, blue and white with a gold rim. In the center of that plate was the image of a strange-looking house like none ever known in the state of Missouri.

He held up the plate so the midwife could see. "My wife's prized possession, belonged to her mother." He carried the baby and the plate to the bedroom doorway and said to his wife, "She's prettier than this here plate of yourn, Yvette. Don't you think?"

"Parnell," she said, drawing out his name like a plea.

"What do you love most, Yvette? This baby or this plate?"

Her eyes went to the plate first, and he raised his arm as if to dash that Spode china against the foot of the bed, but she said, "Why, neither one, Parnell. I love you most. Maybe I don't tell you enough."

"Maybe you don't." He took extra care, though, when he gave her the baby.

Yvette turned the child toward her husband. "Look here, little one. That's your papa, a brave, strong man who will protect you from anyone with intent to harm."

"Hell, Yvette," said Parnell, "why do you always think somebody's going to do you harm? This here is Taney County. We're all good folk."

She gave him a trembling smile and set the baby to suckling.

Parnell watched a moment then said, "Here's her name—*China.* That's what we'll call her."

Yvette made a face.

"I thought you'd like that," said Parnell.

"Angèle is a beautiful name."

"Your ma's name? I ain't gonna have no daughter of mine named after some fancy French woman. The baby's name is China. I said that and I meant that. Ya hear?"

She sighed. "I hear."

"I did want a boy," Parnell said. "Ya know, to carry on *my* name." He lifted the Spode plate, smiled at it.

His wife's face took on a look of resignation, her mouth set in a grim line.

Parnell dropped the plate. It broke into three pieces. "I'll leave that for you to clean up, Yvette."

He nudged the pieces under the bed with the toe of his boot and left the room, closing the door. He looked at the midwife. "You know what a man wants at a time like this?"

"I don't believe I ever wasted a thought upon that," she said.

"You're uppity for all your Injun blood."

She didn't reply.

"A man wants shine. That's what a man wants. Not any old shine, but the pure stuff, stout as oak, clear as water, Mort Dibbler's shine."

At the dry sink he batted aside the flour sack that curtained off the storage area. He pulled out three jugs, uncorked each, and lifted them in turn to his mouth. "Empty," he said. He heaved a giant sigh and dug into the biscuit tin where Yvette kept his money. He opened his palm toward the midwife.

"Twenty cents. All I got to my name. Whatever does my ol' woman do with all my money? She pay you without me knowing?"

Jesse Settle stood up. "She did not."

"Twenty cents won't hardly buy a jug of the worst stuff, but maybe Old Man Dibbler will give me a deal when I tell him about the baby." Parnell donned his red-wool coat and walked out on the front porch.

He left the door open, cold air funneling in, and Jesse saw him stop with a jerk.

"What the hell?" He started laughing. Then he shouted, "Come out here, Miz Settle. I need me a witness."

Jesse Settle wasn't a young woman; she wasn't an old woman either, but her legs ached, and she was tired. On the other hand, Parnell Creed owned a quick temper. She joined him on the porch where she saw a pyramid of gallon jugs. Parnell was counting out loud. Fourteen total. He grabbed the top jug, jostled it, and said, "It's full. You brung these?"

"How could I bring 'em? I been in this cabin for twelve hours with your wife. You know that."

He uncorked the jug and took a swig. "Dibbler shine."

The sharp yeasty tang rising from the cork bung told her he was right.

"You know what, Miz Settle? I'm thinking this is a mean prank. Somebody stacked them jugs on the porch right when Yvette was workin' hard to push out my baby. They're stole, and I ain't about to hang for something I didn't do. You yourself know I'm an honest man."

She did not deign to agree. "Take them back to Mort. Maybe he'll give ya a reward."

"How'm I gonna do that? I don't own no buggy, and if I load them on my mule, he's likely to throw a snit and break 'em all."

"Carry over one or two. Tell Mort he can pick up the rest."

Parnell raised the jug in both hands and took another drink. "If that ain't a joyous sup, I don't know what is."

He sat down in the rocker Yvette kept on the porch. That year of 1851, December 23 fell into the new-moon-time of the month. Night already lay dark as pitch over the Hollow. Jesse Settle could not see Parnell's face, but she could tell his next words came to her through a smile.

"I got me a pretty wife and a new daughter. I'm a blessed man, Miz Settle. I wish I didn't break that Spode plate."

"It weren't a necessary thing," Jesse said.

Parnell snorted but gave no contradicting argument. "I'll buy Yvette another one someday. When she gives me a boy."

He drank more shine, then set the jug beside the rocker and picked up two full jugs by their curled handles. "I'm off to the Dibbler place. Tell my wife."

When Miz Settle was satisfied that Yvette and her baby were well recovered, she put the red-feathered chicken in a flour sack, slung it over her shoulder, and took for home. A thin glaze of snow crusted the ground, and it picked up the faint glow of stars. In her right hand, she carried her punched-tin lantern, which cast a fitful light. The hen squawked every now and again, and Jesse tried to allay its fears by crooning a song. She walked about a mile before she came upon Parnell Creed. He'd shed his wool jacket and left it in a heap on the ground.

When he saw her he said, "I worked myself into a sweat. I'll get my coat on the way home." He set down the jugs. "Them two handles is about to break through my finger bones. Maybe I should drink some off."

"If you get drunk," Jesse told him, "you'll wind up lost."

"Lost? Me? I been wandering these woods since I were two years old." He already sounded drunk. "Here, you carry one."

"I got my chicken and I got my doctoring bag and I got my lantern. I ain't carrying no jug of shine."

"Shouldn't of gave you that chicken."

He made a grab toward the flour sack. Miz Settle sidestepped, and he fell. She went on ahead, stopping when she was out of reach. "You all right?"

"Yeah."

"You need to go back home, Parnell. It's too cold out. I'm your witness that you didn't steal that shine."

"Just what I need, a Red Injun for my witness. You think they'd believe either one of us?"

"Maybe not you," said Jesse.

He snarled, got back up on his feet, and took a few running steps toward her. She easily outpaced him. She had no intention of dealing with a drunken Parnell Creed, him being known for his intoxicated violence.

"God helps children and fools," she said to her chicken. "Maybe he helps drunks, too." That night, she wasted no further thought upon Parnell Creed.

Early the next morning, Mort Dibbler, the old man himself, found Parnell lying in a foot of new snow half a mile inside the Dibbler property line. Two jugs of shine sat on the ground next to him, each well-sampled. A wide smile was frozen to Parnell's cold dead face.

On January 11, 1852, the Widow Creed dedicated her new daughter to the Lord during the Sunday morning service at the Milksnake Baptist Church. As per her late husband's request, she christened the girl China, but she added a middle name she deemed appropriate.

The congregation's gray-haired widows—twelve strong on a healthy Sunday—agreed that, in their long Lord-blessed lives, China Deliverance Creed was the most beautiful baby they'd ever laid their eyes upon.

CHAPTER TWO

CHINA DELIVERANCE CREED, AGE 6 YEARS, 8 MONTHS
AUGUST 1858

I lie awake on my prickly straw tick. The heat of the day lingers. I got into chiggers that morning, and they left a ring of welts under the waistband of my pantalets. Ma Mère painted their bites with coal oil, her medicine for every malady, and the smell of it in the close hot space pummels my skull into a fierce ache.

During the warm months, if Ma Mère and I aren't camping out in our cave, I keep my straw tick near the attic vent, which lets in an Ozark breeze. One of the vent slats has warped, and the gap gives me a view out. I like to see the fireflies beam their tail-lamps in the dark.

As I watch, Ma Mre walks into the clearing twixt our cabin and the cowshed. I recognize the woman who comes to her from the woods, and I clamp my hand over my mouth to hold in my surprise. Miz Jesse Settle. I've never heard much good about Miz Settle, maybe because of her dark Indian skin, or maybe because she's rumored to be a Goomer Doctor, and thus a woman of odd powers.

Goomer Doctors are necessary. After all, if some wicked crone throws a spell, you need to have that goomering removed. Yet, who wants to spend time with an old woman who works in a battleground haunted by hags, haints, and booger dogs?

The minute Miz Settle appears, Ma Mère escorts her to the cowshed. A crack in the door lets out the feeble glow from Miz Settle's punched tin lantern. She and Ma Mère stay in there for a goodly long time.

When my mother returns to the house, I slide from my straw tick and spy down at her through the gap between the attic floor and the stovepipe. She draws a handful of coins from her skirt pocket and dumps them in the biscuit tin, and then, with a great sigh, she goes to bed.

The next morning, when Ma Mère is milking our cow, I climb down from the attic and flit around the cabin, battering like a blue bottle fly, trying to detect any change due to Miz Settle's visit. All seems in order until I open the lid of Ma Mère's sewing box, and there lies a square white cotton bag, no larger than the palm of my hand. I drop the lid like it's poker hot. That Goomer Doctor must've paid my mother to sew charm bags. Ma Mère and I don't wear charm bags, although she does believe in the medicinal properties of asafetida, camphor, and green pennies. I myself hold a great dislike for asafetida, purely for its stink alone.

I'm still standing there by the sewing box when Ma Mère comes in. She's hefting a full milk can, carrying it by the handles, the weight of the thing forcing her into a straddling walk, one foot on either side of it.

"Stay out of there, China," she says as she sets down the can.

"I saw you last night with Miz Settle, Maman. Are you making charm bags for her?"

"It's nobody's business if I do or I don't." She holds up her hands. The knuckles are gnarled with rheumatism, her fingers heading off in peculiar directions from their middle and top joints. "I can't make bobbin lace for Mr. James's store like I used to. I can scarcely tat. I need some way to support us. Miz Settle gets good money for her charm bags, and you know she's a Goomer Doctor, which means she's doing the Lord's work, no matter what anyone else might say. And I'm doing the Lord's work when I keep us fed."

The held-back weeping sound in her voice scares me. "Teach me to make lace, Maman. Teach me. I'll do it."

She smiles, which eases my heart. "I will teach you, but not yet. Your fingers aren't long enough and neither are your fingernails."

I spread my fingers wide. The nails are bitten to the quick. With bobbin lace you need long fingernails to separate the threads.

That evening, we sit out on the front porch, me on the steps and Ma Mère in the rocker. We wave fans of folded newspaper to keep away mosquitoes. I say a silent prayer that God will grow my fingers and help me stop biting my nails. I've finished the third repeat of that prayer when Ma Mère begins to sing. She sings in our secret language, words that are ours alone, and I am not to speak them to anyone except her, nor am I to say *Ma Mère* or *Maman* when others might hear. More than once, I've asked why. She always says, "Secrets are for keeping."

Ma Mère's singing, trembling and deep-of-throat, sends shivers up my arms. When she's done with the hymns, she says, "One last song," and it's ever the same, and I always join in.

> *Something you covet deep to the bone.*
> *But nothing alive with will of its own.*
> *Nothing too large. The earth stakes its claim.*
> *Nothing unseen. The eyes play the game.*

Afterward, I fetch a comb and a brush, and Ma Mère starts in on my hair, which flows in cream-colored curls to my waist. Hair-brushing is the only time my mother comes nigh unto touching me. She never holds my hand. She never kisses my face. She seldom gives me a hug. Even if I cut myself or scrape my knees, she keeps a rag between her fingers and my skin. I long for her touch, and, in that regard, I live a starving life.

In September, Ma Mère sends me to school. I walk the three-mile trail to town each morning. Each afternoon I trudge home. I entertain myself during those long walks by whistling and chattering to the birds. I'm good enough that they answer me, another secret language, but one that even Ma Mère does not speak.

The schoolhouse is located at the eastern end of the town of Milksnake. We little ones, first grade through third, are taught in the cloakroom, which is long and narrow with pegs on the walls for coats and caps. Shelves above hold our lunch buckets. A two-door cabinet stores primers for reading. We youngers have no desks, only benches, and most of us do not own a slate.

Our teacher, Miss Otten, speaks with a stutter, which the older children mimic when she's not close enough to hear. Her eyes are brown like her hair and round like her face, but those eyes carry kindness.

The only new thing I have for my first year of school is a pair of blue mittens Ma Mère knit with ribbed cuffs that almost reach my elbows. My wool jacket, cut down from an old red barn coat, is stained and faded, but the mitts brighten it nigh unto beautiful. After our first snow, Ma Mère lets me wear them to school.

Within sight of the schoolhouse, I cross my arms over my chest, the palms of my hands flat against my shoulders to show off my mittens' high ribbed cuffs, but no one seems to notice. The boys are playing a game with a black leather ball, big around as a baby's head. The girls gather in a huddle near the door. A grade-three girl stands in the middle. Her name is Mary Preck but everybody except the teacher calls her Polly. Her yellow hair makes my nearly white braids seem pale and dull; her blue eyes shine brighter than my brown; my skin compared to hers is far too dark from the sun. She owns three dresses plus lace-trimmed pantalets that peek out from underneath, clean and starched.

I push my way up the steps toward Mary-Polly who holds a doll in her arms, not a rag doll but a real store-bought wax-head doll. In Mr. James's general store, I've seen dolls for sale, but nothing like Mary-Polly's. That doll purses her pink lips into a bud and gazes at the world with perfect blue eyes. Her little feet are shod in black leather shoes with white uppers. She wears a pink coat that buttons up the front and a frothy blue dress underneath. Her yellow hair curls like lamb's fleece.

Mary-Polly shows us the doll's lace-trimmed drawers and her pink cloth belly. I can't breathe for the want of that doll. When I'm finally able to take my eyes off her, I notice that I've crowded in beside my friend, Hazel.

"I never-ever seen a doll like that," Hazel says. She smiles, and I wonder how she can, since the doll belongs to Mary-Polly and not to her.

Hazel grabs my hand, and I notice she's not wearing mittens. I take off my left mitt and give it to her. Then we stare at Mary-Polly's doll, each of us wearing one mitten and with our bare hands clasped for warmth. After school, I let Hazel wear that mitten home with the promise she'll bring it back the next day. Then I make the long trek to our cabin.

The smell of new-baked bread greets me while I'm still on the porch. I open the door with a smile on my face. Ma Mère spreads a warm slice with lard, and I eat it as soon as I'm out of my coat. While I eat, my mother pulls the blue mitten from my coat pocket then searches for the other.

Her face turns red. "China Deliverance Creed, surely you did not already lose one of your new mittens?" Although, Ma Mère's accent is barely discernible most of the time, when she's upset, her words take on the cadence of our secret language. "Do you know how much that yarn cost?"

"No Ma'am, I don't know how much the yarn cost, and no Ma'am, I didn't lose my mitten." Despite the stern look on her face, I can tell she almost smiles at my answer, despite my sassiness. "I lent one of my mittens to Hazel. She don't have none."

"She doesn't have *any*."

"No, Ma'am, she don't."

"China, that was truly kind of you, but you're my child, and Hazel is not. I must provide for my daughter first. You understand?"

"Yes, Ma'am."

"You could've frozen your fingers. Hold your hands over the stove until they're warm."

I do her bidding, although my hands are already warm from that slice of bread. As Ma Mère says, arguments are truly won when they're avoided.

That night after our lard, jam, and bread supper, my mother starts knitting a new pair of mittens. For Hazel, she tells me. She crimps her lips as she always does when the pain of her rheumatism flares, but her four needles flash quick as sunfish. She makes the blue ribbed cuffs first and then knits the rest of each mitten with stripes of whatever leftover colors she has until I worry that Hazel's mittens might be prettier than mine. By morning, there, on the kitchen table, lay a pair of striped mittens with bright red thumbs.

"Now you take these to Hazel and be sure you get your other mitten back."

On the way to school, I put my blue mitt into my pocket and wear Hazel's. When Hazel sees me walking down the iced mud of Milksnake's main street, she comes running, her hands palm-to-palm in a prayerful fold and stuffed into my other blue mitten.

"You got another pair?"

"Naw. Ma made them for you."

She stands there with her mouth wide open, and finally she says, "Them be the most beautiful mitts in the whole of Milksnake Holler, China."

I pull my blue mitten from her hands and tuck it under my arm. She puts on the striped ones. As we walk to the schoolhouse, Hazel says, "This is the best day of my whole life."

"They're only a pair of mitts made of leftover yarn."

"But they're from *you*. And lookee here." She opens the top button of her ragged jacket. Snugged up against her chest lies a doll like Mary-Polly's, the same pink coat, the same curly yellow hair, the same wax face. "It was in my bed this morning under the quilt. Pa come home last night from working four months on the railroads up in New York State. When I showed the doll to Ma, she said he must've brung it. I never-ever thought I'd have such a thing."

I'm on fire with jealousy, but the pure joy in Hazel's face soon converts me to selflessness. She walks halfway up the schoolhouse steps, takes off her striped mittens, and hands them to me. Then she slowly pulls that doll from under her coat. She holds it up, face out. Anyone who looks our way can see it.

Then I spy Mary-Polly walking down the road toward the school.

Hazel shouts, "Polly! Look! I got one, too. My pa brung it for me."

Mary-Polly breaks into a run, her face burning bright red. When she gets to Hazel, she grabs the doll and begins to scream until even the boys stop playing and turn to see what's happening.

Hazel opens her mouth, but not one sound comes out, and I realize what Mary-Polly is screaming. "You stole my doll. You stole it. It was gone this morning when I woke up. You stole it!"

The teacher comes outside. "W-w-what's wrong?" She has to ask again before Mary-Polly stops yelling.

"She stole my doll, Miss Otten."

"Who stole your doll?"

"Hazel."

"It's mine," Hazel says in a soft, halting voice. "My pa brung it for me."

The teacher looks at Mary-Polly who makes her eyes go wide. "My doll was gone this morning, Miss Otten. Ask my mother. She's mad as a hornet."

"You b-b-believe Hazel's doll belongs to you?" the teacher asks.

"Yes, Ma'am." Mary-Polly tips the doll upside down. "Look. See?" She points to three initials embroidered on the petticoat in a pink-thread script. *MLP.* "Mary Luna Preck, my initials."

Hazel's face turns white as if every drop of her blood has drained out. Then she gags and throws up over the stairway rail.

"See, she stole it," says Mary-Polly.

The teacher gently clasps Hazel's two long braids and holds them back out of the way. "When did you get the d-d-doll, Hazel?"

By then, Hazel is bringing up yellow bile, and I answer for her. "She woke up with it in her bed this morning, Miss Otten. She thought her pa brought it. Yesterday, he came home from working four months on the railroad."

The teacher turns to Mary-Polly. "You can rest assured Hazel did not walk a mile through the woods in the middle of the night to s-steal your doll."

Mary-Polly turns to me and stabs her finger into my cheek. Her nail cuts my skin. "Then she did it. China Creed took it. She's a thief like her pa was."

I shout into her face. "He was not!"

"How do you think he died?"

"That is enough!" the teacher says. "M-M-Mary, take the doll home and leave it there."

I swipe my hand against my cheek, and it comes away bloody, but the hurt is nothing compared to Mary-Polly's accusation. My pa was a thief?

Mary-Polly turns on her heel and flounces away. The teacher helps Hazel into the schoolhouse. I walk down to the yard and scoop up a riff of snow, press it against my cheek until the bleeding stops.

Hazel stays at school the whole day, and, when she leaves for home, she puts on the mittens my mother made, but her every breath sounds like a sigh. That evening, I tell Ma Mère what happened. I expect her to jump in on Hazel's side, but she only scurries around the house with a wet dust rag and runs it over every log in the walls and even stands on a chair to wipe the elbow of the stovepipe. Cleaning like that, it's what she does when she's upset.

Finally, she says, "That Polly Preck is a rude girl, but I think you and I need a new rule."

"What kind a rule?"

"A rule to ensure no one ever thinks you're a thief."

"I ain't a thief, Maman."

"I know, but you need to be careful, China. Don't be touching other people's belongings. Actually, it would be best if you don't touch other people. Touching is rude."

I want to ask about games like London Bridge and Red Rover, but there's something else I need to bring up. "Polly Preck said my pa was a thief. She said that's why he died."

"He was not a thief, China."

"Then how did he die?"

"He died happy. That's how he died."

CHAPTER THREE

Spring comes to us late, and we can't put in our cold weather crops until April. We dig up bulrush shoots from the creek swales to tide us over, but every night I go to bed hungry. One night I dream that the moon squeezes through the gable vent and floats into the attic.

"Open your mouth," it says, bold as a raven.

Who would argue with the moon? I open my mouth, and it pops down my throat. It fills my belly as if I'd eaten a fine meal. With my stomach full, I sleep so hard that the next morning Ma Mère has to call me three times before I wake up.

I don't bring a lunch bucket to school that day, just a handful of dandelion greens in my skirt pocket. For supper, Ma Mère cooks our greens in salted water. After, out on the porch, she doesn't sing but only sits and rocks.

To fill the space where music belongs, I say, "Last night I dreamed the moon came into my room, Maman."

She smiles at me. "Were you afraid?"

"Me? No. I ate it up."

"And what did it taste like?"

"Butter and cream."

Her eyes get worried. "Oh China," she says in her softest voice. "Oh, my baby girl."

She cups her hands around my face and kisses me three times, her touch sifting into my soul as fine and pure as white flour.

The next morning when I come down from the attic, I stop in amazement. Our kitchen table overflows with fresh bread and cheese and sparkling jars of deep red jam.

"Maman," I say, "where—"

She hands me a slice of bread. "We have good neighbors."

In May, our cow births a little brown heifer calf. That means we have milk again. We harvest new peas. We walk the pole beans, chopping out weeds. School is over, and it looks to be a good summer, but three days into June all things turn inside out.

It's early morning when the Goomer Doctor walks into our cabin without even a rap upon the door. Maman is still in the barn, milking, and I sit chewing on a hard biscuit. Seeing the old woman suddenly in front of me, I draw in and choke. She slaps her hand against my back to get me breathing.

"Big bites," she says in a rusty voice, "not good."

"You scart me, is all."

"You be a rude child, I see." When she says *rude*, she softly rolls the *r*.

"No, Ma'am. I'm very polite." Of course my contradiction proves she's correct. I amend my statement. "Mostly, I'm polite. Except when I choke."

At that moment, Ma Mère comes inside, a bucket of milk in each hand. She doesn't look at all surprised to see the Goomer Doctor.

"China, you're eating but haven't offered Miz Settle anything?"

I feel ornery enough that I very nearly plop the remains of my biscuit in front of Miz Settle, but the look in my mother's eyes tells me it won't be worth the whipping.

I get up and offer Miz Settle my chair. "Please rest a spell," I say.

She sits down and pushes back her poke bonnet until it hangs by the strings. Everything about her is faded—her dress, her bonnet, her pinafore apron, even her dark skin. But her eyes are as alive as any eyes I've ever seen.

I fetch a cup and saucer and set them on the table. I open the coffee-pot where it boils atop the stove and trickle cold water down the spout to settle the grounds. Then I haul the pot over and pour her a cup.

You can tell by the wrinkles around Miz Settle's mouth that her teeth are long gone, and I worry about offering her a hard biscuit. Ma Mère must have the same thought because she takes out the last biscuit, crumbles it into a bowl, adds a dollop of blackberry jam, and floods it with cream. My mouth waters at all that goodness.

"Thankee," Miz Settle says and eats the biscuit while Ma Mère goes up the ladder to the attic. She returns toting a fat pillowcase and my wool blanket. Something of her plan begins to dig its way into my brain, but I'm too horrified to mount a defense.

She meets my eyes. "China, you will spend the rest of the summer with Miz Settle. Every girl needs learning of various types and what Miz Settle will teach you is something never taught in a schoolhouse."

I set my hands on my hips and say, "No, Ma'am, I won't go."

"You have no choice in this matter, China."

"You can teach me, Mama. You know everything. We can go to our cave and you can teach me about bats. We can walk in the woods, and I'll sing you birdsongs." When she pays me no mind, I turn my words into insults. I call Miz Settle all the names I've heard at school. A dirty Indian, a flat-foot old woman, a witch—*sorcière* in our secret language. Ma Mère looks so shocked that it takes her a minute to slap her hand across my mouth. She's not all that gentle about it.

"You hush, child. Hush right now!"

I don't mean to cry, but tears pop out of my eyes before I can stop them.

She leans close and whispers, "You're hurting Miz Settle's feelings."

I pry her hand away. "You're hurting my feelings."

I see by the set of Ma Mère's mouth that if need be she will drag me to Miz Settle's place. I've pitched prior battles against her and never reaped anything but a good hard tanning.

"I'll miss you," she tells me.

The tremor in her voice gives me the courage to say, "I will not miss you."

Through all this Miz Settle remains in her chair, looking off toward the open door that leads into Ma Mère's bedroom, but, as I speak those mean words, that old woman, quick as a jack-snipe, jumps up and sets her hand around the back of my neck. With the strength of her grip alone, she turns me toward my mother. "You won't never in your life have nobody else who loves you as much as your mama does. You will miss her, and you will tell her that. Ya hear me?"

I gag, and she releases her hold. "I will miss you, Mother," I murmur.

While I wash the dishes, Miz Settle and Ma Mère go sit on the front porch, discussing something. Rules, I expect. Then, with my mother's blessing, that old Goomer Doctor leads me into the deep woods where I'm quite sure the two of us will live no better than rats in a barn during the remainder of that long, horrible summer.

Miz Settle's acreage is situated closer to town than Ma Mère's, but in a different direction, the walk between the two cabins being nigh unto five miles. The last mile is an overgrown path through bramble and willow wisp. During most of our journey, I lag behind, but, when greenery closes in from both sides, I hurry until I'm only a step away. If I get lost I'm not certain Miz Settle would put forth the effort to find me, and who knows when she might get around to telling Ma Mère?

The incoming sound of a beast whining and slobbering gathers a chokehold on my courage. A heavy-footed hound, fearsomely black, jumps at Miz Settle from the brush. I drop my pillowcase and blanket, and I crouch with my arms wrapped around my head. I have no doubt it's a booger dog, big as a half-grown calf and with a neck as wide as a boar's.

"Git up, girl. Bessie won't hurt ya."

I think back to what I know about booger dogs, which is not much, but I've heard they're vicious. I peek out at the hound. She's licking Miz Settle with a happy tongue, her tail wagging into a blur. Booger dogs carry the devil's curses. This dog looks a mite too cheerful for that.

"I raised her from a pup," says Miz Settle.

I stand up. If Bessie was once a pup, I'm safe. Everybody knows booger dogs come into the world full-grown. I hold out my hand, and the dog stretches toward me, keeping her feet in the same place but inching close with her muzzle. I start to laugh.

"See? She's scart of you, too."

"I thought she was a booger dog."

"And why did you think that?"

"She's pure black."

"That ain't no reason to make such a judgment."

"I'm sorry, Miz Settle."

"Don't tell me. Tell Bessie."

I offer Bessie my best apology, and she looks into my eyes like she's trying to see if I've spoken true. Then she smiles wide enough to show me all her teeth, and that's the first minute of our friendship.

Bessie leads us to Miz Settle's clearing, if you could call it a clearing. The weeds look more trampled than pulled. The cabin is about the same size as Ma Mère's and also has a front porch, but the whole thing leans to the east like a leeward tree.

"It ain't much," says Miz Settle, "but we *Aniyunwiya* have learned that it's best not to look more prosperous than our neighbors."

"What's *Aniyunwiya*?" I ask, stumbling over that long word. "I thought you were a Red Injun."

"That's what white folks call us. We call ourselves *Aniyunwiya*."

"So Injuns are really *Aniyun—*?" I've forgotten the ending.

"*Aniyunwiya*," she says. "Some Injuns are. Some have other names. Not all Injuns are alike. The same as white people. Not all white people alike, are they?"

"No. My mother says that some white people are good and some white people are bad."

"That about sums it up for everybody, I'd guess."

She climbs the porch steps then points at a wide board in the porch flooring, "Don't step there."

I don't.

The door is bound by leather hinges and has a latch rather than a knob. Inside, the floor is red clay well swept. Her furniture is only a rocker and a dry sink and a table with one chair. The bed is in the front room, too, but it's not really furniture, only a pile of blankets and rags with space for one person. I don't want to share a bed with the Goomer Doctor, especially a bed like that. I glance at the ceiling of rough-sawn boards. A square opening gives me hope for an attic.

"Lookee here," Miz Settle says and reaches as high as she can to catch hold of a peeled log that's lying with its end sticking out over the attic hole. She hauls it down until the base of the log sits on the floor. The log itself is about a hand length in diameter, and somebody cut notches in each side. "That's your ladder. There's a bed up there for you."

I give those notches a serious study, but I cannot for the life of me figure out how they work as a ladder. Miz Settle slips off her shoes—which are moccasins—and clamors halfway up, curving her feet around the sides of the log and using the notches for footholds.

She gets down and looks at me. "See? It's easier if you go fast."

I would like to tell her that it's easier if you use a ladder, but I'm grateful to have my own sleeping place. I spit into my hands and grab hold of that log, pulling myself up through the strength of my arms rather than relying on my feet in those ragged notches. On my second try, I get to the top, and Miz Settle claps for me like I was a trick dog.

I already miss Ma Mère enough that my chest wheezes when I breathe, but the attic is a good place, clean and smelling fresh. The moment I notice the feather bed, I know Miz Settle gave me her own, and my heart softens with the ache of that. I think about her bed of rags, and a welling of gratitude lifts my soul.

"This bed is real soft," I call down.

She looks up at me, and her crab-apple face cracks into a smile. I hear Bessie whine, and I understand that she wants me to come back down, which I do.

I'm barely down from the attic when Miz Settle hands me an empty tin can and a bucket and sends me out to pick strawberries. I walk onto the porch and step in the middle of that wide board. It flips up, whaps me on the nose, and my left leg drops down through the hole. I scream, and Miz Settle hurries outside.

When my leg's out of the hole, she points to the porch step. "Sit down there. Dratted board. I'd fix it if I had a few eight-penny nails."

I wait while she fetches a cloth and a bowl of tepid water. I've scraped my shin from knee to ankle. She washes the blood from my leg and dabs on coal oil. She inspects my flattened nose, which is stuffed up with blood, but she says it's not broken.

Miz Settle disappears into the cabin. The dog stands beside me and sets her chin on my shoulder, which tells me she understands pain. When Miz Settle returns, she has a charm bag in her hand. The bag is puffed up, full of something, and she loops the carry string around my neck. It hangs nearly to my waist.

"Tuck it under your shirt."

I don't really want it next to my skin, but I do as she says. "Tansy and goldenseal to drive out infection," she tells me.

Tansy and goldenseal don't seem too close to witchery. I thank her and pat the lump of the charm bag where it rests against my belly.

"Off with ya, then," Miz Settle says. "And take the dog. She knows where the berries grow, and she won't let you get lost. Fill the bucket, but eat some, too. That'll be your mid-day dinner."

My dinner? I wonder what Ma Mère will think when I return home being merely a rack of bones.

We head out, me following Bessie. Anytime I lag behind, she waits, but, when we come upon the strawberry clearing, Bessie gobbles the berries from the plants almost faster than I can pick them. When I have the bucket filled, and I've eaten my share, Bessie leads me back to the cabin. I carry the berries up the porch steps to Miz Settle who's grinding some kind of dried greenery with a mortar and pestle.

"Well, I see I have myself an expert," she says, smiling, and we spend the rest of the day making strawberry jam.

For six days Bessie and I pick strawberries and help Miz Settle make jam. I have to shake my longing for Ma Mère out of my bones every now and again, but it's not a terrible life. The seventh day is Sunday, and to my surprise Miz Settle takes me to church. Ma Mère is waiting for us, and I'm grateful for the chance to sit beside her. Bessie came, too, but she's not allowed past the front doors. During the long prayer, I hear her high-pitched whine, which continues on through the sermon, and I have to work hard to keep my face solemn.

During one of the songs, Mary-Polly Preck turns and cuts her eyes toward Miz Settle. Then she gives me a smirk. On our way out after the last prayer, she presses close and whispers into my ear. "What're you doing with that old witch?"

"She's not a witch. She's a Goomer Doctor. She does God's work."

I don't wait to hear what Mary-Polly has to say about that. Instead, I hurry past the folks who are shaking hands with the preacher. A chestnut tree grows stately next to the church, and I stand underneath, soaking up its shade. Unfortunately, Mary-Polly joins me.

"My mother says she's a witch."

"Takes one to know one."

"You shut your mouth, China Creed."

I bend down and pick a blade of grass, arrange it upright between my thumbs. When I blow through it, the grass makes a thin, high whistle.

"Witch, witch, witch," Mary-Polly hisses.

Bessie gets up from the place she claimed on the dark side of the church and stands between me and Mary-Polly.

"And that's her booger dog."

"Leave her alone. She's a good hound."

Mary-Polly starts her chant again. "Witch, witch, witch."

Other children crowd close. I know them all from school, and they shout that wicked name as if a ruckus will prove them right. When

Tommy Belnap takes up the chant, my heart cracks. In my dreams of becoming a wife and mother, Tommy Belnap with his black curly hair always stands at my side.

Mary-Polly scoops up a handful of pebbles and begins pitching them at Bessie. The dog turns mournful eyes toward me.

"You quit that, Mary-Polly!" I shout.

She picks up more stones, bigger ones, and Bessie hides her head in my skirt.

"Ya got no call going after a hound, Polly," says Cordell Smith, a ginger-haired boy, scrawny but fearless.

Tommy Belnap squints one eye. "Cordell's right, Polly." He leads the boys away.

Mary-Polly sticks her tongue out at them as they go. Then she says to me, "Some dog she is, big chicken."

"She's the bravest dog ever. She's not even afraid of a wild boar."

Mary-Polly flings a large stone that hits my shin, the one that's still sore from my fall on Miz Settle's porch. I remember Mary-Polly's meanness to my friend Hazel. I consider how she sneers at girls with patched clothes. My blood pumps into a hot fury, and, when she crouches for another stone, I go after her.

Since she's bent over, my hands land first on her fancy white straw hat. I rip it off her head and throw it to the ground. Mary-Polly stands up real quick, and the top of her head meets the base of my chin. Bone strikes bone, and we both scream loud enough that the adults leaving the church turn to look.

Rubbing my chin, I back away from her. "You stop throwing rocks at me and my dog!"

"I didn't throw anything at that dog. I didn't throw anything at you." Her hands are full of stones.

Mr. James, the store owner, comes over and clasps Mary-Polly's shoulder. "Drop those stones, young lady."

Quick as scat, she puts a look of total innocence on her face. "I wasn't going to throw them."

Mr. James tucks a finger under my jaw and lifts my head. My chin drips blood. "It looks like you already have."

He hands me a handkerchief, and I press it to the cut. "Go home, Mary," he says.

"My mother—"

"Should be very unhappy with you."

At that moment, her parents come out of the church. Mrs. Preck, dressed fancy, clings tightly to her husband's arm. Judge Preck is the most famous man in our town, him traveling to far places like Forsyth and Springfield to make judgments. Mary-Polly flounces away, and Miz Settle's dog leans against my legs. I try to return the handkerchief to Mr. James.

"Keep it." He gives me a crooked smile. "I'd stay away from that girl if I was you."

"I'll try my best, Sir."

He gazes toward the church door. Ma Mère comes out, along with Mr. James's wife, Heptabah. She's carrying a little daughter in her arms, and her belly is swollen with another baby that looks to be coming soon.

"I thankee, Mr. James," I tell him.

He nods at me and strides toward his wife, although I notice something strange. He's not looking at her. His eyes are fixed on my mother, and I realize that, despite her worn clothes, Ma Mère's pure beauty shines through. She walks past Mr. James with nary a look and comes directly to me. She takes the hankie from my hand and spits on it then blots it against my chin.

"What happened?"

"Mary-Polly and me cracked heads. Mr. James gave me this handkerchief. He said I could keep it."

"That was very kind." Ma Mère looks at Mr. James, and, when she catches his eye, she mouths *thank you*. Then she turns her attention back to me.

"Mary-Polly was throwing stones at Miz Settle's dog, and she was calling me a witch. Is Miz Settle teaching me to be a witch?"

Ma Mère looks amazed. "Why of course not, China. Why would you think that?"

"She gave me a charm bag." I pat the bag, where it hangs at my belly.

"I'm sure it's only for good luck, China. Miz Settle is a Goomer Doctor. She's not a witch. She breaks witch-spells."

About that time, Miz Settle joins us. She squints at me and then at Bessie. Nodding slowly, she looks off down the street toward Mary-Polly, and I see she's figuring things out.

I'm hoping my mother will invite Miz Settle and me over for dinner, but Ma Mère only smiles and says, "Be a good girl. I'll see you next Sunday."

I clasp her gloved hand and lean close. "Maman, please, can I come home?"

"Not yet," she whispers and kisses the top of my poke bonnet.

Ma Mère heads west out of town. Miz Settle and Bessie and I head east. Pain squeezes my heart, and I have to sigh a hundred times. I try to believe Ma Mère is right about the witchery, but my life with Miz Settle seems odd beyond understanding. What if Ma Mère is wrong? What if I am turning into a witch? How do I turn myself back into a regular girl?

CHAPTER FOUR

The next day, Miz Settle lines up seven small white bowls and gives me a handful of muslin charm bags. She points at the first bowl, which is filled with twelve short crooked pieces of green mistletoe branches. You can tell they're mistletoe because a white ring marks each joint where the branch heads off in another direction. As Ma Mère would say, mistletoe branches are *zickzack*.

"Lay one stick at the bottom of each bag," Miz Settle tells me. "When dishonest folk try to fool you about something, mistletoe imparts the wisdom you need to see through their petty-fogging lies."

The second bowl is filled with short splinters, and I know what they are. Pieces from a lightning-struck tree, a good cure for toothache. After the splinters, we add a black hen's feather to ward off malaria. Miz Settle explains the other things as we go down the line: a cedar chip to scare evil spirits, a crawpappy pincher to ease bellyache, and small yellow beads made from bodark wood, two in each bag to prevent brain fever.

To protect against violent death, we add a ring made from a nail pulled out of a gallows. Where she managed to get twelve of those I have no idea. I can't remember one person in Milksnake ever being hanged. Last of all, we add a buckeye for general good luck.

I sit on her porch steps for morning light and start sewing the bags shut. I've sewn only two when a young man comes riding in on a black mule. "Miz Settle hereabouts?" he asks, quite out of breath.

I've seen this particular man before. I remember him for his giant mustache, darker than his pale brown hair and wider than his face.

Miz Settle comes out of the cabin. She's toting an old black leather bag. "Mr. Larsen, how's your missus doing?"

"Seems to be in a lot of pain for only a birth. I mean compared to a dog or a goat."

Miz Settle blows out her breath at him. "Dog or goat?" She closes her eyes for a minute then seems to get herself back in hand. "Do you get your water from the crik or a spring."

"A spring."

"Good. Boil water for me, nothing from a crik or drained off your roof. Boil it a goodly long time. Twenty minutes. You got a watch?"

"No, Ma'am."

"Well start the water boiling as soon as you get home and keep it hot 'til I get there. How about clean rags?"

He shrugs.

"Go inside, China, and get me some rags, not the housework rags, but them in the quart sealers. Bring two sealers. Don't open 'em."

I bring out the jars. Bessie is up and pacing as if she's ready to go, but Miz Settle tells her to stay, and she lies down with a sigh. I assume I can't go either, but then Miz Settle looks at my hands. "Child, do you never wash?"

I set down the jars and tuck my hands behind my back.

"Take off now, Hiram," she tells the young man. "We'll be there shortly."

He turns his mule and starts it trotting down the path. It's a rocky ride on the back of a mule.

"Go wash your hands, China," Miz Settle says. "Then bring the quart sealers. See you don't break 'em on the way. I'm gonna start out. You'll probably catch up with me."

I don't have one blessed idea where Hiram and his laboring wife live. When I inquire, Miz Settle says, "On the ol' Corbett farm."

"And where might that be?"

"Walk to town. Behind the schoolhouse, you'll see a crabapple tree at the edge of the woods. The path goes right past it. The Corbett Farm lies northeast about one mile from that tree."

She takes off after Hiram and his bony mule. I go around to the back of her cabin where she keeps a tin basin and dipper next to her rain barrel. I scrub my hands. Then I change my pinafore and cradle the two quart sealers against my chest to keep them from clunking together. I don't catch up to Miz Settle until I'm in town where I spy her walking past the church.

The town of Milksnake is situated upon three roads that run east to west. The center road is crowded with stores and storefronts on each side. The north road has the office owned by Mary-Polly's father and their fancy clapboard house beside it. The south road is a pure empty place waiting for what's yet to come.

I run to catch up with Miz Settle. The path is generous enough that we can walk side by side, and Miz Settle begins talking about childbirth.

First off she says, "You need to know there's considerable pain."

"For the baby?"

My question seems to surprise her, as if she'd never thought of such a thing before. "Well my, I would guess so, but nobody remembers that far back in life."

I try but I can't. She's right.

"The mother might be screaming," she says. "Don't let that scare you. It happens. Some women stay quiet and some yell. Ya think you can handle that?"

"Yes, Ma'am, either way."

"Good."

We walk silently for a time, and she shakes her head as if she's arguing with herself. Finally she says, "One more thing, China. Sometimes births don't go the way we want. Sometimes the mother or the baby or both ain't strong enough to get through it."

"You mean they die?"

"Yes."

"You think Miz Larsen might die?"

"No, I don't. It's a rare thing, but I want you to be ready."

"How can anybody be ready for that?" I don't mean to sound rude, but it seems to me that Miz Settle is asking something that's nigh unto impossible.

"You're wise for your age. I see that right off."

I puff up proud to think I've got some wisdom while yet a child.

Then she says, "But remember, pride is wisdom's greatest enemy." I deflate a bit, and she continues. "So first off, the labor pains start—"

"These are the mother's pains?"

She looks irritated at me. "Yes, like I said."

I nod.

"The mother will have one pain and then later another one, but there's usually a restful pause between. It's God's plan, you see. When her laboring begins, a woman has time to get where she needs to be for help and safety. Next, maybe after a lot of hours and a lot of pains, the mother's belly tightens up and begins the work of pushing the baby out."

I know where a baby comes out, at least in a cow, and I assume it's generally the same for a human woman. "Does she lay down when she's doing all this?"

"Laying down is the worst thing you can do, especially at the beginning. Walkin' forces a body into harder labor."

"You want it harder?"

"The harder the quicker. When the pain gets too strong for the mother to keep walking, she should sit with her knees raised and her bottom down. That way she pushes, and the earth pulls."

"The earth what?"

"Pulls. Didn't you learn about gravity in school?"

"No, Miz Settle."

"Gravity—the pull of the earth." She bends over, picks up a fist-size stone, and lets it drop. "See. The earth pulls it down. Otherwise, everything would be floatin' around mid-sky."

The idea has never before entered my head, and I drift off into thought, but a scream cuts the air, and it sounds like the cry of a mountain lion. If you ever heard a catamount's mating cry, you know it about peels off your skin.

Miz Settle stops and takes in a deep breath, her shoulders rising almost to her ears. "Well, that answers that question. She's a screamer. Maybe I shouldn't of brung ya. If you start feeling sick to your stomach or get jittery, you go outside. Ya hear?"

Another scream arises, and it's louder. "This is Laura-Mae's first baby," says Miz Settle. "First babies usually take longer and their births are harder."

I wish we were going to some woman who pops out a baby like a hen pops out an egg. One squawk and it's done. The path takes a curve and opens up to a peeled-log cabin, new enough that the logs still carry the scent of fresh-cut wood. A porch with steps at the center spreads across the whole front, and two shiny windows flank the door, which is painted sky blue. Two pots of bright red flowers crowd the ends of the top step, and somebody planted everbearing rose bushes at each corner of the house. They're yet spindly, but they've sent out a few shy blooms.

Another scream comes from inside. Mr. Larsen runs out, grabs Miz Settle's elbow, and yanks her up the steps. I follow with the quart sealers. The house must face east because the morning sun pours in bright. I see that Mr. Larsen has not done one thing to get a potful of water boiling.

"Girl," says Miz Settle, "boil water."

I light the stove, locate a pot, and fill it. Then Miz Settle walks out of the bedroom with Mrs. Larsen, who looks too young to be having a baby.

"See that wooden spoon over there, China?" Miz Settle says

"Yes, Ma'am."

"Bring it here for us."

I fetch it and stretch out as far as I can to hand it to her, which starts Miz Settle laughing. "You won't catch nothing from neither one of us." Mrs. Larsen laughs, too, a good thing, I suppose, but I feel my face go red.

"There now, we're gonna walk, Laura-Mae," says Miz Settle in the kindest of voices, but, when Laura-Mae grabs her belly and opens her mouth, Miz Settle sets the spoon between Laura-Mae's teeth.

"Bite down. That'll do you more good than screaming. If you scream all day, you ain't gonna have no voice left to sing lullabies."

Although a bit of scream leaks out from the corners of her mouth, Laura-Mae does a good job of silent suffering. They pace the length of the front room. Then Laura-Mae lets out a groan, and the spoon slips from her mouth. The next minute she rends the air with a scream that lifts the hair at the back of my neck.

Miz Settle crouches in front of her and pats the sides of her belly. "You gotta stay on top of the pain, Laura-Mae. You're letting it get the best of ya," She pats her some more and then frowns. "Well now," she says, and I hear the false cheer in her voice. "Let's go check how far you come." She walks Laura-Mae back into the bedroom and closes the door.

The water is boiling, the cookstove heating up the cabin. Sweat runs down the sides of my face, and I swipe at it with my sleeves. Pretty soon Miz Settle comes out, takes a seat at the table, and looks at me with bleak eyes.

"What's the matter?" I whisper my question.

"The baby's breech."

I have no idea what breech means, and she must see that in my face. "Babies are supposed to be born head first. This baby's coming out opposite."

"What's gonna happen?"

"I can't rightly say." She closes her eyes.

I've heard a few things about childbirth from the girls at school. I search the hutch and find a good-size sharp-blade knife. I bring it to Miz Settle.

"Here."

She opens her eyes and stares at me like I've grown horns.

"You put it under the bed to cut the pain."

"Oh child, that don't work."

Disappointment flattens my heart.

"Go get Mr. Larsen for me. I need to talk to him."

Mr. Larsen is at the back of the house splitting wood. I have to holler twice before he hears me over the sound of his splitting maul.

He pauses mid-swing and hope lights his eyes. "Baby born?"

"Not yet, but Miz Settle wants to talk to you."

He has a lot of questions, and all I can say is, "I don't know nothing."

We walk in, and Miz Settle points to a chair opposite her at the table. Laura-Mae cracks open the cabin with another scream. When she's quiet again, Miz Settle looks into Mr. Larsen's eyes, and he starts to shake his head back and forth.

"No," he says. "Don't you tell me nothing bad. Ya hear?"

I move the boiling water to a cooler place on the stove top. Even though I have my back to the table, my ears are pricked.

Miz Settle takes a huge breath. "When babies come into this world, Hiram, they should be headfirst. That's the safest, easiest way. Your child ain't."

His voice is weak. "What is it? Feet first?"

"Butt first."

"Which means?"

"Which means the birth cord might get squashed alongside the baby's head when it passes through your wife's hip bones. That cord gives the baby its breath and its food. It can do without food for a while, of course, but—"

"But not without its breath. It's gonna die?"

"Not if I can help it, but it'll be chancy, and it'll hurt your wife like nothin' ever has."

"My pa claims women make a lot of fuss about something that ain't that bad."

Miz Settle scrapes back her chair, stands up, and sets her hands on the tabletop. She leans toward Mr. Larsen, glaring like she could cut him up with her eyes. "Let me tell you this, young man. Neither you nor your pa has ever been in the kind of pain your wife is about to endure. Pray to God that you won't, because you'd caterwaul like a baby. Don't you make light of what she's doing to give you a child. Ya hear?"

He leans so far away from her that he tips himself and his chair over backward. I laugh, and Miz Settle looks at me with that same fire in her eyes. I shut my mouth with a snap and grab a rag, wiping down anything that comes to mind.

She stomps back into the bedroom, and Mr. Larsen scrambles off the floor. He sets his chair upright then goes out the door, silent as a cat. One minute later I hear that splitting maul bite hard into wood.

Pretty soon Miz Settle comes from the bedroom. "You got yourself in hand?"

I can't look at her. I'm that ashamed.

"Don't you ever let me hear you laugh at nobody's problems again. You hear me, girl?"

"Yes, Ma'am, I do. No, Ma'am, I won't."

"Good then. I'm gonna need your help. Go wash your hands. Use plenty of soap and get right down under your fingernails and twixt your fingers and up your arms."

I'm about to tell her that I already did that, but I decide it's not going to hurt to be twice clean.

"When you're done, come into the bedroom. Then no matter what you see or what you hear, keep your face straight. No smile. No frown. No tears."

When I'm done washing, Mrs. Larsen screams again. I set my face into a mask, take a deep breath, and head for the bedroom. Laura-Mae is sitting upright on the bed, propped in place with blankets and pillows. She's hanging onto a rope that's tied at both ends to the footboard. Her hands are gripping and pulling and shaking.

Right in front of my face, Miz Settle jerks away the sheet that's been covering Mrs. Larsen's legs. She's bare to the waist, and her knees are raised nearly to her shoulders. Her nether regions are covered with a thick down of black hair. I'm so surprised that I close my eyes, like I've seen something against the natural workings of God. I wonder if the same thing will happen to me if I ever get pregnant, that thick growth of fur, animal-like.

I keep my eyes closed long enough to regain my courage, and then I look again. I see the gap in her flesh, an opening about the shape of a hen's egg, and there a flash of pink skin. Mrs. Larsen goes into another pain. I ignore the scream and fix my eyes on that gap. It widens to show more skin, and I surmise that I'm seeing a portion of her baby's bottom.

As soon as the pain is over, Miz Settle leans in close to Mrs. Larsen's face. "Now honey, I know ya need to push, but, if you can hold off, it would be a helpful thing. See. Do this." Miz Settle begins blowing out in quick breaths, one after another. Mrs. Larsen does the same.

"Darlin', you amaze me. Now what I've gotta do is put my hand up inside you, and it's gonna hurt like the blue blazin' devil, but we want your baby to come out whole and healthy."

Mrs. Larsen starts to cry. "Is there something wrong?"

"Only what I told you. Your child's coming out backward."

All the time Miz Settle is talking, she's greasing her left arm with lard, greasing and greasing. "Might help you, honey," she says, "to think of something wonderful and special. You got a necklace or a ring you love?"

"A necklace," she gasps. "My Grandma's. It was promised to me, but my cousin got it."

"Well, that might not—"

I know Miz Settle wants to suggest something less irksome than that particular necklace, but, with the next push, the baby's bottom bulges out. If the baby could see anything, he'd be looking at his mama's spine.

"I'm gonna reach up, right now, Laura-Mae," says Miz Settle. "Lean back and pant. Pant like I showed you."

Miz Settle works her fingers into the birth canal, her hand crawling up and in, spiderlike. I'm standing there staring when another pain comes. I can see by the look on Miz Settle's face that it's hurting her arm more than fierce, and Mrs. Larsen starts screaming again instead of breathing like she's supposed to.

I squeeze past Miz Settle and press my head up to Mrs. Larsen's head, face to face. I start panting and blowing. "Breathe like this, Miz Larsen. Breathe. Breathe. Breathe." My words don't seem to do much good until I add, "Breathe for your baby. For your baby." I scream the word *baby*, hoping she can hear it over her own yelps, and she must, because she starts to blow and blow and blow.

Like some little miracle, Miz Settle pulls out one of the baby's legs. She puts her hand back in and pulls out the other.

"Give me that scrap of toweling, China," she tells me.

She wraps toweling around the baby's hips, and then she turns the child toward Mrs. Larsen's right leg

"You got a boy," says Miz Settle.

It's the first time I ever saw the human male parts. They're quite interesting. When I realize I'm staring, I shift my look to the ceiling.

"A boy!" Mrs. Larsen starts to say, but her words turn into another scream, and Miz Settle brings down the baby's left arm. She turns the baby to the left and pulls down his right arm. He's a fine fat child, but I feel sick to my stomach, seeing his body out with his head still in.

Miz Settle calls to me. "I need you here, China."

She takes my right hand and pushes my fingers into a fist. Then she lays it where Mrs. Larsen's black hair reaches up in a point toward her belly button. "Put your left hand atop your right."

I do that.

"When I tell you, push straight down." She looks at Mrs. Larsen. "You thinkin' about something pretty?"

"That necklace," Mrs. Larsen whispers.

"I'm gonna put my hands in again." Miz Settle squeezes in her right hand as if to cover the baby's face. "I'm pulling on his cheeks," she says to me. "Now he's looking downward." She puts in the other hand. "I'm holding him steady with a couple fingers up the back of his neck. China, when I say, you push."

Mrs. Larsen moans and Miz Settle roars, "Now, China." Then, "Laura-Mae, push-push-push."

Right at that moment, the baby's head pops out. He's red as a rose-hip, ugly as a toad, and his nose is smashed flat, but Miz Settle doesn't seem to notice. She flips that baby upside down, and, as if the poor child hasn't suffered enough, she gives him a smart slap on his hind end. He starts wailing.

Mrs. Larsen begins to cry, and I hear clumping footsteps on the porch. Half a second later, Mr. Larsen barges into the bedroom, and Miz Settle flips a blanket over his wife's legs.

"You got a healthy son, here, Mr. Larsen," she says, "but we have cleaning up to do. Go back to your work. I'll call you in when we're ready. Your wife's as stalwart a woman as I ever seen, and don't you never forget what she's went through to give you this boy."

Then she sends me to the kitchen to get the jarred rags and the boiled water. Mr. Larsen leaves the cabin, his head down, but I see him catch a tear with the back of his hand. I bring Miz Settle all she needs. To my surprise, she hands me that bloody baby. She's already tied and nipped off the birth cord, and I'm disappointed because I wanted to see it done.

"Wash him up and get him wrapped warm." She points at a cradle beside the bed, and I see folded flannel blankets, soft and new-looking, and diapers cut out of diamond weave cloth. On top of them, there's a strip of white cotton.

"That's the belly band," Miz Settle says. "When he's clean, put that on, too."

I have no idea how to put on a belly band, but, as I'm about to ask, Mrs. Larsen gives a squawk, and I realize she's going to deliver again. My first thought is of twins, which are a problem-filled thing, some folks claiming they're good luck and others that they're bad.

Miz Settle looks over her shoulder at me. "Go do what I said. That baby is cold." And I notice how his skin is mottled. He starts crying again, little short bursts of sound, and I hold him up close to my chest, bloody or not.

"Is she having another—"

"It's the afterbirth."

I feel stupid. Cows, cats, dogs, they all have afterbirths. I hurry to the kitchen and wash the baby with warm water. Then I study that belly band. By the name alone I know it goes around his middle. The strip is long enough to wrap him a couple times, and I do. I fold the diaper clout around his hips and between his legs. I pin it with straight pins, being careful to thread them in and out until they stay tight and won't pick. I wrap him in a blanket, wipe his face, and try to fluff up his hair. Then I take him back into the bedroom. He's not crying anymore, only looking around. I'm thinking his mama probably wants to hold him, but she's gritting her teeth as Miz Settle sews her up.

"Show Miz Larsen that handsome son of hers," Miz Settle tells me. "She needs to take her mind off what I'm doin' here."

I hold the baby on a slant toward his mama.

"He looks like his daddy," Laura-Mae says, and I entertain a moment of wonderment. To me, he looks like he could belong to anybody.

Miz Settle finishes up, cleans her needle, and puts it in her midwife bag. "Let's get that baby nursing, and, China, you fix something for Miz Larsen to eat. She's been working hard."

Under the dry sink, I locate a basket of eggs and then a side of bacon wrapped in butcher paper. I slice off enough bacon to feed us all, and I get it frying in a cast iron pan big enough to hold the lot. The smell of food must bring Mr. Larsen into the kitchen. I'm filling a tin plate for his wife when he tries to take it from my hands.

"Not for you. It's for her."

"Men eat first. That's the rule."

I don't know if he's telling the truth. I never lived with a man in the house. Of course, at church potlucks, the men get in line first, but still, I would guess that a woman having just brought forth a baby should be an exception.

"If men were all that important, then you'd be birthing the babies."

He gives me a scowl, but I pull the plate from his hands and add a slice of buttered bread. "Help yourself, Mr. Larsen." I point at the skillet then carry the plate into the bedroom.

When I return to the stove, he's at the table eating more than his share of the food. I'm guessing I shouldn't have been rude to him, but I saw what his wife went through, and I'm short on patience. I fill a plate and call to Miz Settle. She joins Mr. Larsen at the table, and then I serve myself. It's a hearty meal, and I'm ferocious hungry. Mr. Larsen lays a handful of coins on the table and slides them over to Miz Settle. She puts them into her apron pocket, all except one. She lays that one next to me and says, "That one's yourn."

I've never in my life owned even one piece of money. I stare at it like a one-eyed crow, and Miz Settle says, "You know what that is, China?"

"No, Ma'am."

I look up at Mr. Larsen, and he gives me a smile. "It's a Spanish milled dollar," he says. "Real old."

"It won't buy you nothing," Miz Settle comments, "but it's good to carry as a lucky piece. Thank the man."

"Thankee, Mr. Larsen."

While we eat, Mr. Larsen tells us riddles, and they're good ones, hard to solve. I decide I like him more than I first thought.

We stay for a few hours to be sure all is well, but before the sun sets we head for home. It's difficult to walk a woods trail in the dark, and, in our hurry, we didn't bring a lantern. We plod along without talking. When the trail widens, I walk at Miz Settle's side and work up courage to mention something that's bothering me.

"She had a lot of hair down there."

"Grown women do. Someday you will, too."

That thought makes me squirm, but I'm relieved to know that I haven't laid my eyes upon something brought about by a witch or a goomering spell.

"She's going to be all right?" Miz Settle doesn't say anything, and I finally blurt out, "Is she going to die?"

"No, child. No. She's good, but she might not be able to carry another."

I think about the long time Miz Settle spent inside the birth track, sewing and sewing. "She's ripped up bad?"

"Not anymore, but she'll have scars."

"Inside?"

"Yes."

"What does that mean?"

"Scarred flesh don't stretch. If I didn't put in my stitches as I intended, another baby up inside might make her tear, and if that happens—"

She doesn't say more than that, but I know what she means. If that happens, her baby might come out too soon, or Mrs. Larsen might bleed out all her blood.

I pray for that new baby boy, and I pray for Laura-Mae Larsen. For days and days, every time I think of them, I pray.

CHAPTER FIVE

The next morning Miz Settle treks to the Larsen farm again. She tells me to stay home and walk beans. Chopping weeds is not my favorite work, but I'm happy to be outside with the good dog Bessie, and she seems interested as I tell her about the birth.

Halfway through the morning, Miz Settle returns, looking upset. My fear rises, and I call out, "Did that little boy die?"

"Heavens, child, you can curse a baby by askin' something like that."

"Well you look—" I can't say exactly how she looks. Mad? Scared? Worried?

"The baby's all right and his mama, too. Although that young rooster had his wife out chopping weeds. The idiot. She's back in bed now." Miz Settle points at me and says, "Wash your hands. We gotta go to the store."

When I'm clean, I come back to the porch.

"Tie up your bonnet."

I don't like to wear a bonnet. The brim cuts off your view at the top and sides. You lose out on seeing half the world, but I tie the strings under my chin without complaint, because I like going to the store. I can't beg for penny candy like I do with Ma Mère, but maybe Miz Settle will think of it herself.

She doesn't. She buys only the most everyday things—salt, molasses, ten pounds of flour, and two of cornmeal. Before she pays, she studies an odd gadget Mr. James has added to his glass display case.

"That's a doctor's machine called a stethy-scope," Miz Settle tells me, her eyes alight.

"What's it for?"

"To listen to hearts. If I had that, I'd maybe hear a baby's heart while it was being born. I'd know if it was strong or growing weak. I'd know if I should let the mother's labor go on like normal or give her black cohosh to speed it up. Imagine!"

Mr. James walks over to us. He's a florid man with dark red hair. "Wherever did you get that stethy-scope?" Miz Settle asks him.

"Took it in trade from a peddler. I gave him its worth in lengths of calico.

"How much you charging for it?"

"Ten dollars."

Miz Settle's eyes fade.

"I can let you try it out for free."

"For my midwifing?"

"No, of course not. Here in the store."

He unlocks the display case and lifts the glass door. He takes out that strange leggy thing and puts the plugs in his ears. He settles the bell against his chest and squints one eye as he listens. "Yep, still ticking." He laughs like he's told a good joke, and then he takes the ear bits out of his ears and puts them into mine. He presses the bell against his chest again. "Hear that?"

I do hear it, a strange echoing sound of *womp-pump, womp-pump, womp-pump.*

"What is it?"

"My heart. Here, listen to yours." He settles the bell at the left side of my chest, and sure enough, I hear that same sound again, but not quite as blurry at the edges.

"Let Miz Settle hear," I say.

He lifts the ear-pieces out and offers them to her. She's eager in her listening, and contemplates the beating of all our hearts. After that, Mr. James locks the stethoscope back into the glass case. Miz Settle turns her back on it and forces a smile. I carry home the ten pounds of flour, and she carries the rest. Later, in the heat of the day, when I'm hoeing the garden, I realize how much my arms ache from carrying that flour, but I hold in my complaints until nigh unto suppertime. Then I go inside and tell Miz Settle how much my arms and back ache.

"It worries me that you might turn out to be lazy," says Miz Settle.

I look directly into her face. "Today alone, I carried ten pounds of flour for two miles and then chopped weeds for hours in the hot sun. Since when is that lazy?" The minute those words come out of my mouth, I know I'm in trouble.

Miz Settle points up at the attic hole. "No supper for you tonight, China Creed. Fill your stomach with consideration of polite conversation."

I clomp up that climbing log and lay down on the featherbed. I do try to contemplate polite conversation, but distractions intrude. I kill three mosquitoes, and I harry a blue bottle fly. I watch a fat spider make her web above my head, and I'm pleased when the fly gets tangled therein. It's good to see someone besides myself with a few problems, but, when the fly works up into a constant angry buzz, I set him free. Finally, I hear Bessie make herself a bed on the braided rug, digging and turning and scuffling. It's night. The light's fading. I go to sleep.

Near morning, a mockingbird wakes me with stolen songs that she's woven into something beautiful and new. When dawn turns the sky gray, I decide to court Miz Settle's good-will by gathering eggs before she tells me to. I'm climbing down the log when she screeches and scurries out of her bed. I jump to the floor.

At first, I think it's a snake she's pulling out from under her covers. Then I see it's that stethoscope.

"What did you do?" she yells at me.

"I didn't do nothing. I've been upstairs in your attic all night."

"You didn't go to Mr. James's store and steal this?" She holds up the stethoscope by one ear-plug, and it dangles from her hand like something dead.

"No, honest."

Miz Settle sits down on her kitchen chair. She lays the stethoscope in her lap and presses the balls of her thumbs into her closed eyes. Finally, she looks up. "You promise on the Good Book that you didn't sneak out and steal this."

"I promise."

"Get your shoes on. We gotta go see your mother."

We walk the whole five miles without talking, and we don't stop at the Jameses' store to return the stethoscope. When we arrive at Ma Mère's cabin, I spy her in the garden.

The minute she spots us, she frowns and says, "What'd she do?"

I don't wait for Miz Settle to answer. "I didn't do nothing, and that's the truth, cross my heart to God."

"I did not ask you, China. Come here and walk beans. Miz Settle, may I offer you a cup of coffee?"

"Tea," she says, without even a *please*, and they go into the cabin.

Walk beans. Walk beans. It seems I've been walking beans all my life. I notice right off that Ma Mère is behind in her harvesting, but beans are like that, popping up in such a hurried abundance that they grow past their prime before you know it. I eat a few. After all, I didn't get supper last night, and I didn't get breakfast this morning. When my stomach is satisfied, I decide to pick a batch for Ma Mère. If she doesn't want them, maybe she'll let me take them to the store to trade for penny candy.

I head toward the cabin to fetch a picking basket, and I'm barely on the porch when I hear Ma Mère say, "China is a fine child." She sounds angry.

"She's a bit rude, mouth-wise," says Miz Settle.

I wait to see if Ma Mère will make apologies. She does not.

Miz Settle plops something down on the table, and I step quietly to the open doorway to peek in. I assume she's showing Ma Mère the stethoscope, but she's not. It's a small drawstring bag crusted over with red and blue beads.

"This here finger-purse come to me the second night I had China," says Miz Settle. "My grandmother done the beading, and I ain't seen it in years. How'd it get to my cabin all the way from Georgia? That's what I want to know. Then yesterday morning I went to check on the Larsen baby."

"She had her baby?"

"A healthy boy, born breech."

"That poor woman."

"She's a brave one, but during the birth she got to thinkin' about a necklace owned by a cousin. The next day, she found it in her pie safe. She believes her cousin left it there on a visit made last spring, and nobody found it until now."

"That sounds reasonable."

"It does unless you add in my grandmother's finger-purse and this." She reaches into her tote and brings out the stethoscope. "You gonna tell me what's happenin'? Your daughter ain't welcome at my place until you do."

I lean against the doorframe, and it lets out a squeal like wood does when it's bound by a wayward nail.

Ma Mère looks up, and I see the worry in her face. I step inside. "I came for a basket. Your beans need to be picked."

"Please sit down with us first, China."

I do, although I have to share Ma Mère's chair since we only have the two. She moves to make room for me.

"You remember the stories I've told you, China? The ones about women?"

"Which one? Saint Joan?" It's my favorite, her leading an army like she did.

"Tell Miz Settle the Queen of Sheba story."

I like that story, too, but not as well. "I got a better story about Tommy Belnap's dog, a funny story."

"Why don't you save that for later? Right now we need the Queen of Sheba." Ma Mère looks at Miz Settle. "The problem we've been discussing has historical roots."

Maman nods at me, and I begin. "Queen of Sheba lived in Africa. She was very rich." I stop and look at Miz Settle. She doesn't appear to be much interested in the Queen of Sheba. "Queen of Sheba is in the Bible."

Miz Settle narrows her eyes. "I know."

"The Bible makes it true."

"I believe so."

"She goes to visit King Solomon."

"Why?" says Ma Mère. "Why does she go visit King Solomon?"

"He was very wise and very rich."

Miz Settle scowls at Ma Mère. "What's this got to do with anything?"

"We'll get there," Ma Mère says, and I continue.

"Solomon likes her because she's richer than he is. Now this part, it ain't in the Bible." I pause for Ma Mère to correct my English, but she does not. "It's in other old books though."

"Scrolls," Ma Mère says.

"Those scrolls say that the Queen of Sheba could think of anything, and, right there out of the thin air, it would pop up." I tap my head. "With just her thinking about it. Now Solomon wants to show off, so he takes her to see his golden throne. When she's looking at it, she can't help but think about her throne back at her palace, how it's better than his. Then lo and behold, her throne pops up in the middle of King Solomon's palace. There it is, fancy as all get-out."

Miz Settle loses her look of boredom.

"Solomon knows that some kind of magic has happened, and he suspects the Queen of Sheba did it. Quick as a blink, he orders his guards to take the Queen to a dungeon. He keeps her there until she magics up a bunch of other things for him, but somehow she gets hold of enough poison to kill herself. She promises to eat that poison right down unless Solomon sets her free. He does, but—" I stop and look at Ma Mère because I'm not sure of the next part. "Don't they get married?"

"Something like that."

"And they have children, right?"

"They have a son, and he becomes a Holy Man."

Ma Mère stares into Miz Settle's eyes. "The royal line of the country of Ethiopia marks their descent from that son—a Holy Man, not a demon, not a devil." Then, as if she hadn't mentioned the Queen of Sheba at all, she says, "My daughter has a lovely singing voice."

Miz Settle leans back in her chair and studies me for a long minute. "I might appreciate a song."

I like to sing, and I wail right into "Billy Barlow," but, when I arrive at the raw-rat-tail part, I realize my mother is yammering to get my attention.

"Wherever in heaven's name did you hear that heathen song?" she asks.

"School."

"Well, let's leave it there. How about a more churchy song?

I choose the most churchy song I know, "Holy, Holy, Holy."

Miz Settle looks amazed at the whole performance, and Ma Mère seems satisfied.

"Very nice," Miz Settle says then adds, "I wouldn't mind taking home a few green beans if you have some to spare, Yvette."

Now I know Miz Settle already has green beans beyond need, but Ma Mère points at the picking basket. I fetch it, and I walk hard and heavy out of the cabin and across the porch. Then I crawl back up on my belly, staying well away from the open door.

"You had other folks like China in your family?" Miz Settle asks.

"Not in my lifetime, but I've heard stories. They're women. All of them. The gift is rare and often diluted in power, but each new female child in my family is studied for possibilities."

"What happened to those women?"

"Nothing good."

"If you knew your daughter had this fearsome gift, Yvette, why did you send her to me?"

I have a fearsome gift? What kind of gift? Why didn't Ma Mère tell me?

Ma Mère is quiet a long time, but finally she says, "Everyone knows that those of Indian heritage walk close to God and His creation. I thought you might be able to help China control herself. Besides, you're a Goomer Doctor. You know how to cast out hexes."

"Your daughter is blessed with some kind of born-in power, Yvette," says Miz Settle. "Not a hex, a birthright. I'm not strong enough to cast out something like that, and I don't know anybody who is."

"I'm afraid people might accuse her of black witchery, but you heard her sing. A child of Satan can't utter a holy name."

I start breathing again. At least I'm not a devil.

"Why ain't you richer than King Solomon hisself, Yvette Creed?" Miz Settle asks. "Your daughter thinks about something, and it comes to her?"

"Sometimes, sometimes not."

"Your family, Yvette, they ain't local folk?"

"No. I was born in New Orleans. My maiden name is Destrehan."

"Do they know about China?"

"They do not."

"I suppose that's best, but, if your daughter is gonna stay with me, I don't want her to fill my house with things that ain't mine. How do I avoid that?"

"You can't touch her," Ma Mère says. "I'm not accusing you of coveting, Mrs. Settle, but my guess is that wanting something is the key, wanting something and thinking about it at the moment you touch her."

"That can solve the whole problem?"

"Most of the time."

Their words pound against me like fists. I can tell by the quiver in Ma Mère's voice that whatever I have inside of me is a great and serious problem. The worry of it takes over my breathing until my hands shake, and my arms, and my heart.

I slide from the porch and start running as if I could get away from what I heard. I'm well into the woods before I hunker down and gag up bile, spitting it out of my mouth until my throat burns. I stagger to my feet and follow a deer trail into an open space where clumps of little bluestem have begun to sprout their feather tops. I pick a stalk and chew on it until I coax out a taste of sweetness. No wonder Ma Mère rarely touches me, but how can I live my whole life without folks being able to shake my hand or kiss my cheek? Husbands kiss their wives. I know that much. Does that mean I can never have a husband? Anger fills my chest until I feel as fierce as a wild boar. Then I shout out cuss words meanly spoken.

When I'm done with that, tears start, my thoughts bound tight by misery. Why can't I be like other girls? Other girls have a father. Other girls don't live through every winter hungry enough to eat dirt. Other girls get new dresses. Other girls don't have this fearsome gift.

Our preacher says that God can do miracles. Can't God give me one small thing like being normal? Again anger fills me, but I know that boars don't sit there feeling sorry for themselves. They go out into the world and scare up anything they need.

I huff and I snort and I snuffle. I think about the stethoscope. I picture it in my mind. I close my eyes and try with everything that's in me to make it appear out of thin air, but nothing happens. Of course, I really don't want that stethoscope. What I want is candy. I crouch in the grass, my skirt making a catch-all between my knees, and I imagine it bellied out with all the candy in Mr. James's store. I try with my eyes open and my eyes closed, with my hands folded in prayer, and with my head tipped up toward God. I try it with my eyes vicious, like boar eyes, and eyes gentle like deer eyes. Nothing works.

Part of me is disappointed and part of me is glad. Maybe I'm more normal than Ma Mère thinks. I start back toward the cabin and, when I get close, I hear my mother calling my name.

I duck out from the woods. "I'm here."

She looks into my eyes and says, "Oh China," then encloses me in a strong hug. "You heard Miz Settle and me talking?"

I don't want to admit to eavesdropping, but how else can I explain the sobs that again rack my body? "Yes," I whisper. "What's wrong with me, Mère? How did I get this way? Does God hate me?"

"Of course not, China. He's only given you a very . . . difficult gift, and He wouldn't have given it to you without good reason." She leads me to the porch and sits on the rocker, pulls me to her lap as if I were a baby again. She strokes my hair, humming softly. I find comfort in her nearness, and my sadness falls away. I've nearly relaxed into sleep when she says, "We should take the stethoscope back to Mr. James."

"Where's Miz Settle?" I finally think to ask.

"She went home. You're going to stay with me, at least for the rest of this week."

Happiness pours in and a bit of guilt. Poor Miz Settle, she's more alone than Ma Mère or I will ever be.

At the outside water basin, Ma Mère uses a rag to wash my face and my hands, and then she finger-combs my hair. She makes me wear my school shoes. They pinch. She ties my poke bonnet under my chin, and we walk to town.

Mr. James only sputters when he sees the stethoscope, which gives my mother a chance to tell her story first. "A rather disreputable-looking gentleman rode up to my cabin this morning and traded me this device in exchange for two of my chickens, cleaned and plucked. My daughter said she saw it here at your store yesterday. I thought you might be willing to trade for it again. China needs new shoes for school."

New shoes? Hearing those two words takes the pinch out of my toes.

Mr. James frowns. "It's a stethoscope, a medical instrument, and I hate to tell you this, Mrs. Creed, but that very device was stolen from this store last night."

"Stolen! Did they take anything else?"

"It was the only thing that went missing."

Ma Mère sighs and lays the stethoscope into his hands. "I guess I'm the victim now, being out two fine stewing hens. At least he didn't want the feathers."

"Well, that's not exactly fair either, him taking your birds, but I can't run a business by replacing everything that's been stolen in the town of Milksnake."

"Oh, I would never expect that, Mr. James."

He writes out a slip and hands it to Ma Mère. His eyes linger on her face.

"Oh my!" Ma Mère exclaims. "A twenty percent discount on shoes? Very generous indeed."

"You want to see a few pair?"

"Her feet are still growing. I think I'll wait until the week before school starts."

At that moment, Mrs. Heptabah James pulls aside the dark velvet drapes that curtain off the back rooms where the James family lives.

"You will be happy to know, Wife," says Mr. James, "the stethoscope has been returned."

Mrs. James gives Ma Mère a searching, highhanded look. Then she stares right at me. "Your daughter stole it?"

I wait for Ma Mère to defend me, but, when she stands there with her face red and her mouth closed, I experience a moment of righteous wrath that overrides my caution. "I did not."

Ma Mère clasps my shoulder and gives it a hearty squeeze, but at least she finds her tongue. "My daughter did not steal that stethoscope."

"I'll explain later, dear," Mr. James says. The iron in his voice makes me glad that I'm not Mrs. James. She returns to the back rooms, and he says to my mother, "Could I help you with anything else?"

Ma Mère tilts her head and looks into his eyes. "One pound of white sugar."

My mouth gapes. White sugar is a rare treat, if then.

Mr. James weighs out a pound of sugar. He places it into Ma Mère's flour sack. She reaches into her skirt pocket, but Mr. James lifts his hands, palm out.

"No," he says, "we'll add that to the reward."

My mother thanks him, and we leave the store. I wait until we're well down the boardwalk before I ask, "Did you bring money with you?"

"Hush," she says.

"How did you know—"

"I said *hush*. You've had a difficult day, China. When we get home, I'll make us a yellow butter cake. Would you like that?"

"Yes, Ma'am."

"Then we'll talk over a few things. You're old enough now to understand what a very special person you are." She puts her arm around my shoulders, and I try to think happy thoughts. Maybe my abilities will become as strong as the Queen of Sheba's. Maybe I'll lead armies like Joan of Arc. Maybe someday Ma Mère and I will figure out how I can turn into a regular person.

CHAPTER SIX

Y ou're like the Queen of Sheba," Ma Mère says to me. She's standing at the table, mixing cake batter. "You can sometimes make things appear, but not for yourself, only for others."

"That doesn't seem fair, Maman. I should be able to give things to myself."

My mother slides beaten egg whites atop the batter, folds them in with her wooden spoon. "It's an odd gift you have, *Ma Petite Lapin*, and, as far as I'm aware, no one truly understands it."

"A person has to touch me and think of something they want."

"Yes."

"What if I touch them?"

"It's the same whether they touch you or you touch them."

"I can't hug anybody? I can't hold hands? I can't—" At that moment, I remember Hazel and Mary-Polly's doll and all the problems of that. I remember the time we were starving and Ma Mère kissed me, how the next morning our table was piled with food. I remember her telling me that it was best not to touch other people, and I remember our secret song. In gentle and subtle ways, she's been telling me about my gift since I was a very little child.

"I steal those things, don't I, Maman? I steal them like a thief. They'll put me in jail. God will send me to hell."

I thought I used up all my tears, but I start to cry again. I scurry under the table and hunker down. Ma Mère sits on the floor and pulls me onto her lap. She rocks us back and forth.

"Hush, China. It's not theft if it's not intended."

When I finally stop crying, she says. "What you have is a gift, both wonderful and rare."

"But I can't tell anybody?"

"No, you can't."

"Like our secret language, like our secret song?"

"Yes, except now Miz Settle also knows about your gift. And that's fine. She's a trustworthy woman."

I'm worried and I'm scared. The two feelings mix inside me until my stomach aches, but I get up and wipe my face on my sleeve, and I try to keep my tears at bay. When the cake is in the oven, she goes into her bedroom and brings out a pair of white cotton gloves. That evening she sits close to the coal oil lamp and shortens the fingers and narrows one side of each glove. That's when I know they're for me.

"If you're wearing gloves," she says, "you'll be able to shake hands with people and play games with your friends."

"Like London Bridge?"

"Yes."

My heart lifts at the thought.

I wear the gloves on Sunday to church. When I see the covetous look on Mary-Polly's face, I can't help but smile. When the service is over, Miz Settle joins us. She nods at Ma Mère and says to me, "Bessie's been asking where you are."

Then I know I'm doomed to spend the rest of the summer chopping weeds and living on scant meals. Ma Mère leaves me with nothing but a quick kiss upon my poke bonnet, and I follow Miz Settle to her little crooked house.

We end that summer with me learning all about the medicines set out for us in fields and forests. The inner bark of slippery elm is effective against boils. You work your knife upward when you take the bark. That way the elm knows it needs to pull the infection up and out. Miz Settle teaches me to make lavender tea for muscle ache and to use touch-me-not juice to ward off the itch of poison ivy. I think I could about fill a whole book with what she teaches me. She starts calling me Sheba, which makes me think about my cursed blessing all the time, but I don't have the courage to ask her to stop.

A week before school begins, Miz Settle goes off with nary an explanation and leaves me with a long list of chores. At dusk, I stay in the kitchen with the lamp lit. A few hours later I see her punched tin lantern shedding its pattern against the trees. She stomps inside, and the first thing she does is point at that lamp. I lift the glass chimney and blow out the light. She starts complaining about the waste of coal oil, and, when her voice gets screechy enough to break my ears, I start shouting back.

"I didn't know where you were. I was scart here by myself. I thought you might of left me forever."

"By now you shoulda figured I was catching a baby."

"You might've mentioned that before you left."

She thumps her doctor bag on the table. "Don't be telling me what to do, Sheba."

"Politeness isn't something I should have to remind you about, Miz Settle."

She takes in a breath and lowers her head. Her sudden quietness encourages me toward my underlying purpose.

"I have one week left here. My mother wants me to learn some goomering, and you never taught me one thing about that."

"You ain't ready, Sheba."

"My name is China, and I think I'm ready."

"You ain't, and the injury wouldn't only be to yourself but to whatever person you try to help. Think on that."

"If you don't teach me something—at least one little thing—I'm leaving in the morning."

"I'll miss you." She walks over to her corner, that bed of rags. Then she says one more thing. "The baby died."

A shaft of guilt slices directly through my heart. "Whose?" I whisper.

"Miz James, and it's a blessing it didn't live to full birth."

I want to ask what was wrong with it, but I don't. Miz Settle is surely right. There are some things I'm not ready for. I start up the climbing log.

"I shoulda told you where I was going," says Miz Settle. "I will next time."

My feet lose their grip, and I slide down to the floor. I press my forehead against the log and say, "I'm sorry I was rude, Miz Settle. You can call me *Sheba*. I don't mind."

Sunday morning we make the exchange, and, even though I'd like to have my mother all to myself that day, I know she's right when she invites Miz Settle and Bessie to come share our Sunday dinner. Ma Mère made yeast-rising bread and butter. She has new potatoes scrubbed and ready to boil, green beans with fatback, and pinto beans cooked with molasses. To top all that, she roasted a whole ham in the oven all morning while she was at church. The house is hot as blue blazes, but the ham is worth it.

I make milk gravy with ham juice, and we feast. Even Bessie gets some. Afterward, Ma Mère opens the pie safe and there on the middle shelf sits a walnut pie as pretty as you please, which she serves with cream and shavings from a stick of cinnamon.

Before she goes home, Miz Settle tells us a story about herself, when she was young and the world broke her heart. Later that evening, I'm upstairs on my prickly straw tick, not nearly as comfortable as Miz Settle's featherbed, and I watch out the gable end as she and Bessie start home. I'm more than surprised to realize I'm crying.

CHAPTER SEVEN

AMICALOLA FALLS, GEORGIA, JULY 1835
AS TOLD TO US BY MRS. JESSE SETTLE

The Wise Ones say that the Amicalola Falls captured stars at its birth, and it spun their light until Dâyuni'sï, that spry little water beetle, descended from the sky to discover the reason for all the turmoil.

Dâyuni'sï liked what she found, so she dove deep and brought up mud to make land for her home. Buzzard came, and his long wings brushed against the mud and pulled it up into the great mountains of North Georgia. Then animals wandered in: fox and weasel, skunk and snake, worms and catamounts, minks and bear. And they, too, made homes in that place.

Finally, people came. First red people, then white people, and finally black people. The red people walked softly upon the earth, but the white people came with wide dreams and greedy hands. The black people watered the land with their tears.

Years and years later, on a prosperous farm less than two days' walk from Amicalola Falls, the girl Jesse Settle watched two registry men stride down the road to her father's lane. Since Jesse's older sister had married, and her brother went to find gold over in Lumpkin County, she and her father were the only ones at home.

Jesse hid in the barn when she saw those white men, but her father invited them in. He'd heard they were coming to take a census of all Cherokee people. Her father told her not to be afraid. The registry men would realize that the Settle farm was well cared for, their livestock healthy and abundant. Among the *Aniyunwiya,* but also in the white world, Jesse's father was considered a wealthy man.

Eventually, out of curiosity, Jesse slipped quietly into the house. She was proud of how clean she kept their four-room *galitsode* with white curtains at every window and a braided rug under the round oak table.

Her father and the white men sat at that table with a registry book spread in front of them. Jesse stood at her spinning wheel off to one side of their fireplace. Her hands turned sweaty as she spun rolags of wool into yarn, but she wanted to hear what those men said. They asked for her father's name and for hers and if anyone else lived with them. They asked how much Indian blood flowed in their veins.

She was surprised when her father said, "I'm one-eighth." He was seven-eighths *Aniyunwiya* and proud of it. He looked at Jesse. "She's less than one eighth." The white men studied her for a time. Surely with her dark skin they could see she had more Cherokee in her than that, but she trusted her father and smiled in agreement.

The two men looked alike, with sallow skin and lank brown hair, strong-jawed faces. The older of the two filled out the form, but Jesse's father leaned forward and, reading the paper upside down, thumped his index finger on the line that held Jesse's name. Those white men should've realized Jesse's father was educated as were most Cherokee.

Her father said, "I told you that she is less than one-eighth. She's mostly white. Put white."

The man met her father's eyes with a stern stare, but he set a stroke of dark ink through what he'd written. He recorded her as white. Jesse kept her smile hidden down under her tongue. Her mother had been one-half Cherokee, three-eighths white, one-eighth Negro. Jesse didn't remember her Negro great-grandmother, but her father spoke well of the woman. He said Jesse inherited her long-fingered hands and doe eyes, her deep and beautiful voice.

The census men left, tipping their hats toward her, and, when they disappeared down the lane, she asked her father, "Why'd you lie?"

He spoke to her in their true language, as he often did. "Like appreciates like. White people elevate white. If they think we have more white blood, they're more likely to leave us alone and not hold past wars against us."

"And why didn't you tell them I was part Negro?"

"This is their hierarchy. Understand Jesse, it is not mine. First white and several steps below, Cherokee and Creek, Saponi and all the people they call Indian. Many steps down the Negro people. They're wrong, but they're not apt to admit it."

Her father went to her and smoothed her worried forehead with his calloused thumb. "You are beautiful, like your mother. There are no steps down in my heart. You are everything I want in a daughter. Here is the truth that causes all our troubles. White people want what isn't theirs. First, the gold discovered near the town of Da-bi-ni-ge in Lumpkin County. Second, farms like ours."

It turned out that those two men were enrolling the *Aniyunwiya* with a plan to move them off their own land. The list that included Jesse's and her father's names was called the Henderson Roll. If her father had been there alone, he could've claimed that he and his daughter held only a touch of Cherokee, four, five generations back—too little to matter—but Jesse's skin color was the tell for them both. No matter what they wrote in that registry book, those men knew she wasn't white. Why hadn't she stayed in the barn? Why didn't she hide until they left?

Their farm was included in the lottery. No matter the years they put in to clear and build up the soil, it was given to a family that claimed white in all its bloodlines.

Jesse and her father stayed as long as they could, but in 1838, soldiers with guns forced them to leave. She and her father took two mules, a wagon, and whatever they could fit in it. Her father packed her spinning wheel, but to Jesse, the wheel was a reminder of her foolishness. She climbed up, took that thing from the wagon bed, and heaved it to the ground with enough force to break the very wheel itself. She never spun again.

Soldiers stayed with them through Georgia and Tennessee and beyond. Some soldiers were of the People. You could see it in the bones of their faces, in their use of the true language, in their kindness toward the vast numbers of *Aniyunwiya* heading west to government land. The walk was long. The way was terrible. People died of cholera, and measles, and lung fever. People drowned in rivers. The cold broke their bones. The fear shredded their souls. Sorrow ate their hearts.

In Arkansas, the Settle's wagon tipped and smashed down an embankment. One mule died there, and Jesse's father broke his leg, the thigh bone slicing through muscle and skin.

Jesse was knocked unconscious, and, when she came to herself, she and her father were riding in another man's wagon. Poison had already streaked her father's leg with red lines traveling toward his heart. He died a week later.

They buried him near the Arkansas-Missouri border, where Jesse Settle first saw the stern and beautiful face of William A. Duke, a soldier, mostly white, but who spoke his Cherokee grandmother's language. He rode past Jesse then reined in his mare until she caught up. To hide her tears, she kept her eyes to the ground, wishing with every step that the earth would suck her in. Why did she have to live when her father was dead?

"You, woman," William Duke called to her. "What is your name?"

He had to ask twice before Jesse realized he was talking to her. She wiped her face and looked up. It was a cold day with spitting rain, and she was wearing a woolen shawl, wool she herself had spun and dyed and weaved. The rain leeched all color from the wool, but still, it was warm, and she wore the shawl draped up over her head.

"Jesse Settle," she said.

"That was your father we buried?"

How did he know? By then the *Aniyunwiya* had buried so many. "It was."

He walked his horse at her side for a time, and then he leaned down and reached for her. She set her left foot over his on the stirrup, and he pulled her up to ride in front of him. She was cold and wet, and her heart was shuddering like something half-dead. At first, she sat perfectly upright, her hands on the saddle horn, but eventually, she leaned back against him. His warmth seeped through her shawl and her jacket and began to weave the pieces of her heart together again.

The day William A. Duke first kissed Jesse Settle, the sun shone strong enough to pull the wet out of the hides of horses and cattle and mules and dogs. William walked beside her, his horse on a lead behind them. He told her about his life as a soldier, and about his Scots father and his Cherokee and Scots mother. Then he simply stopped, leaned over, and kissed her, a long and lingering kiss that gave no regard to all the others who walked past.

His breath was sweet with mint, and his cheeks were smooth, like the cheeks of most Cherokee men. They said nothing after the kiss was over, but Jesse's heart stopped dripping blood. That evening, he drew her away from the campfire to a place where trees and brush gave them privacy. He pushed Jesse's shawl from her shoulders and looked at her with questions in his eyes.

"I won't if you don't want to, Jesse."

She'd learned much about William Duke since that first time she rode with him. Even on long, terrible journeys, women talk. He had another wife, dead or alive Jesse wasn't sure. Perhaps he would go back to her someday. She knew what Christian preachers said about such things. One wife per man, regardless of Cherokee tradition, but the journey seemed to pull her away from rules.

She looked into William Duke's dark eyes. "I want to," she told him.

He was slow and careful as he undressed her, taking time over each button on the front placket of her shirt, lifting away the clothing as they stood under a bower of longleaf pine. She shivered when he cupped her bare breasts, but she was not cold. He kissed the side of her neck, which made her shiver again. When she shed her petticoat, William Duke picked her up and laid her gently on a soft bed of pine needles.

"Have you ever had a man before?"

"No." Then, because Jesse believed in honesty, she said, "I know you have another wife. I know you have children."

She wondered if he would deny the marriage or make unkind remarks about that other woman. If he did, she would dress herself and walk away.

"My wife died six months ago, and I will love her always. I will love our children, too, but that doesn't keep me from loving you."

So she stayed where she was as he began taking off his clothes. She watched until he was naked from the waist up, but then she closed her eyes.

He knelt and kissed her on the lips. "You need to watch," he said. "You need to see what is yours."

Forcing away her shyness, she opened her eyes and sat up.

He stood there with nothing on except a pair of drawers, and Jesse looked him over well. His legs were long and shapely. The muscles of his arms and chest were thick, his stomach flat. She knew William Duke was ready for her. She'd seen animals mate. Still, when he peeled away his drawers, she could not help but gasp.

He sat down beside her and whispered into her ear, "Hush, dear Jesse, hush. I will not hurt you."

Of course, he did hurt her. There's no other way for a virgin except through pain, but his caresses made her feel cherished, and, when he collapsed upon her, sated, she foolishly believed the pain of their union had ended.

PART II

HOLLOW

From Ma Mère's Song:

But nothing alive with will of its own.

CHAPTER EIGHT

THE MISSOURI OZARKS
MAY 1864, CHINA DELIVERANCE CREED

The piece of chalk is worn thin, and as I write I scrape my gloved fingertips against the blackboard. Shudder bumps rise along my arms. I've sweated great circles under my sleeves, something Mary-Polly points out to anyone seated close enough to hear.

Today is Tommy Belnap's last day at school. He's leaving to join the Union forces in Northern Missouri as a bugle boy. His uncle, a Union officer, has convinced him to go.

I'm scared for him, and my every breath scalds my lungs. Not that Tommy Belnap ever in his life noticed me, except to pull my hair or tease me about my dark eyes. His are nearly as dark. His father is Milksnake's blacksmith. Tommy inherited his large frame, but he slumps as he stands beside me at the blackboard, murmuring oaths under his breath. "Fractions are God's gateway to hell," he says, "and common denominators are a curse." He erases his current guess with his fingertips, and I take pity on him.

"Thirteen," I whisper.

He gives me a hard look, and I wish I'd kept my mouth shut, but he uses the number and finishes his problem before I finish mine.

"Good job, Tommy," Miss Otten says. She's looking peaked as is almost every adult in Milksnake. Worry pares people down.

Jayhawkers and Bushwhackers, renegades from both sides of the war, attack our town every few months. Mr. James's store was robbed just last Sunday when folks were attending church. Thank God they have yet to find us or Miz Settle. Ma Mère says we live too deep within the byways of the Hollow.

I complete my ciphering and return to my desk. Miss Otten nods at me, but that's as much appreciation as I get. Then again, I'm not about to go off to war like Tommy, and I don't have to put up with the name-calling and disdain of the boys in school whose parents have rebel leanings. But war is a hellacious thing, even for those left behind. Every time I steal a glance at Tommy Belnap, I know that fact to my bones.

The morning ends with a schoolboard visit. The men sit at the back to hear our recitations. When the youngest in the school have finished reciting, the older students spell off in a bee. We start with words like *canyon* and work our way into *paraboloidal* and *fissirostral*. Finally, only Tommy Belnap and I are left. I know what I'm going to do, but I don't want to be too obvious about it. I spell the next two words correctly, holding my breath, hoping that Tommy will do the same. He does. My chance comes with *ridgepole*.

I stare into Miss Otten's eyes as I spell, "R-I-G—"

The boys cheer and stomp their feet at my failure. "I'm sorry, China," Miss Otten says. "Tommy?"

Tommy doesn't hesitate, and I prepare myself to congratulate him. "R-I-D-G-P . . ." he spells, leaving out the *e*.

I look at him with amazement, and he winks at me. Miss Otten's eyes spark fire at both of us, and I almost laugh. All right then, I decide, no pity. I'll match Tommy word for word.

We compete, eyes locked, staring each other down until that fateful word arrives, *ultimogeniture*. It's my turn, and I make the first *i* an *a*. Tommy sounds it out, like I should have, and spells it correctly.

"Tommy wins," says Miss Otten.

He gives me a nod, and the boys cheer. The girls groan, except for Mary-Polly who claps for Tommy. The schoolboard members present him the trophy. It's a narrow silver cup, shining bright. Two side handles frame the words incised on the front. Milksnake School Spelling Bee Winner 1864. I have coveted a spelling trophy since I was eight years old.

Since it's the last day of the school year, at noon ladies of the town descend upon us with picnic baskets and high-rising cakes. They spread blankets on the ground, and we all go outside for a feast. The school-board members stay, too, and I notice the outline of a pistol under Mr. Belnap's coat. Before the War, you'd never see a man with a gun unless he was heading out to hunt.

Pine boards across three sawhorses form a makeshift table for the food. I take a tin plate and fill it with as much as it will hold. I find a place to sit, with my legs crossed, stretching my skirt to cover my knees. Ma Mère agreed I could wear my good blue calico on this last day of school. My breasts have begun to grow, and she darted the bodice to give me extra room.

The ringlets she brushed into my hair form a fall at the back of my head, held there by a dark blue satin ribbon. I glance sideways at Mary-Polly and her friend Devine Dreyer. My friend Hazel and her family moved west some years ago, and I've been lonely ever since.

Since the War started, Mary-Polly has added a layer of arrogance. Her father, Judge Preck, has organized a group of men into a posse to protect our town, and I would swear that every other word out her mouth is about her father's courage and expertise with a gun. Mary-Polly is fourteen years old, and she shines as fair and golden as the sun. Devine is also beautiful, her hair dark as bottom-land dirt. She wears dresses as fancy as Mary-Polly's, and their faces are pale from days spent sunless. They walk past me with their plates scantly filled.

Devine Dreyer glances my way and says, "Hungry, China?"

"You never starved a day in your life, did you, Devine?" I say. Her scorn changes to pity, and I wish I could eat up my words.

Tommy walks over and looks down at me, his plate heaped higher than mine. He gives me a nod. "I like a woman with a healthy appetite, China Creed."

Devine Dreyer starts to snicker, and I say, "I've heard that a healthy appetite is evidence of a strong mind."

Tommy bursts into a belly laugh, nearly spilling his food, and that makes me laugh.

"Mind if I sit here?" he says to me.

"Not at all."

Devine and Mary-Polly settle nearby, ignoring me but asking Tommy questions about the army. Can't they tell he doesn't want to talk about it? When they line up for cake, Tommy and I stay where we are.

"Wish I didn't have to go fight this god-awful war, China Creed."

"Can't you stay home?"

"My dad says I gotta go, but I wish—" He stops.

"I wish you didn't have to go either, Tommy." I look off toward the trail that leads to Ma Mère's cabin. "It's not going to be much fun to come to town, knowing you're not here."

He chuckles, and I realize I've been too truthful. At that moment, Miss Otten rings her little silver bell and calls us to entertain the town folk. It's a surprise we've been planning for two months, and something I didn't tell Ma Mère. She wouldn't have let me participate. What if an inadvertent touch triggered my penchant to thievery?

Miss Otten's face is glowing, and she hardly stutters when she announces that we will perform the Virginia Reel. Before Devine Dreyer can come over and claim Tommy—as she usually does—he pulls me to my feet and links his arm with mine. I've never been his partner before, and I can scarcely keep my heart from pounding out through my chest.

Miss Otten tucks her violin under her chin and hollers, "Tommy Belnap, "you and your partner are the first head couple. Mr. Dreyer is our caller today."

We take our places, boys and girls in two facing lines. When Miss Otten's violin begins to sing, girls and boys take a few steps toward each other and bow. Then we start the actual dance, forward and back, passing each other to the right and then the left. We link elbows and dance in a circle, which is when I realize I left my white gloves tucked into my skirt pocket where I put them while I ate. Before I can remedy the situation, Tommy grabs my hands. We face each other, lift our arms outward, and dance down between the two lines and then back again. I look into his eyes, and I wish the dance could last forever, but no dance ever does.

When the reel is over, everyone claps and Tommy lifts himself up on his toes as if he could take off and fly. To my surprise, he clasps my hand. A giddy warmth steals over me until Devine Dreyer walks up and begins a conversation, her eyes never once looking my way.

All too soon, Tommy releases my hand. "Well, ladies, it's been charming, but I gotta go to work."

He walks down the street, and I hope he will look back and wave, but he doesn't. I return to the schoolhouse to fetch my shawl and slate, and I waste a moment or two as I stare at Tommy's empty desk.

Then I turn and almost run into Miss Otten. "Thank you for the picnic, Ma'am."

"You're a f-fine student, China. You'll come back in the fall?"

"My mother says I can finish up my eighth-grade year."

I know that's a sacrifice on Ma Mère's part. Rather than spend winter days at the schoolhouse, I could be running a trapline to bring in meat. Both Union and Confederate armies regularly stop at stores and farms and houses to commandeer supplies. How can you barter for a chicken from a neighbor when almost every bird in the county has been stewed and eaten by soldiers?

I leave the schoolhouse and wave at the women who brought us the picnic. Then I walk up the street and cut off homeward. The path is shrouded at each side by a heavy cover of white-flowered ninebark, which abounds with fragrant blossoms. Someone steps out of the brush, and I gasp and drop my slate.

"Hush, China, it's me."

Tommy Belnap picks up the slate. "I didn't get to finish our conversation. That Devine Dreyer." He rolls his eyes. "You know I couldn't let you get away with throwing our spelling bee on a word like *ridgepole*. Why'd you do that?"

His eyes pull the truth out of me. "You're going off to war. I wanted you to have the trophy."

"You're a crazy girl, China. Pure crazy." He's smiling, and he lifts his hand to catch the ends of my hair ribbon. He has a dimple beside his right eye that deepens when he smiles.

My belly curls into itself, and suddenly I'm trembling. What if he kisses me? I'll be in a stewpot of trouble if Ma Mère or Miz Settle find out, and what if something shows up at Tommy's house, and he or his dad or his mother are accused of thievery? These thoughts judder through my mind, but Tommy is so close that suddenly, I don't care about the consequences.

I breathe in his pure scent—lye soap and some strange hint of brimstone. He presses his cheek to mine, and we stand there like that. Then he kisses me, a gentle kiss at the corner of my mouth. He slides his lips to cover my lips, and it's an awkward kiss, but I'm glad he's clumsy. That means it's probably his first, too. When he pulls away, I'm breathing like I've run a mile.

He touches my lower lip with his fingertip. "You take my breath,

China. You're so beautiful." We kiss again, and we're better at it this time. Then he asks, "How old are you anyway?"

"Twelve years, five months."

"Pretty young."

"I'll get older."

"You promise?"

I laugh and say, "I promise."

"And will you wait for me?" He sets his knuckles under my chin and lifts my head until I'm looking straight into his eyes. "Will you?"

"I will."

"And you'll write to me?"

I'm not sure what Ma Mère or Miz Settle will think of that, but I promise anyway.

He leans close again, and I feel like I'm made of candle wax, melting under a heavy flame. His kiss lasts a long time, like we realize how much we'll need to remember it. I'm the one who finally pulls away.

His eyes are soft. "I believe I could fall in love with you, China Creed. Some minute right soon."

I want to say that I already love him, but I'm too shy.

"Here." He hands me my slate and then gives me his spelling bee trophy.

"I can't take this, Tommy. It's yours."

"I want you to keep it for me, and, when I get home, you can give it back. And don't you forget what else is mine."

He kisses me again then disappears into the brush, I feel so empty that tears flood my eyes. Is that what love is? Pure joy braided tight together with pure pain? How will I endure all the weeks and months he'll be gone?

The next morning, Ma Mère and I can't find my blue hair ribbon anywhere.

"That ribbon cost four cents, China. I can't believe you could be so careless."

I haven't told Ma Mère about Tommy Belnap's kiss, and I don't plan to, but I climb up to the attic and come down with his trophy, hand it to my mother.

"You told me Tommy Belnap won and you took second place."

"I did."

"He gave you the trophy? Why?"

I make myself look square into her face. "Mère, he's off to war today. Joining up with the Union in St. Louis. He asked me to keep the trophy until he comes home."

She presses her lips together, and her forehead crinkles. My heart starts aching. She's going to return it to Tommy's mother, but she says, "You are only twelve years old, China. That's too young to be courting."

"Tommy thinks so, too. He's going to wait for me, and I'm going to wait for him."

"It'll be a long wait."

"It surely will."

She starts to roll up her sleeves. There's always more work. Then she stops. "China, I do believe you had that ribbon in your hair when you came home yesterday afternoon."

"I did."

"I expect Tommy Belnap has your ribbon now."

I smile at her. "I expect he does."

CHAPTER NINE

A few weeks later, I pack a flour sack with necessary belongings and head to Miz Settle's to spend the summer with her, as I have done since I was a child. The first day I'm there, she puts me to work cleaning the cabin while she's off to visit new mothers. I'm sweeping the porch when I hear someone call my name.

Cordell Smith walks out of the woods, and he's waving a letter. "From my cousin for you," he shouts. He hands me the letter and tips his hat. His bright red hair springs up jubilant. "Wonder why he doesn't write to me?" He's still laughing as he heads back toward town.

I sit on the porch steps and break the envelope seal. I can hardly breathe over the commotion in my heart.

My Dear China, Tommy begins. *I'm hoping you remember me, your friend Tommy Belnap.* Of course I remember him. How could I forget? Then I realize that he's teasing me like he did at school. I laugh, but my laughter is choked with something akin to sadness. The good dog Bessie presses her nose into my hand by way of comfort, and I read the rest of the letter out loud so Bessie can hear. She seems interested in what he says about his horse but not what he says about his rifle.

At the end, Tommy writes, "*Although I intended to fight out of St. Louis where my uncle lives, I find myself north in Hannibal, an altogether smaller town. It reminds me of Milksnake. I don't know how you managed to sneak your blue ribbon into my room before I left town, but I will keep it always. Ever your Dear Friend, Tommy.*

I'm glad to know the ribbon is in his hands and not off in some unintended place, but he's living such a strange and far-away life, that the separation between us seems vast. An ache layers itself over my heart, and I begin to shake.

Then I hear Miz Settle call Bessie. The dog runs to greet her. I fold the letter into my pocket and start sweeping again. Miz Settle walks into the clearing, talking about her visits. My throat is tight with longing for Tommy, and I can scarcely get out one word. My prayers rise silent.

A week later, Miz Settle deems me old enough for my first lesson about goomering. "The underlying idea of goomering is simple, Sheba," she says. "As you know, charms rely on the power of like. You move your knife upward when you peel the inner bark of slippery elm to treat boils, because you want the fester to work upward like your blade."

"Yes, Ma'am," I say.

"Goomering, on the other hand, uses the power of opposites. You understand?"

"About opposites?"

"Yes."

I think for a moment and come up with a possibility. "For sadness, you might make up a charm of daisy petals because daisies are joyful."

"I can't say I ever tried that," says Miz Settle, "but you got the general idea. Now, think on that for a few weeks."

I'm disappointed that our goomering lesson is so short, but then she says, "Today, we'll make love charms."

That idea lifts my disappointment. If Tommy's fancy ever strays toward another girl, it would be beneficial to own a charm that would draw him back to me.

I soon learn that making love charms is a messy enterprise. We split peach pits, removing the shriveled seed, and fill the empty pits with crumbled fat and flour paste.

Miz Settle explains that we need a full moon for the next part, and she's planned well because it is the full-moon time of the month. Unfortunately, since there's nothing else to do until the moon rises, I spend the rest of the day in the garden.

That night I'm fairly rung out from hot sun and ornery weeds, but I'm scarcely asleep when Miz Settle wakes me. The moon's up high, bright, and full. On a flat rock not too far from the porch, we lay out red-dyed strings, twelve inches long, one after another, none touching.

"Ya see, Sheba," Miz Settle says, "each string needs to take in the like-unto-like powers of the moon, which control a woman's bleeding times."

Next we sleep a few scant hours then, at early dawn, Miz Settle wakes me again, and we gather in the string, which is wet with dew. She shows me how to tie the pit halves together with that string, using strong square knots.

"As the string dries," Miz Settle says, "it'll tighten around the pit and keep the two sides joined. If you wear that charm around your neck, the power of those joined halves will draw your beloved to you."

"Like unto like."

"Exactly, but I better not catch you wearing a love charm before you turn sixteen. Ya hear me, child?"

At that moment, Bessie starts baying. Miz Settle nods at the door. "Sheba, go see why that hound's yappin'."

I don't see anything amiss, although there's an odor of something burning, and suddenly I know what's got Bessie upset. I run inside.

"Something toward town is burning fierce, Miz Settle!"

"Git your things, Sheba. Just in case."

I scramble up the climbing log and stuff a pillowcase full of my clothes. As I slide back down, Miz Settle says, "Food. Whatever you can carry."

Minutes later, we're out the door, Miz Settle with her old Harper's Ferry blunderbuss cradled in her arms and her doctor bag hung from her belt. We run the two miles to town, Bessie at our heels. When we reach Milksnake, we hunker down behind a thick growth of black-berry canes.

I see three men, then two more. They wear ragged Confederate uniforms.

"Bushwhackers," Miz Settle says.

It's the third time since April that they've raided us, but they've never set fires before. Tommy Belnap told us that some of them were kicked out of the army for misdeeds and others are deserters. Jayhawkers—renegades from the Union Army—are no better.

It's the schoolhouse that's burning, that precious place, and I pray nothing else has been torched. The three men whoop and holler and shoot their guns into the church, taking out one of the fine arched windows. Down the street, two others kick in the door of Mr. James's store.

Miz Settle and I skirt the town, breaking through vines of new-growth muscadine. Bessie follows, whining high and soft.

Then Miz Settle stops. "Sheba, stay here. Hang on to Bessie."

She lays down the blunderbuss and takes off running. A volley of shots rings out from the blacksmith shop, and I'm suddenly glad that Tommy Belnap is off somewhere north with a true, organized army. Here everything is chaos. Mr. James comes around from behind his store, a long-barrel gun in his hands. He shoots at the Bushwhackers. One staggers and falls. I feel sick to my stomach, but I can't look away. Two men from Judge Preck's posse start shooting from the middle of the street, and the other Bushwhacker falls.

Then Miz Settle crashes in through the blackberry canes. She has hold of a woman, and it takes me a minute to realize it's my teacher, Miss Otten. Her brown hair hangs in tangles to her waist, and her right cheek is blazed with a burn. She has a long tote bag strapped to her back, and she's carrying a few books. I let Miz Settle take the blunderbuss while I ease Miss Otten's books from her arms. She seems bewildered, and I'm not sure she recognizes me.

"Look at me, Miss Otten," I say. "Look at me."

Her eyes clear, and she whispers, "China," a note of relief in her voice.

"We're going to find a safe place, Miss Otten. Come with us."

I take off, Bessie tucked close to my heels. Miss Otten limps down the trail after me, and Miz Settle follows her. We finally get far enough from town to pull in a few breaths of untainted air. We stand there coughing smoke out of our lungs, and then we continue on.

At the last bend of the trail, we come upon Ma Mère. She's loaded herself with needed goods, including our Hawken rifle. "Oh, thank God," she says and grabs me in a tight clench.

"It's the schoolhouse, Maman," I tell her when she lets me go. "It's burning right into the ground, and Bushwhackers are shooting up the town.

"I saw the smoke rising."

Ma Mère clasps Miss Otten's wrists. "Did they hurt you?"

"They didn't t-t-touch me," says Miss Otten, "but our beautiful school—"

My mother looks right into her eyes. "We'll build it back. Meanwhile, we have a safe place to go, right China?"

I suspect she's referring to the cave where we stay during town celebrations and most revival meetings, both of which work Ma Mère into a frazzle of worry. "Yes, we do," I say.

It's an arduous walk, four miles through heavy brush and then up the side of Prophet's Mountain. Sometimes we have to stop and rest, but we finally arrive. Ma Mère makes us wait outside while she lights her lantern and eases in. The mouth of the cave is not much taller than Ma Mère, but it opens into a cavern as large as a good-sized barn. Sometimes we find various animals that have taken up abode within— snakes, skunks, raccoons, and once a bear.

Bessie sidles up to Miss Otten who crouches to pat her. Miss Otten notices me watching, "I nearly f-forgot, China. Mr. James gave me this for you. I planned to bring it to your house, with s-some books I knew you'd enjoy over the summer, but—"

She sighs and gives me a letter from Tommy Belnap. Miz Settle's eyebrows rise up almost to her hairline, and I can tell she's ready to ask me a passel of questions. Luckily, Ma Mère's voice echoes out at us, "All clear."

I tuck the new letter in my pocket, next to the other, and we haul in our supplies. The cave wraps us in a cool wind, and chill bumps rise on my arms.

"It's g-good to be out of the sun," Miss Otten says. She unstraps her tote bag, and I realize by the shape that it holds her violin. "Do you believe any Bushwhackers might come this way?" she asks.

The quiver in her voice ramps up my fear, and I have to breathe out hard to get my heart back to a reasonable cadence.

"They haven't during all the previous three summers of this confounded war," says Ma Mère. She points at an old trunk up on a shoulder-high ledge. "The cave floor is always damp, Miss Otten. We keep blankets in that trunk. Help me here if you would." She stands on her tiptoes and opens the trunk, removes a pile of blankets, which are tied quilts, heavy, old, and ragged. "Here, you can store your violin where it won't get wet. China, go fetch some cedar branches."

The cave seems like a proper haven, and I don't want to go outside, but I think of Tommy's letter in my pocket and head out into the hot day.

A blue-gray snake slides through the sparse grass in front of me. Snakes always cut my breath short, as does this one. Although it's a blue racer and not poisonous, it is capable of giving a goodly number of quick, vicious bites.

I climb upward to the closest cedar tree, my eyes scanning the ground for more snakes. Seeing none, I sit down and open the letter. Before I read one word, I whisper what I wish I would've told him. "I love you, Tommy Belnap." Maybe the wind will carry those words to his ears.

He starts out like he did in his first letter, *My Dear China.* Then he talks about his commanding officer, evidently a gallant man. In the middle portion of the letter, Tommy tells me things about himself that I'm happy to know. His favorite color is blue. His favorite food is hot bread slathered with butter. He gives me an address where I can send a letter, and I wish I was home so I could write him one at that exact moment. He ends by saying, *You are in my heart, China. I watch the moon each night and think of you. I hope you'll watch, too, and think of me. Ever your Dear Friend, Tommy.*

I try to imagine Tommy far away fighting vicious battles, and I pray for him with every bit of my soul. I must spend an inordinately long time on those prayers, because, when I open my eyes, Ma Mère is standing in front of me with her face pinched tight in anger.

"Even if you're not going to finish your chores, China, at least tell me where you're going. I was scared to death."

I hand her the letter.

"What's this?"

"My reason. Miss Otten brought it for me."

As she reads, she sets her hand at her throat. "My word, that poor boy. His father ought to be scalded skinless for sending him off like that." She gives me back the letter. "We'll pray, China. That will make a difference."

Generally, I suffer from weakness when it comes to faith, but Ma Mère's certainty comforts me, and I resolve to cling firm onto the mustard-seed portion that is mine.

I don't have much appetite for supper that night, and a measly meal it is, us four sharing the half-loaf of bread Ma Mère brought with her. Night falls, and we sit at the back of the blazing fire Miz Settle started to keep animals at bay. For a long time, we don't talk, but finally Miz Settle says, "You got a letter, child?"

I look into the fire until I can shut my eyes and still see the flames glowing there behind my lids.

"It's from Thomas Belnap," my mother says, which sets me into a contrary mood. I shared that letter in confidence.

"Where is he now?" asks Miz Settle.

I sigh loudly and hope Ma Mère realizes I'm not happy with her, but then I answer Miz Settle's question. "St. Louis." I pause. "Well, no, that's where he went first, and now he's somehow part of Major A.V.E. Johnston's Mounted Regiment out of Hannibal."

"He's still their bugle boy?" asks Miss Otten.

"I don't know. He owns a rifle and a horse."

Miz Settle hums low in her throat, a worrisome sound, and Ma Mère says, "His father ought to be whipped, sending a boy off to war."

"It's a necessary war, Yvette," says Miz Settle. "Any country that keeps people as slaves is setting itself in the path of God's retribution."

"I'm against slavery," Ma Mère says, "with all my heart I'm against it, but there should be better ways to solve the problem than a hideous war that kills innocent people."

When Miz Settle replies, her voice is quiet but fierce, and what she says shocks me to my bones. "Yvette, my great grandmother was a Negro and a slave, an amazing woman, according to them who knew her. My great grandfather loved her, bought her, and married her. Besides that, we Cherokee weren't treated any better than slaves. My father was a wealthy man, but his farm was stole by the U.S. Government and put into a lottery for a white family to claim."

"I'm sorry, Jesse," my mother whispers, and I know she means it, but it comes to me that just being sorry doesn't measure up to the height of the sin.

Miz Settle's next words carry a bitter edge. "My father died of the gangrene on that march we were forced to take—all the way from Georgia. Did you know about that? Or is it still a secret? Governments do a fine job of hiding evil intent. They paint over it with elegant words, while we all smile and say, 'Now ain't that glorious.' My father broke his teeth, grinding them to keep from screamin' in pain. You talk against war, Yvette?" Miz Settle has begun to shout. "How else could the problem be solved?"

"Hate only begets hate, Jesse," Ma Mère says.

To escape their rising anger, I conjure up Tommy Belnap's handsome face, until it seems that I can see him sitting there on the other side of the fire, the night at his back. Maybe that's why I don't react when something moves beyond the circle of our light. Maybe that's why my brain doesn't click in until a giant of a man steps up and stares at us across the flames.

"Thank you kindly for the welcoming fire, ladies, and for your argument. Your voices called to us while we were yet in darkness."

Ma Mère does not hesitate. Stronger than I could've guessed, she grabs me at the waist and heaves me back into the nether portions of the cave. As I scramble to my feet, she pulls a hefty branch out of the fire by its charred end, likely burning her hands, but she lifts that flaming limb as if it were a pitchfork, tines out.

Bessie, growling, crouches beside Miz Settle, and I try to decide what I should do next.

The cave has a natural niche in its near wall. That's where Ma Mère always puts our Hawken gun. The powder horn hangs from a peg pounded into a nearby crevice, as does the leather case with its caps, patches, and balls. I lift the gun, set the stock between my feet, and fumble until I locate the case and powder horn.

Miss Otten screams, and I look toward the fire. Two other men have joined the first. One has hold of Miss Otten, pressing a knife at her throat. He backs her against the cave wall, and I realize that looking at the fire has blinded my eyes to everything but its light. I close my eyes to restore my sight, and, when I can see again, I set about loading the Hawken, but my hands are clammy, cold, and trembling.

It takes me half a lifetime to open that leather case and remove the small cup we use to measure the gunpowder. I sift powder down the barrel of the gun then rap the barrel sharply with the heel of my hand. I balance the patch and ball on the muzzle. I shove them inside with the starter rod then snug it all the way down with the ramrod. I pick up the gun and cock the hammer, put a cap on the nipple, and pray, pray, pray that I can send that ball toward a useful destination.

I stand with my face at the corner where the cave narrows out toward our fire. The gun is heavier than it's ever been, and my shaking hands mimic the stuttering rhythm of my heart.

There are four men now. The biggest looming over Ma Mère. "Shit, missus," he says, "you yourself are reason for celebration."

"If you know what's good for you," my mother says, "you'll get out of here before our husbands return." She feints toward him with the stick, but he knocks it out of her hands.

"Husbands?" He glances at the others. "Did we run across any husbands hereabouts?"

One of the men spits into the darkness. "Nope. No husbands."

Another looks my way. I tell myself he can't see me, addle-eyed as he must be from the brightness of the fire, but my stomach clenches, and my supper rises into my throat. Ma Mère lifts her left hand as if to slap the man in front of her. He leans away with a smirk on his face, but that raised hand is a ploy. With her right hand, she punches him hard in the crotch then catches hold and twists. He screeches and drops to his knees.

The man with Miss Otten laughs at his compatriot's misery then slashes with his knife, laying open the bodice of Miss Otten's dress. He rucks down her chemise and grabs her right breast. She screams, and he bites her nipple. Blood flows.

Bessie tears around the fire toward that monster of a man. He lets go of Miss Otten to face the dog. "Come get me," he says to Bessie, lifting his long-blade knife.

The two men at the far side of the fire finally venture into the cave, and I stand there, brainless, trying to decide which one to shoot.

Miz Settle scuttles toward me, and the nearest of those two throws his knife at her. It pierces her left shoulder. She hisses, drawing in breath, screams as she yanks it out. Gripping the bloody blade, she hurls that knife so hard that it flips mid-air and embeds itself deep into the man's thigh. He screams and grips his leg with both hands.

Bessie leaps on the Bushwacker who bit Miss Otten, knocking him backward, and rips into his neck until his shouts become whimpers.

My mother has found a fist-sized rock, and she's pounding it against the skull of the man who kneels in front of her. That leaves one attacker standing. He's no more than ten feet away from me, and he smiles, his teeth black with rot. I raise the Hawken.

"You gonna shoot me, little girl? Sure hate to see a child hang for killing a well-meaning man."

Ma Mère taught me to aim for the largest area of any target. I point the barrel at his belly, no mercy, and pull the trigger. He goes over with a roar, but I don't wait to see if he gets up. Bessie has lost hold of that other Bushwacker's throat, and he raises his knife as if to bring it down into her ribs. I don't know how I get over there, but I do, and I strike that man's hand with the stock of the Hawken. He howls, and I hit one more time. His knife flies away into the night. Miz Settle goes after it.

Finally, I return to the man I shot. He's lying on his back, and the gaping hole in his belly looks dark in the firelight. *Gut-shot*, I think and feel a moment of pity. Then he lifts his right hand, and I see a long-barrel revolver aimed directly at my face. I know I should run, but my legs weaken, and I drop to my knees.

I look outward at the star-filled sky, the moon bountiful with its light. "I'm sorry, Tommy," I say, and then, "Please God, don't let it hurt."

In a most terrible voice, the man asks, "How old are you?"

"Twelve," I shout the word. "Twelve years old." Vaguely, as if she were miles away, I hear Ma Mère's voice. She's speaking—maybe screaming—in our secret language. *Mon Dieu, s'il vous plait.*

The man lays his left hand over the shreds of his belly. "I got me a twelve-year-old sister," he says, the gun trembling but still aimed my way. "Her name's Molly."

"That's my name, too. Molly." I hope the lie will buy me mercy.

"Pray for me," he says and steadies his gun.

I close my eyes and brace for death. The sound of the shot echoes, but there's no pain. "Don't look!" Ma Mère cries, but I open my eyes.

His right hand has fallen to his chest, the gun barrel caught in what's left of his mouth. I stare at the blood, at the shattered skull, at the broken teeth. In case that Bushwhacker's soul lingers, I say, "I'll pray for you, and I'll pray for Molly, too." Then I turn away, gagging.

Ma Mère catches me up, her arms so tight they almost split me in half. I flick my eyes toward Miss Otten. She's tucked the blood-soaked remains of her bodice into the top edge of her chemise. The man who attacked her lies at her feet, his neck half ripped away. Bessie is sitting on his chest. Our cave holds as gory a scene as any I could imagine, but we lived through it, all of us.

I'm just regaining my breath when Miss Otten screams. I follow her gaze to a circle of men who stand at the far rim of our firelight. What chance do we have?

Then I hear the strident voice of Judge Preck, a prideful and arrogant man, but at that moment his words sound like an angel chorus. He has others with him, seven, including Mr. James and Mr. Belnap. The men tromp in, and Mr. Belnap asks Miss Otten if she was shot or stabbed. Miss Otten crosses her arms over her chest.

"Worse," I say without thinking.

Ma Mère covers my mouth with her hand, whispers, "Hush." And at that moment, I realize that sometimes men can't be told those secrets that flay a woman's heart.

Mr. James comes to my mother. "Are you all right, Yvette?"

She looks surprised when he uses her first name.

"Yes, I am. Both me and my daughter."

We're all right? I look into her face, and I see how brave she is, her lips clamped tight against the pain of her burnt hands. I gaze at Miz Settle and Miss Otten, and I wonder if I look as horrified as they do, and as strong.

CHAPTER TEN

Two of Judge Preck's men lend us their horses, and in the moonlight we head back to Milksnake. I ride double with Ma Mère, and Miss Otten rides with Miz Settle. When we arrive at our cabin, Miz Settle continues with Miss Otten to Milksnake. Judge Preck says she's needed to help those hurt in the skirmish. One small boy was killed. Another man was shot in the leg. The Judge makes a vague reference to other women, and I realize that those women, too, have been hurt in ways that will never be mentioned.

I feel as if I'm made of glass, that any step could shatter me. The man I shot—his broken face—is imprinted upon my brain, and, when I close my eyes, I live those terrible moments again and again.

That night, I sleep with Ma Mère in her bed. She seems to forget that my gift might cause us problems, but perhaps she wishes for nothing more than me alive and unhurt because no stolen goods come to us.

Miz Settle stops in the next morning and treats Ma Mère's burnt hands with crushed calendula leaves pasted on with honey. Miz Settle can scarcely produce a smile, but Bessie seems to be her normal self, overjoyed at the visit.

"The Judge sent a message to the Springfield sheriff," Miz Settle says.

Ma Mère narrows her eyes, her usual sign of concern. "Men died. Do you think we'll be held accountable?"

"He says not to worry."

We spend that day as if it were a Sunday, with nothing to do but rest. After dinner, Miz Settle heads home, but I'm to stay with Ma Mère for the remainder of the week. We trek to town on Friday and learn that we four women have been declared heroes not killers. The sheriff and his men leave that day, and Miss Otten travels with them, planning to stop off in Christian County to stay at her mother's farm, maybe forever. I already miss her so much that, on the walk home, I have to rest twice, my heart too weak to keep my blood coursing.

The summer passes, and we are into September but the new schoolhouse is still under construction and won't be ready for students for at least a month. Ordinarily I would be upset about that, but we have a new teacher—a young man whose face and mannerisms remind me of a weasel, quick but sneaky. I long for Miss Otten and welcome the delay as a gift.

The last day in September, I'm in Miz Settle's garden cutting winter squash from their tough stems when I hear the sound of hooves. I look up to see Cordell Smith riding a white mule. A smile comes to my face unbidden. Tommy must have sent another letter. He's sent five already, and each one seems more personal than the one before. I didn't even let Ma Mère read the last. According to Tommy, I owe him quite a few kisses.

I set my hoe against the side of the cabin and go meet Cordell, but, when he comes up close, I see that his eyes are bleak with sorrow, and I lose all my strength.

"My uncle in St. Louis sent a telegram," he says. "Seems there was a battle—" He has to stop.

"No, Cordell, don't you dare utter one more word."

He swallows and says, "A battle, in Centralia against the outlaw Bloody Bill Anderson."

"I shake my head at him. "Hush, Cordell."

"He and his men killed a whole batch of unarmed Union soldiers on a train, gettin' transported somewheres."

"Cordell," I scream, "stop!"

"China, listen now. I can't say this twicet. Major Johnston, he took his men after Bloody Bill, but the Major was outnumbered, and—" Cordell starts crying, sobbing, "and, and Tommy. . . ."

"It's a mistake," I tell him. "Tommy just wrote me a letter. He's not dead. He can't be."

"China, he wrote that before the battle."

I'm screaming again, "You lie, Cordell! You're a liar! A filthy liar!"

Ma Mère rushes from the cabin. She gathers me into her arms. Cordell gets down off his mule, and she gathers him in, too, and the three of us stand there on the trail. She cries and Cordell cries, but I scream.

Tommy Belnap's uncle ships him home in a pine coffin. The Reverend Caldecott leads a service of honor and memory. Ma Mère and Miz Settle and I sit three pews back, behind Tommy's parents and his little sisters and brothers. Someone gave Mrs. Belnap a bouquet of pink roses, and I find comfort in their wafting scent.

When the pastor talks about what a good boy Tommy was, I want to stand up and shout, *He wasn't a boy. He knew the worst of life. How could he still be a boy?*

I'm wearing my best dress, the one Tommy saw me in the day before he left. Ma Mère pinned a black ribbon around my neck as a sign of mourning. That dress has two long pockets, one sewn into each side seam of the skirt. In one I have a hankie, but in the other, I carry Tommy's spelling bee trophy.

When the service is over and the last prayer is said, the pallbearers carry Tommy out of the church. Mr. and Mrs. Belnap follow them, but, when they come to our pew, Mrs. Belnap stops and reaches over Ma Mère to clasp my gloved hand. She looks at Ma Mère with questions in her eyes.

My mother nods and whispers, "Yes, of course."

Mrs. Belnap draws me up into the aisle. I walk beside her that long, long way between the pews. When we get outside, she pulls a rose from her bouquet and gives it to me, and I give her Tommy's trophy.

"He asked me to keep it for him until he came back home," I say.

That night, Ma Mère and I eat supper in silence, and after, I try to study one of the books Miss Otten left me, a history of Africa, with drawings of strange animals you can scarcely believe exist.

I try not to think about Tommy, but every hour that passes seems to pull me further away from him. I want my life to stop. If I can't have him with me, at least let me stay only a few months away from our kiss.

Life, however, does not stop. When I get up later from the kitchen chair where I was reading, I look down and see a red stain on the seat. I gasp, and then I realize what it is.

"China?" Ma Mère says.

She looks at me and at the chair. She goes to her bedroom and brings out a handful of catch rags. She gazes into my eyes. "You're old enough now to have children of your own." She smiles. "Although I hope you won't for some time yet."

"I won't." I don't tell her that I've already decided to never give my heart away again. The pain isn't worth the love.

"I understand your sadness," my mother says, "and I'm not going to tell you that sorrow passes quickly, but the days will become easier to face, and you will find joy in life once again. When you're ready, come outside to the porch. I need to tell you a story."

Later, when I go outside, Ma Mère is sitting in the rocker. I sit on the steps. I lift my hands to cup the waxing moon as if it were an apple, ready to pluck, and I whisper a prayer that Tommy Belnap can see it, too, from somewhere up in heaven. Then Ma Mère begins her story, one that surprises me so much that, for a little while, it eases the weight of my sorrow, and I breathe in the perfume of the night as if I were still an innocent child.

CHAPTER ELEVEN

THE DESTREHAN PLANTATION, NEW ORLEANS, LOUISIANA
1851—AS TOLD TO ME BY MA MÈRE

When their carriage stopped before l'Habitation Vivienne, Ma Mère—then seventeen-year-old Yvette Marie Destrehan—forgot to breathe. She had not seen l'Habitation since she was four years old, and she retained few memories of it. Her mother, Angèle, had drilled the facts into her head—three thousand acres, three hundred slaves—but the reality was more than Yvette had imagined.

When she was born, her grandparents Henri and Vivienne Destrehan recorded the date and her name in their Book of Accounts, untroubled that their youngest son Édouard had taken a mistress, his mother's gifted French lacemaker. As long as the boy eventually married for social and financial status, what did they care?

Unfortunately, Édouard fell in love with his mistress. More unfortunately, he married her.

As a footman helped Yvette and her mother from the carriage, the front door of the mansion opened, and a man strode out. He greeted them in a deep, loud voice so much like Yvette's father's that her throat ached in remembrance. She met her grandfather Henri on the veranda steps. A barrel-chested man, he wore his mane of silver hair in a pompadour that made him seem taller than he was. A widower, he still honored his dead wife Vivienne with candle-lit prayers.

He looked down into his granddaughter's face and murmured, "Exquisite."

Henri had invited Yvette to attend the Destrehan Ball, which he sponsored every winter after the New Orleans Debutante Ball. He'd not arranged for his granddaughter to grace that New Orleans fête. He would spring her upon the world under his own roof. After all, 1851 was modern times. Let the old women murmur their disapproval.

When the invitation arrived, her mother told Yvette they could not go, but Yvette begged until Angèle reluctantly agreed. After all, wasn't some small portion of l'Habitation Vivienne Yvette's birthright?

Henri gestured toward the door. "You first, my dear." He looked back at his daughter-in-law. "Angèle, you might as well join us." When Yvette scowled at his condescending words, he pinched her chin between his thumb and index finger. "We will provide your mother with elegant accommodations during your visit, Ma Petite, even though she is only a lacemaker, but don't forget her roots are your roots. You are only one-half Destrehan."

It was her first moment of doubt, but Yvette forced a smile. Under the protection of a good husband, she could provide her mother comfortable quarters for the remainder of her life, and obtaining that good husband was Yvette's goal. Already Angèle's fingers were misshapen with rheumatism. How much longer could she help Yvette craft their exquisite lace, their only source of income?

That night, Angèle Destrehan came into Yvette's large elegant bedroom and crept into her daughter's bed. "I have things to tell you," she whispered.

The tremor in her voice puzzled Yvette. Her mother was the bravest person she knew.

"Remember the song I always sang to you?" Angèle whispered the words of the song. "*Something you covet deep to the bone. But nothing alive with will of its own. Nothing too large. The earth stakes its claim. Nothing unseen. The eyes play the game.*"

Yvette sighed and fell back against her pillows. "About the curse carried by women in Grand-mère Destrehan's family? That song never made sense to me, Maman. Those stories you told me about Jeanne d'Arc, Eleanor of Aquitaine, and the Queen of Sheba—if they could grant wishes, how is that a curse?"

"In more ways than you and I can imagine, Yvette."

"And we're related to them?"

Angèle laughed. "Your Grand-père Henri makes that claim—very distant cousins. Whether or not it's true, I can't say. Henri's always had an elevated opinion of his family. But you must realize that the Destrehans watch for any child who might possess the gift. Like your great aunt, who could move small items across a room. Your father said it seemed like nothing more than a parlor trick, a small trinket in one place and then almost instantly in another, but he was only six when she died. Highwaymen stole her."

"I know, Maman. You and Papa told me the story many times."

"A woman like that could make a great deal of money for a master who groomed her to entertain highborn gentlemen. A beautiful face and magic hands."

"If she could make them money, why did they kill her?"

"They did not kill her."

Yvette frowned. She hadn't heard that part of the story. "Who did?"

Angèle clasped her daughter's hands and looked into her face. "She killed herself, Ma Chérie."

Yvette drew in her breath.

"I brought you something, Yvette." Angèle struck a Lucifer and lit the oil lamp on Yvette's bedside table. "Look here, beside your lamp."

"You brought me a book?" Yvette picked it up, studied the scarred cover. "A Bible, Maman? Written in French? The priests prefer Latin."

"The priests don't need to know."

From between the pages, her mother drew out a folded sheet of paper. "Read it."

It was a list of names, all women, several marked with a crosshatched star. Her grandmother's name, Vivienne Destrehan, was the last on the list, that name also starred.

"This is my grandmother's pedigree?" Yvette asked.

"Yes, and, of course, yours. The stars mark those who had some form of the gift."

"My grandmother did?

"Do you remember your grandmother's white hair?"

"I do."

"It was always that white, not just something that came upon her in old age. White hair is a sign of the gift."

"Did she give Grand-père this plantation?"

"No. Her gift was very small. Do you remember waking up with a hen's egg on your pillow?"

"I do. More than once."

"That was her gift. She could give eggs."

Yvette laughed. "A very small gift indeed."

"Not for someone who is starving."

"Of course, Mère. I did not mean to be flippant, but this list. It's all women, and Grand-mère Vivienne had no daughters."

"Sons can pass the gift, although they never possess it."

"Why not?"

"How should I know, Ma Chérie? I simply want you to be aware that your grand-père is very interested in any daughter born into this family."

"He did not seem much interested in me. At least not until now."

"Because you do not have the gift, but now you are old enough to marry and have children."

"What if one of them has the curse?" Yvette whispered.

"We must be wise as serpents, fierce as wolves, sly as foxes."

"And keep her hidden?"

"Oui, Ma Fille Chérie."

One tailor, four seamstresses, two beaders, and Yvette and her mother—the lacemakers—completed Yvette's ball gown during a month of eighteen-hour days. The bell skirt was edged with yards of Bayeux lace, and the bodice was deep-cut and patterned with diamanté. The entire dress glowed a deep garnet red, inappropriate for Yvette's age and status, but then Yvette was not a typical debutante.

As she stood through the final fitting, sweat ran down her sides, but she kept her back straight and her knees locked. She did not let herself contemplate how she would dance for hours carrying the weight of that gown. She must; therefore, she would. Her father's death after a long illness taught her that life was difficult. Although they were not wealthy when her father was alive, her grandfather had provided his errant son a stipend that allowed them to lease a good house, keep a kitchen maid, and send Yvette to finishing school.

After her father's death, her grandfather sent no more money, and Yvette left school to join her mother as a lacemaker. They lived in stifling attics at one mansion or another, employed to create the lace needed by a debutante or a wealthy wife.

Yvette's education seemed useless to her then—piano and voice lessons, drawing classes, the equestrian arts, Latin, French, English, and, of course, deportment—but now she realized that her education had prepared her for life in her grandfather's home, and it had prepared her for the Destrehan Ball, which would be held during the height of Mardi Gras, another winter diversion for the wealthy until the forty days of Lent demanded more solemn events.

The evening of the ball, a knock on the sitting room door sent Angèle scurrying to answer. The butler, Henri's messenger, held a brief murmured conversation with Yvette's mother. When he left, Angèle came into the bed chamber carrying a flat velveteen case. Inside lay an exquisite necklace.

"It's yours for this night," she told her daughter.

Yvette skimmed her fingers over the deep red stones. "Rubies?"

"I would think so, Ma Chérie."

"We could run away with it, Maman. It would pay for a voyage to Europe. Grand-père would never find us."

"Or you could marry well and receive it as a wedding gift."

"Which do you prefer, Maman?"

"It is not my choice to make."

"Then it shall be marriage. Surely that would be better than having Grand-père hunt us down like foxes."

The festivities were underway for an hour before Henri Destrehan escorted his granddaughter down the marble stairway into the ballroom. The music stopped, and a number of young men left their quadrille partners to walk to the foot of the stairs.

Her grandfather laughed. "Well, Ma Petite, take your choice." Then he leaned close and whispered, "Consider the two Le Roy sons most carefully." He nodded at a young man who had stayed at the side of his partner, a homely girl dressed in white. "Monsieur Paul Le Roy," Henri said. "And," he motioned toward one of the men at the foot of the stairs, "Monsieur Anselme Le Roy."

Anselme stepped forward and clasped her hand, led her to the dance floor. The musicians resumed their music, and the quadrille continued, gentlemen scrambling to reclaim their abandoned and disgruntled ladies. Anselme did not speak to Yvette during the complicated steps of the dance, but, when the music ended, he stared down at her and said,

"A man might decide to give up his card games for a woman like you, Mademoiselle Destrehan."

"And he would be expected to," she replied as he escorted her from the floor.

Her grandfather had provided her with a list of dance partners. Paul Le Roy was scheduled for an allemande, a new dance to the Americas, with partners held close. Paul was a tall, handsome man with yellow-white hair. He came to her shyly smiling, a reprieve from the bravado of his brother and others, who had tired her with boasts about their horses and carriages and their fathers' plantations.

She and Paul had danced only a few minutes when he glided her to a corner where potted palms partially shielded two padded Rococo chairs. She sighed as she sat down, and, under cover of her skirts, she slipped her feet from her heeled shoes.

"It was that obvious, my exhaustion?" she asked.

"Not at all. You are a gifted actress, and I mean that in the best sense of the word."

"Then I thank you."

"Your grandfather chose your partners?"

"So I was told."

"I suspect you will have many suitors."

"Should I remind them that Grand-père has two living sons? My inheritance will be modest." As soon as she uttered the words, her face colored. What foolish impulse made her say that? "Gracious, I apologize. I didn't mean to imply that—"

"That I was merely interested in the Destrehan fortune?" He looked into her eyes. "I've seen more lives ruined by reticence than by truth. Thus, I will be more than honest in my request."

"Which is?"

"Please, Mademoiselle Destrehan, consider me among those suitors. Although I have little interest in your grandfather's wealth, I do covet the kind regards of his granddaughter."

Her heart stuttered. Could it be that simple to find a good husband?

He clasped her hand and gently squeezed her fingers. "And will you consider me?" He leaned toward her, kissed her forehead.

"Of course," she said, a whisper scarcely voiced, but she saw by his smile that he heard.

* * *

More than a week passed before Yvette saw Paul Le Roy again. She'd begun to think his comment about being a suitor was only a polite reply to her faux pas. Other young men came to visit, and, with her mother acting as chaperone, she listened to their stories and rode in their carriages.

On February 24, a Monday, Yvette's grandfather summoned her to his office. She was wearing a faded day dress from her life as a lace-maker, her hair in a messy bun. Henri peered at her with disapproval, which was puzzling. He'd seen her in day dresses before and never objected. Then Paul Le Roy stepped from a shadowed corner of the room.

She quickly curtseyed. "Monsieur Le Roy, as you see by my dress, I do not waste each day hoping for callers."

Her grandfather's mouth twitched, and she prepared for a reprimand, but he said, "And you are sure, Monsieur Le Roy, you want to court my granddaughter?"

"Quite." Paul's answer was directed at Yvette.

That Sunday, he escorted her to church, and during each prayer, he placed his hand over hers.

The following Monday, her grandfather summoned her again to his office. He sat behind his desk, a ledger book open before him. He did not look up when he said, "Paul Le Roy has asked me for your hand. May I have the banns read?"

Tears gathered in Yvette's eyes, and she had to blink them away. Her mother had been wrong. Their visit to l'Habitation was the wisest choice she ever made.

When she did not immediately answer, Henri closed the ledger and leaned back in his chair. "Am I wrong in my assumption that you are happy with the thought of Paul Le Roy as paramour and then husband?"

She blushed at his use of the word *paramour*.

"Perhaps I assume too much," Henri said. "Not even yet a kiss? If you don't make yourself available, Yvette, he will find another. Most husbands do anyway."

Yvette bristled. "How sad. How spineless. A man who does not honor his vows." Surely her father had never taken a mistress, but then she remembered that her mother had been his mistress.

Henri burst into a rolling laugh. "The banns?"

"I have one question, Grand-père."

"Yes."

"Why did you choose the Le Roy family?"

He gazed through the bank of windows on the east wall, which provided a wide view of the horse pastures. Then he opened a desk drawer and took out a small drawstring bag. "You will keep this information to yourself. No one else, not even your mother, needs to know." He spilled the contents of the bag over his ledger.

Yvette stared at the pale brown granules. "Seeds?"

"Cotton seeds. There will be more than these few, Granddaughter, enough to plant one thousand acres. The land is ready; the soil is hungry. If the banns are read this Sunday, the seeds will come to me Monday morning. Both Le Roy brothers have agreed. You know that their parents are dead, and the brothers own the plantation in joint partnership."

"Ma Mère told me."

"Of course. House servant gossip."

Yvette ignored the barb. "You have been planting cotton for years, Grand-père. I'm sure some of that must be seed cotton. Yet you need Le Roy seed? Why?"

He smiled as if pleased with her question. "For the same amount of work on the same amount of land, the plants that grow from these seeds will yield an increase of nearly one-third over the crop that currently grows in Destrehan fields."

"Where did they get it?"

"I don't know. I hope to find out. Perhaps, once you are married, your husband will tell you, and perhaps you will be inclined to tell me. Paul might appreciate inheriting a share of l'Habitation's acreage. One-third for him and one-third for each of my two living sons, both of whom are in Europe, dedicating their lives to debauchery." He sighed. "The banns?"

"Yes," said Yvette.

The summer of 1851 saw an abundant cotton crop growing on Henri Destrehan's thousand acres, but the mosquitoes were particularly vicious, and everyone knew they heralded the miasmas that brought the dreaded chills and delirium of yellow fever.

The first Monday in June, Yvette planned an early breakfast with her mother then a horseback ride with Paul. She and Angèle had completed their meal when a maid brought Yvette a note written on the yellow stationery used by the Le Roy brothers. She broke the seal, read the note, and closed her eyes in dread.

"Paul has canceled our ride this morning, Maman. He's not feeling well. Do you think he might have yellow fever?"

"Ma Chérie, he's grown up here. Surely, like you, he survived the fever as a child. He will be immune." She reached over and patted her daughter's hand. "No worries, Yvette. He's a strong man, but we have other problems. Last night something happened that concerns me far more."

They retreated to her mother's boudoir where a small blue plate lay at the center of Angèle's bed.

"You remember this, Yvette?" she asked. She picked up the plate.

"Of course, it's from the set of Spode dishes Papa gave you. I didn't know you'd brought them with us, Maman."

"I didn't."

"Then how—"

Angèle interrupted her. "Tell me true, Yvette. Is there any chance you might be carrying a child?"

Yvette's cheeks flamed. She walked to the window, opened the thick drapery, and looked out. The sky was crowded with heavy clouds. "I do not regret it, Maman. Paul is a most tender lover, but I doubt I carry his child. Leastwise, I have no sign of it."

Angèle picked up the plate and ran her finger around the gold rim. "The other night, I dreamt about those dishes, particularly that small plate made for petits fours. I believe your child brought it to me."

"Maman, non, non, non. Grand-père, he must have had our belongings packed and—"

"Yvette, after your father died, I sold the whole set to put food on our table." She walked to Yvette's side and handed her the plate. "Keep it for your baby. Tell her that she gave it to me as a gift, and my heart was happy."

"Maman, you're being foolish. This child—if I carry a child—could not give you that plate. You must have forgotten that you kept it."

"Non, Ma Chérie." Her mother blinked back tears. "You will have a girl, and her hair will be white, and her gift is already amazing. Marry your handsome Paul, and, when your daughter is born, tell him the truth about her, but be ready to leave Louisiana, because someday Henri will take her away from you. Don't ever doubt it. No matter how jovial his laughter or how sincere his promises."

The next morning, Paul's brother Anselme came to escort Yvette to the Le Roy plantation. Paul was very sick, the doctor said. No doubt he'd contracted yellow fever—yellow jack as it was often called. Anselme led the way to Paul's chambers, and, when they entered the room, even before Yvette saw him, she knew the doctor was right. The cloying odor of the disease was unmistakable.

"I have brought Yvette," said Anselme.

Paul, sunken deep in his pillow, didn't open his eyes, but he lifted his hand. Yvette stepped forward and caught it in a tight grip. She stroked the hair back from his brow and kissed his forehead. She looked up at Anselme, tears bright in her eyes.

"I will give you some privacy," he said.

He left, and Yvette whispered to Paul, "I have great good news, my love. A reason for you to live."

Paul opened his eyes.

"I am with child."

He smiled, and his teeth were stained dark with blood.

"Oh my darling," Yvette said and began to weep.

For three days she sat beside Paul's bed while the yellow jack ate him alive.

The day after Paul Le Roy's burial, Yvette's grandfather told her that a year of mourning would be adequate. Then she would marry Anselme. The Le Roy cotton seed was already growing in the Destrehan fields, as she well knew. Henri owed the Le Roy family a wife.

A few days later, Yvette's mother arranged a visit to New Orleans where Yvette would be fitted for more black gowns. Anselme would accompany them. It was noon when they disembarked from the paddle wheeler that carried them from her grandfather's wharf to the city. Anselme escorted them to a hotel and into the restaurant that took up one side of the first floor.

"Order for yourself, dear Yvette, dear Madame," he said. "I have business to attend. An hour, no more." He kissed Yvette's cheek and set her tapestry bag at her side then disappeared into a back room. A few minutes later, Yvette and her mother cashed her grandfather's notes of credit, intended as payment for her dresses. Not a great deal of money, but perhaps enough.

"I will not be long at l'Habitation, Ma Chérie," her mother said. "Your grandfather will not put up with me. After all, his son loved me more than he loved Henri. Worse, he loved me more than all Henri's riches, and Henri will never forgive me for that. I have cousins in Canada."

"The dreaded Acadians?" Yvette said, her voice lilting into a tease. She hoped to make her mother smile.

Angèle did not smile. "Your father and I did not tell Henri about that side of my family. Why make my lowly estate even more abhorrent in Henri's estimation?"

"What will you tell Anselme?"

"A very sad story about your request to walk along the river, and that you threw yourself in, distraught over Paul's death."

"They will search for my body. When they don't find it, they'll know you are lying. Please, Maman, come with me."

"Bodies are lost in this river every day, Yvette. They will see my grief and believe that I have lost my daughter, for I truly have." Her voice broke. "But if I go with you, they'll know you are still alive."

"We could meet in Canada."

"Yvette, I cannot trust my Acadien family with your child's curse. Greed is more powerful than loyalty."

"But how can I find someone who is not driven by greed?"

"You won't, Ma Chérie, but our ruse may keep your daughter and her secret away from the Destrehan family. The more powerful the family, the greater the chance of harm."

They walked to the docks where traders brought their pirogues and flatboats loaded with market goods. They stood in a shadowed alcove between two wretched shacks and studied the dockworkers—most of them Negro, Irish, or Acadien.

A great deal of commotion arose from one area, the men there surely from the north, some of them wearing buckskins, all of them boisterous and loud. A man like that might fight for his wife, Yvette thought. And, for her child, if he believed it was his.

"An American, Maman. Grand-père would never believe I'd go with an American."

"An American? No, Yvette."

"For my little one, Maman." Her mother began to cry, and Yvette wrapped her arms around her. "Oh Maman, how will I live without you? I'm foolish and silly and prideful. How can I survive without you to guide me?" They held each other and wept, but finally her mother pulled away. She wiped Yvette's tears with her gloved fingers, and she looked into Yvette's eyes. "You are not alone, dear daughter." She set her hand gently at Yvette's belly.

Yvette kissed Angèle on both cheeks. "You are right. I'm not alone."

They looked out over the wharfs, their arms around each other's waists. One of the traders leaped ashore and secured a flatboat to the dock cleats.

"Beaver furs from the Rockies," he shouted, speaking English. "Missoura tobacca and the best damn shine under God's good sun."

He removed his hat, and Yvette caught her breath. Before her mother could stop her, she stepped from their hiding place, and shouted in English, "The best damn shine, you say?"

The American bowed in her direction. "Yes, Ma'am. Parnell Haddeus Creed at your service."

She eyed his mop of white-blond hair and made herself smile.

PART III

HAINTS

From Ma Mère's Song:

Nothing too large. The earth stakes its claim.

CHAPTER TWELVE

CHINA DELIVERANCE CREED, JULY 1873

Miz Settle and I take seats near the back of the visiting preacher's open-sided tent. If the man deserves more than polite attention, I'll add the penny in my pocket to the offering. I'm quite sure Miz Settle has no money to give. A doctor has taken up abode in Milksnake, and some of our customers—the fools—have changed allegiance, but Ma Mère taught me to make lace, and I eke out enough money from the ladies in town to spare a penny.

Dusk is near, and the hills crowd close, blocking the westerly sun. The revival service is about to begin. Milksnake descends unto darkness. Someone has set several rows of upright barrels at the outermost edges of the canopy tent. When people come in, they set their coal oil lanterns atop those barrels or across the foot-high platform at the front. That much coal oil, burning in unison, adds a choking miasma to the air.

During the years of the Civil War and its aftermath, few traveling preachers dared venture into the torn and bleeding state of Missouri. Even yet, women wear mourning for sons, fathers, or husbands. Most soldiers who returned to our town seem broken one way or another. Haggar Johnson stumbles through the streets, drunk by ten in the morning. Dale Torik's left leg is an oak peg, and more men than I can name—from Milksnake, Prophet's Mountain, and Grit's Hill—roll and pin an empty shirtsleeve.

Milksnake has not had the benefit of a revival service since 1860 when I was still a child. At that time, Ma Mère, a respectable widow, sang in a choir, and the preacher was taken with her pure, high voice.

He asked her to sing a solo the last night of his visit. There will be no such request by this preacher. Although I am mystified by my mother's actions, I am her daughter. Her foolish decisions do not lessen my love for her, but I am well aware that the people of Milksnake believe she is a harlot, and if she is, what does that make me? Nonetheless, I boldly meet the eyes of any woman who looks my way.

Our Reverend Caldecott walks in, a straight narrow-boned man. Mrs. Caldecott hangs onto his right arm, and she's frowning as if a layer of dread has settled over her. Perhaps she worries that her husband's sermons will not live up to whatever hellfire is unleashed upon us during this service.

I expect the revival preacher to come in next, but neither of the two men who enter looks like a preacher. They are dressed much too city-fancy. Both are handsome, the tall one with fine-boned aristocratic features, tawny eyes, and light brown hair. The shorter gentleman looks ruggedly Celtic, his eyes a vivid blue, his hair black and curly.

"The new doctor, Sheba," Miz Settle hisses into my ear.

"Which one?"

"The one with brown hair. The other's a friend, or so I heard."

The doctor's coat and pants are brown serge cut in the new style called a sack suit because of its looser fit. His friend wears a pale grey fitted frock coat unbuttoned to reveal a blue jacquard vest underneath. Their collars are high and very white, and their ascots shine like silk, which I suppose they are.

The two gentlemen sit a few rows back from the front platform, the doctor nearest the aisle. The next person to enter the tent is Mary-Polly Preck, walking gracefully. Heads turn as people catch sight of her. The dearth of young men who survived the war has left her a spinster, but I have no doubt she will find a husband, her father still being a judge acquainted with people who live far beyond the roads and trails of Milksnake Hollow. According to rumor, Judge Preck brought the doctor and his friend to our town for Mary-Polly's benefit.

She's styled her hair into an elaborate mass of curls atop her head, and I waste a few thoughts on the bun that sits low at the back of my neck, likely a mess after our trek from Miz Settle's house. Mary-Polly wears a cascade of my point plat appliqué lace pinned to her bodice, and I try to cultivate gratitude. She doesn't select a seat, but instead steps up on the platform and stands behind the slender podium at the center. She pulls a tuning whistle from her skirt pocket and blows into it. It emits a thin, silvery sound, and she hums until she finds her first note.

The pride I carry about my own voice falls before Mary-Polly's rendition of *Rock of Ages*. Each note is fragile yet perfect. She's gifted, and she's still lovely in a golden way. I'm a wraith compared to her, too tall, too thin. An unbecoming tan darkens my face and hands. Still, men notice my white-blond hair, and Ma Mère claims I'm beautiful.

Mary-Polly finishes her song, the audience sighs, and she descends from the platform. She stops beside the doctor, and he stands. She claims a chair between him and his friend who moves over once he realizes her intent.

The sudden wail of a fiddle cuts the air, and Mr. Grant Teller of Poplar Bluff, a man famous for his violin and loud nasal voice, capers down the aisle in a fragmented dance that makes some folks smile and others murmur disapproval. To dance? In a church meeting? But the tent preacher walks close behind, clapping his hands in rhythm, and the disapproval is swallowed down whole. I look at Miz Settle. Her eyes twinkle, and we both smile. I hold that smile until the preacher faces his audience from behind the narrow pulpit. I see hubris in the set of his lips, and at that moment I suspect that his touted godliness is more theatre than truth. His deep fluid voice rises above the fiddler's song, and I shrink back in my chair as he proclaims us all sinners.

Mr. Teller lowers the fiddle.

"Stand!" the tent preacher bellows. "Stand in the presence of the Lord."

I stand as does everyone except Miz Settle. I lean down. "Are you all right?"

"Doubt's caught a holda me," she says. "I doubt we're in the presence of the Lord."

I don't allow myself to laugh. After the opening prayer, we sing several songs, including a new one that is loud and fun and inspires Miz Settle to stand up and join in.

Then we sit, and the preacher preaches. He's a man of simple words, long arms, and a loud voice. The ends of his mustaches twist up into points. As he speaks, his dark hair overcomes its pomade and falls over his ears. For fifteen minutes he preaches, for half an hour, and finally a full hour. My nodding head wakes me with a jerk. I glance around in guilt, but Miz Settle is also asleep as are a number of others. The preacher must notice, because he wraps up his sermon and asks the fiddler to play something strident. When everyone is awake, ushers pass the offering baskets. I'm prideful when I add my penny, checking the reaction of the farmer next to us. He pretends not to notice and lets the basket pass him by.

Mary-Polly gets up and sings another song, this one quiet and intended to pinch the heart. Then the preacher begins to coax. We need to repent, all of us, he says. People lean forward in their chair as if his voice draws them, but I assure myself that my sins are not of the caliber to require me to walk the aisle in shame and repent under the heavy hand of this particular preacher.

Miz Settle tugs on my arm. My guess is she's ready to go home. It's dark, and I don't want her to walk alone, even though she brought a lantern. I'll spend another night with her and return to Ma Mère in the morning.

I look at Miz Settle and nod my head toward the open sides of the tent, but she points at the front of the tent. My heart sinks. People are kneeling there. She wants to go up, and who can blame her? Half the people in Milksnake believe an Indian needs more repentance than other folk. Why not conform? It might bring Miz Settle more customers. On the other hand, it might be God himself who has spoken to her. Who am I to contradict? As I step into the aisle, I'm greeted by the avid shout of the tent preacher. I gaze up at him, but he's not looking at me. His eyes are fixed on a young woman who stands in the aisle in front of the pulpit. She's frothing at the mouth. Her dress is torn at the waist and droops in a gap that offers a glimpse of the bare pink flesh of her hip. She reaches toward the preacher with wild, fierce hands. Others who have come forward move away.

Miz Settle grabs my arm and says, "That girl is goomered."

Heavy dread settles deep in my gut. "You think the preacher can help?"

"Maybe. Maybe God gave him the power to cast out spells, but be ready just in case."

The new doctor is the next one to step into the aisle. He escorts Mary-Polly to safety several rows back. Mrs. Preck rushes forward and hugs her daughter. Then the doctor strides up the aisle and clamps hold of the girl's arms. She screams, and the revival preacher shouts at the tormenting demon.

"Fool," whispers Miz Settle. "It ain't demons. It's a spell. Were it demons, they'd jump from her to the preacher. He ain't got enough God inside to hold 'em off."

I shudder.

"Come on." Miz Settle says.

We begin a difficult journey up the aisle, pushing past people who have crowded in to see what's happening.

"Pray, Sheba," Miz Settle tells me. I don't need the reminder.

We're finally in front of everyone, a few feet back from the girl, who's kicking at the doctor with her hard-soled barn boots. Her right foot lands with such force against his shin that it rips through the fabric of his pants. The minister commands the demons to come out.

The girl is suddenly still, frozen in place, her skirt rucked up to her knees, her bright ginger hair hanging down over her face. She's breathing hard, but at least she's quiet. The preacher begins to praise God.

"Too soon," Miz Settle says.

All things happen at once. The girl bites the doctor's hand then rips herself out of his grip. She steps up on the platform and crouches like a catamount. Babies begin to cry, and mothers gather their children close. The girl leaps to the tent preacher's chest, her arms around his neck, her knees knuckling in at his belly. She snaps her teeth close to his cheek, and he screams.

The doctor's friend jumps onto the platform and clasps the girl by the waist. He coaxes her to let loose of the preacher and lowers her to her knees. He kneels behind her, his right arm wrapped around her shoulders, the left around her waist. I'm close enough to hear him say, "Hush, hush, little lass. Hush. All is well."

Of course, he's wrong. All is not well. The doctor cradles his bitten hand, blood welling from deep tooth marks, and the tent preacher is trembling.

Miz Settle steps up to the platform. She bends over the girl and says in a low, calm voice, "What's your name?"

"Patience Camry," the girl says, as if it were an ordinary introduction with no attendant problems.

"Patience Camry, what hex-maker done this to you?"

"I'm the hex-maker. I done it to me." She hacks a gob of bloody spit toward the preacher, but he jumps back, and it falls short.

"That's a lie, and you know it," Miz Settle tells her.

Patience Camry snarls. "Says who?"

"I do and this girl here." Miz Settle points at me. We're both Goomer Doctors."

I'm standing near the platform but satisfied to remain on lower ground. Patience Camry turns her eyes toward me, and they are the strangest eyes you might ever see, pale green and bugging out of her head, the whites bloodshot nigh unto red. She wipes her mouth on her sleeve. "You're young to be a Goomer Doctor," she says to me in a most civilized voice.

The doctor's friend maintains his grip on her, but he gives me an encouraging look.

"Young or not, I am a Goomer Doctor. Able to cast out hexes. Tell me, what happened to you?"

"I'll tell you but not her." She stabs a finger toward Miz Settle. "She looks like a witch to me."

"She's not."

"But she's Injun."

"She is."

"She got Injun spells?"

"She's never put a spell on anyone."

"That true?" the girl asks Miz Settle.

"I don't cast spells. I remove 'em."

"And you?" She squints at me. "What's your name?"

"My name doesn't matter, Patience. I'm a Goomer Doctor. You were goomered."

The girl begins to cry, which gives me hope that she will soften toward us.

Unfortunately, the preacher recognizes his opportunity. "You need the Lord, girl. Right now, repent and ask him in."

I look up at that preacher, and he gives me an evil eye if I've ever seen one. "She's not ready yet. Please back off."

He seems amazed by my boldness, but at least he stops talking. I turn my attention to the girl. "Do you know who goomered you?"

She clamps her mouth tight-shut.

"You know, don't you?"

When she speaks, her lips scarcely move. "Her name's Miz Theodore Bixby, and she lives over in Polk County. She's mad because her son has took a likin' to me.

A woman stands up from the audience. "I ain't no witch, you dog!"

The indrawn breath of the congregation rises like a rush of wind.

Although Mrs. Bixby's crooked nose gives her face an odd, misaligned appearance, she's respectfully attired in a dark-colored dress that shimmers of silk, but meanness pours off her like sweat.

Miz Settle looks at me with determination in her eyes. For us and our goomer doctoring, family battles are the worst, but Miz Settle is nothing if not courageous.

She clasps the tent preacher's arm and points to Mrs. Bixby, who is screaming curses at Patience Camry. "There's your hex-maker," Miz Settle tells him. "I'd say in most circumstances a preacher should be the one to take care of her, but I'm afraid you're not strong enough."

"What do you know about strength?" he says. He leaves the platform and starts down the aisle toward the woman.

I speak to the doctor's friend, "Would you bring a chair for Miss Patience?"

He gently lets go of her and brings a chair. She sits down, and he stands behind her, his hands on her shoulders. I approach Patience Camry like I would a fearful dog, my gloved hand extended palm up to show I bear no weapon and intend no harm. "Patience, I'm going to touch you now. A gentle touch on your wrist." She twitches but doesn't try to shake me off. "Does that hurt?"

"No, Miss."

I pray, but I keep my eyes open. When I'm done praying, I slip a buckeye from my pocket and press it into her hands. A buckeye doesn't have the power to chase off a goomered hex, but it can calm a person in trouble. Miz Settle leans over my shoulder, a white muslin charm bag dangling from her hands.

She gives me the bag. "Show her what's in it."

I dump the contents onto the girl's lap—a pebble with a hole through it to siphon in good luck, a string for knotting off sickness, and one small roll of paper no larger than the tip of my finger.

I reach for the paper, but Miz Settle stops my hand. "It's Ezekiel 16:62."

Ezekiel 16:62 is a short, strong verse. I recite it. "'And I will establish my covenant with thee; and thou shalt know that I am the Lord.'" I press the curl of paper into Patience's hand. "This verse is God talking to you, and He's far more powerful than any goomering you have endured."

She and I say the verse together, and Patience wipes her eyes. "I feel my heart waxing strong again," she says.

Miz Settle leans in toward the girl. "You stay away from that woman, ya hear? Her son can come see you. Don't you go see him."

At that point, Miz Theodore Bixby starts up the aisle, and people part before her as if they were the Red Sea. Although the platform is only a foot higher than the trampled dirt aisle, she leaps upward and extends her arms. The full sleeves of her dress take on the appearance of raven wings.

Patience Camry slides from the chair and huddles on the floor, her arms over her head, her hands protecting the back of her neck. My heart shudders, but I stand firm beside Miz Settle, the two of us between Patience and the hex-maker. Goomer Doctors use scripture and prayers and the plants growing on God's good earth to stop hexes and defeat curses, but we are not adequate to face demons. Still, Miz Settle holds fast. How can I do less?

Mrs. Bixby stands over Patience Camry, looks down at her with her lips curled into a sneer.

"You will not hurt that child," Miz Settle says.

Mrs. Bixby's body jerks as if she's been hit by a bullet.

Miz Settle's voice grows stronger. "You demons, listen! You will not hurt this child. You will not! Ya hear?"

I can't explain what I do then. Only that God's hand was surely upon me. I reach out and clasp that wicked woman's right wrist. Then her left. She screams, and it's a scream of pain. Three times her head jerks backward.

"Three demons," Miz Settle says, quietly enough that only I and Mrs. Bixby can hear.

Mrs. Bixby falls to her knees.

"Don't let go of her," Miz Settle tells me. "Hold on for all you're worth. Demons come in sixes."

The woman whimpers. Two more times her head jerks.

"Let go," Miz Settle tells me.

"There's one more."

"It ain't in her."

I'm puzzled until I look up and see the revival preacher hovering over us. The viciousness on his face is explanation enough. I let go of Mrs. Bixby's arms, and she slumps to the floor. Patience scuttles out from behind us. She's panting hard, and Miz Settle says to her, "You're free. Go home."

"Thankee. Thankee so much."

Patience runs from the tent, and the tent preacher's eyes fade back to normal. He nudges Mrs. Bixby with his foot. "Get up, you foul beast."

To my surprise, she does. "I'm empty," she moans. She sits on the edge of the platform with her eyes closed.

"And you two—" The preacher points at Miz Settle and me. "—what are your names?"

For some reason, my eyes are drawn to the doctor's friend, who remains standing behind Patience's empty chair. As if he understands hexes and curses, he mouths, *Don't tell him.*

I wouldn't. Names are not to be bandied around by a person who offers you nothing but hate.

The tent preacher's face burns red, and Miz Settle wags a finger at him. "Demons don't catch comfort floatin' free," she says. "They need to find a body. Beware. Only God is strong enough to keep them away."

The preacher tilts back his head and laughs. Then he addresses the audience. "These two women, they're the ones who are demon-possessed."

"They are not," the doctor's friend says and offers his right arm to Miz Settle and his left to me. His body heat, radiating through the fine wool of his jacket, makes me shiver.

"Don't you take those women out of here," the preacher shouts as we walk down the aisle. "They're demon-possessed."

Half the congregation seems to agree with him, hissing at us and raising crossed fingers to ward off any hex or demon we might carry. Tears burn my eyes, and our escort looks down at me. "You did God's work here," he says. "Don't doubt your faith or His strength."

It seems such a strange thing for a man to say, especially someone we'd never met before, but it brings me comfort, and my steps grow firm as I walk down that dirt aisle. When we pass the Reverend Caldecott, he stands. I assume he will also condemn us, but to my surprise he lifts his open Bible toward the tent preacher and says, "'Judge not.'" Then he begins to sing. The fiddler takes up the tune, and soon the whole congregation joins in.

"My land, who could believe all that?"

I recognize Mary-Polly's voice and glance over my shoulder. She and the doctor are walking out behind us. The doctor watches me with puzzlement on his face as if I'm a riddle he needs to solve. Outside the tent, the doctor's friend introduces himself.

"Royce Cooper," he says. His voice carries a deep brogue.

Miz Settle doesn't hesitate to offer up our names and Mary-Polly's as well, although I see by his acknowledgment that Mr. Cooper has already made Mary's acquaintance. "And Dr. Stephen Grey," says Mary-Polly, clasping the doctor's arm with both hands.

"Well done, ladies," says Dr. Grey. "A difficult situation."

He stares into my eyes, and Mary-Polly says, "Doctor, I would appreciate an escort home."

Royce Cooper looks at Miz Settle. "May I walk you home?"

"We're all right, once I claim my lantern," she says. "It's only a couple miles to my cabin, but I thankee for your help. Much appreciated."

The singing ends, and I feel a ruffle of unease. I have a double curse against me now. My mother's most embarrassing difficulties and the fear carried by those who didn't understand what just happened in that service. Miz Settle goes off to fetch her lantern. Mr. Cooper stays with me, and I realize I still have my hand tucked around his arm.

I release my hold, and he smiles at me. His left front tooth has a sizeable chip off one corner, but for some reason, that imperfection adds to his appeal. "Safe journey," he says.

His words seem strange, but I guess to someone from the city, our short walk in the woods might seem to be a fearful trek.

CHAPTER THIRTEEN

The next day Miz Settle and I make the arduous excursion up Grit's Hill to check on a woman named Marie Cort whose baby is nearly due. When we come to the Cort farm, we see a horse tied to the porch rail.

Miz Settle sighs. "Doctor's horse." Her voice carries a tremor. Mrs. Cort has had a difficult pregnancy and only came through into her ninth month because of Miz Settle's herbs and wise counsel.

I turn to leave, but Miz Settle clasps my arm. "I ain't giving up that easy." She raps at the door.

A boy opens it. "Pa don't want you," he says. "We got a real doctor here."

Miz Settle walks past him and into the back bedroom.

I stay near the door, but I hear the long groan of a woman at the pushing stage of childbirth. The moaning stops, and a conversation begins. I can't decipher what's being said, but I recognize the doctor's voice, then Miz Settle's, and Mrs. Cort's. Shortly, Miz Settle comes from the bedroom. I follow her outside.

"Told ya," the Cort boy says before he shuts the door in our faces.

"It ain't her," says Miz Settle. "It's her husband. He says I'm a witch."

"Why would he think that? I seem to recall that you released him from a goomer spell two years ago."

"Some folks got undersize memories."

"All this because of last night at the tent meeting?"

"I would say so."

"What'd the doctor think?"

"He invited me to assist. As if he knows anything, him never giving birth."

Miz Settle has told me some of her life story, and I'm quite sure she's never given birth either. She must sense my thoughts because we haven't gone far when she says, "I told you about the toilsome walk from Georgia to Milksnake."

"You did."

"Well, here's the part I didn't tell." She pauses while we walk a steep path that requires more concentration to keep our balance. Once we're on more level ground, she says, "When I told William Duke that I was carrying his child, we snuck away, and he brought me to Milksnake Hollow. He looked more white than Cherokee, and he pretended he was white when he bought me my land. The cabin was already on it. He said he'd come back for me and our child when his army time was done. Two days after he left, I lost the baby. I couldn't even tell yet if it was a boy or a girl. A few months later, he got killt over in Indian Territory."

I shiver at the sorrow in her voice.

"That's why I'm a midwife, Sheba. I want to help other women hold onto their babies. I don't want them to feel as empty as I have ever since mine died. My people, the *Aniyunwiya*, don't have midwives. Women just go off and give birth by themselves, but I wonder, could a midwife have saved my baby?"

"You've saved babies that were determined to be born too early."

"I have, Sheba. I spent a lifetime finding the right plants to help their mamas keep them inside."

I hope she will tell me more about her early life in Milksnake, but, Miz Settle must think she's said enough. The rest of the way to Milksnake, not a word passes between us.

In town, the streets are unusually crowded, women going to Mr. James's store, men at the new barber shop. We do notice one strange thing. Most folks walk past us with nary a greeting. Miz Settle takes to calling out their names. Some are embarrassed into politeness. Others are not.

At the path that leads to her cabin, she says, "Best we stay to ourselves for a while, Sheba. Your mama's not far off from birthin'. Bessie and me, we'll keep busy in the garden. Come get me if you need me—for your mother, I mean."

She walks away, and I look back toward town. It's hard to believe our lives have changed that quickly, all because Miz Settle and I helped in a situation where no one else could. Of course, it's more than what happened at the revival service. It's also Ma Mère and what she did. It hasn't been easy between us since she told me she was carrying.

The shock of her announcement left me speechless, and for days I couldn't even ask her about the father, but finally I did, hoping he'd be a single man willing to marry her. Of course, that could carry troubling consequences, but I could always go live with Miz Settle.

When I worked up the nerve to ask her, Ma Mère and I were clearing a new winter's snow from porch, Ma Mère with a broom and me with a garden shovel. I asked her in light, almost playful voice, hoping that would mask my discomfort and growing anger, as if every day widows got themselves pregnant.

"I think I should know who the father of your baby is, Ma Mère."

Her cheeks turned deep red, and dread flooded my heart. What had she done?

My next words are not kind or polite in any way. "Whatever stupid thing did you do, Maman? Are you involved with someone important like Judge Preck or Reverend Caldecott?"

"Do you take me for a fool, China?"

"Right about now, yes."

She leaned her broom against the cabin wall and looked directly into my eyes. "Mr. James," she said.

I choked on my own breath. "Mère! That's terrible. Does Mrs. James know?"

"I hope not."

"He hasn't promised to leave her and join you in holy matrimony?"

She caught my sarcasm, and her nostrils flared. "I didn't ask it of him, and I will not."

"How could you two get yourselves into such a mess, Maman?"

She didn't seem to have a ready answer, but finally she said, "On his part, lust, I suspect."

"On your part?"

Her next word was soft. "Love."

I had to turn away from her. How on earth could she ever love Mr. James? Full of himself, he was, and obnoxious about it. I still have my back to her when I say, "You once told me you loved Paul Le Roy, and you were pregnant when he died. Was he my true father or did you lie about that?"

She grabbed my shoulders and turned me around. Then to my shock she slapped my face, hard enough that I bit my cheek. "Yes, China, Paul Le Roy was your true father, and yes, China, I loved him—I still love him—and, until you have a child of your own, don't you dare judge me."

I didn't try to hide my angry tears. "But it was wrong, Mère."

"I took up with Mr. James last winter. Do you remember that time? Even in early November the snow was too deep for you and Jesse Settle to go out and deliver babies."

"Of course I remember."

"We were starving, China. Then you caught that croupy cough, and I was afraid you were going to die. We couldn't afford to buy food."

"I could've stolen food for us, Mère. All it takes is a wish."

"And risk that someone figures out what you can do?" Her dark hair had come loose of its bun, and she tucked the stray strands behind her ears. "I went to Mr. James with a request for food and medicine. I promised to pay for it in the spring. He gave us what we needed, and he said it was a gift. Do you understand what he meant?"

I was too ashamed to answer.

She was wearing her woolen shawl, old, moth-eaten. Whatever color it had once been, it had faded to gray. She took it from her shoulders and wrapped it around me. "My beautiful daughter, child of my heart, how can I look at you, alive and healthy, and consider my choice to be a sin?"

"I'm cursed, and you know it, Maman."

She wiped the tears from my face with the tails of the shawl. "You were given a gift, China. Not a curse. I'm more than sorry about any consequences you will suffer because of what I did, but I don't regret it. What would my life be without you?"

She picked up the broom and went into the house, but I stayed outside scraping snow from the porch steps. It was a long time before I felt worthy to join her inside the cabin, Ma Mère brave and strong, me foolish and self-righteous.

As I walk home from Milksnake, reliving that conversation, I'm so caught up in guilt that, when I arrive home, I don't sense that anything is amiss. Then our cow lows from the shed, a plaintiff cry, and I realize that she and the calf are still locked up inside. I hurry into the house and set my midwife satchel on the table. My mother is in her bedroom, sitting on her feather tick. She's breathing hard, her hair drenched with sweat.

"Baby's coming," she says then whispers. "I'm thirsty. Water, please."

I run for the pitcher in the dry sink.

I fill a tin cup, return to the bedroom, and hold it to her lips. As she swallows, another pain takes her. She chokes, spewing out what she drank. I grab a handkerchief from my pocket and blot her face dry. I help her sit back against the pillow then return to the kitchen, tie on my pinafore apron, and fill our cast iron teakettle. I light the stove. The day is already hot beyond comfort, but boiled water is clean water.

Ma Mère groans. I grab my satchel and a wet dishrag. In the bedroom, I wipe the perspiration from her face until a contraction makes her cry out. She grits her teeth, arches her back, and screams.

When the pain fades, she says, "I need to push, China."

She pulls her nightdress to her belly, and I check up inside her birth channel. She's full-dilated.

I've helped in the delivery of more than one hundred babies, and, long ago, I lost my inhibitions about the nude female body, but I drape a flour sack towel across her hips to save Ma Mère from embarrassment.

"I don't mind, Ma Petite," she whispers.

She grimaces in the agony of a hard contraction, and I lift the cloth. A thin white scar marks the taut flesh between her vagina and anus, a fragile marker of Miz Settle's knife on the day of my birth. Ma Mère's birth channel gapes, and I see the white of the baby's water sac.

She asks in a worn-out voice, "Anything wrong?"

"Nothing, Maman. Nothing at all."

I open my satchel and remove a vial of olive oil, expensive beyond necessity, but I want the best for my mother. I rub the oil into the skin of her vulva. "This is to keep you from tearing, Maman." I hope I don't have to cut her.

Her eyes are closed, her face puckered. I cap the vial and set it aside. My mother gasps and gropes for my hands. She braces her heels against the quilt, but, as she bears down, her feet slip, and she cries out in pain. I climb on the bed and kneel to face her.

"Put your feet up against my thighs."

Her eyes flash open at the word *thighs*.

In reference to a fried chicken, a woman is allowed to say *thighs*. In reference to herself—no. Then, as if that hypocrisy hits her, she starts to laugh, and her laughter prompts mine until we approach hysteria and lose all our strength. When the next pain begins, we aren't ready. She curls down and knots up, which doesn't do her or the baby any good, but we're ready for the contraction that follows. When it comes, she clenches my hands until I think my fingers might snap off. Then with a great splash, the birth sac splits and douses us both, releasing a smell of musk and witch hazel.

She lets out a sigh that sounds like relief, but, with scarcely a breath between, the next pain rolls in. I look down and see a wet thatch of red hair. For a moment I picture my mother in Mr. James's arms, but then I banish him from my thoughts.

The baby's head comes out crown first. The flesh at the opening of Ma Mère's birth canal rips, and she mews like a kitten. I use my scalpel to add an inch to the tear.

"Red hair, Maman, lots of it."

Through the next pain, the baby remains where it is. I work my fingers between my mother's flesh and the child's. When she pushes again, I gently pull. One shoulder inches out and the other, and then, in one quick rush, the whole baby lands on the draped skirt of my apron.

I sing out, "A boy. It's a boy. Fat as a hog."

Ma Mère begins to weep, and I sit there atop the bed looking at my baby brother, his mop of bright hair, the slick of the birth sack against his belly, and the twisting blue and white cord, the source of which is still caught up within my mother's body.

I clear his mouth, and he erupts into a wail.

I take two pieces of well-boiled string from my satchel. I tie the cord, one string close to his belly, the other an inch or two farther along. I use scissors to cut between the ties. It isn't an easy cut. It never is with a baby's cord, which is tough as a piece of grizzle.

Ma Mère reaches down, her hands trembling, and I lay my brother on her chest, opening her nightdress to lessen the amount of blood that will stain it. He begins rooting as soon as he's tucked in close to her neck. She closes her eyes as the afterbirth slithers out. I study it to be sure it's whole with nothing yet attached to my mother's womb. All is as it should be.

I set a layer of clean padding under Ma Mére's buttocks and stitch her up. Then I rise from the bed and slip off the pinafore apron and my skirt, wet and bloody. Wearing nothing more than my shirtwaist and pantalets, I pad out to the kitchen and set the mess into a metal tub. When I return, I see that my mother is already nursing her son. I clean her and pad her nether regions with thick toweling. She surrenders the baby, and I clean him as well, counting his fingers and toes. Then I give him back to her and go out to bury the afterbirth. Despite whatever sin Mr. James and Ma Mère committed, I can think of nothing better than a new baby living with us.

When I walk into the cabin, I call, "Do we have a name for him, Mère?"

She answers, her voice drowsy and drifting, "Daniel James Creed."

Likely a poor decision, but perhaps she'll change it after a day or two of consideration. I slip a clean skirt on over my head, button the waistband, and peek in at my mother. She's sitting up, a pleased look on her face. I brew tea, which will help bring in her milk. Although, from the wet stains on the front of her nightdress, that doesn't appear to be much of a problem. Still, tea is a comfort, and I'm glad to make it for her. By the time it's ready, the baby has fallen asleep at her breast. I tuck him into his cradle.

"What can I do for you now, Maman?" I ask.

My mother's teasing smile makes me feel like a child again. "Milk the cow. Strain the milk. Gather eggs, make butter. Sweep the kitchen. I could use some breakfast when you have time."

"Which first?"

It should be breakfast, but she never thinks of herself. "The cow, poor thing. Her udder must ache."

I take the milk pail from its place in the kitchen and walk outside where I stop dead. A cornucopia of boxes and bags clutter the porch. A bolt of bleached plain-weave muslin lies across the seat of the rocker, enough to clothe little Daniel James for all his toddling years. Another bolt is propped beside it, this one of diaper-weave cloth. A bundle of cinnamon sticks rests atop a pyramid of canned peaches, and a multitude of bulging totes lean against the cabin wall. I'm amazed, appalled, over-joyed.

I pick up the cinnamon and inhale that wonderful dusky-sweet scent. I feel a sudden longing to make a batch of sticky buns for my mother. Unfortunately, we have no sugar. Then I notice a large cloth bag slumped between the rockers of the chair. I untie the twine at the top. White sugar.

I whisper the first line of our song, "*Something you covet deep to the bone.*" Strange what a woman will covet during birth throes. I search through the other totes. Our bounty includes two ten-pound bags of flour and a pair of high black button shoes, their uppers soft as butter.

Since our cognizance of my adept thievery, a portion of my mind continually wrestles with the puzzle of that ability. At least we have the song, which partially explains my limits. Ma Mère has no idea who first sang it and how old it is. Although I learned it in English, she remembers it in an antique French, forerunner of what she and I speak when we're alone. She's told me rumors about gifts similar to mine, snippets of stories passed down within her family, mostly as fairy tales: a tablecloth that could produce a hearty meal, a goose that laid golden eggs, and, of course, stories about the Queen of Sheba, Solomon's paramour, and Eleanor of Aquitaine, wife and mother of kings. Most of all, Ma Mère speaks about Joan of Arc, whose armies were equipped through the highest grace of God. Was Joan thief enough to steal that grace?

I think back to the story Miz Settle has often told me about the night of my birth and Parnell Creed's wish for Dibbler shine, the cause of his death, which bequeathed me a great amount of guilt.

The cow begins lowing, and I leave the other treasures for later. The cow is still in her stall, kept away from her calf. I fill a pail with milk then put her out on a picket line to graze the grass that grows at the north side of our cabin. Her calf bunts the cow's udder with her little polled head. I wish we could keep that calf. She's such a pretty thing, soft brown in color with a wide blaze of white on her nose. Imagine having two milk cows.

Before I attack my remaining chores, I bring in everything from the porch. I hope Ma Mère doesn't expect me to sneak it all back to Mr. James's store. After what she went through to birth my brother, she's earned the whole lot.

I peek in at my mother. She's asleep, snoring lightly. My brother gazes up from the cradle, discovering his wide new world. As I work in the kitchen, he begins to squeak and eventually coaxes himself into a fury. He's close enough that my mother can reach him from the bed. If she wants to let him cry, that's her choice. Miz Settle claims crying is good for the lungs. I take my time setting the sponge to rise for the sticky buns. The baby's wails continue, and I decide Ma Mère must expect me to change his diaper clout before she feeds him.

I walk into the bedroom and lift him from the cradle. He turns his head to root at my blouse. "I don't have anything for you, you greedy little bug," I tell him. Then I carry him into the kitchen, calling to my mother, "Mère, wake up. Your baby's hungry."

I unwrap his swaddling and use baking soda dissolved in water to clean his bottom. He looks into my face, which steals the heart right out of my chest, and I entertain a strange thought about this brother. If Ma Mère and I can get him through his first perilous year, he might live my entire life, a person I won't ever have to lose.

Where that thought came from, I still cannot say. Maybe we know more about the future than we allow ourselves to admit, the good things being too good to hope for and the bad too terrible to contemplate.

I return to the bedroom. My mother's still asleep. I stroke her face. When she doesn't stir, I gently shake her.

She wakes up and looks off over my shoulder. "I need more time."

So certain is the fixation of her eyes that I turn to see the person she addressed. There's no one.

"Mère? Maman?"

She clasps my hand and stares into my face. "China, I called for you. I called."

"I was milking the cow, Mère."

She looks off over my shoulder again, and her words turn frantic. "Remember, remember, remember." Her eyelids flutter.

"Remember what, Mère?"

"My family. Our family. They're waiting for the next one with the gift."

"Yes, Maman, you've told me many times." I stroke her hair back from her forehead. "You don't need to worry about them. They'll never find us."

"Stay free, China. Stay free, my love."

Fear grabs a tight hold on me. Her voice is too weak. Something's wrong. I fold back the sheet that lies over her, lift the hem of her nightdress, and gasp in horror. The pads under her buttocks are saturated with bright blood. I close my eyes to ward off a sudden vertigo.

Miz Settle and I have dealt with such bleeding. We've saved three women and lost two.

At age thirty-nine, my mother is older than many who give birth. Sometimes with older women, the womb remains pulpy and weak. I press down on her belly and hold tight, hoping the pressure will lessen the flow. When we deliver the babies of women with red hair, Miz Settle does such a thing as a matter of course, but my mother's hair, dark as pitch, should have no effect on her womb.

Ma Mère moans, and I know I'm hurting her. I lean forward, pressing down. "I'm sorry, Maman, but I have to stop the bleeding."

I keep a packet of dried yarrow in the kitchen. Why didn't I make her a yarrow tea before I went out to milk the cow? My eyes fall upon the Bible resting on the bedside table. I reach for it and lay it over her belly as a weight to maintain pressure on her womb. I run out to the kitchen and rekindle the coals in the firebox, and then I return to my mother and again press against her belly. When I hear a hiss of steam from the kettle spout, I make quick work of dumping a handful of dried yarrow into a cup of hot water. After it steeps, I dredge out the yarrow and fold it into a clean flour sack towel. I squeeze until the towel is wet with juice and take it into the bedroom. I set my left hand upon the Bible and with my right push the towel up her vagina.

My mother adds her screams to my tears. I wipe my face against my raised shoulder and startle as hands clasp my arms. I know those hands well. Jesse Settle.

"Thank God," I say.

"She's bleedin'. Why didn't you come for me, Sheba?"

"The placenta was whole. I thought everything was fine, but I can't get this stopped. I have a yarrow compress up inside. There's yarrow tea in the kitchen."

Miz Settle fetches the tea. I raise my mother's head and shoulders.

"Yvette," Miz Settle says. When Ma Mère doesn't respond, she shouts. "Yvette!"

My mother's eyelids open.

"You got a new baby here that needs you. And China needs you. Drink this."

My mother chokes on the first mouthful but is able to take in the rest of it.

"I'm sorry," she whispers. "I'm sorry."

She slips away from us again, and my soul turns ignorant, battering against the casement of my brain. "What about the doctor, the one in town?" I ask Miz Settle. "Would he know something we don't? Would he have medicine?"

Miz Settle shakes her head, her eyes full of sorrow. "No."

"If there's any chance—"

"Go if you got a mind to, Sheba."

I bend down and kiss Ma Mère. She tries to smile. "God's will," she says. "God's will."

Miz Settle looks at me. "Run."

Two miles later, I stop to catch my breath. A pain stabs hard at my side, and I press my fist into my belly until the hurt fades and I can run again.

In town, as I pass the church, Mrs. Caldecott comes out. When she spots me, she calls, "China Creed, whatever is the matter?"

I bend over and set my hands on my knees, pull in enough air to gasp, "My mother's poorly." How can I tell her about my brother? "I'm going for the doctor."

"He's at the Jameses' place." I don't need to ask how she knows. In a town as small as Milksnake, information rides the wind. Mrs. Caldecott lays her hand on her belly. "Mrs. James, well, you know."

Mrs. James is also delivering? How lovely for her husband, both his women bearing him a child on the same day.

At the store, Mr. James stands behind the counter. I hear the sudden squawk of a baby. Mr. James smiles. Anger chokes me, and I must clear it from my throat before I'm able to speak.

"You have a son," I say to him, and he stares at me in puzzlement.

"But the doctor hasn't—" He stops and meets my eyes.

"Lots of red hair. His name is Daniel James Creed."

"She can't call him that."

"She did."

He looks as if he could take a whip to me.

"I need the doctor," I tell him. "My mother is poorly."

"Dr. Grey is here, and I'm paying him to stay here."

"Did you not hear what I said?" I'm shouting. "My mother—"

He interrupts me. "Where were you this morning?"

Somewhere at the back of my brain, I register the strange wailing cry of his other newborn child, as if each breath is hard won.

"Were you here at my store? Sneaking in?"

I frown in disgust. "I was delivering a baby this morning. That's what I was doing. Why would I be at your store?"

The doctor walks out of the living quarters, and Mr. James turns his attention away from me.

The doctor is wiping his hands on a flour sack towel, and he seems to take more time than necessary. "Your wife's good, Daniel."

"Doctor Grey," I say, but my voice is soft.

He goes on with whatever he intends to tell Mr. James. "Your wife is a strong woman, and it was a hard birth, but she's fine." He speaks with sharply cut vowels, his accent very different from ours here in Milksnake. "You have a son, but he's small, and almost two months early. I can tell by his breathing that his lungs aren't fully formed."

"Can you . . . do anything?"

"I can try. We need to keep him warm. Do you sell medicine droppers in this store?"

"I do."

"Your son won't be strong enough to suck. Your wife can milk her breasts and feed him with the dropper." I see sorrow in the doctor's eyes. A caring man. Pray God he will condescend to help my mother.

Mr. James threads his fingers into his thick red hair. "She's lost three boys, my wife has. This would be the fourth. I don't know what that might do to her."

As if he needed that information to spur him on, the doctor starts back through the velvet curtains. I take two giant steps and grab his arm.

"My mother. I think she might be dying." I speak loudly enough for Mr. James to hear.

The doctor stops and stares. "China Creed?"

"Yes. We met at the tent meeting."

"I remember. What's wrong with your mother?"

"She just gave birth. I can't stop the bleeding."

"I have to tend the James baby, Miss Creed."

"My mother is in desperate need."

"I'll get there as soon as I'm able. Where do you live?"

"West down the Hollow about three miles. There's a trail that begins a few rods this way from the schoolhouse."

"I'll come as soon as I can. Meanwhile, try alum."

Alum? A styptic? "It's worse than a small tear." But the doctor has already disappeared behind the curtains.

I glance toward Mr. James, who turns away.

I lift my chin and grit my teeth. "Your wife might live in ignorant bliss, Mr. James, but rest assured God is aware."

Mr. James fetches a tin of alum and places a small square of cloth on the countertop. "How much you need?" he asks me.

I grab the whole tin and leave the store.

When I arrive at the cabin, Miz Settle is sitting in our front porch rocker, my brother in her lap.

"She's gone," I say.

"Yes."

I fling that alum as hard as I can. The tin bounces off the side of the cabin and lands in the garden. I walk up the steps, past Miz Settle, and I don't even look at my brother. My mother lies on the bed, her best quilt—a blue and yellow wedding ring pattern—covering her from feet to chin. I lay my hand on her forehead. Her body hasn't yet cooled, the day being warm, but already blue bottle flies drink from the corners of her closed eyes. With all the running and the hoping and the begging, I'm dry to the bone. I have no tears.

Miz Settle used pennies to weigh down Ma Mère's eyelids. I snap them away with my fingertips, swearing the vile oaths I've heard from drunken men, and for some stupid reason, that harsh wickedness helps lift the crushing weight from my heart.

I return to the porch, and Miz Settle hands me my brother. In his bright hair, I see Mr. James. Otherwise, he takes after my mother—her eyes, her mouth, her nose. He's fussing, and I place the tips of my fingers into his mouth, which calms him. I take him inside. Miz Settle follows and fetches a clean flour sack towel. "You have scissors," she says.

I nod toward the bedroom where the scissors I used on my brother's birth cord still lie on the bedside table. Miz Settle brings them to the kitchen and wets them in the water pitcher then chips off the dried blood with her thumbnail. She cuts the towel into strips. "You got sugar, China?"

I point at the sack of white sugar I set among our other supplies. Little Daniel James might as well enjoy the best. He has little else to comfort him.

Miz Settle uses a teacup to dip milk from the milk pail, which I haven't yet moved to the spring shed. She adds a few pinches of sweetness then dangles a knotted tail of the towel into the mixture. "Let him suck on it, but, if he sucks too hard or the strip gets worn out, he might pull threads down into his throat and choke."

I already know this, but still, my armpits prickle with a sudden cold sweat.

"You're gonna need a wetnurse for him, Sheba. He can't survive on cow's milk. It'll either bind him up or give him the scoots. A day or two, maybe three, that's what ya got. After that—" She leaves those words hanging. I've heard her say similar to despondent fathers who've lost a wife in childbirth. I always believed my heart ached as much as theirs. Now I'm aware my sorrow was inadequate for the loss. My mother is dead, and I must give my brother to a wet nurse? Who else do I have in this wide world but him?

Miz Settle places her hands on my shoulders and looks up at me. I'm a full head taller than she is, but when I'm with her, I feel like a child. "Sheba, women all over this holler, good women, got babies. You might offer yourself to a family to work for a year in exchange for the mother's nursing."

The suggestion chases away some of my panic, but still, a hard-scrabble farmer as my master? And what if he found out about my gift? I'd do better—my brother would do better—if I could earn real wages and pay for his care with cash money. I wonder if Mr. James would hire me in his store. He surely owes for what he did.

"We gotta bury your mama. You need to dig a grave, Sheba. You know where your pa lies?"

"I do."

I'd passed through a time in my childhood when I pulled the weeds off Parnell's grave and sometimes left a handful of wildflowers. My mother neither helped nor discouraged, but I outgrew the urge, and it's been years since I've cleared the plot. A quick sweep of regret makes the blood rise to my face.

I give my brother sugar tits until he seems satisfied, and I consider that I should change his diaper cloth, but he's asleep and I have a great deal to do. I place him in the cradle. By then Miz Settle is well into preparing my mother for burial.

"I ain't strong enough to lift her myself," she says. "Help me turn her over. You got any special clothes you want her in?"

My mother has a dress that she wore for church. Miz Settle points at it. "How 'bout that green dress? It owns some good lace."

"My mother made that lace."

"I know."

Together we place her on her stomach, and Miz Settle begins washing my mother's back. Her skin is flawless. Ma Mère had been a beautiful woman. No wonder Mr. James wanted her.

"Is there . . . was there . . . anything I could've—" I choke, and tears fill my eyes.

"Tell yourself it's God's will. That'll help."

"Why would God take away my mother when my brother and I need her so much?"

Miz Settle keeps washing. "Don't expect me to explain the Almighty to you, Sheba. I got enough trouble trying to figure out normal human beings. Come on, now, and help me get the dress on over your mother's head."

When we're done, I leave Miz Settle to comb and braid Ma Mère's hair while I go outside to dig her grave. As I dig, twilight descends, and I decide to wait until morning to bury her. Miz Settle refuses to take any payment but does accept a flour sack towel knotted around two cups of white sugar. We bring the cradle to the front room and shut the bedroom door. I wish Miz Settle could stay, but there's a woman downriver from her cabin ready to deliver at any time. They're a poor family and unlikely to call in the doctor. I want to walk Miz Settle home, but she refuses.

"That baby needs you more than I do. If I can, I'll stop by tomorrow. Besides tonight is your mother's wake. You need to sit up with her throughout."

I understand the reason for that traditional all-night vigil. On rare occasions, a person declared dead comes back to life. I don't hold any hope for that with my mother. How could she live again nearly bloodless?

Miz Settle leaves, and darkness falls. A great and terrible dread takes hold of me. However will I keep my brother alive? However will I find a woman willing to take a bastard to her breast? However can I act as midwife with a brother too small to leave alone? I remember all the terrible ways children of the Hollow have been injured or accidentally killed. I sit down and whisper prayers to keep the horror from eating me up.

A rap on the door startles me. My brother begins to wail from the cradle.

"Who is it?" I call out.

"Dr. Stephen Grey."

I pick up my brother and invite the doctor in. He sets his black leather bag on the table and removes his fancy bowler hat, clutching the brim of it in both hands.

My grief lashes out in a sudden and unbidden way. "You're too late. She bled to death." My words sound harsh, and they shame me.

He ducks his head, and in that one motion I see the little boy he must have been–shy and penitent. "I'm sorry."

I press my lips to my brother's bright, warm head. "I didn't mean that like it sounded. Maybe she couldn't be saved, but I was out milking the cow when the bleeding started, and I'll always wonder—" I can't finish my sentence.

"You have my sincere condolences. Is there anything I might yet do?"

All my needs fly into my head. A way to feed my brother. Money. Fodder for the cow. A winter supply of wood. What can the doctor do? Not much.

"Advice," I finally say.

"About?"

"This baby. Do you know anyone who might nurse him? I've spoken to Jesse Settle. You may be aware that she's a midwife."

"I am."

"She says sugar tits aren't enough. What do you think?" In my heart, I beg him to tell me that a baby can survive quite well on watered-down, sweetened cow's milk, but, of course, he does not, and he gives me the one name that will do me no good.

"Mrs. James."

I can't keep from looking at my brother's red hair. The doctor's eyebrows lift for a brief second, and I surmise that he's putting everything together.

"My father's long dead," I say to help him out. "My mother's been a widow—was a widow—since shortly after my birth." I stop.

He rubs the side of his nose. "Have you already buried her?"

"I will tomorrow."

"Would you like me to check the body?"

It seems a strange question. Perhaps he's concerned she's not dead.

"I assure you she's passed. I'm also a midwife. I'm not ignorant of these things."

"I'll come back in the morning and help you bury her."

"I only need help lifting. I've already dug the grave, but I can find someone."

My brother lets out a short, fitful cry, and I raise him to my shoulder.

"May I?" the doctor says.

He takes him from my arms and lays him on the table. When he unwraps the swaddling, my brother opens his mouth and wails. Dr.

Grey taps the baby's belly then turns him over and runs his hand down the spine.

"A healthy, hungry baby," he says, and wraps him in the swaddling with a fair amount of skill. "I'll go now, Miss Creed, but I'll be back in the morning. Wait for me. Meanwhile, I'll ask concerning a wet nurse."

"I can't pay you."

"I don't expect pay."

"I'll wait then. And thank you."

He settles his bowler on his head and picks up his doctor bag, turns, and places his hand on the doorknob. It's a real brass knob. My mother was prideful about it. I choke at that thought and have to clear my throat before I ask, "The James baby, how is he?"

"Not good," the doctor says without looking at me.

"I'm sorry for Mrs. James," I say. "I'm sorry for the child. I don't hold much sorrow for the baby's father."

CHAPTER FOURTEEN

The next morning Cordell Smith and Dr. Grey come to help me bury Ma Mère. Cordell works for Tommy Belnap's father at the blacksmith shop, the job Tommy most likely would have taken had he survived the war. Cordell's thin arms and narrow shoulders don't seem to hold much hope for his abilities as a blacksmith. The sleeves of his blue cotton shirt are rolled past his elbows, and his forearms are dotted with scars and half-healed burns. I feel a moment of sadness that Cordell must live a life someone else chose for him.

When the doctor and Cordell come into the house, the baby is asleep, exhausted after a night of colic. When Dr. Grey stops at his cradle and presses a gentle hand over the baby's tight stomach, his concern rips into my heart. He looks at me and says, "Cow's milk."

"Yes."

"Goat milk might be better if you can get some."

My thoughts flit to a family that owns a farm on the other side of Grit's Hill. They raise goats, but their farm is a four-hour walk one way. The milk would sour before I could get it home, and what would I do with the baby? He'd surely die of heatstroke if I carried him a full eight hours in the sun. I open the bedroom door.

Ma Mère lies at the center of the bed, the wedding ring quilt wrapped around her but folded back from her beautiful face. My heart squeezes tight as I cover her completely.

I sew the quilt's edges into place with the threaded needle I left there for that purpose. When I'm done, I bend close and bite off the thread, breathing through my mouth to block the smell that arises from her body, but that sickly odor of cellared apples and putrid meat haunts my dreams to this day.

I leave the room to give Dr. Grey and Cordell space. They lift her easily and carry her outside to the hole I dug, two feet to the right of Parnell's grave. Somehow the two men balance her weight as they get to their knees. Then they lower her into the hollowed earth. Cordell picks up the shovel I left in a pile of dirt near the grave.

His kind intent warms my heart, but I shake my head. "No, please. You did what I couldn't do myself. I prefer to finish this alone."

"Whatever you want, Miss Creed," the doctor says.

Cordell thrusts the shovel back into the dirt, stepping on one shoulder of the blade to set it deep.

"Don't wait too long," the doctor tells me. "Miasmas rise from open graves." He nods toward the house. "I left my hat on your table."

The doctor leaves Cordell and me standing beside the grave. Cordell looks down the path that leads to town as if his eyes could take him away. He clears his throat. "You hear that Holly Barnes and me are steppin' out?"

I hadn't. "That's good, Cordell. I'm happy for you both." Was he trying to ward me off? He need not worry. If I can somehow support myself and my brother, I'll be content all my days.

"What I'm saying," he continues, "is that if you need anything, Holly and me can help ya. I got a good mule and a plow. Holly's got a patch of pie plant if you want roots."

His kindness takes away my words, and I'm grateful when the doctor returns. "Keep in mind that cow's milk is hard on a baby's stomach," he says.

Again Cordell gazes off at the townward path.

The doctor's horse is a fine red gelding with socks and a blaze. Cordell rides his white mule without a saddle. They disappear from sight where the trail curves into its first wide bend. I pull the shovel from the pile of dirt and slowly fill Ma Mère's grave.

The next morning the baby's scat appears black and thick, as it should for a newborn, but by noon it's turned runny and greenish. Cries wrack his body, and I fear for his life. I knot a flour sack towel around a bundle of my brother's clothes—flannel diapers and a tiny shirt and soft nightdress I made before he was born. I bring milk in a small corked jug, already watered down and sweetened, plus fresh muslin to twist into sugar tits.

I set out in my best dress, a blue sprigged gingham without bustle or flounces, its only affectation being sleeves that flare at the wrists. I wear my straw sunbonnet and the new black shoes that came to us after Daniel's birth. The shoes are tight at the toes, but better-looking than any pair I've ever owned. They would've fit my mother perfectly. I doubt I stole them from the Jameses' store. They're too fine. But if I did, Mr. James be damned.

By the time we get to town, wide wet circles have bloomed under my arms. My bun hangs damp and bedraggled against my neck. I stop at the doctor's storefront first. He comes to the door after my second knock. His shirtsleeves are caught up with garters and rolled to his elbows.

"How may I help you, Miss Creed?" His voice is gentle.

I'm frightened about what I plan to do and tears spring into my eyes. I have to cough before I can speak. "May I come in for a moment, Sir?"

He opens the door more widely, and I walk into the welcoming shade of his front room. A desk claims pride of place a few feet from the back wall. Cubbyhole shelves top a credenza behind it. Six knobbed pegs are set into the south wall. His coat hangs from one, and another coat, grey tweed, hangs beside it. I remember the gentleman who accompanied him to the tent meeting. Royce Cooper.

The doctor gestures toward a spindleback chair, one of two facing the desk. I'm glad to sit. My arms ache from clutching my brother. I ease him to my lap.

"He's not doing as well as I hoped."

The doctor perches on the corner of his desk. He seems overly close to my chair. I notice again how handsome he is with a strong chin and wide-spaced golden eyes. I like that his mustaches are trimmed neatly without waxed curls. He looks into my face with such open interest that I gain the courage to speak.

"The diapers . . . his diapers—" How on earth do you talk to a man about a baby's scat? Surely it's not a subject to be discussed in polite company.

"Greenish and malodorous?"

I clear my throat. "Yes."

"It's the cow's milk. Some babies react that way. You need a wet nurse, Miss Creed. Soon."

"I highly doubt, Dr. Grey, that any woman in the Hollow would be willing to nurse my mother's child."

He takes that in without comment, and I continue.

"I love this little boy already, but I'm aware I can't care for him properly." I lift my brother to my shoulder and rock side to side, more to calm myself than to comfort him. "But I have an idea." I pause then ask, "How is the James baby?"

The doctor grimaces. "He's not doing well. He might yet live, but his lungs are weak and perhaps his heart."

I lower my brother into the cradle of my arms. "Look at this baby, Dr. Grey."

"A strong boy."

"Yes, Sir." Daniel James wiggles but doesn't wake up. "I told you my mother was a widow. She never remarried."

"I don't judge your mother for her choices."

In saying that, he proves himself kinder than I. "Thank you. At this point, though, my interest is more taken up with my brother's father." I ruffle Daniel's deep red hair. It already holds a good deal of curl in it, like my own, which has always been a riot of spirals.

The doctor levels his gaze at me. "His father, Mr. James."

"Yes."

"Would you like me to approach him?" he asks.

"No. This is my business, and I'll take care of it."

I stand up and walk to the door. I'll say no more at the moment, but I hope I've planted a seed that will bear fruit. I carry the baby to the Jameses' store and find Mr. James there alone, no daughters in evidence, no town folk either. He looks up as I enter, and, before I can utter a word, he hurries over and locks the door. He flips the open/closed sign that hangs in the front window. Then he ushers me into a storage room.

He shuts the door, which limits us to the dim light glowing through a small dusty window. My gaze falls upon his hands—fingers short and blunt, nails bitten and ragged. I shudder to think of those hands on my mother's body.

"Could I see the boy?" Mr. James asks.

I peel away the white muslin in which I've wrapped him.

Mr. James addresses me in a near-whisper. "I know what you think. But I care deeply about your mother. I'm willing to extend her credit at my store until she's on her feet again."

"Mr. James."

He continues. "And anything—"

"Mr. James!" Sorrow turns my voice harsh. "Stop talking and listen to me. My mother died. She's dead and in her grave."

He begins to cough, a choking sound, and, when he's quiet again, I speak a lie, yet I feel not one whit of guilt. "I've heard that your wife's baby will not live out the day."

He blinks at me, a flutter of his eyelids. "He might. He might."

"Mr. James, you know better."

He presses his fingers to his temples.

"Does your son have red hair, Mr. James?" His daughters are both redheads, although his wife's hair is a cloud of golden blonde. Too much depends on one small happenstance of heredity.

He lowers his hands and stares at me. "He does."

I let out my breath. "You've not been the best husband to Mrs. James, have you?" I don't give him time to answer. "You know a woman's worth is measured in the accomplishments of her sons. If your baby dies, and may God prevent such a thing, but if he dies, doesn't your wife deserve a little red-haired boy to raise? Don't you think, in her current state of mind, she might not admit to the difference between the two babies?" I whisper the last words, and he bends close. I smell the pomade he uses on his hair. "Right here, in my arms, this strong healthy baby—also your son—is turning sickly for want of mother's milk."

"I don't deserve all these problems."

"You most assuredly do, Mr. James."

I thrust my brother into his arms. He balances the baby awkwardly at first but then lifts him against his shoulder and begins to pat little Daniel's back.

"I've seen your wife in recent years after the death of a son. You've lost three?"

"Yes."

"And in that regard, I want you to think again about the possibilities I've raised concerning my brother. Let me know your decision."

I leave the store with little Daniel James in my arms. My hope and grief draw out my tears, and I duck my head to hide my face. When I reach the doctor's office, two women turn the corner—the pastor's wife and her widowed sister. They press their hands against their skirts to allow me passage. I use the tears on my face to my advantage as I stop and turn toward them.

"This week I've lost my mother to childbirth. Now I'm losing my baby brother. The doctor says there's no way to save him, but I've come in the hope that the Lord will give me a miracle."

The sister wrinkles her nose, but the minister's wife lays her gloved hand on my brother's head. "We will hold you both in our prayers."

The sister adds additional assurances, but her voice is filled with condemnation, and I barely check my tongue against a rude reply. In my hurry to get away from her, I enter the doctor's office without knocking. He stands when I come in, and he listens intently as I tell him about the ploy I've engineered.

I'm quite sure I see admiration in his eyes as he makes me one small promise. "I'll do what I can."

The walk home is pure hot misery, and we've just arrived back at the cabin when I hear the pounding of hooves. It's Cordell Smith on his mule.

"Doc wants you to bring the baby back to town." Without another word, he spins his mount and trots down the path, leaving me to walk.

I drink down a cup of water and feed my brother, taking less time than I should. Then I start him toward a new life—a good life, I hope.

By the reckoning of the sun, the three-mile trek takes me better than an hour. I wipe my face on my sleeve and walk into Dr. Grey's office. He's at his desk, a thick book open before him. He stands when I enter and scarcely pauses before saying, "Mr. James wants your brother."

"And their baby?"

"He's dying, Miss Creed."

"Does Mrs. James know that?"

"She doesn't. She won't. Mr. James will bring him to me within the next hour or so, and he'll take your brother home to his wife."

Despite my relief, a cloud of grief overtakes me. I want to see my brother's face when he takes his first step, and I want to be the one who teaches him to talk. When he needs comfort, I want him to come to me. I want to show him that a planted seed can mean the difference between living and dying, and that a man's honest work best measures his worth. But Dr. Grey takes him from my arms.

I walk to the door, stop there and turn, thinking to catch one more glimpse of my sweet little boy, but the doctor has already carried him into the back room.

I go outside and press my hands against my chest. Otherwise, my heart will surely burst out through my ribs and drop me dead right there on the street.

CHAPTER FIFTEEN

The day after I give my brother away, Miz Settle comes to the cabin. It's late morning, and she's carrying her mid-wife bag. Grief has squeezed me dry as dirt. Every breath scalds my throat, but the sight of Miz Settle calms the hurtful beat of my heart.

She makes no reference to my loss, nor would I expect her to. She merely says, "A woman's in labor, halfway up Prophet's Mountain. You wanna come along? We could take your brother. It's a shady walk from here."

I come down off the porch and hold out my arms to her. I see the surprise on her face. She and I keep a no-touch rule, but sorrow has flayed me alive. I need the comfort of her embrace.

She gathers me in and hugs me hard. Then she backs up a step. "You didn't lose him, did you, Sheba?"

"No, no, sorry to scare you. I gave him to the Jameses."

"You what?"

"Their baby boy, delivered the same day as little Daniel, was dying. Mr. James and the doctor are hoping that Mrs. James might not see the difference between the two."

"Most mothers know their own baby."

"Both boys have red hair."

"Well, I hope that works out." She looks off ke she needs to switch her thoughts toward better things. "My offer stands, Sheba. You wanna come with me?"

"Next time. I'm not fit to cradle another newborn right yet."

She presses her lips into a tight crimp, nods, and then heads out on the trail that passes my cabin, the one we took to the cave long ago. She's no sooner into the trees when I see the doctor on his horse coming down our path. A small oblong box of new wood is fastened behind his saddle. My heart begins rattling. The box looks a lot like a baby's coffin. Why would he bring it here?

I fall into a moment of panic. "That's not my brother, is it?"

"No. It's the James baby. The other James baby. Your brother's fine." He dismounts and ties his horse to the porch rail. "The Reverend Caldecott won't allow the burial of the child he believes to be your brother in sacred ground."

Anger burns a path to my heart. I twist my hands into my skirt, and my words come out mean. "What's more sacred on this earth than a newborn child?"

"I agree, Miss Creed."

I stand there until my civility returns. "I'll fetch a shovel."

When I come back, the doctor removes his coat and rolls up his shirtsleeves. He takes the shovel from my hands and asks me where to dig.

I choose a place to the right of my mother's grave, and he begins. He's down about three feet when the earthen wall between the baby's grave and my mother's gives way, refilling most of the new hole and revealing the quilt wrapped around my mother's body. The bright fabric is already discolored, and a shaft of pain slices me wide open. I groan and sit down within the puddle of my skirt.

To my surprise, the doctor sits beside me. When he places his arm around me, I give in to the temptation of his sympathy and hide my face on his shoulder. I'm content to stay that way for a long time, but finally I say, "I'm sorry."

"If we are to assign blame, Miss Creed, surely it's more my fault. I couldn't convince the Reverend to bury an innocent baby in his cemetery."

"It's Mr. James's fault," I say. "He's not brave enough to claim the poor child."

I pull away from the doctor, and we get up. He fills the little grave and sets the shovel blade at a place below Ma Mère's feet. "Here?"

I agree, and he digs again. When the baby is buried, the doctor brings a small cross from his saddle ties. It's lovely in its simplicity, wrought iron painted black. An oval wooden plaque, affixed at the juncture of the arms, reads *Peace*.

"A gift from Mr. James," the doctor tells me.

He pounds the cross into place with the shovel blade, and it seems not only to mark the baby's grave but also my mother's. "We should pray," I tell the doctor.

He narrows his eyes. "I stopped praying some years ago."

"I have not." I bow my head. "The child deserves better than this, Lord," I say, which is as honest as I can be. "Amen."

Dr. Grey repeats the *Amen*, although he directs the word at me and not upward toward God.

I point at the outside washbasin. The doctor cleans his hands, and we walk to the porch. He dons his coat, but slowly. I sense his reluctance and make an offer of hospitality. "I have fresh baked biscuits with plum jam and cream."

He follows me into the cabin.

I turn my back to the open bedroom door, which provides an indecent view of the bed, and gesture toward the table. A wide strip of lace I've just completed is draped over the back of a chair. He looks at it with questions in his eyes. "My mother taught me to make lace. I'm making a series of samples in the hope that Mr. James will agree to sell them for me."

"Do you mind?" The doctor picks up the lace and studies it. It's an English bobbin lace that features motifs of flowers and leaves, an edging strip.

"Very fine," he says. "You sell it in lengths?"

"I do."

"So I could buy some for my mother, perhaps five yards?"

"You could." I hold my breath in the hope that he will decide to order the lace. In Milksnake, few women can afford bobbin lace, and most are satisfied with tatted lace that they make themselves, narrow edging to decorate undergarments or pillow cases.

"I can order it directly from you or . . ."

"I should have more sales if Mr. James carries samples of my work in his store."

"Then tell him that I'll take five yards of—Does it have a name?"

"Honiton."

"Five yards of Honiton—in this pattern."

"Thank you. Your order should be most helpful."

The doctor sits down and watches as I split a biscuit, butter it then spoon on the jam. From the well of the dry sink, I fetch the cream in its small blue pitcher and drown the biscuit. I make another serving for myself.

At the first spoonful, he closes his eyes and murmurs, "Perfect."

Then we eat in silence until I can no longer restrain my curiosity. "May I ask where you were raised?"

He sets a solemn look on his face. "New York."

By his accent, I'd guessed he grew up somewhere in the North, but I thought it might be closer to Missouri. "The city or the state?"

He looks surprised that I should know the double designation.

"My mother used to draw maps in the dirt of our front yard," I tell him. "She used a stick, and her foot was the eraser."

"Good for her."

"And good for me, but which is it the city or the state?"

"The city. Have you ever been there?"

He assumes that distant travel is a possibility for me? Perhaps he's only being polite. "No."

He goes on to tell a few stories from his growing-up years. His family is wealthy, but he wanted to be a doctor. "I enrolled at the Bellevue Hospital Medical College and served as a Union surgeon during the War, in the states of Virginia and Pennsylvania."

"Heavy fighting in those states. It must've been terrible."

He looks into my eyes. "That's why I came to Milksnake. I needed to live in a quiet place."

"How did you hear about our little town?"

"Judge Preck's advertisement in the New York Times newspaper."

"Are we worth the journey?"

"I like Milksnake. You have good people here, and they seem to appreciate a doctor living in town."

I think about Miz Settle and me, the financial difficulties Dr. Grey has inadvertently brought upon us. My silence must make him believe our conversation has ended because he finishes his biscuit and stands up from the table. We walk outside, and he pulls his horse's reins out of their tie. He rides off but stops and waves at me where the trail turns its first corner. My stomach suffers the same strange drop as when I kissed Tommy Belnap so long ago.

* * *

For a week, long into each night, I make lace, and I try to live above the sorrow that dogs my every step. The fourth day I slip my last three pennies into my pocket, pin on my homemade but stylish Fonchion bonnet, and start for town. I've completed edging samples of five different types of European lace, a yard of each, and I also finished the five yards of Honiton requested by the doctor. The lace swings in a flour sack at my side.

It's still early in the day, and Mr. James hasn't opened his store. I sit on the bench he keeps on the boardwalk and listen for the sound of my brother crying, but all is still. I look across the street at the doctor's office and wonder if he's there or out on a call. I shiver as I remember the comfort of his arms at Ma Mère's gravesite.

When Mr. James finally unlocks the door and sees me waiting, he says, "The baby is doing well, as is Mrs. James."

"Glad to hear it. Please know I'm grateful." I slip my hand into my pocket and jingle the pennies.

He rubs his knuckles across his chin. "What can I do for you?"

"I need some baking soda, and I have a business proposition."

I follow Mr. James into the store. He stops to straighten a row of men's work boots, black with high bulbous toes, and a sign beside them that states the outrageous price of four dollars a pair. Who can afford that?

He takes his place behind the counter, plucks his round-lens spectacles from his shirt pocket, and loops the stems over his ears.

"Baking soda, you said?"

"Yes."

"Nine cents."

"Baking soda cost three cents last time my mother bought some."

"Your mother earned a discount."

I drill him with my eyes. "Perhaps, I deserve a discount as well, but not for the same reason." I pull the lace samples from my flour sack tote and lay them on his counter. "I'd like to make bobbin lace for your store, Mr. James. I think we might have a market if the word gets out."

His face darkens, and I can tell he's about to refuse my offer, but Heptabah James walks in from the family quarters and says, "That sounds like a possibility, husband."

She's holding my brother. He's swathed in a pink knit cape that makes his red hair look aflame. I hurry across the store to peer down at him. He opens his eyes and turns his head my way.

"He's beautiful," I say. "I'm very happy for you." With a swish of her skirts, Heptabah walks past me to her husband's side.

Mr. James begins to arrange a pyramid of tinned meat beside his accounts book, and Mrs. James studies the five short lengths of lace.

I walk over to the counter. "Two Honiton patterns," I tell Mrs. James and point them out. "One Battenberg and the two thicker samples are Guipure." She looks at her husband. "This is very good work, Mr. James. I'm sure we can sell it."

"The doctor's already placed an order for his mother," I say. "She lives in New York City."

Mrs. James looks impressed. I take the Honiton lace I made for the doctor from my flour sack. "Five yards of Honiton." I drape it across the countertop. "He's willing to buy it from you or directly from me if you prefer not to sell my lace in the store."

Mr. James stands there like a stone. With a brittle smile, his wife hands him the baby. "Men and yard goods," she says, shaking her head.

She walks to the dry goods side of the store. "You use crochet thread?"

"Yes, but it must be fine. Size 80."

She removes several balls—two white, one ecru—from a drawer in her display counter. I select a white with a high sheen. "Do you have more of this?"

"I do. It's very fine cotton."

"And expensive," says Mr. James from across the store. "You can cover the cost?"

Heptabah's eyes flash. "This is a speculative venture, Mr. James. China, we'll pay you ten cents a foot and supply the thread."

"Fifteen cents a foot."

"Done." She smiles as if she's won a victory, and likely she has. "When can we expect your first strip of completed lace? Let's say the same length as what you made for Dr. Grey."

"The Guipure will take me longer, a week for five yards. Several days for this Battenberg pattern."

She chooses the Battenberg.

Shaking his head, Mr. James says, "Women's work. Using up all that time to make a few pennies. I gotta see Clay Belnap about the leather straps he ordered."

He leaves the store, and Heptabah James leans toward me. "I know more than my husband thinks." Her voice catches. "Where is my little boy? Where did you bury him?"

I have to take in more air before I can answer. "He's buried beside our cabin. A clear shady spot. You're welcome to come and visit the grave any time. It's marked with a wrought iron cross. All I ask is that you give my brother whatever love you can spare."

Her eyes flood. "Don't worry about your brother. I already love him like my own." Then she gives me seventy-five cents out of the cash register for Dr. Grey's lace and hands me a box of baking soda. "The baking soda will make up for you using your own thread on that Honiton."

I leave the store a rich woman.

I'm halfway down the boardwalk when I hear the hollow thump of feet. I turn. Mr. James is striding toward me. He stops when we're toe-to-toe.

"Since my wife is satisfied with your work, I'll sell your lace, but, if you tell Heptabah about my son, rest assured I'll make your life a misery."

I come close to saying that his wife already knows, just to see the horror on his face, but why give up such an advantage? "Then we have an understanding, Mr. James. I won't tell your wife, and you won't ever again mention the relationship you had with my mother to me or to anyone else."

He steps away, and someone behind me says, "Miss Creed?"

I jump and look back over my shoulder.

It's the doctor's friend, Mr. Cooper. He stares at Mr. James. "All is well?"

Courage fills me up. "Mr. James has hired me to make lace for his store."

"Dr. Grey mentioned that possibility. I understand he ordered lace for his mother."

"He did. It's waiting for him at the store."

"Would you consider making some yardage for my sisters?"

"Of course. I left samples with Mrs. James. You can tell her your preference."

Mr. Cooper takes my tote bag and offers his arm. We turn our backs on Mr. James. It's the second time Mr. Cooper rescued me from an uncomfortable situation, and I realize I'm more at ease with him than with the doctor, probably because Mr. Cooper doesn't make my heart rattle.

A large pasteboard box sits outside the door of the doctor's office.

Mr. Cooper gestures toward the chair on the porch. "Have a seat, Miss Creed. I'll tell the doctor his lace is at the store. He should pay you?"

"No, he pays the store. I'm all set." He picks up the pasteboard box and bids me farewell.

I'd like to wait. Maybe the doctor will come outside, but I also know that, with a woman like Mary Preck in our town, I don't have a chance. I head toward the path home, cutting across a portion of the schoolyard where several boys are playing.

"It's the witch," one of them says, and they begin to pelt my skirt with small stones and clots of mud. "Devil take ya," another boy yells. His stone lands a painful blow on my shoulder. I turn and stare them down.

"Evil eye! Evil eye!" They sound like a chorus of crows.

"And God bless you all," I call out.

The goodwill I felt when I was with Mr. Cooper falls away, and my walk home is beset with a chilling sense of dread.

CHAPTER SIXTEEN

A week later I return to town with ten yards of Battenberg. At the store, Mrs. James stands behind the counter. I'm quick to notice my brother lying in a small cradle near a butter churn. I lean down and smile, and he coos as if he remembers my face. Mrs. James scurries to the cradle and lifts him to her shoulder.

"You finished more lace?"

"Ten yards of Battenberg."

"My word, you work fast. I'll put it in the display case, and, when we sell some, I'll pay you. Meanwhile, we received an order for eight yards of Guipure, four of each pattern. It seems Mr. Royce Cooper has two sisters back east. Mrs. Preck has also promised us an order." Mrs. James bounces on her toes as women do when they hold a baby. "Can I get you anything else?"

I tell her no. The food that landed on our porch the day my brother was born will feed me for some time yet. I stroll to the deep shelving on the opposite side of the store and stare with longing at the bolts of dress fabric on display. One is a pale blue plaid striped through with shiny copper-metallic thread. That's the one I would buy if I had the means, the most expensive in the store. I'd make a fashionable dress and boldly wear it to church. Then what would people say?

They'd say *like mother like daughter.* How else did a harlot's whelp buy expensive fabric except by whoring? At that moment I entertain my first longing to leave the Hollow and find a town where I could make a life untainted by my mother's choices. I glance out the window and see the doctor walking down the street toward his office. I remember again how he held me in his arms. Maybe, if I was the doctor's wife, I could stay in town near my brother. Maybe I'd be a considered a respectable woman in our little community.

I turn my back on the bolted fabrics and leave the store. I cross the street, lifting my skirt to avoid horse dung. I walk into the doctor's office. He's there and seems to be entranced by some odd-looking machine set upon his desk. The apparatus is black and brass, as every device of importance seems to be. It's about the height of a half-gallon crock and sits upright upon splayed legs. Dr. Grey is looking downward through its long cylindrical eyepiece.

I'm not sure he knows I'm here until he hooks his index finger toward me. "Come and look, Miss Creed."

He steps away from the machine and says, "It's a Zeiss Microscope. It magnifies minuscule things until the human eye is capable of viewing them. I saw a Zeiss when I was in Europe last year but never believed I would own one."

Under his direction, I press my right eye to the ocular piece. I see a length of thread, red-brown in color, covered by overlapping scales.

"It's a strand of my hair," he says.

I glance at him in surprise. Hair? Scaly as a hen's leg? He removes a thin rectangular piece of glass from under the eyepiece, selects another from a small black pasteboard box.

"The piece of glass is called a slide," he tells me. "It's used to trap very small things so people can look at them."

I peer down and see a series of crowded and misshapen circles with dots at their centers, like fried eggs with tiny yolks.

"What are they?"

"Skin cells. Bright pink isn't their true color. It's a stain to make the details stand out. Our entire bodies are made up of tiny bits of tissue, Miss Creed, smaller than the point of a pin, each a living entity in itself. They're called *cells*, and by studying them we hope to discover the roots of disease." He smiles, dimples showing deep at either side of his mouth. My heart thuds. "The Zeiss is a gift from my mother, or at least I believe it is. That in itself means a great deal." Perhaps in response to the puzzled look on my face, he adds, "She was angry at me when I turned my back on the family business. Doctors don't make as much money as investors do."

"Well, they should. They save lives."

"Thank you. How is the lace coming along?"

"Fine. I certainly appreciate your order. Mr. Cooper has ordered some for his sisters."

"Good." He waves his hand toward one of the spindleback visitor's chairs. "Sit, sit. Can you stay a while? Did you walk the whole way from your cabin?"

"It isn't that far and, this early in the day, not overly warm."

"I wish I had a spare horse I could lend you."

"No need. The trail's rocky. Why bother a horse?" I dare to look into his eyes. They're bloodshot. "You've had a busy week?"

"A man with an ornery ax, an infection in Cordell Smith's hand, and a baby stubborn in its delivery. The past two nights I've had little sleep."

A baby stubborn in its delivery. Likely, Miz Settle could have eased that mother's pain and speeded the delivery with herbal medicines.

The doctor tilts his head. "Is there anything else I can do for you? Do you need any medicine?"

Whyever would I need his store-bought medicine when our woods and swales are filled with herbs? "No, I simply wanted to let Mr. Cooper know that I should have his lace completed in about ten days." I'm not bold enough to mention that I won't be paid until the Jameses receive their money.

The doctor looks away for a minute then asks, "Do you plan to attend church next Sunday? I understand they've organized a reception to celebrate Reverend Caldecott's twentieth year as pastor."

Is the doctor asking me to accompany him? I haven't attended regularly since Ma Mère's pregnancy became the prime subject of town gossip.

"Perhaps."

Mr. Cooper chooses that moment to come into the front room from a door that closes off the left back corner of the building. He wears a wide-brimmed braided straw hat, and his tall leather boots are crusted with mud. He removes his hat, nods at me. "Miss Creed."

"Miss Creed wants you to know your lace should be completed in about—" He pauses.

"Ten days," I say.

"That's quick."

I wiggle my gloved fingers. "Worn to the bone."

Both men laugh politely, and I take my leave.

* * *

When I set out Sunday morning, I wear white gloves much mended. My mother's good brown skirt and her stiff horsehair and cotton crinoline, which gives the skirt a bell shape. The night before, I removed a piece of lace from an old dress and pinned it at the collar of my white shirtwaist. My flat Fonchion bonnet, also white, sits atop my head.

In the church, Dr. Grey and Mr. Cooper greet me when I walk past their pew, but I sit one pew up with a farm family that squeezes closer together to make room. Their two-year-old—a boy I delivered—sits on my lap for most of the service. Reverend Caldecott is long in his speaking, but sincere, and I appreciate the opportunity to sit and do nothing except coax a sweet child to remain quiet.

When we sing hymns, the doctor's voice rises loud and off-key, another reason to like him. Perfection owns a tendency to blight admiration. I notice Mr. Cooper's Scotts burr when he sings—even more pronounced than Miz Settle's rolled Cherokee *rs*—his voice fine enough to send chills up my arms.

The reception will be held outdoors on the leeward side of the church. When the service is over, I walk the aisle, greet Reverend Caldecott, and leave the sanctuary. Mr. Cooper comes out, looking harried as he sheds mothers and daughters. When he sees me, his face brightens, and he walks to my side.

"Will you stay for the reception?"

Dr. Grey joins us. He evidently heard Mr. Cooper's question, because he says, "She promised me she would." I didn't, but I'm not about to contradict him.

They exchange a glance. Then Mr. Cooper tips his hat and walks away.

Soon both men are surrounded by young women, their mothers pretending not to watch. They wedge me away from the doctor's side, and Mrs. Caldecott clasps my arm. She hurries me toward the makeshift sawhorse-and-board tables.

"Could you help me?" she asks, smiling. "It takes two to spread a tablecloth."

Other women join us, and, for the most part, they include me in their conversations. We arrange food dishes, bat away flies, and serve the men then the children. We choose from the leftovers, hurrying to fill our plates before anyone returns for seconds. The doctor and Mr.

Cooper stand together as they eat, laughing and talking. I'm enjoying a wedge of white layer cake when they approach.

Dr. Grey says, "We were discussing the name of your town, Miss Creed. Milksnake. What on earth is a milksnake? Some type of mythical beast?"

I swallow my mouthful of cake. "No, Dr. Grey, milksnakes are real, and they're quite lovely as snakes go."

He looks surprised. "How so?"

"They're banded across their backs with red, beige, and black, quite colorful. They like to live in barns. I would guess because of the mice that make their nests in the hay."

"Are they poisonous?" he asks.

"No, they're not, but they do bite. Rumor has it they'll clamp onto a cow's teat and suck out the milk, thus their name."

"They're milk thieves? Really?

I smile. "I've never seen it happen, but I have seen milksnakes in our barn. Actually, it's sad. A snake that keeps down the mouse population shouldn't be punished due to a rumor of thievery. A lot of milksnakes get killed because of that."

It's a strange conversation, something a woman like Mary-Polly would've never gotten herself into. I'm relieved when several ladies head toward Mrs. Caldecott's lovely backyard. I nod toward them.

"You gentlemen might be interested in Mrs. Caldecott's garden. She grows herbs and uses them for medicine and cooking.

I set my empty cake plate on the sawhorse table, and Dr. Grey offers me his arm. The three of us walk into the yard. Mrs. Caldecott plants the herbs in blowsy drifts along the edges of a stone path. I pick a sprig of purple flowers, and the fragrance drifts up to us.

It's a common enough herb. Nonetheless, I name it. "Lavender. It's easy to grow and, as you can see, it blooms in late July and early August. The smell relieves anxiety."

"I've heard that," says Mr. Cooper, but the doctor frowns.

I lead them to a shrubby willow Mrs. Caldecott has wisely planted in a bowl-like depression. Unlike lavender, willow appreciates damp roots. I pull away a twig and peel off the bark.

"This green portion here relieves minor pain. Headaches and such."

"Really?" says the doctor, and Mr. Cooper asks, "How do you prepare it?"

"Fresh or dried, boil the green inner bark, strain it, and drink the liquid like you'd drink a cup of tea."

"Interesting."

"Or you can do what I do." I place the strip of bark into my mouth and pull it out using my lower teeth to scrape away the green portion. I chew it and swallow.

The doctor chuckles and plucks a twig, does the same thing I did. "I tend to believe doctors who use their own medicine."

My face colors at his flattery, and I can't think of an apt reply. I go on to show him touch-me-nots for mosquito bites and rose hips for fever, colds, and rheumatism. He fills his pockets with samples of the herbs, and I notice that Mary-Polly and Devine Dreyer are watching from a distance.

When we reach the far end of the garden, Dr. Grey says, "Mr. Cooper and I have been wondering about something ever since we saw it. Perhaps you'd be willing to explain."

"I'll try."

"The young woman at the tent meeting. You were able to calm her when no one else could."

"Mrs. Settle was there, too."

"The both of you then," says Mr. Cooper.

"We're Goomer Doctors."

"You're what?"

"Goomer Doctors. Goomer Doctors break curses."

"Like witchcraft?" Mr. Cooper asks.

"There's no witchery about it. We use herbs and scripture and opposites to break hex spells."

"Opposites?" the doctor says. He seems to be battling a smile.

I call him on it. "Are you interested, or is this just a game?"

"I'm interested," he says.

"All right then. Let's say that a hex spell has been put on someone out of greed. A Goomer Doctor will write down a scripture that talks about sharing and then boil tea from the leaves or branches of a generous plant. Raspberries are good for this, each cane yielding multiple fruit."

Mr. Cooper seems intent on what I'm saying, but the doctor has begun to smirk. When he realizes I'm looking at him, his expression changes to one of careful interest.

"I won't try to convince you, Dr. Grey, except to remind you of what happened with that girl at the tent meeting."

"'Almost thou persuadeth me,'" he says.

I'm familiar with his quote from the Bible, King Agrippa speaking to St. Paul, who was trying to convince him to become a Christian. "Thank you, Dr. Grey, for implying that I have the persuasive powers of St. Paul."

His smile is genuine.

A child's cry, high, thin, pierces the air, and a few moments later Reverend Caldecott spots us and calls out, "The Danner boy fell out of the hickory tree, looks like he broke his arm."

The doctor hurries away, and then Mr. Cooper looks into my eyes so earnestly that I smile. "You're a treasure, Miss Creed. Thank you for a most enjoyable interlude."

His words and Dr. Grey's attentiveness stay with me as I return to the women and help wash dishes. I take the sprig of lavender home and set it on the sill of our front window to dry in the sun. Its delicate scent lingers for days.

CHAPTER SEVENTEEN

My dreams of romance wilt. Although the doctor attends church the next Sunday, he sits with the Preck family, Judge Preck beaming and Mary-Polly simpering. Mr. Cooper sits in a back pew and leaves before the last hymn.

Outside the church, two women confront me. They're spinster sisters who live on a few scant acres halfway up Prophet's Mountain. It seems to me that they've always been old, as faded as their sunbonnets.

"You're the midwife China Creed," one of them says.

"Yes, Ma'am, I am."

"Demons in you, I hear." Her sister draws her skirt in close.

A chill passes over me. "No Ma'am, I'm simply a Goomer Doctor."

The sister points one knobby finger at me and opens her mouth as if to speak, but I have no desire to prolong our conversation. It's one thing to endure the taunts of boys, but quite another to have grown women confront me with such a twisted accusation. I turn my back on them and walk quickly toward my homeward path.

That afternoon, I check the hazelnut shrubs that grow in great profusion near the south side of the house. These hazelnuts ripen a full month before most, and they're ready for harvest. I've promised Miz Settle a hazelnut pie.

A sudden brittle sound stops me. What person of the Hollow does not recognize a rattler's warning? I scan the ground and spot the snake coiled under the shrubs. I back away slowly, but the snake leaps forward from its coil, scales winking at me in the sun. It sinks its fangs into my left hand and clings for a moment, soulless eyes shining. A scream of fear and pain sticks in my throat and blocks off my air. The snake drops from my hand then glides away, and I sink to the ground. When I'm able to breathe again, I run to the cabin and grab a butcher knife. I thrust the point into the wound. Blood bubbles, and I suck it out, spit it into a basin, sucking and spitting four, five, six times.

I know I need plantain leaves to draw out the poison, and I usually find them within a few steps of the porch, but on this day I cannot locate one plant.

Ma Mère suddenly floats near. *Get help*, she whispers.

I start toward the Settle cabin, that five-mile trek. I walk slowly, with my hand below my heart as I've been taught, but, by the time I'm in the edge growth that borders Milksnake, the swelling has crept halfway up my arm. I'm afraid I'll pass out during those last two miles to the Settle cabin, and what if Miz Settle isn't home? I imagine myself without my left hand. What hope would I have to make my living as a midwife or as a lacemaker? I consider stepping back into the shrubbery and lying down to die. Wouldn't that be the easiest solution? But my stubborn heart aches to live.

I walk into town, down the middle of the main street, cradling my bitten hand. A great dizziness catches me, and I close my eyes. I hear voices, a man, women. They all talk at once. "Who is that? Who is that? Who is that?" Finally one of the women says, "China Creed. She's snakebit. Look at her hand."

I crumple into the dust of the street, and they come to me—the minister's wife, her sister, Clay Belnap the blacksmith. I hear the clomp of hard-heeled boots on the boardwalk. Someone raises my shoulders from the dirt. I open my eyes to a wedge of light and see Mr. Cooper. He picks me up and carries me in his sturdy arms. The jostling brings the pain to a level that makes me scream, and then, best as I remember, I faint.

I awaken on a table in the doctor's back room. The minister's wife stands to the right, the doctor on the left, and he's talking to me, boldly using my Christian name.

"China, hold still, hold still." I can tell by the odor that he's washing my hand and arm with carbolic acid. "I must relieve the swelling or it'll split your skin."

The bite of a knife follows the outer edge of my hand and down over my wrist. The pain of that somehow eases the greater injury. I gather enough strength to beg. "Don't cut off my hand. Please. Please. Please."

"People here use herbs for snakebite, don't they?" the doctor asks, his voice tight, strained. He wears a long apron over his clothes, and it's splattered with blood, mine I suppose.

I try to say *black cohosh, plantain leaves*, but the names won't leave my throat.

The minister's wife answers. "The midwife, Jesse Settle. I don't know where she lives, but she would have something."

Dr. Grey says, "See if you can find her, Royce. See if anyone knows where she lives."

The minister's wife smooths my hair back and kisses my forehead, such a kind and gentle touch. *Wish for something*, I tell her in my thoughts, and then she morphs into my mother. Would dying be terrible if I could be with Ma Mère? The doctor washes my arm again, this time with something that burns like hellfire in the slices he made with his knife.

A wet rag descends upon my face. Someone's wiping away the sweat and grit that burns my eyes. I let myself drift off, and the voice that awakens me belongs to Mr. Cooper. Did he find Miz Settle? I call for her, and she's there. Her dark hands layer leaves over the bite and along the doctor's cuts.

A spoon butts up against my teeth.

"China," Miz Settle says, her breath upon my cheek, "black cohosh tea. It may save your hand. More than that—it may save your life."

I swallow the tea. Strangely, I don't care much about my life, but I'd dearly love to save my hand.

The next time I awaken, I'm lying on a cot. My hand is wrapped in gauze, the skin on my fingers tight as sausage casings, an itching torment.

The curtains on the windows are open, and the sky carries the gray hue of early morning. The whole night has passed? I prop myself on my right elbow and gaze at the wreck that is my left arm. Above the gauze, it's swollen to twice its size, purple and blue like a giant bruise. The gauze is marred by blooms of blood. I lift my hand and gasp. The tips of my fingers are black. I groan, and the doctor comes in.

I lie back on the cot and nod at my arm. "Tell me."

"You'll live."

"My hand?"

"I believe I can save it."

"My fingers?"

He doesn't answer.

"No hope?"

"I don't know, Miss Creed. They may be all right, or you might lose all feeling or even the ability to move them. I can't say for sure."

Bile burns my throat, and I clap my right hand over my mouth. Dr. Grey holds a small tin basin under my chin, and I vomit up what little is in my stomach. When I'm done, he wipes my lips and sets his hand gently on my head.

"Sleep, Miss Creed. Sleep."

Within my dreams, possibilities loom monstrous. My left hand is fingerless, without even the nub of a thumb, and then even the hand is gone, and finally the whole arm. I wake up and a shock of pain vibrates back to my elbow, but pain is better than no feeling at all. I place my feet on the floor. My head spins, and my stomach twists, but eventually I regain my equilibrium. I hear the outer door of the office open, and I recognize the high, thin voice of the telegraph operator. "From your mother again, Dr. Grey," he says.

The curtains between us do not mask the doctor's sigh. His desk chair squeaks. The curtains sweep aside. "You're awake, Miss Creed. I'll help you to the outhouse."

He's a doctor, I repeat to myself as we make that embarrassing journey.

When we're finally back in the examination room, he asks, "You'll be all right if I leave for a few minutes?"

"Yes." My voice shakes, but he doesn't seem to notice.

When Dr. Grey returns, he comes immediately into the back room, pulls up a stool, and cups my wounded hand. He unties the knots that hold the gauze in place then slowly unwraps the bandage. "Look away, if you want, Miss Creed. It won't be pretty."

Indeed it's not, but I don't look away. It's my hand, whatever becomes of it. The final layer of gauze pulls painfully wherever blood has glued it to my skin. The hand and the lower half of my forearm are still swollen and purple with bruises. The fang marks are the most tender place. The skin there is black. Dr. Grey glances at me, and, when he sees I'm watching, he points at the snakebite. "Here and here, you'll shed some flesh. Maybe into the muscle." He sniffs the wound. "No putrefaction."

He presses at various places on my fingers, especially the nails. "You should expect to lose some of your fingernails."

"Forever?"

"Probably not."

He leaves my smallest finger for last, dark as stove blacking.

"Does it hurt?" He pinches down hard on the nail.

I press my lips into a tight grimace. "Like blue blazes."

"At least you retain feeling."

"Can you save it?"

"I hope to, but no matter what I do, this nail will come away, and you might not grow another."

I shrug my shoulders. It seems a small sacrifice.

"Most women would be—" He stops.

"Upset?"

"More than upset."

"I'm not exactly delighted."

He meets my eyes, and my heart sends shivers toward my belly.

"I need to go home, Dr. Grey. I don't even know what's become of my cow and her calf."

"Cordell went out to check on them. He let the calf go back to nursing."

"Bless him," I murmur.

"I'm not sure you should return home yet. You'd be by yourself."

"I'm capable."

"Promise me no stressful activity. Keep your hand clean, especially around the wounds." He fishes a roll of gauze from a drawer and re-wraps everything. "I'll stop and see you tomorrow. If I don't like what you're doing or the way the wound is healing, you'll be right back here with me."

He stands, and a slip of paper falls to the floor. It's buff-colored, a telegram. I pick it up and notice the short message when I hand it to him.

He balls it in his fist, a dreadful waste of paper, the message taking up less than one-quarter of the sheet.

I realize that he's looking down at my bare feet.

"You need shoes," he says.

"I'm tough."

"I'll take you home on my horse. I need to check on the Lowry family anyway. They all came down with mumps. Have you had the mumps?"

"I have."

"Good. I'll be back for you in a few minutes."

He leaves, and I close my eyes, pondering what I read. *Mother* STOP *Strange situation here* STOP *Did you send the microscope* FULL STOP

Only those few words, yet they say so much. Pray God she sent that microscope.

CHAPTER EIGHTEEN

M iz Settle stays with me my first night home, and the doctor visits the next day. I sleep in Ma Mère's bed, and I pretend she's there beside me.

In addition to grieving my mother's death, I live in a cauldron of worry about Dr. Grey and Mr. Cooper. Dr. Grey had embraced me after we buried the James baby. What if he received the microscope due to that touch? Surely he'd receive even more from treating my snakebite. And what about Mr. Cooper? He picked me up. He carried me.

When worry and grief become too heavy, I concoct strange and reckless plots of how to steal my brother away from the James family. We'd take a horse and set out for the West, my brother strapped to my back. Always, those foolish dreams end in tears.

As the days pass, the swelling of my hand subsides as does the muscle-ache in my forearm and the bone pain under the bite. At the ten-day mark, I take out the stitches, and I'm embarrassed by my vain grief over the red and puffy scars. What are a few scars to an Ozark woman? We all live hard lives.

My little finger continues to bother me. Pus seeps out from around the nail, and I notice the odor of rot. The twelfth day I awake feverish and decide to seek out Miz Settle's help. By the time I arrive in town, my fever's so high that my thoughts are muddled and strange. I walk to the doctor's office where I see a sign posted on his door. *Out on calls.* I sit in his porch chair to wait for him, and I fall into a troubled sleep. The clatter of hooves arouses me.

In the strange half-dreaming world where I live at that moment, it seems as if the doctor flies down from his horse and swoops over me like an archangel. Has his skin become unusually pale, his breath caustic?

"You're sick, Dr. Grey?"

He seems flustered by my question, but perhaps his concern is more for my hand because he curses under his breath when he sees my finger. "Can you stand, Miss Creed?"

"Yes."

"Go inside. I'll be there shortly."

It takes every ounce of my strength to make it to his desk. I sit down in his chair and try to fend off dizziness. Someone walks across the porch. I expect Dr. Grey, but, when the door opens, Mary-Polly Preck comes in. Her eyes narrow at the sight of me.

My befuddled brain pictures her with the wax-head doll in her hands. Strangely, she's grown to look like that doll with the same round face, small mouth, and bright blue eyes. The shiny black points of her shoes peek out from under her skirt, a fluttery confection of pink with layers of pleated ruffles.

I point to my hand. "Snakebite."

She looks relieved. Dr. Grey enters his office from the back rooms. He gives Mary-Polly a grim smile, and she sits down in a visitor's chair.

She directs a smile of pity my way. "I will pray for you."

I hear no kindness in her words.

The doctor escorts me to the examination room, to a wooden chair with wide, flat armrests. As he washes his hands in a basin of water, the curtains of the room open, and Mary-Polly peeks in.

"Stephen," she says, "how much longer? I told Mother I'd be home in fifteen minutes."

He turns to Mary, his fingers dripping. "Miss Preck, I'm working. Go home, please."

She looks startled by his terse command, but she leaves, and a mean gladness grows in my heart.

Dr. Grey fetches a magnifying glass and studies my finger. He presses against the top joint. "Does that hurt?"

I feel nothing, not even the pressure of his hand. "No."

"Here?"

"I can feel that."

He lifts his eyes to mine.

"How much do you have to cut off?" I ask.

"To be safe, halfway between the top knuckle and the middle."

He dons a clean apron and sorts through his scalpels, which allows me time to bid my finger goodbye. I was born with long, slender hands, and, despite their scars and callouses, I'm vain about them. "Better you than the whole hand," I say to that finger.

The doctor turns toward me. "Pardon?"

My face reddens. "I couldn't let the finger go without an explanation."

"Fingers are that way."

I raise my eyebrows. "What way?"

"In need of philosophic justification." He hands me a spit basin. "Hang onto this."

"I'm good with pain," I say.

"It's the crunch of the bone that bothers most people." He picks up an instrument that looks like a small hoof nipper. "This will quickly separate bad bone from good, and I'll also use this." He lifts a knife with a short blade set into a bone handle.

"Scalpel," I say.

He looks surprised that I know.

"Midwives use scalpels, too, Dr. Grey."

He taps the point of the knife on a curved needle. "You recognize this then."

"Yes. For stitches."

He carries the tools to a table where he applies various sharp-smelling liquids. "To disinfect," he explains. "A new medical concept, but you and Mrs. Settle have been using some type of disinfectant for years, haven't you." It's not a question.

"We boil everything."

"I suspected that within a week of coming here. The death rate due to childbirth is very low in Taney County, even compared with New York." He washes his hands again, looking over his shoulder at me. "I can offer you whiskey."

"My father was a whiskey drinker. Rumor is it killed him." I feel my face redden as I realize that my nervousness has coaxed out more truth than the doctor needs to hear. "I don't want to get drunk."

"Just enough to relax you. I promise."

The first taste burns deep, and I choke.

"Damn," he mutters. He pats my shoulder until I regain my dignity. "There now, close your eyes. One more sip."

My breathing grows easy, and my shoulders take on a pleasant weight. Dr. Grey cleans my hand then ties it palm up on a board. "A pillow," I say, "to bite on."

He hands me a pillow from the cot, and I cram a corner into my mouth. The scalpel slices through my flesh, and the pain is hideous. Tears leak from my eyes. Dr. Grey uses a compress of gauze to catch the blood, and it soon fills the pad.

"This will burn," he says as he swabs on carbolic acid. Again, I bite hard into the pillow, and this time I picture new snow—cold and pure.

He adjusts the ties and turns my hand over. The pain of the next cut is worse, as if the flesh there is more alive.

I pant, trying to rise above the agony. My finger bone crunches, and a moan escapes from my throat. He probes within the severed edges of my flesh, and my feet begin a peculiar dance upon the floor as though I have no control over them.

"Checking for bone chips," he tells me.

More carbolic acid, more probing, more pressure on the severed nerves. *I will not scream.* He folds a flap of skin and flesh from the back of my finger over the site of the amputation and begins to place the stitches. The pain eases into bearable. When he finishes, he wipes the sweat from my face. I close my eyes and force my muscles to relax, my breathing to slow.

To my surprise, the doctor kisses my forehead. "Hush, hush, hush, China," he says, "the worst is over."

And I trust he's telling the truth.

CHAPTER NINETEEN

My finger heals well. If I overuse my left hand, the bone aches, and, when I tie the knots necessary to make lace, I bind the stump to my ring finger to keep it out of the way. Dr. Grey refuses payment for his treatment, but the debt disturbs my peace of mind. To ease my guilt about his generosity, I decide to make him a hazelnut pie. I'm taking the pie from the oven when I hear the approach of a horse. I wipe my hands on my apron and walk to the door. My heart leaps in a most unseemly way when I recognize the rider, Dr. Grey. He has Cordell Smith's white mule on a lead line.

As I greet him, he ties his horse to the porch rail. "Your finger?" he asks.

He doesn't remove his riding gloves when he cups my left hand in his. "Very good," he says after a moment of study.

"May I invite you in for coffee?" I ask.

I'm disappointed when he says no, but then he grins and asks, "But would you join me for a picnic?" He gestures with his thumb to the back of his horse where he's strapped an ashwood basket. "Mrs. Fenster filled it for me."

The Fensters own a storefront in Milksnake and have begun to sell smoked meat and jams and jellies. I glance down at my ragged skirt and bare feet, but the doctor must assume I'm hesitating for other reasons.

"We won't be alone. Mr. Cooper is surveying a portion of land where there's a waterfall. He says it's beautiful."

I know those falls, a mile down the Deer Lick where a narrow stream of water spills from a rocky ledge into the creek. I consider changing my skirt and blouse but decide that my attire is appropriate for a mule ride.

"One moment," I say. I take off my pinafore, put on stockings and shoes. That's as fancy as I'll get. I swipe my sunbonnet from its hook and pick up the pie.

"I made a hazelnut pie for you. Now I won't have to tote it to town."

"Much appreciated." He places it inside the picnic basket.

I untie the mule's lead rein. "Miss Creed," says Dr. Grey, "I'll ride the mule. You take the horse."

With a good grip on the mule's short brushy mane, I heave myself up to my stomach and swing into a straddle, adjusting my skirt. "Dr. Grey, when was the last time you rode a bareback mule?"

He stutters a bit. "Umm, never."

"I have adequate experience with mules, although none whatsoever on a saddled horse."

He laughs and mounts his gelding. We direct our animals to the woodsy path that leads to the waterfall, me following him as if I'd lived my whole life ignorant of what lies just beyond the borders of Creed property.

When we arrive, Dr. Grey calls out, "Brought you lunch!"

Lunch. I file the word in my memory. In Milksnake we call our midday meal *dinner.* Our third meal of the day is supper.

Mr. Cooper comes to us, smiling. He's carrying a brass mechanical object, skeletal in its appearance and about half the size of a camera. It's affixed to a long-legged tripod, and it looks heavy, but he seems to carry it without much effort. Mr. Cooper's smile fades when he catches sight of me. He leans his tripod against a tree and greets me solemnly. He's trailed by a boy who looks so much like Tommy Belnap that my breath catches. I know him, of course. Robert Belnap. He was a toddler when Tommy went to war, which would now make him about eleven or twelve.

"Hello, Robert," I say, and he greets me by tipping his hat, his dark eyes shifting back and forth between the doctor and me.

The doctor dismounts and unfastens the picnic basket. I slide down from the mule and point out a wide flat-top rock, large enough to hold a picnic lunch. Dr. Grey brings the basket to me, and says to Mr. Cooper, "Miss Creed wants to see this waterfall you've found."

I'm not thrilled that he implies I instigated our journey, but I don't contradict him.

"It was Robert who found it," says Mr. Cooper.

"Was Indians who found it," Robert says.

Mr. Cooper leads the way to a tumble of boulders overlooking the falls. A rainbow glows within the rising mist, colors waxing and waning.

We watch until Dr. Grey asks, "Anyone hungry?"

Mrs. Fenster has kindly provided a red-checked cloth, and I spread it over our table-rock. Then I lay out the food, my pie with its woven top crust as our centerpiece. We perch at the edges of the rock and eat boiled eggs, fried chicken, and molasses cookies.

To my amusement, the men begin to compete, both trying to pass food to me and speaking over one another as we discuss the weather and other benign subjects.

In an attempt to cut the tension, I ask, "Mr. Cooper, what do you call that fancy device over there?"

He casts the doctor a sidewise glance and a smile tugs at the corners of his mouth. "It's a transit theodolite, Miss Creed. I use it to survey land. It takes the two of us, Robert and me, to use it, and it measures both the horizontal and vertical angles—"

The doctor interrupts. "For heaven sakes, Coop, Miss Creed isn't interested in that. Why don't you pass me the pie?"

"I'm very interested," I say, but Mr. Cooper closes his mouth and passes the pie.

The doctor takes a folding knife from his pocket and cuts four large pieces. Mrs. Fenster provided no tableware, and we make a mess of ourselves eating the pastry with our hands. The waterfall rushes and hisses, background music to our laughter. A meandering wind carries the anise perfume of sweet coneflowers, and both gentlemen seem as reluctant as I am to end our picnic, but Dr. Grey finally says he must get back to work.

As I repack the basket, I ask Mr. Cooper how he obtained his surveying job.

He plucks a few maple leaves and uses them to wipe his hands. "You probably know about the recent amendment to the Homestead Act."

"Not really."

"It opens new land for Union war veterans," he says. "I was aware when I took the job that it wouldn't make me a popular man hereabouts, but the job is short-lived and pays well."

I understand what he's not saying. The town of Milksnake lost men and boys in that war, and most of them fought for the confederacy.

I fold up the tablecloth and say, "I abhor slavery, Mr. Cooper."

I'm quite sure I see admiration in his eyes, which emboldens me to continue.

"I understand why you'd take the surveying job, but perhaps the Federal Government should think again before placing unsuspecting families into areas where they'll be shunned or even hated."

Mr. Cooper is a handsome man, his blue eyes mesmerizing. "A good point, Miss Creed."

The doctor interrupts. "Enough. This is far too serious a subject for a beautiful day and a beautiful woman. Mr. Cooper, Robert, we'll leave you to your work."

"Always work," says Mr. Cooper.

Do I detect a look of regret in his eyes? Or am I turning into a faded version of Mary-Polly Preck, sure that every man who speaks to me has romantic interests in mind?

During our return to Ma Mère's cabin, the doctor tells me more about his life in New York City. "Concerts, balls, and receptions," he says. "Stores filled with everything imaginable. I would love to show you New York."

I'm not sure if that's an invitation or only a polite comment, and I don't ask. When we arrive at the cabin, the doctor quickly dismounts and helps me down from the mule, his hands lingering for a few seconds at my waist.

I back away from him, but he walks to the porch. "Sit with me a minute, Miss Creed." He takes off his riding gloves, and we sit down on the top step.

Although he checked my left hand before the picnic, he does so again. He strokes my palm, and goosebumps rise along my arm.

"May I call you China?" he asks.

I'm surprised, but maybe in New York, doctors call their patients by their first names.

"You may."

"And you'll call me Stephen."

I hesitate. "You're my doctor. Shouldn't I address you more formally?"

"But if we were seeing one another?"

My heart jumps. What?

"Perhaps I'm being forward," he says, "but is there someone who would give me permission to call on you? Maybe Mrs. Settle?"

"The only one to ask is me."

He looks off toward the path to town, a strange smile on his face. Then he turns and stares into my eyes with an intensity that cuts my breath short. "Miss China Creed, would you allow me the honor of calling on you?"

My mouth drops open.

"I know this is sudden," he says. "Do you need time to think about it?"

If Ma Mère were alive, she'd insist that I get to know him better, because, if we're entering any kind of relationship, I must to tell him about my curse. Is he a greedy man? If so, I might destroy him just as I destroyed my father. Finally, I stammer out, "I'm honored, Dr. Grey, but what would the people of Milksnake think? You know, considering my mother."

"I don't care what they say." He smiles into my eyes. "But I won't rush you into any decision. Let's begin simply—please call me Stephen."

I think about Mary-Polly who already uses his first name. Why shouldn't I?

"Thank you, I will."

Then as if we'd been friends forever, we talk. He tells me about his joys and aggravations, about his schooling, and his love of medicine. I learn that his father, always a role model for him, died three years before, and his mother continues the family investment business. He has a younger brother named Philip, but he has no sisters.

Finally, he releases my hand and checks his pocket watch. "You're a difficult woman to leave, China, but leave I must."

He mounts his gelding and tips his hat. Cordell's mule seems content to stay where he is, but Stephen able to convince him otherwise, and then all three of them head toward town. Again the doctor pauses at the first turn of the path, and, for the second time in my life, I deem to hope that a good man might come to love me.

Two days later, I bake Stephen another pie—an excuse for a visit. When I enter his office, he doesn't look up, his attention caught by whatever he's studying through the microscope. I set the pie down on the desk corner. He glances at it and leaves his microscope. He comes to me, gently clasps my gloved hands. His fingers are trembling, and his eyes look strange, the pupils so tiny I wonder how he can see.

"As you might guess, China," he says, "I'm having a relapse of malaria."

I stutter out a few words of sympathy. In Milksnake Hollow, malaria is no mystery. East in Missouri's Boot Heel region, the Mississippi River generates swamplands where malaria breeds, a chronic sickness that waxes and wanes. Modern medicine has given us Warburg's Tincture, but not even that is a complete cure. It hurts my heart to realize that Stephen suffers from a disease that will plague him all his life.

Before I can ask how I might help, the front door opens and a young man walks in. He wears field clothes, and he's jittery on his feet. From his dark, soft eyes, it's easy to tell he's of native ancestry. His family, like Miz Settle, must have slipped away during the removal to Indian Territory. He looks past me to the doctor. "My woman needs help bad."

"What happened?" Stephen asks.

"Cut her leg with an ax. I can't get it stopped bleeding."

Stephen stares up at the ceiling and does not respond. I dare to place my hand on his shoulder. "This man needs you, Dr. Grey."

He shakes himself, like a person might do upon waking, and hurries into the examination room, emerges with his suit coat and black leather bag.

"Wait for me, Miss Creed, if you would," he says.

On his way out the door, he stumbles and falls to his knees. The young man looks at me with wide, frightened eyes.

"You have a horse, Sir?" I ask as Stephen gets to his feet

"No."

"Give me a minute."

I rush to the backyard. The doctor's gelding stands in the lean-to that serves as his stable. I've never saddled a horse or even put on a bridle. I call for help, and several men come over from the blacksmith shop. They quickly get the horse ready, and I lead it to the street. Dr. Grey mounts, and the young man springs up behind him, manages to stay on even when the horse tucks its rump and leaps into a gallop.

I return to the office and pick up my pie, carry it to the kitchen. Dirty dishes are piled high in a zinc-coated basin, including my pie tin from the picnic. I wash everything then carry my tin out to the desk. I study the microscope from all sides and finally lower my eye to the viewing apparatus. The glass slide appears to hold a drop of liquid. I jump when I see little rod-like creatures swimming within that drop.

In my surprise, I sit down hard in the doctor's chair, and at that moment Mr. Cooper comes in the front door. He's wiping sweat from his face with a large blue bandana.

"Miss Creed, good to see you again," he says then asks, "What's he looking at now?"

"I'm not sure, but they appear to be alive."

He joins me at the desk and leans forward to gaze into the microscope. "Amazing what a person might see in a drop of water."

"In every drop of water?" The thought makes my skin crawl.

"I'd prefer not to know."

We laugh together, and I say, "I brought another pie."

"You suppose Dr. Grey will share it with me?"

"He'd better."

"I'll tell him you said so."

Mr. Cooper shuffles his feet, and I realize that, unlike Stephen, he's quite shy.

"The doctor's out on a call," I tell him. "He asked me to wait here."

I look into the microscope again. The tiny beasts continue to swim. Mr. Cooper stays beside me, and the silence between us begins to feel awkward.

Stepping back from the desk, I ask, "How does a man train to become a surveyor, Mr. Cooper? Did you attend a college?"

"I studied architecture at a university, but I learned surveying during my employment with a man named Frederick Law Olmsted. A genius really, he designed the landscape of Central Park."

Mr. Cooper must notice the blank look on my face. "Central Park is a greensward in New York City," he explains.

"And what is a greensward?"

"A place where people can relax among lawns and woods. When your life is bounded on all sides by noisy streets and large buildings, a place of greenery renews your soul."

"I'm sure it would. And are you from New York like Dr. Grey?"

"I was born in Scotland." He broadens his accent. "Are ye not surprised, lassie?" He chuckles. "I've tried to corral my speech, but sometimes the Scots does leak through."

"It's a beautiful accent. Don't try to change it."

He turns away from me and walks to the front window, looks out. "I was nine when my mother died. A few months later, my father brought me and my two sisters to this new world. He thought we might thrive better in a place that didn't remind us of her. He passed away some ten years ago. I miss him. I miss them both. Every day."

I can't allow myself to think about Ma Mère. Instead, I cast my thoughts toward Parnell Creed and Paul Le Roy—the two fathers in my life. I can't say I miss them, but I do feel the lack. "What did your father do, Mr. Cooper? His occupation, I mean."

"He was a farrier, and Stephen's family hired him. We lived above the Grey family stables. It wasn't long until Stephen and I became friends." He turns and grins at me. "Actually, I was more of a tag-along than a friend. Stephen's three years older than I am."

I want to ask more questions, but I hear a horse trot up and stop in front of the building. When someone calls for help, Mr. Cooper and I run to the door. Stephen and the Indian man are astride the gelding, and I can tell by their faces that nothing good came of Stephen's efforts.

The man slides down over the rump of the horse. He stomps up to me, his eyes blazing. "You're his wife?"

"No. A patient." I hold up my hand to show him my shortened finger.

"I hope he wasn't drunk when he did that to you."

"The doctor has malaria," I say, and I don't miss the surprise on Mr. Cooper's face.

The man shouts, "You don't know nothing."

Mr. Cooper places a protective arm around my shoulders, keeping me at his side as he leads the gelding behind the building, Stephen slumped in the saddle.

"Hold the horse, Miss Creed," he says, and he pulls Stephen down.

We leave the gelding in the fenced yard and support Stephen between us as we walk him into the office and then to the examination room. I've been with Miz Settle when she gives treatment with Warburg's Tincture and wormwood, but the malaria I've seen causes headache, fever, and vomiting. Not the lethargy that seems to plague Stephen Grey.

When Mr. Cooper and I finally get him into the cot, I say, "It's not malaria? Is he drunk?"

"Does he smell like liquor?"

"Not at all."

"It's a private problem, Miss Creed. I'll leave it to Dr. Grey to explain. It'd be best if you go now, but thank you for your help."

As I leave the examination room, I notice an elegant mahogany side table set in the corner, and I know I haven't seen it before. A variety of medical bags, some old and worn, others new, are lined up on top. Stolen goods?

CHAPTER TWENTY

The next day, I sit on the porch in Ma Mère's rocker, watching the sky as a gathering of clouds grow tall and dark. My left hand aches from hauling buckets of water to the garden. We need rain. A rise of dust blooms down the trail, and I soon hear a thunder of hooves. Dr. Grey? I stand and tuck stray curls into the bun at the back of my head, but the rider is Cordell Smith, and the animal is his white mule. When he alights, he gives me a smile, and, without invitation, he sits on the porch steps. He removes his straw hat, bats it against his leg a few times, then launches into a meandering conversation.

Finally he says, "Ya got a fine little heifer calf, China."

I know where this is going, and my heart starts to ache. Anyone who has heard the bawling of a cow when her calf is taken understands, but I know I must agree. "What price will you give me?" I say even before he asks.

He reaches into the side pocket of his overalls and pulls out a three-dollar gold piece, the bust of an Indian in feathered headdress stamped on the front side. I sit speechless. I've not seen a gold coin since the war and rarely a silver one.

"Where on earth?"

As if we were still schoolmates, he says, "Mine to know and yours to wonder." Did I touch Cordell, skin to skin? If so, I may have stolen that gold for him. Pray God, it didn't belong to someone otherwise penniless. "This for your calf," he says.

I ignore my feelings of guilt. "Would you let her have another month with my cow?"

"Fair deal." He flips the gold coin with his thumb, and I catch it midair.

"Cup of coffee?" I ask as he ambles down the porch steps toward his mule.

"Thanks but my uncle expects me back at the smithy. How's your hand?"

"Doing well. Have you heard anything about Dr. Grey? He was poorly yesterday when I was in town."

"I saw him up and about this morning. Didn't notice anything wrong."

I'm relieved but also foolishly disappointed that I won't have reason to offer Stephen some of my herbal cures.

Cordell climbs on his mule and is about to turn the animal toward the trail when he smacks his hand against his forehead. "I forgot the main reason I came." He pulls a letter from his breast pocket, leans down, and hands it to me.

My belly clenches. The postmark is from Louisiana. Have the Destrehans found me? How could that be possible?

When Cordell and his mule are out of sight, I study the sealed envelope. I'm accustomed to Grand-mère Angèle's occasional letters and her gifts from Canada. Whoever wrote Ma Mère's name and address upon this letter possesses a bold hand, not at all like my grandmother's. I break the seal.

The letter is edged in black, and new sorrow adds weight to my burdened heart. I know before I read one word that Grand-mère Angèle has passed. At least I won't have to write her about Ma Mère's death, something I've been putting off.

A lawyer in New Orleans expresses his condolences to Ma Mère upon the loss of her mother. He doesn't mention how my grandmother died or why she retained a lawyer in New Orleans when she lived in Canada. Folded within the condolence letter is a smaller paper envelope. Written on the back in my grandmother's hand is my mother's full name, Yvette Destrehan Creed, and below it my name, simply China. The envelope is sealed with a glutinous paste. I open it and gasp. American greenbacks in denominations of ten and twenty fall down the steps of the porch. I scramble to collect the bills, and then I count them.

One hundred dollars—a fortune—and most precious of all a slip of paper in my grandmother's handwriting. *I will always love you both.*

I waste the remainder of that day on regret. Regret that my true father died before I was born. Regret that, because of me, my mother had to leave her family. Regret that I never knew my Grand-mère Angèle. Regret that Parnell Creed died of Dibbler shine, which I likely stole for him. I've hurt too many people.

I weep until my throat is parched, and, when that weeping has passed, my tears flow again with the fear that somehow, through the lawyer's letter, despite all my mother's and grandmother's precautions, the Destrehans will find me. I tuck that fear into my heart where it keeps me awake all night.

In the morning, I rise up from my grief and walk to Miz Settle's, good company being the best palliative for sorrow.

She's sitting on the porch steps, stringing a mess of green beans. We nod at each other, and I sit down beside her, gathering a double handful of beans and dumping them in my lap. "Many hands, light work," says Miz Settle. We have no further need of conversation until we're done. Then she clasps my left hand and studies the scars left by Dr. Grey's knife. "He done a good job."

"He did."

"But that finger ain't the reason you're here."

"No." I tell her about my grandmother's death. Bessie comes up and looks at me with doleful eyes. "I haven't been around much, have I girl?" I stroke her head. The fur around her muzzle has turned gray.

"There's something else I should know," says Miz Settle.

"I can't keep any secrets from you, can I?"

"Probably not."

"Dr. Grey—"

"He's courting you?"

"Why would you say that?"

"I seen him in church. He can hardly take his eyes off you."

"He asked permission to call on me. I haven't said yes or no. I think I should tell him about my curse before I agree to any kind of courtship."

"You're sure you can trust him?"

"Pretty sure." I've caught some beggar's ticks in the hem of my skirt, those prickly little seeds. I pick them out. "The doctor's sick, Miz Settle. He claims it's malaria, but I don't think it is."

"Could it be consumption?"

Her words punch out my breath. "Surely not."

"Ya need to know, Sheba. If he has it, he could give it to you. Maybe that's why he left the city. Ozark air is good for the afflicted."

My first impulse is to confront him immediately, that very day, but Miz Settle interrupts my misguided thoughts. "You strong enough for a trip up the Deer Lick? I'm thinking to coax Janie Myrtle Aubright toward birthing. She's two weeks over."

Janie Myrtle Aubright has always kept to a regular schedule, giving birth every two years. "Her ninth child?"

"Tenth. Remember the twins?"

Who could forget the Aubright twins? Two small boys likely to destroy anything they set their hands to. "I'll go."

We leave within a few minutes, but Bessie stays home. Trips tire her beyond necessity, probably because she's too slow to chase squirrels. As Miz Settle claims, unresolved longing weakens the heart.

The easiest way upstream is down the middle of the creek. We take off our shoes and stockings and wade in. The water lies ankle-deep in late summer and, as in most years, a soft ridge of sand has accumulated at the center. It's a soothing walk, but we watch carefully for cottonmouths. Although disinclined to bite humans, their poison is worse than a rattlesnake's.

The Aubright cabin, a cobbled place, has grown with the family. They've added multiple rooms to each side and the back, every roofline a hand-length lower than the one preceding. In the clearing, two boys work at a chopping block. A girl, not much bigger than a mite, comes from the hen house, her apron heavy with eggs. Despite the heat of the day, someone's started the kitchen stove, and a heavy flow of smoke pours from the central chimney.

Janie Myrtle's husband, Del, greets us. He's blond with squinty eyes and a ready smile. "Perfect timing," he says. "I were about to go get ya. Janie's holding on tight to the sides of the bed."

"Pushing already?" Miz Settle asks.

"She is."

Miz Settle takes the porch steps in one high bound. I start after her, but Mr. Aubright catches my sleeve. "Sorry to hear about your ma," he says. "We sent up some prayers for ya'll."

"Thank you."

"Iffen you need extra work, I could hire you on. Pay you in flour and eggs."

It's a kind offer, but I hold up my gloved hand with its truncated finger. "I appreciate that more than you know, but I'm not going to be much good to anybody for a while."

He raises his eyebrows.

"Snakebite," I tell him.

"Troubles, they come threefold."

In practical day-to-day living, I've found that old saying to be true. If so, I'm due for a little mercy.

"Well, keep us in mind for next year," Del says. "I can always use extra help to stook my grain. Meanwhile, stay away from snakes."

Janie Myrtle lets out a squeak. "I better get in there," I say.

"'Preciate it."

I enter the backmost bedroom at the very moment the baby crowns.

"Next push," Miz Settle says.

I know that's the cue for me to take my station atop the bed. Miz Settle's rheumatism relegates most baby-catching to me. Janie groans, and somehow grabs hold of my right hand. She pulls, skinning off my glove, but, before I can worry about that, a squalling boy lands in the skirt of my apron. He's blessed with red hair, as are half the Aubright children. A stray thought about my brother sears my heart.

"A boy," I shout. I try to remember how many of each they have, but I've lost track. "Good lungs on him."

Janie Myrtle, laughing, reaches for her baby.

"Wait a minute, mama," Miz Settle says. "I need a little slack on his birth cord."

The thick cord is wrapped once around his chest.

I find my glove among the bedclothes and wiggle my hand into it. When the placenta slides out, I place the baby against his mother's chest. Del comes into the room about then, and I scramble to cover his wife's private parts, although he surely is familiar with that region of her anatomy.

He sits on the bed and kisses his wife. I'm overtaken by a sudden longing for a strong husband and a houseful of children. I look at Miz Settle, and her sad eyes tell me she's yearning for the same, but for her, it's a threadbare wish.

"Cut the cord," Miz Settle tells me.

As Miz Settle places the afterbirth into a metal tub, Del lifts his baby's right fist and commences counting his fingers, but, as the baby stretches out his hand, a golden ring drops away from the infant's tight clasp. Miz Settle's eyes grow large.

"What kind a witchery is this?" Del says in a strangled voice.

I don't know where the idea came from, but I remove my glove and slip the ring on my index finger. "I'm sorry. It was my mother's. It must have come off when Janie Myrtle caught hold of my glove."

"I pulled that glove clean off her hand," Janie says. "Didn't mean to."

I try to laugh. "You have a powerful grip."

Miz Settle turns her voice gruff. "I told you, China, no jewelry. Didn't I say that?"

"More than once."

Del Aubright gives me a studied look, and I'm not sure our performance has convinced him. I'm relieved when he turns his attention back to his wife and child.

Miz Settle and I clean the mother and the baby and the bedroom. I manage to put a passable supper on the table—reheated molasses-laced beans, sliced onions fresh from the garden, and catfish rolled in corn-meal and fried golden. When everyone is fed and the baby content, Miz Settle and I start down the creek for home. Mr. Aubright paid us in coin, which puts Miz Settle in a talkative mood. She speaks about sundry things, mostly experiences catching babies. We arrive at her house before sunset, and she finally addresses the subject we've been avoiding.

"Let me see the ring."

I pull it from my finger and hand it over. She sniffs it, her nose crinkling. "That one came from a grave. Pray hard the Aubrights don't recollect which grave."

"I've been praying," I say. "You want the ring?"

"No. And if you're smart, you'll heave it into the crik."

I know she's right, but it seems like double thievery to throw it away. I slip it into the pocket of my skirt. It's a moon-bright night, an easy walk home. I bring the cow into the barn and milk her by lantern light then close the door on her and her calf, each in a separate stall.

That night, in Ma Mère's bed, I dream about a baby growing inside me, a baby who wants everything in the world until my belly is filled to bursting with all the treasures that child covets.

* * *

The next day I walk to town. I need pickling salt, but I also plan to visit Stephen and ask him if he has consumption.

If he does, I'll offer my services as his nurse.

I visit the store first. My brother is propped in a basket lined with a striped blanket. He's trying to focus on his hand but keeps batting himself in the nose. I'm fascinated.

"He doesn't understand he's the one doing it to himself." Mrs. James's voice comes to me from the dry goods counter. She's pushing needles through rectangles of white paper, a variety of sizes on each, a novel idea. Every seamstress needs various sizes. How convenient to buy them as a group.

I crouch in front of my brother. He smiles, and my heart warms. We've been endowed with the same shape mouth. I wonder if Mrs. James has noticed. Mr. James comes into the store from the back room, and my brother begins to fuss.

"Would you mind picking him up out of the basket, China?" Mrs. James asks.

My heart expands in gratitude. Little Daniel is a sturdy boy, and I'm pleased to see how much he's grown. I carry him across the store, and Mrs. James takes him from my arms.

I study the pile of papered needles. "A smart idea."

"Choose one. You've earned it."

I thank her and tuck the needles into my pocket.

Mrs. James coos baby words, calling him *Danny*. I turn away from her happiness, disgusted that I'm unable to share her joy. I must have been born with a miserly heart, wanting everything for myself.

I tell Mr. James I need pickling salt, and I place a few coins on his counter.

When he gives me my change, he says, "You hear about the doctor?"

I draw in my breath, and Mrs. James gasps. "What? Did he die?"

"Of course not."

"You almost scared the life out of me, husband."

"You scare too easy," Mr. James says. "He's not dead, but he does have malaria. Got it bad. I hear somebody's keeping watch over him day and night."

I pretend I'm not much concerned, although I say, "He'll need prayers."

Mr. James squints at me. "From the likes of you?"

Mrs. James stares daggers toward her husband. "I'm sure Miss Creed's prayers are more effective than yours, Mr. James," she says, and she strikes me as a woman who has finally come into her own. "China, would you mind carrying over a pot of soup? I've got one simmering."

The moment she asks, I know I've betrayed my true feelings, but I volunteer for the task.

She places the baby in his basket and a few minutes later brings out a blue splatterware pot, the rich smell of beef seeping out from around its lid. I load the pickling salt into my tote and take the pot. With a reason as innocent as any, I walk to Stephen's office.

Inside, I catch a strange odor, vinegar but not vinegar and it carries a smoky overtone. Cordell Smith comes out of the examination room, eating an apple. We exchange greetings, and Stephen calls, "Miss Creed is it?"

"I brought you soup from Mrs. James." I set the pot on his desk.

"Oh go back and see him," says Cordell. "I'm a suitable chaperone."

I bat aside the curtains and go in. Stephen is sitting up in a chair. He's pale, and his hair is rumpled, but his color has improved. The smile he gives me makes my trek to town worthwhile. He gestures me over and catches my hand. He studies my stumped finger as if he could see it through the gauze.

"You're swabbing it?"

"Three times a day."

"Carbolic acid?"

"And vinegar." I pull my hand away. I've had enough conversations about my finger. "Stephen, may I ask you something?" My words come out shaky.

"Yes."

"You'll tell me the truth?"

"I always tell the truth."

"Do you have consumption?"

His smile lifts my heart. "Dear China, of course not. You were worried about that?"

"Your malaria isn't anything like I've seen before."

"It's an odd type, only that, and it seldom bothers me, but when it does I'm very sick. I'm sorry it came upon me just when we were—" He pauses. "—pursuing our friendship."

"A worthwhile friendship is strong enough to weather poor health."

"Well said." He hesitates then asks, "China, would you accompany me to church this Sunday?"

How can I refuse?

On Sunday, Stephen looks weary, but his smile is warm. As soon as the service ends, and we are out the door, he asks, "May I walk you home?"

"It's three miles."

"A walk will do me good."

He offers his arm, and I'm filled with both joy and nervousness. At the very place where Tommy Belnap kissed me, Stephen stops and reaches into a pocket of his frock coat. "I don't want you to feel like I'm rushing you. I'll wait as long as necessary. However—" He pulls out a ring, its blue oval stone rising from a circle of shining crystals. "Would you be willing to wear my ring as a sign of our friendship?"

Surprise robs me of words.

"Please," he whispers. He turns the ring, and in the sunlight, the blue stone glows red, as if a burning coal lived inside. "The center gem is an opal. The others are diamonds. The ring is a family heirloom. Will you wear it?"

Suddenly there's nothing else in this world that I want more than that ring. I lift my hand, and he places it on my ring finger. "Would this mean we're courting?" Stephen asks.

I look into his eyes and every resolve I've held about courtship falls away. "I would say so."

We kiss, and my stomach drops deliciously toward those nether parts of me that want much more. I lean toward him, hoping he'll kiss me again, but he says, "One kiss each time we meet, China. I'll not ask for more until we're married. I don't want to compromise your moral standards."

When we arrive at Ma Mère's cabin, he refuses my reckless invitation to sit down for a cup of tea, and then he thanks me.

"For what?" I ask.

"For being everything I need."

He kisses me again, a long, slow kiss that sends chills down my spine, and then he smiles ruefully. "There, you see how much power you have over me. I've already broken my first promise to you."

"Perhaps we should change that promise to two kisses," I say.

"Agreed."

I cup his face in my hands, and the look in his eyes is every bit as powerful as a kiss. "Three?" I ask.

He steps back and lifts his index fingers in a cross as if against a hex. We're both laughing as he walks away.

CHAPTER
TWENTY-ONE

The next Sunday morning, I wait for Stephen in the shade of the chestnut tree. Although I've worn his ring for a week, I still fight the inclination to swat at it, as if were an insect perched upon my finger. Mary-Polly trails her parents down the street. Even though my glove covers the ring, I tuck my left hand into the side pocket of my skirt. She glances at me, her lips curled in a stiff smile.

"I hope your hand is much better, China," she says.

"Thank you. It is."

The Aubright family passes us. Del doesn't look my way, but Janie Myrtle pulls aside the light blanket that protects her baby's face from the sun. I compliment her beautiful child, and the family disappears into the cool shadows of the church. A few minutes later, Del walks outside and heads my way.

He takes my elbow and leads me across the street. "I been thinking on that ring, Miss Creed."

I widen my eyes as if I have no idea what he's talking about.

"Don't look at me like that. You know what I mean. The ring that was in my son's hand." His fingers tighten on my arm. "It took me a few days, but I finally remembered where I seen it. In a coffin. On the finger of my wife's dead grandmother. I visited her grave not two days ago. It's sunken and old. What I'm saying is, ain't nobody dug it up. That ring should still be down there buried with her. Something strange happened, and if my son carries a witch's curse, I will do all in my power to destroy that witch. All in my power, ya hear?"

"Do you have any idea how many plain gold rings there are in the world, Del?"

He lets go of my arm and gazes off toward the church, waves at Cordell Smith who's escorting Holly Barnes toward the open door.

"Here's what I'm saying, Miss Creed. I want that ring back. Maybe it wasn't buried with the grandmother. Maybe somebody leaned close over the body and slipped it off. But I want the ring, or I'll go all the way to Forsyth and bring the law down on you and that thieving Injun Miz Settle."

"I'll say it again, Del. The ring is mine." I marvel at the certainty in my voice. "But if you promise you will cause no harm to Miz Settle, I'll bring it to you tomorrow as a gift for your son."

I don't wait for his answer. I walk toward the church. I'm nearly to the door when someone taps my shoulder. I turn. Stephen's friend, Royce Cooper, smiles at me.

"Dr. Grey asked me to express his regrets."

"He's not sick again, is he?"

"He's fine." Mr. Cooper inclines his head and offers his arm. "Shall we?"

I don't want him to escort me into the church. People might think I'm after every available man in town. I may wear Stephen's ring, but I've told no one except Miz Settle about our courtship. I'm careful to release Mr. Cooper's arm when we enter, and I slide in at the second pew from the door. He sits beside me. Mary-Polly's mother glances back, glowering. Mr. Cooper and I share a hymnal and recite litany in unison. Unlike Stephen's, his voice is deep and beautiful, and I enjoy listening to him sing.

At the end of the service, he says, "Dr. Grey was hoping to invite you on another picnic. He had Mrs. Fenster fill a basket. I'd be most happy to accompany you instead."

I'm uncomfortable enough about Mr. Cooper escorting me to church. "Mr. Cooper, I thank you for the invitation, but it's time I return home. My animals rely on me for safety and comfort. In other words, I need to milk my cow."

He chuckles, which makes me laugh, too.

"At least take the picnic basket home with you," he says.

"You're sure? Wouldn't you and Stephen appreciate Mrs. Fenster's fine cooking this afternoon?"

"We appreciate her fine cooking almost every day." He pats his middle as if he'd grown stout.

We walk to the office, and he steps inside, comes back in a moment carrying the basket. Several families pass us on the boardwalk.

One of the women—Lemmie Branet—hisses, "Like her mother."

Heat rises to my face, and Mr. Cooper says to me, "I'll take care of this."

"Please don't, Mr. Cooper."

Nevertheless, he sets down the basket and hurries after Mrs. Branet. Miz Settle and I delivered her last baby only a few months before. The child was lying crosswise in her womb. I wonder if she realizes how few mothers or babies survive such a delivery.

"Mrs. Branet?" Mr. Cooper calls out. "Do I have your name correct?"

The woman stops and looks at him. Her husband, a genial person, carries their new baby in his arms. Mrs. Branet is clasping the hand of their toddler.

"Concerning your comment as you passed Miss Creed and me," says Royce Cooper. "I believe it was a slight, not only of her but also of her deceased mother."

Mrs. Branet puffs herself up. "You might as well know the truth, Mr. Cooper. She's stepping out with the doctor one Sunday and with you the next."

"Miss Creed is not stepping out with me, and rest assured the doctor has only honorable intent." He looks my way. "May I share your good news?"

Of course, with that remark, he already has. I remove my glove and hold up my left hand, blunted finger and all. The ring sparkles.

"You see, Mrs. Branet," Mr. Cooper says, "a doctor can't always plan on a day of rest. Jesus Christ himself healed people on the Sabbath."

I tuck a smile behind my teeth.

Mrs. Branet fairly spits her words. "Do I understand that you're comparing Dr. Grey with Jesus Christ?"

"Not at all, Mrs. Branet. What I am doing, as per the doctor's request, is giving this picnic basket to Miss Creed. Even though he must miss their planned dinner together, there's no reason to waste the food."

Mr. Branet shifts the baby to his left arm. His whisper is loud. "Lemmie, whenever will ya learn to keep your trap shut?"

She looks at him, her eyes blazing, but she closes her mouth, and they walk away.

Mr. Cooper returns to my side. "You're amazing," I tell him.

"Thank you." His eyes are soft as he looks at me. "Dr. Grey is a lucky man." To my surprise, he kisses my cheek as he hands me the basket.

I take a quick backward step. "Good day, Sir."

I hurry away, thoroughly agitated. If Mr. Cooper believes me to be an innocent young lady, why would he kiss me? The more I think about it, the angrier I become, and it's on that walk home that I first begin to wonder how Stephen obtained that ring—a family heirloom—here in Milksnake.

I spend the afternoon in my garden, chopping what remains of the bean vines into the soil. I attack clumps of dirt until they're fine as buckwheat. I don't hear the beat of horse hooves until the beast is snorting behind me. I turn around. It's Stephen. His riding boots shine black and slick as mica.

Before he can even greet me, I say, "I need to talk to you about something."

His smile fades. "What's wrong?"

I wrap my hands around the haft of the hoe. "It's difficult enough to keep a decent reputation in this town without the complication of two escorts. I had no need for Mr. Cooper to accompany me to church and especially for him to kiss my cheek."

Stephen's face colors. "Well—"

"Well what?"

"Well don't blame him." He dismounts and looks at me from across the saddle, but he can't meet my eyes.

"Why did he kiss me, Stephen?"

He rubs the bridge of his nose. "Mr. Cooper kissed you because I asked him to."

"You asked him to?"

"Hear me out, China. I have a good reason."

"You'd better."

"How do I say this?" When he finally speaks, his words come in a rush. "I've begun to believe something rather odd, and I wanted Mr. Cooper's input."

I lay down the hoe and walk to the off-side of the horse. "Your mother did not give you the microscope."

"She did not."

I look him full in the face. "I'm not a witch."

"I never thought you were. Science precludes witchery."

"Then why don't you tell me what you think I am."

"A fine young woman."

It's a flippant answer, and it makes me even angrier. "The whole truth."

"I believe you're a Goomer Doctor."

"Goomer Doctors are rare, Stephen, and they're gifted, but they are normal people."

"You're more than that, aren't you?"

I lift my chin. "You tell me."

"You're a telekine."

"I'm not familiar with that word."

"You transport things with the power of your mind, China."

I'm suddenly cold, as if fear has unleashed winter upon me. "I've been working hard in this garden, Stephen, and the sun is beating down like blue blazes. If I could move things with my mind, I'd have a dipper of water in my hands right now, wouldn't I?"

He strokes his gelding's neck. "China, did you—somehow—give me the Zeiss Microscope? Did you do that for me?"

My stomach twists. "Not to my knowledge." A compromised truth. "Suppose you tell me more about the microscope, Stephen. Did you want it? Had you seen it before?"

"I saw one in Europe, and I wanted it. What did you do, China? Did you wish for it?"

"How could I wish for it? I'd never heard of a Zeiss Microscope, and I didn't know you wanted it." I walk toward the cabin. "Are you hungry? I have a bountiful basket of food inside, thank you kindly. You're welcome to join me if you wish. I'm guessing your horse needs water. I filled the trough as soon as I got home from church."

Inside, I wash my face and hands and dry off with a rag. I take Stephen's ring from the biscuit tin where I store it. I slip it on my finger. I'm weary, and I'm frightened. Ma Mère and I and Miz Settle kept my secret for such a long time. What will happen now that more people know? The image of the Aubright baby comes into my mind, that terrible moment when I saw the ring in his hand.

I'd almost convinced myself that I could trust Stephen with my secret, but if he sent Mr. Cooper to kiss me, purely on suspicion alone, is he worthy of my trust?

I open the basket and take out a piece of cold fried chicken and a soft white-flour roll. I place them on a plate. When Stephen comes in, I hand him the food. He sits down, and I serve myself. I sigh as I ease into the other chair. Polite, Stephen waits for me to take the first bite.

We eat without conversation, but, when Stephen's plate is empty, he says, "Mr. Cooper was only an experiment."

I lean my elbow on the table—quite rude Ma Mère always claimed. I set my chin in my hand. "I'm listening."

"We're trying to figure you out, China. You have a talent, a gift beyond anything I've seen. Touch—skin on skin—has to be involved. Am I correct? And perhaps your ability connects some way with the recipient's mental imagery."

"I don't deny I have a gift, Stephen, but it's God-given, not some evil satanic power. Nor is it a scientific marvel to be dissected. Even if you began to suspect my abilities, you had no right to tell Mr. Cooper without my permission."

He rubs his eyes then stares at me. "Please accept my apologies. From now on, I'll keep your secret between you and me. I promise. Tell me only as much as you want, and don't go beyond your own level of comfort, but perhaps you'll share this one thing with me. Who else knows?"

It's a fair question.

"Miz Settle knows. Both my mother and my Grandmother Destrehan knew."

His eyes widen. "Destrehan?"

"You've heard the name?"

"I have."

"My mother was the granddaughter of Henri Destrehan."

His mouth drops open. "My lord, China, he was the wealthiest man in all Louisiana, and your mother was content to live here? Why?"

"That's something for another day and another discussion, Stephen."

He reaches across the table as if to take my hand, but I pull away. "And this ring? How did it get here? It's a family heirloom?"

"You tell me." He gives me a grim smile. "I want to understand your abilities, China, not as a scientist, but as a man who loves you."

It's the first time he's mentioned love. Why tell me in such an off-hand way? Fourteen-year-old Tommy Belnap was more romantic.

He waits a moment, as if he hopes I'll respond with a declaration of love. I don't.

Finally, he leaves his chair and crouches beside me. "I apologize, China, and I promise to protect you from anyone who might take advantage of your gift. I promise. I know we can work out any problems your abilities might cause us."

He looks at me with such longing that I close my mind to the possibility that he might not be longing for me.

"And Mr. Cooper?"

"He's a good man, China. Not at all greedy. You can trust him. Come here." He stands up and pulls me into an embrace. "As for now, tell me everything or tell me nothing. It's your choice."

I'm quite sure Ma Mère would urge caution, but this is Stephen, who wants to be my husband. I lay my head against his shoulder, and he begins to sway as if he were rocking a child.

I sigh, and then I say, "There's a song my mother used to sing, actually a riddle. Maybe we can solve it together." I lift my voice in the simple melody.

> *Something you covet deep to the bone.*
> *But nothing alive with will of its own.*
> *Nothing too large. The earth stakes its claim.*
> *Nothing unseen. The eyes play the game.*

I look up at his face. His eyes are closed, and his lips are moving. I'm quite sure he's repeating Ma Mère's song.

CHAPTER TWENTY-TWO

That night, besieged by doubt, I sleep fitfully. Is Mr. Cooper trustworthy? Does Stephen love me for myself? When I awaken, I find the world swathed in early morning fog. It's the first day of September, summer waning. The past three months brought so many changes that I feel the need to reclaim my life. When an obliging sun lifts the fog, I walk to the Aubright homestead.

When I'm close, I hear the heavy rhythm of Del's splitting maul. I approach from the side to avoid his backswing. He startles when he sees me, finishes a split, and tosses the two pieces of oak into the woodpile. Then he sets the maul head-down against the ground. I hold my hand open flat, the ring upon it. He plucks it from my palm and lifts it toward the sun.

"I'm prit-sure it's hers," he says, squinting at it.

"I'm prit-sure it's mine," I tell him.

He wipes the sweat from his forehead, leaving a smudge of dirt. "Then thanks for the gift."

"We're all settled?"

He says two words that freeze my heart. "For now."

Without another word, I turn toward the path to town and walk away. My unease lasts until I arrive at Stephen's office. I let myself into the front room where he stands at his desk studying a stack of papers, some large enough to cover the entire desktop. He glances up and, when he sees me, a smile lights his face.

"China," he says, "come here and see your most recent and generous bequest."

I walk to his side and look down at the top sheet. It's a drawing of an elegant series of spindles that uphold a long arched railing. The illustration was made with black ink, pencil, and some type of paint, which lends a light wash of color.

I run my fingers over the heavy paper. "Beautiful, but what on earth is it?"

"It's called the Southwest Reservoir Bridge and it stands in a park in New York City."

"The greensward Mr. Cooper told me about—Central Park?"

"Yes."

"You know he helped design that park?"

"He didn't mention it."

"He's a modest man, China."

"And this is what Mr. Cooper wanted most of all? These papers?"

"You'll have to ask him, but my guess would be yes."

"What did he think when he saw them here?"

"He doesn't know yet. He's surveying a farm about two miles north. I expect him to be back soon. I found the roll of drawings on the porch after he left."

I contemplate Mr. Cooper's reaction, and, instead of dread, I feel a rise of exhilaration. Have I become enamored with both men? No, of course not. Stephen has claimed my heart.

He flashes his mesmerizing smile. "China, I've had a thought."

By the tone of his voice, I suspect he means to coax me into something. I must be strong enough to refuse him or our relationship will never work.

"I've been thinking about a horse I had to leave in New York. A beautiful bay thoroughbred I obtained with the help of Mr. August Belmont."

"August Belmont?"

"Mr. Belmont is a Prussian gentleman who immigrated to this country some years ago. He's earned considerable acclaim for his knowledge and love of horses. He's known for his thoroughbreds."

"This horse of yours. You care deeply about it?"

"I do."

"I sang my mother's song to you yesterday. Remember the line, 'Nothing alive with will of its own?' The horse might be injured or killed."

He paces across the room and back. Then with a stubborn set to his lips, he clasps my upper arms and pulls me close. He kisses me, a harsh kiss that I don't enjoy.

I step back and stumble. He grabs my arm to steady me. I jerk away. "Don't you ever do that again! You understand?"

Mr. Cooper walks in the front door. His eyebrows lift when he sees us. "Am I interrupting something?"

"Of course not," says Stephen. "We're celebrating Miss Creed's most recent gift."

"And what has she given you now?"

"It's for you," I say, quelling my anger at Stephen.

Mr. Cooper sets his tripod against the wall, slides off his boots, and walks to the desk in his stocking feet. As soon as he sees the drawings, the breath hisses from his lungs. He begins to leaf through them, his hands trembling. The ones under the first page are merely parallel and intersecting lines, crosshatched and shaded for definition.

"Are you going to tell us what those are, Coop?" Stephen asks.

He doesn't look up as he answers. "The first page is the plan for a bridge."

"I can see that. I mean the page you're looking at now."

"Central Park's underground drainage system."

I almost laugh. That's the treasure he coveted? Sketches of the drainage system in Central Park? Surely that's the oddest thing I've ever given anyone.

He turns away from the desk and looks at me. "Miss Creed, I'm awash in guilt. Please forgive me for kissing you. Dr. Grey told you about our experiment?"

"Yes." I meet his eyes. "You're forgiven."

Mr. Cooper splays his hands over the sketches, as if they might vanish as quickly as they appeared. "I didn't realize how much I wanted them."

"I'm happy for you. Especially if you can devise how to use them wisely. The park has extra copies?"

"I would think so," he says. "Rest assured, Miss Creed, I'll never again take advantage of your gift nor tell another living soul."

"Thank you."

We smile at each other, and Stephen clasps my arm. "Allow me to show you something." He escorts me into the examination room where he opens the doors of a cabinet. A large glass jar filled with liquid sits on a middle shelf. A brain rests inside. "Do you know what it is?"

"A brain?"

"You're correct."

"I'm guessing it's human."

"Correct again."

Mr. Cooper joins us. Gazing at the brain, he asks, "Where in thunder did you get it?"

"From a corpse, where else?"

"The corpse's family is aware?"

"He had no family."

"It seems immoral to keep it."

"You think it's better for a brain to molder away in a grave, Coop?" He doesn't wait for Mr. Cooper to answer him. "China, during the War hundreds of soldiers paid ahead—just in case—to have their bodies embalmed and returned home."

"The art of embalming," Mr. Cooper says, "it's opened new horizons of knowledge?"

"It has. However, like every branch of science, embalming is an evolving discipline. Scientists don't agree about the chemicals that should be used. I chose a mixture of arsenic, zinc, mercuric creosote, and turpentine." He tapped the side of the class jar. "At the bottom of the brain, there's a halo-like ring of arteries. That ring is called the Circle of Willis. Did you know that?" He doesn't give either of us a chance to answer. "The Circle of Willis does a fine job of conducting blood—or in this case embalming fluidto smaller arteries throughout the organ. Once I injected the embalming fluid, I immersed the brain in an emulsion of those same chemicals diluted by locally manufactured alcohol. In other words, moonshine. A brain isn't easy to work with. It's soft. You can easily poke your finger right into it. Nonetheless, I believe my experiment turned out reasonably well."

I don't comment. The brain is already deteriorating. Its perimeter appears hazy within the liquid preservative.

"You've heard about the experiments done by the Russian author and psychic researcher Alexander Nikolayevich Aksakov?" Stephen asks.

"I have," says Mr. Cooper.

"And you, China?"

"No."

"Mr. Aksakov found people who could move things by using thought alone."

Royce Cooper looks at me. "At best Aksakov is a gifted sleight-of-hand artist. At worst, a charlatan."

Stephen sighs. "Study that brain, Coop. The size of it. Those convolutions are a mystery. We have no idea concerning the untapped powers that lie within."

"All right, Stephen, for the sake of argument, let's assume Miss Creed is a telekine. How did the Zeiss Microscope transport itself to Milksnake from wherever it was? Did it swim the ocean? Did it fly like a bird? Could people see it pass overhead?"

"Coop, have you heard about the theories proposed by James Clerk Maxwell?"

"Isn't he the physicist who claims that electrical and magnetic waves travel in space?"

"Yes." Stephen flings his arms wide. "We can't see them. We can't feel them, but they're there." He picks up a sheet of paper and folds it into a fan. "What if electrical and magnetic are only two of many types of waves? And what if distance can be compressed?" He unfolds the fan. "I'm here." He points at one end of the paper. "The microscope was here on the other side. All this great distance apart, but then—" He collapses the fan into a narrow strip. "Look how close we are now. Sometimes the most difficult ideas can be reduced to utmost simplicity."

"All right, let's say the microscope traveled through compressed space. How did Miss Creed know you wanted it?" Mr. Cooper addresses me. "Did Dr. Grey tell you?"

"No."

"He didn't show you a photograph?"

"No."

"Then we must assume you're also a mind reader."

"You think so?" says Stephen.

"No! I don't think so, but evidently you do. How else would she know what to give you?"

"That's part of the mystery, and the three of us are going to solve it together."

"I don't know, Stephen. Mind reading seems too complicated. Miss Creed, do you know what other people are thinking."

"No, I don't."

"Frick, Coop," Stephen says. "Why do you make everything so damned difficult?"

Royce Cooper squints as if he's trying to visualize something. "All right, Stephen. Then let's define all parts of this puzzle as telekinesis. Telekinesis being the common denominator, I mean. No mind-reading, no psychic abilities, only the gift to move objects with a thought. What if Miss Creed's powers are strong enough to draw forth the small telekinesis ability that each of us possesses within the convolutions of our brains?"

Stephen points at Mr. Cooper. "You know what? That makes sense."

"It's more reasonable than mind reading."

"It is. It is! I'm impressed, Coop. China, are you game to figure out the rest of it?" He clasps my arms. "I promise that Mr. Cooper and I will keep you safe."

I can't give him an immediate answer. There's a war going on between my brain and my heart. To trust or not to trust. "Let me think in it," I tell him and pull away from his grip. I'm out the door before he can summon an argument.

I walk home in a troubled state. Are Stephen's experiments for my own good, as he claims, or does he plan to use my gift for personal gain? I remember his rough kiss. I contemplate his wish for the horse. I hope with all my heart that the poor beast is still safe in his far-away stable.

I think back to a story Ma Mère once told me about a sea captain named Odysseus. He and his sailors nearly wrecked their ship in their desire to possess the women known as Sirens whose amazing songs lured crews to their deaths on the rocks of their island. Odysseus tied himself to the mast where he could hear their singing but not be drawn into destruction.

What rope constrains Stephen? What mast offers strength enough to keep him and Mr. Cooper safe? If I link my life with theirs, will I also fall victim to the lures of power and ownership? Will I pit king against king like Eleanor of Aquitaine? Will I lead righteous armies until the fear of my abilities drives men to destroy me? I dare not let myself imagine the anguish Joan of Arc suffered when the flames devoured her tender flesh.

CHAPTER
TWENTY-THREE

A day later, my unease prompts another visit to town. I'm disappointed to discover that both Stephen and Mr. Cooper are away. I'd hoped for continued discussion. Perhaps because of my disappointment, I decide to buy the blue plaid fabric that very day. If I do become the doctor's wife, I'll need finer clothing than anything I now own.

When I enter his store, Mr. James doesn't deign to greet me. "Looking at dress goods," I tell him as if I didn't notice the slight.

I've just pulled the bolt of material from its cubby hole when the door opens. Two men clad in tailored suits enter the store. Since the end of the War, carpetbaggers from the North have invaded our land. They're best ignored, especially by young unmarried women. I turn my attention back to the fabric. It's yarn-dyed, which is good. The colors will last longer, but Mrs. James has priced it at fifty cents a yard. Do I really want to spend that much?

One of the visitors clears his throat and addresses Mr. James. "An interesting store. You are the proprietor, Mr.—"

"James. Daniel James. Yes, I am."

The visitor's accent catches my interest. Although Ma Mère's accent was apparent only when she was upset, there is a similarity.

The taller of the two extends his hand across the counter to Mr. James. "How do you do, Sir. I am Julien Destrehan and this is my brother, François."

My heart leaps toward my throat.

"Just so you know," says Mr. James, "my store is not for sale."

I slide the fabric back into its bin and take soft steps toward the far corner of the store. Mrs. James pokes her head out from the curtains that guard their living quarters.

She straightens when Julien says, "We are here in hopes of finding our cousin, Yvette Destrehan. We believe her married name to be Creed." His resemblance to my mother is unmistakable, the same wide forehead and dark hair. The same cleft chin.

Mr. James scans the store until he locates me. He raises his eyebrows, and I mouth *no*. I crouch behind a barrel.

He pulls out his handkerchief and wipes his lips. "I'm most distressed to have to tell you that Mrs. Creed passed away this summer. An illness of some type."

"How unfortunate," says François, "for her and for us. Our father, her uncle, will be greatly distressed."

Mrs. James beckons me, and I weave a crooked path across the store. She opens the curtains for me, and I scurry into their folds. I've barely caught my breath when the bell on the front door jangles, and Mary-Polly Preck and her mother walk in. Mary notices the Destrehan brothers and smiles, folding her parasol. The men tip their hats and resume their conversation with Mr. James.

"We understand our cousin had a daughter, possibly a grown woman by now. A Miss China Creed."

I gasp, and Mary-Polly looks my way. I press my forefinger to my lips and shake my head, but I have little hope for mercy.

"China Creed," she says.

The men turn toward her.

"Long gone, I'm sorry to say," she tells them. "Lit out of this town not more than a few days after her mother died. I understand she has a beau—one of the Doolin brothers—down in Johnson County, Arkansas."

Mrs. Preck looks at her daughter as if Mary-Polly has grown two heads. "Mary dear?" People in southern Missouri know that any stranger asking after one of the Doolin family has already landed himself into a great deal of hurt. Gratitude and amazement war within my breast.

Mary clasps her mother's gloved hand. "Now Mother, you know how highly I treasure my friendship with Miss Creed, but I will not lie for her."

Mrs. James places her arm around my waist. My impulse is to slip out the backdoor and run, but she holds me there, and I realize she's right to do so. Information may be my best protection.

Of the two brothers, Julien seems to be the spokesman. As he continues his questions, Mr. James does a fine job of misdirection, placing Ma Mère's cabin in the adjoining Stone County rather than in Taney, its true location. Otherwise, he answers most questions by saying, "I don't rightly know."

Finally, the Destrehans leave. Mrs. James draws me into her kitchen, where biscuits, still warm, send up a fragrant steam that makes my stomach growl. My brother lies in his basket, now nearly too small for him. He starts fussing.

The curtains of the living quarters open. Mary-Polly and her mother peer in. "Are you going to tell us what all this is about, China?" Mary-Polly asks as she closes the curtains behind them.

"I'm sure it's her own private business," says Mrs. James. She lifts my brother from the basket.

Mrs. Preck squints at me. "Would those men be from your mother's family?"

"Likely."

"Why not introduce yourself?"

Plausible answers scramble through my brain, and I finally say, "My mother's family is not exactly known for their kindness or morality. We Creeds always avoided interaction."

Mrs. Preck pats my hand. "Your secret is safe with us, China dear."

"I think we still might have a problem," says Mary-Polly. "The Reverend Caldecott will never lie for you, China, and it's likely those men will seek out any local minister."

I draw in my breath with a hiss. She's right.

"I'll talk to him," she says. "I'll tell him that I heard you went to Arkansas."

"That's a sin, daughter," says Mrs. Preck.

"Somehow I don't think so, Mother."

I look into Mary's eyes. "I thank you from the bottom of my soul."

"We might not be the best of friends, China, but you're homefolk, and I am loyal."

They leave, and Mrs. James bundles a generous share of her warm biscuits into a flour sack, hands them to me. I thank her and kiss my brother. I'm not three steps outside when I hear Mrs. James say, "And where on earth did you get that, Danny? Give it here."

He starts to wail, and I consider Stephen's theory about each person having telekine abilities, some more than others. I wonder what suddenly came into my brother's hands due to an innocent kiss.

My first impulse is to walk to the cave where we tried to hide from the Bushwackers, but I change my mind. Instead, I head to Miz Settle's house. I need to inform her about the Destrehans' visit and also discuss my relationship with Stephen. I haven't yet told her that he and Mr. Cooper know about my gift.

I find her behind the cabin, a shovel in her hands and tear tracks on her face. I know as soon as I see the grave. Bessie.

"Foolish old woman blubbering over a dog," she says, but, when I hold out my arms, she comes into them as if she were a child. We both cry.

When we part, I ask, "How did Bessie die?"

"The way we all hope to go. During her sleep."

"It's best, I know, but I'm sad for you. You'll need to get a pup and start again." I see by the look on her face she's not ready to think about that. Mourning exacts due time. "Someday," I add.

We link arms and walk back to her cabin. She fusses at her stove and then heads toward the dry sink, leaving one task undone to start another. I stoke the stove and reheat a cast iron pot of rabbit stew. I dish up a serving for each of us, adding one of Mrs. James's biscuits to each plate. The discussion about the Destrehans can wait until Miz Settle's sorrow backs off a reasonable distance.

When we're done eating, she looks into my eyes and asks, "What else is going on with you? You gotta problem with that doctor?"

"You're too smart, Miz Settle."

"Not smart. Schooled by life."

"You know he's given me a ring."

"Which means he intends to marry you."

"I suspect so."

"His family's from New York?"

"Yes."

Her face crumples. "Sorry," she murmurs. "He'll likely want to take you there, and I'm a selfish old woman, ya know."

"I know."

We both try to smile.

"What would you do if you were in my place, Miz Settle?"

"If I was young like you, I'd go. Now, looking back with added wisdom, I wouldn't."

I consider telling her that Stephen and Mr. Cooper have figured out my curse, but I don't want to add to her worries. "If we go, maybe you'd go with us."

"You know I love you more than any other living person, Sheba, but I have patients and obligations."

"I know. Do what's best for you."

My heart moils itself into a veritable mess of trouble and loss: Ma Mère, my brother, Bessie. And now those two Destrehan men, if they survive the Arkansas Doolins. Worry burns into my brain, and my hands start to tremble.

"Let's wash the dishes," I say.

I stay for another few hours, and, when I leave, Miz Settle follows me onto the porch. She pitches a high whistle, and says, "Where's that ol'—" She stops.

"I reckon she'll come in for the night, Miz Settle."

I say that, and I believe that.

Later, in the evening, I sit down at my table, shamelessly using up lamp oil to sketch possibilities for a dress if I buy that plaid fabric. When I hear a rumble of hooves, I look up. The malignant light of pine-tar torches wavers through the front window, and I'm thrust backward in time, remembering Bushwhackers and Jayhawkers. Outlaw bands still roam Missouri. Have they found me here alone in Ma Mère's cabin?

I grab the Hawkin rifle from its braces over the door and have it loaded by the time someone clatters up my porch steps.

"Who is it?" I shout. "My husband's here with me."

"Your husband?" I recognize Del Aubright's voice. "What husband?"

I greet him with the gun resting easy in my arms. "Blue blazes, Del. I thought you were Bushwhackers."

Five other men sit astride their mules a few feet beyond my porch. I recognize our new town barber and a farmer from Grit's Hill. Miz Settle and I delivered his wife's firstborn. Del tries to push past me into the cabin, but I brace myself at the doorway. "I didn't invite you in, Del. I'm a woman alone as you well know."

He gives me a sour look. "We come to tell you somethin'."

"So tell me."

He leans close, and I smell the shine on his breath. "My baby son cries morning, night, and noon. He barely stops even to eat."

All this commotion about a baby? No. Of course not. Who would bring a posse for something as normal as infant colic? Nonetheless, I let him believe my concerns are totally about his son.

"You smoke a pipe?" I ask.

"And what does that have to do with anything?"

"Tobacco smoke breathed over a teaspoon of mother's milk is a fine cure for colic."

"It ain't colic. It ain't anything like colic. He's bewitched."

"A goomer spell? We don't have anybody in Milksnake doing that sort of thing right now, Del, especially to a baby."

"It's worse than a spell." He squints at me. "You or that Injun woman, one of yous is a witch. I recollect that tent preacher saying you got the devil in you."

His men back him up with catcalls. I consider shutting the door in his face, but wouldn't that confirm his suspicions?

"I'm no witch, Del. Nor is Miz Settle. We are Christian folk. How dare you accuse us of such a thing?"

He opens his right hand. That thin gold ring lies in his palm, and dread takes a firm hold on my heart.

"There's no way this ring came to my son during the birth except by witchery. I've known you a long time, Miss China, and I seen what you did against that witch at the tent meeting, but I need more security in this matter. You got a Bible?"

"I do."

"Would you fetch it?"

I retrieve Ma Mère's Bible and ruffle the pages. "There. Are you satisfied? Look. It's a Bible." I hope he doesn't realize the words are in French. Who knows what he'd think about that.

"Put your hand on it and swear to God you ain't a witch."

I speak slowly and with a bite to my words. "In the name of the Lord, Mr. Aubright, I am not a witch."

He steps off the porch and clambers up on his mule. As he turns the animal, a stay beam from one of the torches illuminates the blued barrel of a long-gun. They're carrying weapons? Suddenly, I know where he's going. When they're off a ways down the path, I run to the table, pick up my lantern by its bail, clutch the Hawken to my side, and take off as if demons were at my heels.

Like most mules, Del's animal is in no hurry, and I'm able to keep them in my sight as I trail behind, using my skirt to direct the lantern light down toward my feet. When they get to Milksnake, Del's mule suddenly heads toward the blacksmith shop, and two of the other mules do the same. The men howl curses, and I make my way past the church to the path that leads to Miz Settle's place.

I'm there before Del and his men catch up. I fly across Miz Settle's porch and run the handle of her broom through the latch string hole, lift the inner latch, and let myself in. Miz Settle rises from her bed, her hand flung up to block my lantern's light.

"It's me, Miz Settle."

"Sheba? What's wrong?"

"Del Aubright. He's coming here with a gun and five other men. He thinks you bewitched his son."

She scrambles from her bed. "Get my blunderbuss," she says as she buttons herself into her skirt.

"We are not fighting those men, Miz Settle. If we kill or injure any one of them, we're dead."

"What we gonna do?" Her voice trembles.

"We're going to hide in the woods. You choose the place."

She leaves the blunderbuss but takes her midwife bag and leads me to a thicket of swale canes and willow. I lift the chimney of my lantern, marveling that it didn't fall and shatter during my flight. I blow out the flame, and we wait.

The men arrive within minutes, shouting, their voices ragged and mean. A scattergun blast takes out the front window. Miz Settle begins to moan, and I wrap my arms around her. Her hens wake up, cackling, and the men take their fury to the chicken house. I cup my hand over Miz Settle's mouth to muffle the sounds of her grief. The men's mules bray in the way of animals overcome by fear, and one of them tears past us as it makes a new path through the woods to escape the chaos.

The last thing those men do is douse the porch with coal oil and light the cabin afire. When they finally leave, cursing Miz Settle and the devil and the escaped mule, dawn is gray over Prophet's Mountain.

I hold Miz Settle as she weeps for the ruins of her life. Yet, in all her sorrow, she curses no one. I cannot say the same for myself.

One chicken survived the massacre, a large red-feathered hen. When the fire has burned itself out, we take the chicken with us and start toward my cabin. We make use of detours to avoid the town. The closest thing we have to law is Judge Preck, but you can't expect a judge to buckle on a firearm and chase down perpetrators. Besides, would anyone believe Miz Settle and me if we testified against Del Aubright? I'd have believed him myself a few weeks ago had he denied his part in the ruin of a homestead.

My cabin is as I left it. The chickens ruffle their feathers at the new hen, but after a skirmish or two, she establishes a high place for herself in the pecking order.

I prepare a breakfast of biscuits and eggs, but Miz Settle can't eat more than a bite or two. When we hear another rider, I grab my gun. Then a voice as beautiful as a song comes to us, Stephen calling my name.

I set my Hawkin butt-down against the wall and open the door. He's astride his horse, its flanks lathered. As soon as I see his face, I know he's heard what happened. He dismounts, and I run to him. He pulls me into his arms.

"There's word in town about the men and the fire. You're all right?" He smooths my hair back from my face. "They didn't hurt you? They didn't—" His voice breaks.

"We're fine. Unhurt, untouched."

Miz Settle looks out at us from the open door, and he beckons to her. "Come here." To my surprise she does. We're both in his arms when he says, "My mother sent a telegram. She wants me to help her through her latest bout of dropsy. I fear her heart grows weaker with each year that passes."

It seems a strange, unsuitable thing to mention, and all my courage leaves me. How will I survive without him? Stephen loosens his hold on us, and Miz Settle tightly clasps my hand.

"Why don't you both come to New York with me?" he says.

Surely some of the most welcome words I've ever heard in my life.

"Mr. Cooper can join us if he wishes. You'll be safe there, Mrs. Settle, as will China. I can't live without her, and I know that she doesn't want to live without you. Cordell Smith has already promised to watch over my office and China's cabin. Would you go? It doesn't have to be forever."

I look down into Miz Settle's dark, sad eyes, and she nods at me. I answer for both of us. "We'll go."

PART IV
HEIGHTS

From Ma Mère's Song:

Nothing unseen.

CHAPTER TWENTY-FOUR

ST LOUIS, MISSOURI–MONDAY, SEPTEMBER 22, 1873

We've been ten days on our journey from Milksnake to St. Louis, the first portion on horseback, the second by train. Mr. Cooper decided to join us and required an extra horse to carry his surveying equipment. Miz Settle has nothing left except her midwife bag and the clothes she was wearing the night of the fire, but we altered a couple of Ma Mère's skirts, and I made her two new shirtwaists. Other than clothing and my midwife accouterments, I packed very few of my belongings, although the broken pieces of Ma Mère's Spode plate are well wrapped and tucked at the center of my tapestry tote bag.

St. Louis is as large a town as I ever hoped to see. Shops crowd every street. The rush and flurry of the city's inhabitants lead me to comment on their prosperity. Stephen replies with a grim smile, and Mr. Cooper takes it upon himself to tell us about the bank failure a few days earlier in New York City. Neither Stephen nor Mr. Cooper seems overly concerned; therefore, my thoughts center on those families in Milksnake who turned against Miz Settle and me. How could they forget the many women and babies we kept alive through arduous childbirths? How could they believe we are witches?

I miss my mother's cabin. I miss our cranky woodstove, the dry sink, and the pie safe. I miss my milk cow and her calf, safe with Holly and Cordell. I want to lay flowers on Ma Mère's grave. I grieve over my brother Danny who I'm sure has already forgotten me. I tell myself that someday I'll return, but fear steals my hope.

We are three days in St. Louis, staying at a well-kept boarding house with plentiful if tasteless meals. When Stephen secures a place for us on a train to New York, and I'm surprised to see we have an elegant passenger car all to ourselves. The walls are paneled in dark mahogany, and the sofas and settees are upholstered in thick red velvet. Sconces feature gas lights, and windows line both sides of the car. At the far end, a narrow door opens into an aisled area with sleeping compartments on each side. The whole arrangement is finer than anything I've ever seen.

I quietly ask Mr. Cooper how Stephen can afford such luxury.

He seems surprised by my question but kindly says, "His mother is heavily invested in this particular railway."

And in what else? They must be wealthier than Stephen let on.

When Miz Settle and I are done with our gaping, Stephen escorts me to a wide sofa. Miz Settle and Mr. Cooper choose a settee that forms a right angle to ours, making a convenient area for conversation.

I try to hide my homesickness by remembering that, when I was yet a child, Ma Mère's stories made me yearn to see the Mississippi River. And here I am, in unimaginable luxury at the verge of that wide waterway where we'll cross, west to east.

A ferry carries our train over those muddy waters, one car at a time. My anticipation of the crossing is marred by the sway of eddies and currents, which gives me vertigo. My stomach bucks, and I press my hands over my mouth to hold everything down. Stephen notices my discomfort and places his arm around my shoulders.

"You're motion sick," he tells me. "Look out the windows and focus on the horizon. That'll help."

It doesn't, but, when he opens a window, the rush of river-cooled air does.

I direct my eyes toward the partially completed Eads Bridge that will soon span the river and allow trains to cross directly over. Mr. Cooper leans across the space between us and says, "The bridge will stretch more than a mile when complete."

I merely nod, afraid of the consequences if I attempt to speak.

When we reach the Mississippi's eastern shore, belching engines latch to the cars, and we begin the long journey through the hinterlands of America. I'm fascinated by the variety of towns and fields and forests. Who could believe that our country is so huge?

We stop often at stations, large and small, and we usually disembark for a few minutes of fresh air. Several hours before one scheduled stop, Stephen draws me aside and says, "Our next stop is longer than most, a full two hours." He turns to Miz Settle and Mr. Cooper. "What do you think if China and I get married here? Surely we can find a minister."

It's not the romantic proposal I'd dreamed about, but the idea lifts my heart. I smooth my navy cotton skirt, faded and well-worn. I tell myself I shouldn't care about my clothing. I'm about to marry a kind, educated man, who is not afraid of my curse. I smile at my fiancé, ready to agree. Then I glance at Mr. Cooper, and the emotions on his face startle me. Concern, of course, but also sorrow. Why? Does he believe I'm not worthy to be Stephen's wife?

"Stephen," he says, "you haven't given Miss Creed the opportunity to decline your proposal."

"Decline?"

"Don't tell her. Ask her."

"Ah," Stephen says. "Coop, always wise." He kneels in front of me. "China, will you marry me?"

Mr. Cooper turns away, and I tell myself that I do not see anguish on his face. I look at Miz Settle who shrugs and smiles, and I follow the dictates of my heart.

"Oh yes, Stephen. Yes, yes, yes!" He stands and pulls me to my feet then stops my babbling with a kiss deep enough to make me melt against him.

The rest of the morning, Mr. Cooper studies the drawings of Central Park's drainage system, Miz Settle knits the toe end of a rag-wool sock, and Stephen and I discuss our dreams for a shared life. We'll settle in a rural area and practice medicine together, Stephen as a doctor, me as a midwife. Miz Settle will live with us, and, of course, Stephen and I want children.

We're a half-hour from the stop when Mr. Cooper rolls up his diagrams and takes his usual seat. He leans forward, his arms resting on his knees, and he says to us, "I wish you both the most beautiful life possible. However, allow me to play devil's advocate. If you get married before we arrive in New York, Stephen, your mother may forgive you, but will she ever forgive Miss Creed?"

Stephen's face takes on a haunted look, and a rill of dread crowds into my thoughts. What kind of woman is Mrs. Grey? Strong, unbending, vengeful, or simply a mother who wants the best for her son? Either way, Mr. Cooper is probably right. We should wait. Why do wise choices so often hurt the heart?

Two days later we approach New York's Grand Central Depot. One train and then another comes in, each with hissing steam and screeching brakes. I clamp my hands over my ears in an attempt to preserve my hearing. We coast into an area where the disembarkation platform is conveniently level with the floor of our passenger car. We exit, and Stephen draws my attention to an ornate ceiling that rises above us in a soaring arch. If it weren't for the fumes still seeping from the trains, that ceiling alone would make me believe we've entered the portals of heaven.

Stephen secures a porter to pile our luggage on a wheeled cart. Mr. Cooper follows close behind, Miz Settle on his left arm and me on his right. Our porter is short and fair of skin. He has black hair and an accent that makes his speech sound like a song.

Mr. Cooper leans close and says, "He's Irish."

We follow our Irish man out of the station to the street where people laugh, shout, and curse. The outside of the depot is even more impressive than the inside. Its front façade boasts three square towers capped by what Mr. Cooper calls mansard roofs. The high central tower showcases gigantic round-face clocks on three of its four sides. Stephen tells us that during the night the clocks are lit from within and can be read by passers-by.

I cannot adequately describe the immensity of that building. Mr. Cooper claims it covers more than twenty acres. Ma Mère and I lived on forty acres, and we considered ourselves land-rich.

Hansom cabs wait in line to be hired. Like the Irish porter, the drivers are a ragged bunch, their horses thin and with drooping heads. I feel a great sinking in my belly. I'd heard that New York City was awash in wealth, and the depot seems to prove that assertion, but the workers don't.

Stephen whistles, high and piercing, and snaps his fingers at a driver. The man directs his horse toward us, and the porter loads our belongings. The hansom cab, a two-wheeled buggy, seats only two passengers. Mr. Cooper hails another cab for himself and Miz Settle. The driver sits behind his passengers, above the roof. Stephen and I look out over the horse through a wide front window. Our drivers crack their whips, and we move into the street where the stench of horse urine, manure, and rotting food rises from the gutters.

People of all ages crowd the roads and cobblestone byways, the bluestone sidewalks, and the boardwalks. Most of them don't look much better off than the working people of Missouri, but, as the cab carries us southward, I see people who appear to be more prosperous. Here, most men carry a cane, although it seems they are a fashion accessory rather than something needed. The women walk sedately, their dresses aglow with dyes brighter than any my mother and I could ever coax from boiled plants and alum mordant. Parasols protect faces white as milk. Children wear elaborate clothing decorated with tabs and buttons, the tailoring exquisite.

I gasp aloud at the height of buildings. Some rise an amazing six stories. Huge storefront windows display an array of inventory—shoes, clothing, gloves, and parasols. One store seems to offer nothing but cigars.

New York City steals my breath, a place so busy and alive I'd swear it owns a beating heart.

The Grey home is located off Fifth Avenue on 34th Street, near other magnificent mansions built by families whose names are unfamiliar to me: Stewart, Astor, and Townsend.

Our cab pulls up before the Grey mansion's main entrance. This is where Stephen grew up—a house large enough that half of Milksnake could fit within. I'm speechless.

The building is faced with white marble, and the roof, like the towers of Grand Central Depot, is a mansard. A turret-like structure rises at each corner. Every window is topped by an elegant arch, and wide steps lead from the sidewalk to double doors.

It's a fearsome thing, a home that large, and my hands tremble as if I face a monster, but Stephen only laughs.

"You'd better stop looking up, China, or your neck will break."

I can't help looking up. I need assurance that the sky is yet above us, and I still tread upon the planet Earth.

Whatever Stephen pays the cab driver causes the man to leap down most willingly to handle our baggage. Mr. Cooper's cab pulls up behind ours, and we wait for him and Miz Settle. Fat pigeons strut nearby, their feathers a soft and soothing gray. They appear to be ornamental. If they lived in Milksnake, they'd be roasted in their own gravy under a golden crust.

Stephen extracts a pair of women's doeskin gloves from his pocket. I recognize them from Mr. James's store where more than once I'd sent a coveting glance their way. Why wait until now to give them to me? Then I realize how soiled my cotton gloves have become on our journey. Our eyes catch and hold, and I remove the old gloves to put on the new.

Miz Settle is straight as a soldier when she marches up the mansion's steps, and once again I admire her courage. The doors open wide, and a man wearing a black cutaway jacket, striped trousers, a white shirt and waistcoat bids us a stiff welcome.

"You took a cab, Dr. Grey?" he says. "Mrs. Grey planned to send a carriage."

"The train came in early, and I didn't want to wait. The cab was adequate." Then Stephen introduces us. "China, our butler, Holgrim. Holgrim, allow me to present my fiancée, Miss China Deliverance Creed."

During our journey, Stephen informed Miz Settle and me about family members and a few longtime servants, including Holgrim who has been employed by the Greys since Stephen was a boy. I extend my hand as is the custom in Milksnake, and I don't retract it, even when I see the surprise on Mr. Holgrim's face.

"Where I come from, Sir," I tell him, "men and women greet each other with a hearty handshake."

He follows through on my suggestion, and I offer him my best smile. Stephen introduces Miz Settle as my aunt, a decision we made to give her a higher ranking within the household. She also shakes Holgrim's hand, but Mr. Cooper only nods his greeting.

Inside, a tall middle-aged woman approaches us from an open doorway on our left. With her wide jaw and long face, she's not conventionally beautiful, but her smile makes her seem so, and I have no doubt she's Stephen's mother. Her hair and eyes are the same tawny color as his. When she holds out her arms, Stephen steps into her embrace and kisses her cheek, his eyes closed.

He steps back and says, "You're looking well, Mother."

"My health improved as soon as I learned you were coming home."

I can't help but wonder if Mrs. Grey was entirely truthful about her illness, but New York is a haven of safety, and I can only be grateful for her hospitality.

Stephen extends his arm toward me. "Mother, my fiancée China. China, my dear mother—Alberta Schermerhorn Grey."

Mrs. Grey tilts her head and looks into my eyes. "She's absolutely lovely, Stephen." She leans forward and kisses my cheek then clasps my hands. "I welcome you with great joy, dear China. I've been worried that my son would never give up his bachelor ways." She laughs, and her laughter comforts my heart, which is still fragile from the loss of Ma Mère. "Of course, being Stephen's mother, I blame Mr. Cooper for my son's sense of adventure."

Royce Cooper seems to force his smile, but he comes forward and kisses Mrs. Grey, a quick brush of his lips on her cheek.

"And this dear woman is Aunt Jesse?" Mrs. Grey asks.

"My beloved Aunt Jesse," I tell her.

Our introductions complete, Mrs. Grey addresses Holgrim, naming Miz Settle's bedroom then mine: The Mahogany and The Yellow Rose. I smile at the thought of a house large enough for its bedrooms to be christened.

"Mr. Cooper, your room is ready, too, if you choose to stay tonight. An early dinner at seven for all?"

"That would be wonderful," says Stephen.

"And Stephen, would you meet me in your father's study when you've shown Miss Creed and Mrs. Settle to their rooms?"

Royce Cooper offers his arm to Miz Settle and leads her toward the stairway. Stephen and I follow. Halfway up, I peer down at the foyer. The floor is comprised of square white marble tiles with black diamond-shaped insets joining their corners. Giant ferns grow in pots on either side of the front doors. The walls are figured marble. I'm warmed by the beauty, and, when I speak my thoughts aloud, Stephen hugs me, even though his mother is watching.

At the top of the stairs a wide, red-carpeted hallway extends both left and right. I learn later that that area is called the mezzanine. Its back wall serves as a gallery for paintings—most of them landscapes or portraits of grim-faced men.

Stephen guides me to a second stairway, which is narrower but brightened by the yellow-green flames of gas wall sconces. He opens the first door on the left and says, "The Yellow Rose Suite."

When I gasp, Stephen laughs. "You don't like it?" He kisses my cheek, and we walk in.

The outer area is a sitting room, its walls lined with vertically striped fabric—yellow, buff, and white. The dark wooden floor is accented by gold Turkish carpets. My eyes are drawn to a dainty cherry-wood desk and the narrow bookcase beside it. The rich leather smell of book covers undercuts the fragrance of yellow roses displayed in a vase on the fireplace mantel. Two upholstered wingchairs are positioned to catch the warmth of the brightly burning fire. Holgrim sets my tapestry bag on the floor. Stephen follows him to the door, and they have a short murmured conversation. I gaze up at the coffered ceiling decorated with plaster florets at each corner. A chandelier aglow with faceted crystals hangs from a central medallion.

An archway opens into the bedroom. Surely four people could sleep side by side in that wide bed. A lace canopy is draped above its fancy-weave counterpane.

Stephen returns to me and clasps my hands. "What do you think, China?"

He leans close as if to kiss me, but a quick rap on the door jamb makes us step apart. A young woman enters, a pile of thick white towels in her arms.

"China," Stephen says, "this is Agnes Lillico, your lady's maid."

Agnes is pretty, with a heart-shaped face and a cleft in her chin. Her black hair is caught up under a white cap. I cannot help but notice that her gray dress is much finer than the skirt and shirtwaist I'm wearing. She does the best she can to curtsey, the towels still in her arms.

"Madame asks if Miss Creed would like a bath drawn."

"China?" Stephen says.

"A bath would be lovely."

He kisses my cheek again and leaves. Then Agnes ushers me through one of the doors that flank the fireplace into a smaller room where a white tub crouches upon lion paws.

During the next hour, I experience my first New York City luxury—a perfectly heated bath in a large porcelain tub. Pure heaven.

CHAPTER TWENTY-FIVE

As she helps me dress for dinner, Agnes tells me I should call her by her last name—Lillico. Throughout the cinching, bundling, and buttoning, she kindly provides additional information about etiquette and ladies' fashions.

She pulls the corset strings to force my stays into an unhealthy clench, and I'm fairly out of breath when I ask, "Do New York ladies always wear their stays this tight?"

"I've only gotten you down to twenty inches, Miss," she says as she ties the strings into a drooping bow. "The finest young ladies try for eighteen."

Dear Lord, help us all.

"Did you not wear corsets where you used to live?"

"Only on Sundays and not this tight."

Unfortunately, my torture is not yet ended. My dress is a gift from Mrs. Grey. Evidently Stephen sent her an estimate of my measurements. I soon learn that a fancy dress requires more undergarments than merely a chemise, pantalets, and a corset. Lillico helps me don white silk stockings, which she fastens a few inches above my knees with ribbon garters. Over the stockings and pantalets, I must wear a soft silk petticoat and an awkward tape-strapped garment that serves as a skeleton for the shape of my skirts. Over that, I must have another petticoat.

Of blue silk brocade, the overskirt lies quite flat in front but is caught high at the sides to display an embroidered, ruffled underskirt. A bustle shapes the skirts at the back. The sleeves of the bodice are narrow to the elbows then fan out in pleats over a cascade of ivory lace. The same soft lace—a Battenberg—falls from either side of the square neckline.

As we work to make me presentable, Lillico steals glances at her new doeskin gloves, a gift from Stephen. When he declared that Miz Settle and I must have lady's maids, we knew my maid couldn't touch my skin. Mr. Cooper came up with the idea of Lillico wearing gloves, and she doesn't seem to mind.

I'm in a sweat by the time we finish, and Lillico guides me to the dressing table, where I sit with the bustle pushed to one side so I don't crush it. She pats my face dry then brings out what she calls a combing cape and drapes it over my shoulders.

She pokes and pins and braids my hair into an edifice of curls held in place by scented pomade, diamanté clips, and combs. Then she opens a wide shallow drawer filled with cork-sealed pots and lidded tins. She lightly applies the contents to my face: a red powder brushed on the apples of my cheeks; a concoction of the same red powder plus beeswax, which she smooths over my lips; black sooty paste that she strokes on my eyelashes and brows. She opens another drawer and takes out a pair of pale blue silk gloves, no heavier than a feather. Stephen must have informed his mother about the snakebite because the little finger of the left glove is padded.

Lillico folds the cape to keep stray hair from falling on my dress. As she carries it from the room, Stephen comes in. I stand and turn. For a moment he doesn't say a word, and I wonder at the look on his face. Admiration, but something else as well. Regret? Surely I'm mistaken, I tell myself, content for the moment to live within my fairy tale.

"Lovely," he says, "absolutely lovely." He presents a dark green velvet case. "I asked that this be brought from the family vault, China. It's yours until you decide to pass it down to a daughter or daughter-in-law. It once belonged to my grandmother."

He opens the case, and my mouth gapes.

A necklace of rose-colored gold drips with tear-shaped diamonds. Among the diamonds, pale stones shimmer, such an ethereal blue I could believe someone cut them from the sky. Stephen names them before I ask. They are aquamarine, a type of beryl. I've not heard of either aquamarine or beryl. He fastens it around my neck where it lies cold and heavy against my breast. Placing his hands on my upper arms, he turns me toward the dressing table mirror.

The glow of the diamonds draws forth an answering sparkle from the diamanté clips in my hair, and my eyes shine dark as coal.

Stephen takes my left hand and steps back. "Truly, China, you're the most beautiful woman I've ever seen." Then he begins to laugh. "You're not wearing shoes."

"And much more comfortable that way."

He's still laughing as he ducks into the room where my new clothing is stored. He brings out a pair of blue silk slippers, and I slide my feet into them. To my amazement, they fit more perfectly than any shoe I've ever owned.

Then Stephen says, "Aunt Jesse is already downstairs with Royce."

One question has battered around in my head since we arrived. I don't mean to ask him at that moment, but somehow the words slip out. "Have you told your mother yet about—"

"Your gift."

"Yes."

"I've asked for a private conversation concerning you. Don't worry. Mother will be more intrigued than upset."

I tuck my gloved fingers around his arm, and he squeezes my hand against his side. My stomach ties up in knots, but I navigate the stairways with passable grace, and, when we're on the main floor, Stephen takes me to the Receiving Room. Its blue walls form a pentagon, and a marble fireplace with an enormous maw yawns out heat. Chairs and side tables are arranged in groups of three and four. Miz Settle and Royce Cooper stand near the fireplace. Her gown is simple but elegant, a deep burgundy velvet that sets off the copper glow of her skin. Her lady's maid styled her dark braid into an elaborate knot at the top of her head, which emphasizes the exquisite bone structure of her face.

When Mrs. Grey enters the room, Stephen steps away from me and clasps his mother's hand. She turns sideways and extends her arm toward a young man who walks in behind her. "China, this is my son, Philip."

Unfortunately, my first reaction is to stare, which he doesn't notice, but I'm sure his mother does. Philip is blind, his pupils and irises masked by a white caul. Why didn't Stephen tell me?

Philip wears his chestnut hair long enough to brush his collar, a style not quite suited to his wide-boned face, but how would he know? He holds his shoulders erect and stares off as if he were seeing some world hidden from the rest of us.

"Honored to meet you," Philip says. His voice is at that adolescent breaking point, shifting from high to low, sometimes within one word.

He wears a more casual sack-cut coat, a lightweight burgundy wool dyed to make the colors shimmer. His dark tie is knotted in the simple Four-in-Hand style.

Miz Settle joins us, and I say, "Philip, allow me to introduce my aunt, Mrs. Jesse Settle."

"How do you do?" Miz Settle says in her lovely low voice.

"I do well considering the circumstances." Philip smiles in his mother's general direction. Then he says, "Miz Settle, English isn't your first language, is it? I detect an accent, but I can't place it."

"Philip!" Mrs. Grey reprimands.

"No harm," says Miz Settle. "I'm *Aniyunwiya*, although your people call us Cherokee. I'm glad you can hear the music of our language in my words."

Mrs. Grey looks at me. "And she's your aunt?" she says, some puzzlement in her voice. I'm sure she's considering my dark eyes and the abrupt contrast of my pale hair.

"She is." I don't care what that claim might cost me in New York society. I owe too much to Miz Settle. If Mrs. Grey blanches at the thought of *Aniyunwiya* blood flowing within the veins of her grandchildren then that's her problem.

Royce Cooper speaks up, telling us about the Grey mansion, its various attributes, and odd history. I'm surprised to learn that portions of the house were transported across the Atlantic Ocean from ancient homes and castles in Italy and England.

When Philip and Stephen take up the discussion, Mr. Cooper steps to my side and whispers, "Wait until spring. The gardens are magnificent."

"What vegetables do they grow?"

"You'll have to ask Cook about the kitchen gardens. I was referring to the flowers and shrubbery."

If I'd been speaking to Stephen, I would've been embarrassed, but the gleam in Mr. Cooper's eyes makes me smile. I listen with interest as he names and describes the plants, bulbs, and ornamental trees that thrive in the gardens behind the house.

Holgrim escorts two people into the room, an elderly gentleman dressed in dark evening garb and a younger woman who clings to his arm.

Mrs. Grey introduces them as William Hamilton and his daughter Harriet. Stephen shakes Mr. Hamilton's hand and nods at Harriet. Her dress is as elegant as mine, a bustled green jacquard lavished with lace, but she wears no jewelry, and her brown hair is gathered into a plain bun at the back of her neck. A tracery of crow's feet at the corners of her magnificent green eyes does not detract from her beauty.

"How many years has it been, Harriet?" Stephen asks.

Her face colors. "Three," she says.

How many years since what? Was Harriet a former love? Jealousy, white-hot, rips through me, and I must draw in a deep breath before I'm able to smile at her. I remind myself that Stephen is thirty-five. He's certainly had other women in his life, but he has chosen me. I don't allow myself to ponder the reason.

A footman announces dinner and leads us to the dining room. Philip carries a black cane, its top graced by a heavy silver knob. An ivory tip at its foot taps quietly against the floor. Only once does he extend his hand to a doorframe to orient himself.

Stephen takes my arm and as we follow Mrs. Grey, he explains that the house contains three dining areas. The room where we'll dine that evening is an intimate place intended for no more than twelve. When we enter, I see that it's built as an oval, the muralled walls broken only by a double door where we come in and two single doors that must provide access to the kitchen.

Stephen sweeps his hand toward the mural and says, "This harbor scene depicts New York City in 1794. You can see that the streets were merely country lanes. It was inspired by an etching drawn by Philip-Balthazar-Julin Févret de Saint-Mémin."

Of course, I've never heard of the man, but the walls are a magnificent tribute to his art, and the room is called The Févret.

Alberta Grey sits at the head of the table. Mr. Hamilton takes a place at the foot. Stephen dines at his mother's right with Harriet beside him and Philip next to her. Mr. Cooper and I and Miz Settle sit opposite them.

Daisies and yellow roses make up our centerpiece. Heavy silver-ware borders each delicate plate at the sides and the top.

As two footmen carry out plates of breaded oysters, Stephen motions at my gloves, and I understand that I should take them off before eating. Mrs. Grey stares at my left hand, surely because of my amputated finger. I tuck my hand into my lap and try to keep it there. I don't want to ruin anyone's appetite.

Mr. Hamilton begins our dinner conversation with a description of the recent panic on Wall Street. Royce Cooper leans toward me and whispers, "Wall Street is the heart of New York's financial district."

"Absolute chaos," Mr. Hamilton says, his white hair haloed by the light of the branched gasolier above us. "Men were shouting, running, trying to break into locked banks and brokerage firms."

"This was September eighteenth?" Stephen asks.

"Yes, be thankful you weren't here. It was dreadful."

"I was able to get my hands on a few newspapers during our journey," Stephen says. "I understand that Jay Cooke was one of the first to close."

"And the basic cause of the problem. Over-speculation, you understand." Mr. Hamilton glances at Mrs. Grey. Her lips are pressed into a tight line. He clears his throat and says, "I suppose a business discussion is best left outside the dining room, Alberta?"

She grimaces. "Yes, please."

"My apologies. Perhaps Miss Creed and her aunt would like to learn about Harriet's work at Colony House."

Mrs. Grey nods at Harriet, but Harriet waits while the plates and silverware of the first course are removed and replaced with bowls of consommé.

Finally she says, "Colony House is simply Father's way of sharing our blessings with others."

I'm surprised when Miz Settle speaks up. "And who are the ones you bless?"

"The needy, mostly women and their babies."

Stephen watches Harriet as she speaks, sadness in his eyes, and a shaft of worry catches me under the tight boning of my corset.

Through that second course, Harriet tells us about the various training programs Colony House offers destitute women so they can support themselves and their children. I stay silent, but Miz Settle asks enough questions for both of us.

Our third course features broiled fish accompanied by shredded root vegetables in aspic. I'm already full, and my constricted stomach begins to ache. Mr. Cooper rescues me by whispering, "A taste or two of each course is adequate." I wish he would have told me that before we started.

During a course of roasted beef, Mr. Hamilton launches into stories about the childhood escapades of Harriet, Stephen, and Mr. Cooper. "I blame myself," he says. "My dear late wife blamed me, too." He chuckles. "I was the one who bought Harriet a puppy. Who could believe it would grow into the size of a pony?"

Mr. Cooper begins to laugh. He glances at me and says, "We hitched it to a wagon and took an adventurous ride down Fifth Avenue."

I'm amazed. "Fifth Avenue?" I've already seen how busy that street can be.

Harriet says, "Royce is the one with a permanent reminder of our escapade. The rest of us survived with only a few scrapes and bruises."

He looks at me and points at his mouth.

"The chipped tooth?" I ask.

He nods and laughs, but Stephen frowns. Evidently, another man's chipped tooth is not something a fiancée should mention.

Philip speaks up. "Mr. Cooper isn't the only one who suffered lasting effects. Mother has never allowed me to have a dog, and I blame you three."

Everyone laughs, and I turn my attention to my wine glass, but I only sip, alcohol being a rare drink in my life. Even that small amount makes my face feel like a lit candle. The kitchen door opens, and Holgrim brings out a cake swathed in creamed frosting. The starving days of the past winter flit into my mind then fade like a nightmare well-forgotten.

When the meal ends, Stephen directs a congratulatory smile my way. Evidently, despite my mention of Mr. Cooper's tooth, I've passed my first test. Mrs. Grey sends Philip to his room, and, even though he complains that he's old enough to join the men, she doesn't relent. Royce Cooper, Stephen, and Mr. Hamilton stay in the dining room for brandy and cigars, and we women *retire*—Mrs. Grey's word—to the Withdrawing Room where a maid serves us tiny cups of thick, bitter coffee.

During a lengthy hour, ticked off by an enormous long-case clock, we four sit in padded wingback chairs while Stephen's mother quizzes me about my preferences, particularly regarding food and recreation.

Her questions are difficult to answer. I doubt she would serve my favorite foods at her table—cornpone and squirrel stew. I offer a safe answer of warm bread and fresh butter. As to recreation, I've known little of it, although I dearly love to wade barefoot in a fast-flowing creek.

"Making lace," I finally say.

Mrs. Grey leans forward in her chair. "I would love to see how it's done, China."

"I brought my mother's lacemaking pillows, pins, and patterns. I'll be happy to show you when you have time." Then to redirect her questions, I say, "Aunt Jesse's life is more interesting than mine. She's been a midwife for thirty years. Aunt Jesse, how many babies have you delivered?"

She muses for a moment then says, "Five hundert I guess, maybe more."

Miz Settle looks at Mrs. Grey, perhaps in hopes of approval, but the expression on Mrs. Grey's face indicates she finds the subject repulsive.

I glance at Harriet Hamilton, expecting the same reaction; however, she smiles and says, "Very impressive, Mrs. Settle. We're in great need of midwives at Colony House. It's volunteer work, of course, but if you're interested, please consider coming for a visit. Miss Creed, I'd enjoy showing you how our charitable enterprise improves the lives of the city's indigent—"

Mrs. Grey interrupts. "A perfect diversion for Mrs. Settle, Harriet, but China will be far too busy putting together her trousseau and helping me with preparations for the engagement party."

Engagement party? I try to keep a smile on my face.

Harriet Hamilton leans back in her chair. "I wish you and Stephen every happiness, Miss Creed. The celebration of your engagement will lift people's spirits during this ghastly financial panic."

I cut my eyes toward Miz Settle. Ghastly? It's that bad?

"China," says Mrs. Grey. "I should give you and your aunt some background information about the panic. Mr. Hamilton and I are business partners, and Harriet is quite accustomed to our open discussions, which is one of the reasons, I'm sure, that her father brought up the Wall Street panic during dinner. Did Stephen share the particulars with you?"

"Not really." *Not at all,* I think.

Mrs. Grey gazes up at the ceiling as if to gather her thoughts then says, "Actually, the crisis began in Vienna. You've heard of Vienna?"

"Yes."

"Of course, you have." She gives me a condescending smile. "The problems spread from there to all of Europe and eventually to us. The causative factors are varied and perplexing." She ticks them off on her fingers. "The Franco-Prussian War, demonetization of silver in Germany, devastating fires in Chicago and Boston, and over-investment in railroads. Needless to say, those issues impacted our banks and lowered their cash reserves. Do you follow me, China?"

"For the most part."

"Then allow me to shorten this dreary tale. Our banks have become seriously weak. Mr. Jay Cook, a giant of finance,"—I hear sarcasm in her words—"speculated beyond his means. I warned him, and, when he asked us to back his Northern Pacific Railway bonds, I turned him down. It seems I wasn't the only one. Cook's bank failed and others have followed suit. Each new day brings tidings of another bankruptcy among the nation's railroads or another bank that has become insolvent.

"Let me assure you, China, the Grey family is financially secure. My dear husband and I always believed in land as a wise investment. Several of our bank accounts will be impacted, of course, but I won't burden you with that minutiae. Rest assured we are far from ruin."

I hope she doesn't sense my unease, but I see my uncertainty reflected in Miz Settle's eyes. One errant thought rises above all others. Has Stephen brought me here to bolster his family's coffers? I can scarcely breathe as I entertain the possibility. What if he has? He knows my abilities rely on thievery. Would he ask that of me? How can I stay if he does? Yet how could Miz Settle and I leave? How far could we travel on Grand-mère's one hundred dollars?

"When my husband and I wed," Mrs. Grey says, "we united two strong families, the Greys with ties to nobility in Great Britain and a secure financial base in New York, and the Schermerhorns, one of the city's founding families, and also quite well off. As a part of our family, China, you and Mrs. Settle will never want for anything."

Her assurances act as balm, and my worry begins to fade. When the men join us, Mrs. Grey rises, clasps Stephen's arm, and they lead us through double doors into their music room. A black triangular pianoforte with red velvet skirting sits in one corner. Stephen asks his mother to play.

"Johann Sebastian Bach," she says.

She adjusts the piano bench and sits down. To my uninitiated ears, the piece she plays sounds complex but also staid and overly mathematical. As accomplished as she is, Alberta Grey doesn't seem to enjoy her own music. When she yields the instrument to Royce Cooper, the notes come alive. His fingers fly over the keyboard, and I cannot look away.

Later, when Stephen escorts me to my room, he kisses me goodnight with a hold tight enough to stop my breath.

The next morning, Lillico suggests I wear a pale yellow muslin dress, and I find it almost as comfortable as my Missouri clothes. She arranges my hair in a simple braid wrapped around my head. My gloves are white cotton. I meet Stephen at the foot of the main stairs, and he escorts me to the breakfast room where food is served on a long sideboard. We've not yet filled our plates when Holgrim comes with a message for Stephen.

Stephen reads it then pats my shoulder and whispers, "Business beckons."

It seems odd to me that, if the Grey investments are secure, Stephen's first morning at home must be interrupted by financial matters, but what do I know? As he walks away, I remind myself that I've survived more difficult situations than eating breakfast alone in an elegant room. I choose from an odd assortment of food: fat sausages, breaded kidneys, eggs scrambled with green herbs. A casserole turns out to be fish in a cream sauce, and various toasted breads stay warm on dishes set above short flaming candles. Chilled bread pudding rests in a white pottery bowl, and fruit, including bananas, is stacked whole on a platter. I choose a banana. I've eaten only one in my entire life, but I remember its exotic taste.

Each of three round tables is set with silverware and napkins for four people. I place my plate on the closest then r eturn to the buffet for tea. I'm filling my cup from a silver pot when Royce Cooper and Miz Settle come in. She looks rested and is wearing one of Ma Mère's skirts with a new long-sleeved white silk blouse. She's added elegance with a pearl necklace. She piles her plate and sits beside me.

"I like your necklace," I tell her.

Her smile is full of mischief. "You should, Sheba. You gave it to me."

I try not to show my consternation. Mr. Cooper sits down across from us and asks the whereabouts of Stephen.

"Holgrim brought a message, and Stephen had to leave."

"Sad," Mr. Cooper says, but he doesn't sound sad.

Philip joins us, and a few minutes later, Stephen returns.

"I must spend the morning unraveling monetary mysteries," he tells us. "Perhaps this afternoon we four could tour the city. Maybe a visit to City Hall with its rotunda dome? Did you know, China, that Abraham Lincoln's body laid in state there on the staircase landing?" He doesn't give me time to answer, but, of course, I didn't know. "Since we'll be downtown," he adds, "we can see the progress of the bridge construction across the East River."

Royce Cooper lifts his napkin and wipes his lips. "Why don't we plan a late afternoon meal at Delmonico's, Stephen?"

Miz Settle asks before I can, "Who are the Delmonicos?"

Stephen struggles against a smile. "It's a restaurant."

Miz Settle's look conveys her delight. Not even during our train trip did we eat at a restaurant. Again, I wish my mother were with me to share the luxuries that have suddenly become mine.

"May I come, too?" Philip asks.

"It's a *sightseeing* tour, Philip," Stephen answers, and I'm surprised that he would say that to his brother.

Philip is not cowed. "You who are sighted miss more than I do. You need to take a smell-sniffing tour, and a sound-hearing tour, and a—"

"That's enough, Philip," says Stephen. "You have school this afternoon."

Stephen's rudeness makes me uneasy. I hope it's only because he must spend the morning on financial issues.

When we finish eating, Miz Settle and I walk upstairs together. Lillico waits for me at the door of my room.

"A city tour?" Lillico says to us. "How fun. Mrs. Settle, you'll find a walking dress laid out on your bed. Meanwhile, you both might like to take a nap."

Miz Settle grumbles as she leaves. "We got too many clothes for our own good, and I ain't tired."

I agree with her, but I don't mind the time alone. I'm anxious to look over the books in my sitting room. Lillico directs me into the bedroom area of my suite. A tailored orange silk dress with a matching plaid jacket lies upon the coverlet.

"At noon, I'll return to help you, Miss Creed. Meanwhile, relax."

As soon as she leaves, I head to the bookcase. I'm delighted to find a thick biography of Eleanor of Aquitaine. I settle in a wingchair, basking in the gentle heat from the fireplace. I take off my shoes and set my feet upon a footstool. Then I lose myself in twelfth-century France.

When Lillico returns, we make quick work of my toilette. I dress, and she rebraids and drapes my hair, applies scant coloring to my lips and cheeks. She uses a broach of carved ivory to secure a deep brown velvet ribbon at my neck. We complete my outfit with brown kid leather gloves and a pair of matching walking boots. When Stephen raps at the door, Lillico excuses herself.

"Absolutely beautiful," he says.

I relax into his embrace, scarcely able to believe the dream I'm living. Why should I be upset for his rudeness to Philip? In Milksnake, I've seen brothers go after each other with knives. Boys and men, you can never quite tame them.

We visit all the places Stephen suggested, and his attention makes me feel precious and beloved. Despite the financial crisis, the city thrums with life. Boys hawk newspapers at every corner. Men sell apples, ropes of sausage, and meat pies. Ragged girls peddle tuzzy-muzzies in small metal vases made to be held. Stephen buys one of those dainty bouquets for me and another for Miz Settle.

Later that afternoon, he takes us on a chartered steam boat. A girl raised in Missouri never hopes to see an ocean, and I vastly enjoy my first unobstructed gaze of that endless expanse of water. The fall weather is chillier in New York than in the Ozarks, but Stephen takes every opportunity to place his arm around me and hold me close.

We eat supper in a private alcove at Delmonico's triangular building, one of several locations they have in the city, Stephen tells us. Waiters bring us many courses of food, and I remind myself to pay attention to the rising discomfort of my compressed middle. It would not do to split my seams.

We arrive home in time to dress for an evening with Mrs. Grey and Philip. Stephen and I sit together on a settee and endure an hour of his mother's stilted playing. When Stephen takes me to my room, he asks, "You had a good time, China?"

The concern in his eyes makes me smile. "I did. I love your city. I love being here in your home, and most of all I love being with you." His kiss hints of deeper sensual pleasures, but he resolutely sets me away and holds me at arms' length. "I can't wait to marry you," he says.

"And when will that be?" I blurt out.

He laughs. "I'm glad you're eager, but a New York wedding is complicated, and my mother is a woman who loves to organize and plan. I hope with all my heart we'll be married before Christmas."

He kisses me with gentle passion, and I float into my room where Lillico waits to peel off my evening dress. She helps me into a lace-trimmed bedgown. As she neatens the dressing table, I linger at the windows, looking out at the lamplighters who chase off the darkness with their fired wands. My dreams loom large, the stars fade, and I lose sight of the infinite.

CHAPTER TWENTY-SIX

Miz Settle and I are swept up by society life, but in different ways. I'm amazed how easily she seems to fit in. Then I remember the stories she's told me of her past life. Why be surprised about her ability to adapt to life in New York City? She's survived much more difficult situations. She's teaching Philip Cherokee words, and they've made plans to plant an herb garden in the spring. I envy her the afternoons she spends at Harriet Hamilton's Colony House.

Meanwhile, I keep to a hectic schedule of more frivolous activities arranged by Mrs. Grey, shopping for clothes and making calls upon her friends—the crème-de-la-crème of society, as she refers to them. She arranges for a governess to give me etiquette lessons. Who would believe that it's a terrible faux pas to cut open a dinner roll with your knife? No, you must tear it with your fingers. It's also frowned upon when a woman wears last year's fashions, even if the dress still looks new. Hats, gloves, shoes, silverware, visiting schedules, dining venues—may God save us from interminable, prissy rules.

Miz Settle and I manage to squeeze in a few carriage trips to Central Park where we are enchanted by Mr. Cooper's greensward and the genius of its designers, Frederick Law Olmsted and Calvert Vaux. However, I rarely spend time with Stephen. He's increasingly occupied with the family business. Even our evenings together are curtailed by demands that he attend this function or that, and seldom are fiancées welcome.

Riding lessons are also a part of my new life. Heaven forbid that I should appear in public astride a bareback mule. The Grey's stable manager, a small wiry man named for his ancestry—Scot—agrees to be my riding master. He's generous with his criticism, but, after a mere week of daily lessons on the sidesaddle, he gives me a rare compliment. "She's tooken to it." And I'm assumed ready.

On a sunny morning, dressed in my new riding habit, which includes a veiled brown hat adorned with ostrich feathers, I walk into the Receiving Room to meet my escort. I hope for Stephen, but Royce Cooper awaits me.

The ostrich feathers choose that moment to tickle my nose and I must catch a sneeze with my handkerchief. "Bother," I say, "I'm sure the ostrich needs those feathers more than I do."

Mr. Cooper laughs, and I must admit I enjoy his sense of humor.

The Grey stables were built on another street some blocks away, but Scot brings my horse to the garden area behind the house, where a mounting block is cleverly hidden amongst stone statues of nymphs and angels. I slide onto the sidesaddle, hooking my right leg around the top pommel and placing my left foot into the stirrup. My mount is a mare, an American quarter horse dappled in grays and whites. Mr. Cooper rides a chestnut gelding.

"Ye got yourself a natural horsewoman, here," Scot tells Mr. Cooper as he checks my stirrup. "I might believe ye are a wee bit wise, too, Miss China," he adds. "Unlike most women, ye dinna clutter your ride with trailing ribbons and such."

I'm not sure *wise* is an apt descriptor, but a woman doesn't grow up in the Ozarks without understanding a horse's inventory of weapons—quick reactions and the ability to run at great speeds. Balanced on a sidesaddle, I'd probably be thrown if my mount took off at the sight of a windblown ribbon.

Mr. Cooper and I spend the first portion of our ride silent, negotiating the unexpected events that occur along busy streets. We follow Broadway to Central Park and enter at The Circle through the Merchant's Gate.

The park provides three separate roadways: one for pedestrians, another for carriages, and a third for those on horseback, a convenient trinity of paths. Mr. Cooper and I ride side by side as he points out various aspects of the landscape. Much of what he tells me is about Frederick Law Olmsted, park designer and humanitarian. According to Mr. Cooper, Mr. Olmsted cares not only about Nature, but also about individual people, their needs and their hopes, no matter whether they're wealthy and privileged or everyday ordinary.

Although Miz Settle and I have been Royce Cooper's appreciative audience on carriage rides, it's the first time I've seen the park on horseback. Every curve of the bridle path opens new vistas, which allow me to forget the busy roadways beyond the park's outer boundaries.

We pass a small lake that has been designated The Pond, and from there we make our way to the Terrace and Esplanade, an area of greens and paving. The Bethesda Fountain stands at the center of the Esplanade, and I reign in my horse to appreciate the fountain's splendor.

Mr. Cooper brings his gelding close. "Have I told you it's the largest fountain in the city?"

He has, but joy deserves an audience. "Tell me again," I say.

"Twenty-six feet high." He stands in his stirrups as if by his will alone the fountain is able to ascend to that amazing height.

He draws my attention to the winged woman at the top, a bronze statue by sculptress Emma Stebbins. The statue was unveiled only within this year of 1873. That a woman could create such a thing amazes me. Most of all, I treasure the realization that the falling waters of the fountain and the rills and eddies of far-away Deer Lick Creek speak the same language.

The natural and manmade beauty of the park, the crisp scent of autumn leaves, and the brightness of the foliage enhance a day that Ma Mère would have called *a cercle de joie*.

As we watch and listen, a honey bee takes a bold path between our horses.

"We have bee hives," Mr. Cooper says.

"I noticed the hives near the Esplanade."

"Our Hungarian carpenter made them. Have I told you about him?"

"Stephen has. Anton Gerster?"

"Yes, a gifted and exacting man."

"Amazing how many talented people—including you, Mr. Cooper— came together to plan and build this wilderness within the city."

Mr. Cooper strokes the neck of his gelding. "I don't consider myself talented."

"You should."

He stares at me with such intensity that I must look away. I've given my heart to Stephen, and I won't betray him. I cast my thoughts toward the familiar comfort of birds singing, but Mr. Cooper is not done testing my resolve.

"You grant the wishes of others, Miss Creed. If you could make a wish for yourself, what would it be?"

A strange question and something I've never been asked before. I answer without considering the repercussions of my words, but they are true words, the wish of my heart since I was a child. "A kind touch."

At first, Mr. Cooper looks surprised, but then he whispers, "I understand."

My throat tightens, and I look away then see another honeybee. I point, and Mr. Cooper scans the sky.

The bee flies in a high arc as if in pursuit of something further afield than Mr. Gerster's rustic hives. I take advantage of the opportunity to end our uncomfortable conversation. "I wouldn't be surprised if you have a honey tree in the park, Mr. Cooper. Is there a place where a dead tree might be left to its own fate? Honey bees often locate in a hollow trunk."

"Perhaps in The Ramble," he says. "Let's launch a search. We'll have to leave our horses behind."

Mr. Cooper hails a mounted member of the park's police force who agrees to watch our animals. His deference as he speaks to us enlightens me. My companion has understated his role in the development of the park.

"All right, you're the expert," Royce Cooper says. "How do we pursue those elusive wild bees?"

"We wait until we see another one."

We find an ornate iron bench, the sky overhead unobstructed by branches or foliage. We sit down, and I say, "If you see a bee, pay attention to the direction of its flight and watch it as long as you can. That's the tricky part."

We sit there for quite some time, but finally, Mr. Cooper points up. The bee flies toward The Lake.

We're at the center of the Bow Bridge when Mr. Cooper spots yet another bee. They gradually lead us into the most rugged portion of the park. Our path is not easy. Brambles tug at our sleeves and catch our ankles. We scramble up a rocky incline, which borders a fall of water. A muskrat scurries away into the understory of the forest. A blue jay swoops close, bright in his colors and rude in his comments. Gray squirrels abound, not at all reticent to remind us that we are intruders within their kingdom.

Maples, oaks, poplar, and ash crowd close nearly blotting out the sky. Then I hear what I'd been hoping for. "Listen," I say.

"For?"

"The bees. They're singing. Don't you hear them?"

"Yes, I do!" His enthusiasm is catching.

We hurry along the turns and wanderings of a narrow animal path until we come upon a small clearing. Outcroppings of grey rock define its edges.

"This is bedrock," says Mr. Cooper, "the very bones of the earth."

He looks into my face, and I feel a discomforting kinship. To distract myself, I adjust my riding hat which has slid to the side of my head. The bee-song grows louder, and Mr. Cooper plunges into the edging woods, pulling me along with him. We take only a few steps until we find a second smaller clearing, and there it is, a dead oak, most of its bark and limbs lost. A wide hole gapes halfway up the trunk.

"Ha!" says Mr. Cooper. "Found it. Can we gather honey?"

"Only if you want to be stung."

"I guess not."

"But isn't it a joy to watch them?"

Neither of us says a word as we listen to the bee songs, a lovely never-ending concert. The sun leaves its apex, and we return to our horses. When they see us, they whinny, telling us they've been idle long enough. We exit the park, and the noise of the streets envelops us.

Back at the Grey mansion, Mr. Cooper helps me down to the mounting block and then to the flat, safe earth, and his eyes look everywhere but at my face.

CHAPTER TWENTY-SEVEN

The Greys attend an elegant Episcopalian Church named Trinity in lower Manhattan, and Mr. Cooper usually goes with us. The Sunday drive is pleasant, many of the street vendors, drays, and shoppers being absent, the loudest noise, our own iron-bound wheels and the hooves of our horses. Stephen says the church is the tallest building in the city, and I can't help but think that Trinity's steeple must surely pierce the floor of heaven.

Our third Sunday at Trinity, a rotund gentleman of medium height pauses at our pew, his wife by his side. Stephen introduces Miz Settle and me then says. "Mr. August Belmont and his wife Caroline Perry Belmont."

Ah, the gentleman who sold Stephen his beloved thoroughbred. The horse has come to recognize me when I visit the family stables.

Mr. Belmont's mutton-chop whiskers and bright eyes make him seem as young as Stephen, but the gray in his hair speaks of late middle age. His wife, Stephen says, is the daughter of the great Admiral Perry, which puts me quite in awe of her. The Belmonts retreat to their boxed pew, and another service commences, alight with music so exquisite that it draws tears from my eyes.

On our way home, Mrs. Grey asks, "Why the tears, China?"

"I'm sorry," I say, sure that I've broken another rule of etiquette.

Stephen speaks in my defense. "I suspect she has good reason, Mother."

I take a juddering breath, grateful for the opportunity to explain. "I wept for the beauty, Mrs. Grey. The magnificent window behind the high altar, the voices of the choir. I can feel God in that church."

Mrs. Grey rolls her eyes and sighs. "Deportment, Dear China."

"Who of us most pleased the Lord then, Mrs. Grey?' says Royce Cooper. "We who sat still as stone or Miss Creed with her quiet tears?"

Mrs. Grey looks into his face. "I would be careful if I were you, Mr. Cooper," she says. "I would indeed."

We ride the rest of the way home in uncomfortable silence, and I'm filled with longing for my life in Milksnake—the earthy scent of the woods, the melody of bird song, rain on the cabin roof. The carriage stops at the Grey home, and Stephen smiles at me. I push away my thoughts of home and return his smile.

The next day the morning papers carry the news of our engagement and the celebration party to be given in our honor. Stephen brings the newspapers to me in my room. He pulls me up for a long kiss, and he whispers how much he loves me.

Then he hands me the paper. When I read the announcement, my breath catches in my throat. "Stephen, your mother wrote my name as *China Destrehan Creed*. Did you know that?"

"What?" He pulls the paper from my hands.

"I told you about my Destrehan cousins trying to find me in Milksnake."

"I had no idea she'd do that, China. I'm so sorry."

Fear makes me numb. "They'll take me away from you."

"China, the Grey family is every bit as powerful as the Destrehans. It's impossible for them to take you away from me."

He holds me in his arms until I feel safe.

That afternoon, to my delight, Mrs. Grey suggests I go with Miz Settle to Harriet Hamilton's Colony House. Harriet drives us there in her chaise, the horses a smartly matched pair of chestnut geldings.

"I'm kidnapping you," she laughs, as the three of us crowd together on the chaise's one seat.

She deftly maneuvers through the traffic to an area two blocks shy of the infamous and dangerous byways of Five Points, where, Harriet says, even police officers hesitate to enter.

Colony House takes up half a block, its brick façade staid and sturdy. We enter through a front hall, where young women greet us, some far advanced in their pregnancies. One of the bolder women sets her arms akimbo and plants herself in front of me. Her hair is a very deep red, and she's wearing a flamboyant striped dress. Her waist has only begun to thicken with her pregnancy.

"And what sort of fancy creature have ye brung us today, Miz Hamilton?" she says, and I wish I would've worn my own Missouri clothing instead of the brown silk walking dress I chose.

"Miz Settle's niece," says Harriet, "Miss China Deliverance Creed."

"China?" She brays. "Whoever heard of a name like that?"

She dips in a mock curtsey. I return the curtsey, which makes her laugh. "No accounting for my mother's taste in names," I say. "And you are?"

"Colleen McCarthy, also known as Blue." She points at her eyes. They are a most startling hue of aqua. "Not at your service, your highness."

"But I'm at yours," I tell her.

She scowls. "How so?"

"I'm a midwife."

"Fancy-dressed like that? Ain't you afraid you'll get bloody?"

"I've never worn a dress I wouldn't sacrifice to help a mother or a child."

Some of the belligerence leaves her stance. "I like her middle name," Blue says to the women around her. "Deliverance. Good name for a midwife." She cackles.

"You'd better watch your manners, Miss McCarthy," says Harriet. "We have other needy mothers who covet a place in Colony House."

"Don't worry, Miss Hamilton. I'm loyal to you, not her. I know what she done to you." Blue insolently lifts her middle finger at me then saunters away.

I'm shocked, not at the gesture but at the accusation. Whatever did I do to Harriet Hamilton?

Before I can gather wits enough to inquire, more young mothers and children drift out from the shadows. They accompany us as we visit the dayroom, which is painted a cheerful yellow. Women sit knitting or mending. Several hunch over treadle sewing machines. I can scarcely imagine the ease of sewing with a machine. I've heard that it stitches ten times more quickly than the most able seamstress.

As I watch, Harriet says, "I'm sorry about Blue."

I'm not refined enough to be anything except forthright. "Harriet, if I've done something to hurt you, I apologize."

"Stephen and I were friends," she says. "More than friends, affianced, some years ago."

My heart drops.

"I suppose he didn't tell you."

"I'm sorry. He didn't."

"You have no reason to be sorry. I was the one who broke the engagement."

I don't have the courage to ask her why, but she volunteers the information.

"When Stephen went off to war, I started Colony House, not so much out of the goodness of my heart, but to preserve my sanity. By the time he came home again, all my dedication was centered here." She pats my gloved hand. "I want you and Stephen to be happy together. Just remind him once in a while that Colony House needs financial support." She smiles.

I have the feeling that she's not telling me everything, but I return her smile.

She suggests a tour of the kitchen, which is even larger than the one in the Grey mansion. Platters of leftover food clutter the work tables, and I realize that the women at Colony House enjoyed a more substantial luncheon than ours of crustless watercress sandwiches and broiled whitefish.

"Ya see why I try to eat here mid-day?" Miz Settle says.

Harriet and I laugh together, and my heart lifts. Perhaps I've made a friend.

CHAPTER TWENTY-EIGHT

That evening Mrs. Grey asks Stephen and me to join her in the library. I could happily spend hours perusing the shelves of books in that room, but Mrs. Grey has told me more than once that reading for pleasure is a frivolous pastime.

As we enter the room, she hands me a copy of the invitation she mailed to those fortunate enough—her words not mine—to be invited to our engagement party. Then she picks up a battered book from the desk. We sit down in the leather armchairs that front the fireplace, and I study the invitation.

Elegant black script embossed on heavy cardstock announces the fête, three weeks away, to honor Dr. Stephen Schermerhorn Grey and his fiancée Miss China Destrehan Creed. Again, I wince at the change in my middle name, but the invitations were sent only to a select few. If my cousins notice anything, it will be the engagement announcement in the newspapers.

Inside, the card informs recipients that the party will be a costume ball with a buffet supper and a sit-down breakfast. I had no idea that a party could last through the night.

After giving Stephen a list of those invited, Mrs. Grey leans back in her chair and smooths the rich dark fabric of her skirt. "Now, onto something else." She takes a deep breath. "I don't want to sound like a lunatic, but strange things are happening in this house."

Mrs. Grey opens the book on her lap. A whiff of mildew rises from its pages. "*The Pilgrim's Progress from This World to That Which Is To Come,*" she reads, "written by John Bunyan. This book was one of my childhood treasures, a moral compass so to speak. It's been lost for years, but I found it on my pillow last night. She pulls a round golden watch from her skirt pocket. "And there's this. I believe we buried it with your father, Stephen. Perhaps I'm mistaken."

"You're not mistaken," Stephen says softly. I know by the look on his face that he hasn't yet told her about my curse.

"And the opal ring." Mrs. Grey motions at my left hand. "I assumed, Stephen, that you asked for it the evening I sent Holgrim to fetch your grandmother's rose-gold necklace. Please don't misunderstand, China. The ring is yours, but Holgrim said he didn't remove it from the vault. When did Stephen give it to you?"

"Mother," Stephen says, "let me explain."

"What possible explanation could there be?"

"An odd one."

Stephen takes the scientific approach, and I'm glad for that, having had enough accusations of witchery in my life. As he explains his theory of telekinesis, Mrs. Grey's eyes never leave his. He ends by saying, "It must remain a secret, Mother, or China's life and mine will become hell on earth."

Mrs. Grey is silent, a stunned look on her face. Finally, she stands and clasps my hands, leans down, and kisses my cheek. "An experiment," she says.

A chill lifts goosebumps on my arms, and I'm suffused with a sense of dread.

Mrs. Grey gazes into my eyes. "I'm very good at keeping secrets."

My costume for the engagement fête is completed a mere two days before the event. Lillico and a kitchen maid carry a life-size wooden figure of a woman into my boudoir. She comes complete with arms and hands and a swanlike neck but alas no head. They both huff a sigh as they stand her in a corner. She's wearing my engagement dress.

"Our wooden lady is heavy for all that she's headless," Lillico comments. "'Course the dress is almost as heavy as she is. I can't think how you'll have strength enough to dance in it, Miss Creed."

I answer her flippantly, "I'm strong," and I laugh, but, during the fittings, I worried about the same thing.

Lillico adjusts the train of the gown into a semi-circle around the wooden lady. A fleur-de-lis pattern details the deep red velvet of the overskirt. Each gold jacquard sleeve is a separate article of clothing, each secured at the top of the shoulder with a velvet tie. The red and gold brocade bodice is accented by a low-cut square neckline and laced up the front.

Lillico and the maid leave my room, and Mrs. Grey sweeps in, her arms extended toward the dress. "Well?"

Gratitude trips up my words. "It's, it's beautiful. It looks like it belongs in the Middle Ages."

"You have a good eye. Can you guess who you'll be?"

"No," I say.

At that moment Stephen steps into the room holding a gold circlet inset with sparkling gems—obviously a crown.

"Now can you guess?" his mother asks.

"A princess?"

"More than a princess. A queen."

My heart sinks. I told Stephen about Eleanor of Aquitaine, purported to be my distant cousin, but I'd asked him to keep it secret. I don't need the Grey family to latch upon any connection I may have to ancient women of great wealth or ability. My powers are lesser, but I'm sure Mrs. Grey's choice is not a coincidence.

"Eleanor of Aquitaine," I say my voice flat.

"You're not pleased?"

I muster a smile. "It'll be great fun, Mrs. Grey."

She strokes my face. "Mother Grey, please."

"Mother Grey."

She spends a few moments telling us about the menu she plans for the party, and when she leaves I confront Stephen. "How does she know about Eleanor of Aquitaine?"

He picks up a book from the seat of my wing chair and points at the gold embossed title, *Eleanor of Aquitaine*. "Mother noticed."

I apologize with a kiss.

Miz Settle is overjoyed with her dress. A sheath made of pale deerskin, it's exquisitely beaded in red and blue. Long fringes adorn the sleeves, hem, and over-bodice, but, when she sees the moccasins, she sends me on an errand to Mrs. Grey.

Mrs. Grey sits at her desk, writing a letter that she quickly covers with a blank sheet of paper. "My dear," she says.

I thank her for both dresses, pretending I didn't see that surreptitious move. After all, letters should be private. "Aunt Jesse and I love them."

She clasps her hands at her bosom. "I'm delighted."

"However, there is a small problem with the moccasins."

"They don't fit?"

We'd been measured to distraction the second day after we moved into the Grey Mansion. Even the clothing Mrs. Grey ordered for us prior to our arrival was altered in small and unnecessary ways.

"Everything fits wonderfully well, but Aunt Jesse's moccasins must be changed." I pull them from their velvet drawstring bag. Red and blue beads form a sunburst on the vamp of each. "They're exquisite as you can see. But—" I turn the moccasins sole up. The bottoms are also beaded. "My aunt wants permission to remove the beads on the soles."

"Slippery perhaps?"

"I suppose they would be, but Aunt Jesse's concern is that sole beading marks them as burial moccasins."

Alberta Grey's eyes widen. "Oh dear, my sincere apologies. I'll contact the artisan."

"Please don't. We can do it ourselves. Again, thank you, Mother Grey."

She gifts me with a lovely smile, and I return to my room, assuring myself that every problem in the Grey household will be as easily resolved.

The night of the engagement party, Lillico weaves my hair through and around the filigree circlet in a complex and flattering style. My dress makes me feel closer to that distant cousin who battled a heartache I hope I'll never have to bear. According to the biography I'm reading, despite being Queen Consort of France and then England, Eleanor of Aquitaine also endured sixteen years of imprisonment.

My thoughts are interrupted by Miz Settle's laughter as she catches me gazing in the mirror. "Yes, you're beautiful, Sheba," she says. "Don't let it go to your head."

I smile sheepishly at her. Truly she looks the Cherokee maiden, her gown falling gracefully in a trim line from her shoulders to her ankles where it meets the tops of her now smooth-soled moccasins.

She carries a fan of feathers, dyed blue. "It's also a mask," she says, holding it up to cover the lower half of her face.

A knock interrupts us, and I answer the door. It's Stephen, but not the Stephen I know.

"Good evening, ladies," he says. "Allow me to introduce myself, John Paul Jones, ready and willing to fight for freedom and an end to all tyranny."

He certainly looks the part of a Revolutionary War hero, dressed as he is in a blue and red naval uniform and knee britches. A black tricorn hat sits upon his head. Miz Settle claps her hands in delight, and I laugh.

He hands me my mask—a confection of stiffened white fabric, gold feathers, and diamante. Stephen's mask is merely a swath of dark fabric, pierced with eyeholes. As he ties it around his head, he says, "Mr. Cooper waits for you in the hallway, Aunt Jesse."

When she leaves the room, he kisses me twice, deeply enough to set my heart racing. Then he leans his forehead against mine. "As I promised, only two kisses."

He escorts me from the bedroom wing to the other side of the upper floor where the ballroom is located, along with its necessary adjoining chambers: a ladies' salon, a gentlemen's smoking room, powder rooms, the essential pantries, plus a large dining area. Shortly after nine p.m., our guests begin to arrive.

We are who we aren't. That is how Philip describes us as we form the receiving line. Mrs. Grey is first. She's dressed in what she calls Egyptian, a white pleated silk sheath with a draped neckline. Wire bracelets adorn her upper arms and a small snake is affixed to her left wrist. It's only a snakeskin padded to look real, but I startle when I see it. She wears a black wig, the hair parted at the center then hanging long and straight. A leopard skin is draped over her shoulders.

Stephen stands next in line then me and Miz Settle, last of all Philip who's dressed as a jockey in bright green silks and white knee britches, a quirt tucked under his arm.

When Holgrim announces each couple, he presents them only by their character names. Thus I've met General George Washington and his wife Martha, Julius Caesar and his slave-girl Olivia, Quasimodo and his beloved Esméralda, and a bounty of other characters, historical or from plays and novels.

Perhaps a guessing game is in store later before guests remove their masks. I'm ready for whatever the evening might bring.

We greet nearly one hundred people. After the last few pass through our receiving line, Miz Settle says to me, "Lots of these folks been goomered, Sheba."

I'm startled by her comment. Who would curse these elegant people? Then I remember the woman Blue at the Colony House. Certainly the poor of this city might wish to curse the wealthy. "I hope you're wrong."

"I'm not."

Royce Cooper joins us. He wears black knee-britches and a blousy white shirt with full sleeves. A red bandanna is knotted at his neck, a striped cummerbund tied around his waist. His eyepatch and sheathed dagger leave little doubt. He's a pirate.

As Mrs. Grey leads Stephen and me to the center of the ballroom floor, the conductor of the stringed orchestra raises his wand, and the musicians play a short fanfare. Footmen in black uniforms carry trays of crystal flutes filled with a bubbling wine called champagne. Our guests help themselves, as do we, and then Mrs. Grey lifts her glass and says, "We're overjoyed that China Destrehan Creed has accepted my son Stephen's marriage proposal. A toast to a joyous and bountiful life together."

Everyone drinks then Stephen proposes a toast to our assembled friends, as he calls them. I catch Harriet Hamilton's eye, and she beams a smile. Whatever she and Stephen had together hasn't turned her against me, and I'm grateful.

Other toasts ring out: to our health, to long lives, and one slightly unsettling—to golden years of wealth. The footmen take our empty flutes, and the orchestra begins a waltz. Stephen pulls me into his arms.

"You are magnificent," he says. I'm breathless with the moment.

Soon Mrs. Grey and Philip join us on the dance floor, then Mr. Cooper and Miz Settle, after them Harriet and her father, who are dressed as Quakers. When Stephen teases Harriet about her plain dress, her eyes light, and I have to turn my head. Stephen's clasp on my extended hand tightens, and, when our dance ends, he kisses my forehead before handing me off to Philip for a lively polka.

A quadrille follows, and, although Stephen has taught me the dance, I'm awkward. More than once, to the laughter of other dancers, I blunder. Finally, Harriet leaves her partner to instruct me, the two of us paired like carriage horses as I mimic her steps.

Servants bring in more champagne. I take another glass and drink it far too quickly. My head buzzes, and everything becomes hilarious.

During a pause between dances, Holgrim seeks out Mrs. Grey who beckons Stephen. When I hear her say, "Bring China," I walk to Stephen's side.

"Two gentlemen, Sir," says Holgrim. "A Mr. Julien Destrehan and his brother François, plus another man, a Mr. Blisset. I told them to remain in the foyer."

My joy drops away, and the heaviness of the Aquitaine gown nearly pins me in place. Stephen guides me into the hall. His mother follows us.

"The Destrehans!" he says. "Shall I take you to your room, China?"

"Let her come," says Mrs. Grey.

"Yes," I reply. "I need to know why they're here."

The three of us walk downstairs to the mezzanine that overlooks the foyer. Our uninvited guests stand just inside the double doors. The Destrehans are beautiful in the same way that Ma Mère was beautiful, with fine-boned, sculpted faces and perfect posture. They're still wearing their overcoats. Holgrim has quick access to the foyer via the maze of servants' passages, and he soon joins them.

"Those three are the ones who came to Milksnake?" Stephen asks me, sotto voce.

"The taller two. I don't know the third gentleman. Mr. Blisset? Is that what Holgrim called him?"

"Yes," says Mrs. Grey.

Blisset stands a few steps behind my cousins. His coat is not of the same quality as theirs. His mustache is heavier, his nose bulbous. He's very still, but his eyes move constantly, as if he expects to face enemies.

As we start down the stairway, Stephen calls out, "May I help you, gentlemen?"

Holgrim introduces the three men. Then Julien begins what sounds like a short rehearsed speech.

"We've come on a mission of congratulations, Dr. Grey. We thought we'd cause less interruption if we joined your celebration now rather than when you were first welcoming your guests." His English, although accented, is perfect. If I didn't know who he was, I'd be charmed. "As you might guess by our names, we're related to your fiancée." He nods at me. "Our grandfather and Miss Creed's grandfather were brothers."

He reaches for my hand, but I step away. "You're beautiful as we knew you would be, dear cousin. And of course, the white hair is stunning."

"A thief beyond compare," his brother says in French.

I glance at Mrs. Grey and wonder if she understood his comment. Does she realize the repercussions she brought upon us simply by gilding my heritage?

"Mother," says Stephen, "why don't you take Miss Creed back to the festivities. I'm sure our guests have noticed her absence. Please make my apologies, China. I'll join you as soon as possible." He presses his cheek to mine and whispers, "I'm here for you."

Mrs. Grey links arms with me, and we climb the stairs. In the gallery, she says, "What a surprise that the Destrehans should arrive at your engagement party. You haven't been in touch with them?"

I tamp down my anger. "My mother severed ties with her family long ago. I suspect your use of the Destrehan name in the newspaper announcement helped them locate me. Don't you think?"

She pats my hand. "We're your family now, China. Whatever relationship you decide to pursue with your cousins, or lack thereof, we'll back you." She tries to pull me toward the third-story stairs, but I stop.

"It's to my best advantage to hear what Stephen tells them, Mother Grey."

"Come, come, dear. All will be well."

"Please make my excuses."

She scowls at me but walks away, her spine stiff. I linger, hidden in the shadows of the mezzanine.

Evidently, their conversation has already ended, because Stephen says, "I bid you goodnight, gentlemen. I must return to our guests."

"Again our congratulations, Mr. Grey," one of them says.

"Dr. Grey," Holgrim tells him.

"Pardon. Dr. Grey."

I hear the outside door open, and, I step to the edge of the mezzanine, but I am too quick. François has not yet left the foyer. He lifts his hand my way and dips his head then says, "Dear Cousin, we know the Grey family fortune suffered due to the recent collapse of Jay Cook's empire. If they can't provide the opulent life you deserve, we're willing to offer assistance."

"Leave now!" Stephen pushes my cousin out the door.

The Grey family fortune suffered? Is that why business matters have overtaken Stephen's life? Perhaps Stephen has not been totally honest with me. I wait, hoping he will escort me back to the ballroom. I need his reassurances, but he walks toward the library, asking Holgrim to bring him a brandy.

What if the Grey family expects me to shore up their finances with thievery?

Simple. Miz Settle and I would leave New York. Not so simple. Where would we go? Who would protect us? Not only from the Destrehans but also the Greys.

Still, François could be lying, and I should doubt him before I doubt Stephen. After all, Stephen loves me. I square my shoulders and return to the ballroom where I search out Mrs. Grey. "Stephen's still downstairs," I whisper and hope I do not betray my unease.

At that moment, a footman announces the opening of the Regal Dining Room. Mrs. Grey offers her arm and lifts her chin. I take a deep breath to calm my nerves. Miz Settle partnered by Mr. Cooper follows us and then Philip and a young woman who wears gauze wings attached to the back of her gown. After them, our guests enter two-by-two as if they were boarding Noah's Ark, each woman a step ahead of her escort.

The dining room is ablaze with gas sconces, and in each corner tall beeswax tapers shine atop clustered groups of candelabras. The buffet table is piled with food. At its center, a full-feathered black swan—dead, of course—seems to swim within a pool of blue asters. A table of desserts sits against the far wall, including a magnificent multi-layer cake topped by a mound of glacé fruit. I glance back at Miz Settle. She lowers her fan-mask and simply stares.

Mrs. Grey takes very little food, as do I, making choices that pose less of a threat to my gown. Then she leads our family group to a small room off the gallery where King Louis chairs are arranged in a cluster. I sigh as I sit, the great weight of my dress no longer crushing my collarbones.

"You may remove your gloves to eat, dear," she says to me, and then, "I'm sorry for that unfortunate interlude. I don't mean to insult your family, but those men were terribly rude."

"They were."

"What men?" asks Philip.

"Nothing to be concerned about," his mother tells him. She turns to me. "Otherwise, what do you think of the party?"

Before I can answer, the door opens and Stephen joins us. "Mother, the party is magnificent," he says then leans close to me and looks into my eyes. "All is well, China. Truly."

He's left the door ajar, and August Belmont, dressed as Benjamin Franklin, peeks in. "Ah, I've discovered your eyrie."

I quickly don my gloves.

"And what do you think about this lovely evening, Miss Creed?" Mr. Belmont asks. He comes to me, lifts my right hand, and leaves a lingering kiss upon my knuckles.

"It's quite overwhelming."

"You're truly a beauty, my dear."

"Yes, August," says Stephen, "and well-educated, her French being as fine as anything you or I might attempt."

Mr. Belmont looks surprised, but he says in French, "Honored to meet you."

I respond in kind, and he asks if I have any German.

"My apologies, Sir, I do not."

He glances sideways at Stephen. "May I offer my services as a tutor?" He leans toward me as if to place a kiss upon my cheek, but Stephen pushes him away with a good-natured smile.

"Only her fiancé is allowed to kiss her."

Mr. Belmont bows at the waist and leaves us to our repast. I eat enough to drive away the fuzziness the champagne left in my head, and, when the music resumes, Stephen suggests we participate in a quadrille.

We rejoin the others in the ballroom, and I perform with scarcely a misstep. After the quadrille, we dance a breathless polka. Stephen's smile drives away my worry, but I notice that Miz Settle is looking tired, and, after the dance, I take her to her room.

I help her into a flannel nightdress and then tell her about the Destrehans' visit.

She climbs into her bed and settles back against the pillows. "That ain't our worst problem at the moment, Sheba. The other guests, they're here for a reason beyond celebrating your engagement. They been told."

"Why would you think that?"

"They got greed in their eyes, plain as anything I ever seen."

"Who would tell them? Mrs. Grey promised to keep it a secret."

Miz Settle pats my hand. "Enjoy your party, Sheba. Tomorrow we'll make plans for just-in-case. Wise plans are a strong weapon."

When I return to the ballroom, Stephen is waiting for me. "Miz Settle was not feeling well?"

"Just tired. I helped her to bed."

"And how are you?"

"I'm good."

At that moment, Mr. Belmont-Benjamin Franklin happens upon us.

"Might I have this dance with your fiancée, Dr. Grey?" he asks.

Stephen agrees, and Mr. Belmont and I dance. Later, he guides me to a gathering of chairs where tall palms offer a modicum of privacy. "Champagne is surely in order," he says. He walks away, and I scan the room for Stephen. Where did he go? Mr. Belmont returns, carrying a flute of champagne in each hand. Bowing, he offers one to me. "Liquid courage."

He's about to sit down when the orchestra begins another song.

"Bother," he says, "I promised my wife this waltz. It seems I've been neglecting her. Or at least she thinks so."

I raise my champagne to him as he walks away and then carefully set the full glass into the pot of the nearest palm. Almost immediately, Mr. Cooper takes the empty chair beside me, and I feel like I can breathe again.

"Are you all right, Miss Creed?" he asks.

"I am."

"Where's Mrs. Settle?"

"She was tired. I took her to her room."

He studies my face. "There's something else, isn't there?" He meets my eyes and doesn't look away.

How does he read me so easily? I gather my thoughts and finally say, "I told you that my Louisiana cousins came to Milksnake, trying to find me."

"I recall."

"They were here tonight."

"Surely Mrs. Grey didn't invite them."

"No. She was almost as upset as I was, but she used the Destrehan name in the newspaper announcements."

"I noticed. She probably thought the prestige would pave your way into New York society. Not a wise decision?"

"No. It wasn't."

I gaze out at the dancers, the women's bright dresses swirling. George Washington strides toward us, a determined look on his face, and I remember Miz Settle's warning. Mr. Cooper stands and pulls me to my feet.

"She's promised this dance to me, George," he says as we walk past.

"Thank you, Mr. Cooper," I whisper, and we glide onto the dance floor.

Royce Cooper is a fine dancer, and I soon relax. Although we maintain a polite distance, his warmth comes to me through our clasped hands.

I smile up at him, and the intensity of his eyes makes my heart catch. I've seen that look before, but where? Stephen? No. Then it comes to me. Tommy Belnap.

Mr. Cooper says something, but the music is too loud for me to hear. I try to read his lips, and I can't look away. Breathe, I tell myself. What kind of woman am I that he can make me feel like this? I love Stephen.

The waltz ends, and Royce Cooper bends close. "Are you sure about Stephen, China? Are you sure?"

The concern in his voice frightens me. A few hours before, I would've been able to answer him, but now, I can't. I don't doubt that Stephen needs me, and that's a strong foundation for any marriage, but Royce Cooper seems to understand me at a far deeper level than Stephen ever has. I release my hold on his hand and press my fingertips to my temples.

"Headache?"

I try to smile. "Too much champagne."

"Could I get you something to eat? That should help."

"A cup of milk would be wonderful."

He walks me back to the alcove of palms. I sit down and watch as he crosses the room. Mr. Cooper is no sooner gone than Mr. Belmont is at my side. A polka begins, and, despite my protest, he pulls me to my feet. Halfway through, my stomach begins to churn, and I plead for a respite. He guides me from the floor and fetches two small crystal glasses filled with a pale liquor.

I shake my head no, and he says, "Merely sherry, Miss Creed. Very mild. It'll settle your stomach."

I take a sip. He's right. It helps. I catch a glimpse of Stephen talking to George Washington. Both men look upset. A waltz begins, and General Washington approaches. Mr. Belmont removes the sherry glass from my hand, and George whirls me away.

From Washington, I go to Julius Caesar, an elderly man whose slower pace allows me to breathe. From Caesar, I'm pulled into the arms of Napoleon, and after Napoleon, Attila the Hun. The three huge gasoliers that light the ballroom sparkle above me. Their hanging crystals and gold-plated arms shimmer. I tip back my head and watch them spin. My worries lift, and I begin to laugh. Attila laughs with me.

"Are you dizzy?" he asks.

"I am."

"I have just the thing." He takes me to the alcove, leaves me for a few moments then returns carrying a small glass of pale green liquor. "This will help."

I push it away. "No more spirits."

"It's medicine, Miss Creed. Good for headaches and general weariness."

I take a cautious sip. It tastes of anise and fennel, healing herbs. I drink it, and we return to the dance floor. Despite masquerading as Attila, my dance partner must be a gentleman. His left hand is smooth with no callouses, but as we dance I begin to wonder how I know that. Etiquette dictates gloves for all dance partners, and, if he isn't wearing gloves, are mine that thin?

With effort, I fix my gaze on my extended right hand. His hand is bare and so is mine. I lift my left hand from his upper arm. At least I retain my left glove, which strikes me as hilarious. One glove, what must Mrs. Grey think? I realize that I don't care, and my laughter rises above the dance music. Attila delivers me into another man's arms. He's dressed in red, and his mask extends up into a hideous helmet of feathers and antlers. I don't remember him coming through our reception line. I try to pull away, but he holds me in a tight clench. The rhythm of the music pounds up from the parquet floor. Drums? Surely there are no drums in the string orchestra.

I begin to feel motion sick, and I cling to the red devil to keep my balance, but he whirls me until I can scarcely stay on my feet. My hair tumbles down to my shoulders. I lose my remaining glove. Another dancer claims me, a pirate, but not Mr. Cooper. Then I'm back with the devil. How many dances? Two? Three? Finally, Mr. Belmont wrestles me from the demon's arms.

"Enough!" he says, as he pulls me away.

"Could we sit?" I gasp.

He takes me to a chair and somehow procures a delicate fan, which he waves before my face. Suddenly Stephen is with us. "What's wrong?"

"Too much liquor, I'd guess," Mr. Belmont says.

"What happened to your gloves, China?" Stephen asks.

A familiar smoky fragrance clings to him, and his pupils are so small that his eyes look pure gold.

"Your gloves?" he asks again.

"I lost them. Stephen, I don't . . . I don't feel well."

His mother comes to us and addresses Mr. Belmont. "Thank you for your help, August." She clasps my right arm with her talon claws. The snake on her wrist flicks its tongue. I shudder.

"She's drunk, Stephen," Mrs. Grey hisses. "Get her out of here. She's a disgrace."

"She's a disgrace, Mother? I told you that her gift was ours alone, but you've informed everyone here, haven't you? Don't lie to me." Stephen's voice sounds strange, too high. Is he slurring his words?

"Only a necessary few. Blame your father's foolish investments."

Stephen pulls me to my feet and takes me into an adjoining chamber. From there we enter the servants' hall.

I apologize, but he pinches my arm hard enough to make me cry out at the pain. "Shut up and watch where you're walking, China. I can't believe you allowed yourself to get drunk."

He opens a door, and we stumble out into the bedroom wing. Royce Cooper is there, engaged in a conversation with Holgrim.

"What's happened?" Mr. Cooper asks. He bends near, and, in my befuddled state, I think he's going to kiss me, but he simply inhales and says, "Someone gave her absinthe, Stephen. Absinthe."

Stephen squints at him. "What did you say?"

"I said someone gave her absinthe. You know it causes hallucinations."

"It wasn't me." Stephen reaches out as if to pinch me again, but Mr. Copper pushes him away.

"Don't touch her."

Stephen staggers, and Holgrim clasps his arm to keep him from falling. Perhaps I'm not the only one who's drunk. Then I'm floating in Royce Cooper's arms, down the hall to my room. I rest my head against his shoulder. He opens the door and carries me to the bed. I fall asleep.

CHAPTER TWENTY-NINE

My dreams are filled with devils and haints, booger dogs, and demons. They dance, and they laugh, and finally they startle me awake. I'm still clad in my regal costume, shoes and all. Memories of the party return. The red devil. Was he real? My head aches.

"You have a hangover, well-deserved," I tell myself.

I leave my bed and fetch my medical bag where I always keep thistle seeds and ginger. Miz Settle and I have treated our share of repentant imbibers. I eat the seeds without the benefit of boiling them and chew a piece of ginger, raw and tough. They settle my stomach. In my water closet, I dampen a face cloth and press it against my eyes.

Then I sit on the edge of the porcelain tub and try to clear my thoughts. A memory surfaces—Mr. Cooper carrying me into my room, pulling away the counterpane, and laying me down on the bed. Did he have tears on his face or was that a wayward dream? Perhaps my befuddled mind only offers what I need most—someone to trust.

"You have Miz Settle," I say aloud, and at that moment I know without a doubt we must leave.

In my sitting room, I light one of the candles on the mantle and remove my silk shoes and golden crown. After I shed my party gown, not an easy task without Lillico, I take off my corset, which has left my skin red and itching. I slip into a flannel nightgown, sit at my dressing table, and pull the clips and combs from my tousled curls. A hallway clock chimes. Five o'clock, I have hours yet before Lillico will come and help me dress for the day. At the moment, sleep must be my priority. Miz Settle and I need clear minds to make our plans.

I've just climbed back into bed when someone raps on my door. My heart jumps, but I get up and put on my wrapper, open the door, and peer out.

It's Philip, dressed as if it was already morning. "Miss Creed," he says, "my brother's quite ill. I thought you should know."

It takes me a moment to process his words. "Ill? How so?" My thoughts stray to common maladies—croup, grippe, fever.

Holgrim and Mr. Cooper rush past us and enter Stephen's room at the end of the hall, leaving the door open.

"Come with me," Philip says.

The hallway is dimly lit, and Philip is more sure of his step than I am. We hurry to the room and walk into a maelstrom. Two wingchairs lie on their backs. Sheets and blankets are tangled in a heap beside the bed. Papers litter the floor. Stephen is slumped on his knees near the fireplace.

"No, no, no, Royce. I need her," he says.

"You'll never survive, Stephen."

"Those damned Destrehans, they'll try to get her away from me. This house, everything, it's too much. I can't do it without her. And I need . . . I need—"

Royce Cooper notices us. "Miss Creed, please go back to your room."

I release Philip's arm and kneel beside Stephen.

"I'm sorry, China," he says. "I meant to protect you. I thought I was strong enough."

He falls against me, and his weight topples me sideways. My head hits the floor, and I gasp in pain. Holgrim and Mr. Cooper lift him until I'm able to slide away. I stagger to my feet, and Philip clasps my hand.

Stephen curls into a fetal position on the carpet.

"What's wrong with him?" I ask.

Mr. Cooper rights one of the wingchairs. "Please sit down, Miss Creed. I'll explain when we get the situation under control."

I'm too agitated to sit. I use a poker to stir the coals in the fireplace, and then I kneel again at Stephen's side. His eyes are closed, and his breathing has become labored. He doesn't respond when I speak to him. A terrible sorrow rises within me, and I lift desperate prayers, but my faith is weak. God seems distant. Mrs. Grey enters the room. Scot from the stables is with her and another gentleman I don't recognize.

"Dr. Broward," Mrs. Grey says, "may I present Miss China Creed, Stephen's fiancée."

The doctor is a man of middle years, hawk-nosed, and gaunt.

Mrs. Grey flicks her fingers at me. "For pity's sake, China, go get dressed." She's wearing a morning gown as if it were the beginning of an ordinary day.

"What's wrong with Stephen?" I ask her.

"That's a discussion for another time. Go. You, too, Philip."

He grabs my arm and pulls me from the room. "Don't fight," he whispers. "You'll never win a battle against my mother. As we walk down the hall, Philip says, "To her, Stephen has always been the perfect son. I'm her greatest disappointment."

His voice quivers, and I attempt words of comfort. "You're a hand-some, brilliant young man, Philip."

"I'm a burden. That's all my mother sees, nothing beyond that. She keeps me here in this house, locked away from almost everything."

"You have no friends?"

"Who wants a friend that must ride a horse with a lead rein?"

"Someone who values good company."

He rubs his eyes. "And what woman wants a blind man for her hus-band?"

"A woman who looks past your eyes to your heart."

"My brother doesn't deserve you." I hear the anger in Philip's voice.

"You know what's wrong with him?"

"Ask Mr. Cooper. He'll tell you the truth. After all, Royce loves you."

"Philip, that's nonsense. I belong to Stephen."

"You shouldn't, and that's my best advice."

He leaves me at my door. Fighting to hold in tears, I walk into my room. Miz Settle is standing beside the fireplace.

"What's wrong?" she asks. "All the commotion woke me up."

"Stephen's sick again."

"It's more than sickness that takes holda that man, Sheba."

I break down, and Miz Settle gathers me into her arms, pats my back as I sob. When my tears are spent, she offers me her handkerchief, not a lace-bound scrap of linen but a large red bandana. I dry my eyes and my face.

"Mrs. Grey told me to get dressed," I say. "I think we have a meeting with the doctor."

"You want me to help you?"

"No, wait for me in your room. We have to make plans. We can't stay here with Mrs. Grey, especially now that Stephen can't protect us."

"He never protected us, Sheba. Don't you know that?"

"I do now, at least in my head. My heart isn't ready to admit defeat." I cup her face in my hands. "Close your eyes and wish for money."

I opt to wear one of my Missouri skirts and my mother's white shirt-waist, familiar clothing to bolster my courage. I finger comb my hair into a single long braid, and, when I return to Stephen's room, he's lying in bed. Holgrim and Scot are gone. Mrs. Grey sits near the fireplace, and Royce Cooper hovers beside the doctor who's listening to Stephen's heart with a belled stethoscope.

Mrs. Grey rises and walks toward me, frowning. She plucks at my shirt. "You look like a scullery maid."

I'm too tired to care what she thinks. "Ladies don't bicker, Mother Grey."

She turns away from me. "Dr. Broward, when you finish here, I'll expect you in the Receiving Room. Mr. Cooper will show you the way. China, come with me."

I follow her downstairs. She must have roused one of the servants, because the coal in the fireplace is ablaze, and the gas sconces are lit. When the two men join us, Royce Cooper sits at my side on the settee. The doctor remains standing and addresses us as if we were an audience.

"I'm distressed to tell you that Dr. Grey is nearly unresponsive."

Stephen's mother presses her clasped hands into her lap. "What should we do?"

"If he doesn't show signs of awareness by evening, I'll arrange a transfer to the Broward Institute. With constant care he may recover." He nods at Mrs. Grey. "I'll take my leave now and return in a few hours."

"See him out, Mr. Cooper," says Mrs. Grey, rising from her chair. She walks over to me, leans down, and strokes my cheek. I clench my teeth to keep them from chattering. "Dear China, please remember that Stephen loves you, regardless of the damage you've done him."

What an odd thing to say. "What damage?"

"Stephen should've told you."

"Tell me now!"

She hisses at me and clasps my left hand. Her face wrinkles in disgust as she eyes my truncated finger. "God sent that snake, you know. Yet Stephen in all his goodness would save you." She releases my hand. "You're an intelligent woman, China. I thought you'd figure everything out before now." She stares into my face and says, "Stephen is an opium addict."

My throat closes, and I struggle for breath. I'm a child again facing the Bushwacker's gun, suddenly aware how helpless I am. I knot my hands into fists. My fingernails cut into my skin. A minute passes, maybe an hour, maybe a year. Mr. Cooper walks into the room, and I lash out at him. "Why didn't you tell me?"

Mrs. Grey answers. "Because Mr. Cooper is my employee, China, and his job–may I remind you, Royce—was to prevent exactly what happened tonight."

He looks off toward a painting that hangs against the wall, horses grazing peacefully. Then he turns his back to Mrs. Grey and addresses me. "Stephen's experiences in the war were nothing short of horrendous, Miss Creed. Laudanum allowed him to sleep between long hours of surgery. Unfortunately, when the war ended, he continued to rely on its medicinal qualities. He was seeing Harriet Hamilton at the time. When she broke off their engagement, he weaned himself from his dependence, which had progressed far beyond laudanum. That's when Mrs. Grey saw the advertisement in the Times, a doctor needed for the town of Milksnake."

Mrs. Grey walks over to the fireplace, stares down into the crusted coals. "I thought he'd do better there," she says. "After all, Milksnake has no opium dens." She turns toward me. "But it had you, China, and you provided him a constant supply of the very best. When he brought you to New York, familiar places and old acquaintances lured him back into regular use. I'm quite certain the appearance of your cousins at our party pushed him over the edge."

How can I pity her? How can I pity any of them? They're so bound by greed.

"Be honest, Mother Grey, it wasn't only the Destrehans. Stephen was appalled to realize that you broke your word to him and told your friends about my gift."

"You expect me to believe that you and your aunt don't appreciate your opulent life here with us? You owe me for every luxury."

"Your luxuries are not worth the damage to my soul. You've turned me into a thief."

"Let's not embark upon a discussion of morality, China. Don't tell me you've never used your gift to get what you wanted. You're in a very precarious position. I can easily convince the police that you're a thief, and I have the jewelry to prove it."

"I'm sorry, China," says Royce Cooper. His face is drawn tight with sorrow, and I'm suddenly sure my memory of his tears was not a dream.

Mrs. Grey attempts a smile. "She deserves no pity and no apology, Royce. China, you'll be wealthy beyond belief, and we'll protect you from the Destrehans. As a matter of fact, Mr. Cooper has come up with a most ingenious idea. He'll leave this morning to take your cousins on a well-planned wild goose chase and keep them occupied until Stephen recovers. Then we'll welcome you into our family as his wife."

"You're willing to risk your son's life for what I can give you?"

Mr. Cooper steps toward me, leans down, and takes my hands. "You must learn to live above your guilt, Miss Creed."

"Is that what you do?"

I feel him slip something—a small piece of paper?—into my fingers, and he releases my hands.

Mrs. Grey narrows her eyes. Did she notice our exchange? To distract her I say, "If I'm to be Stephen's bride, I insist upon one thing."

She raises her eyebrows. "An audacious little thing, isn't she?"

"I'm learning from the best, Mother Grey."

She laughs. "I could almost like you, China." Then she says, "Don't keep us in suspense. What is that one thing you insist upon?"

"When Stephen recovers, you'll help him establish a medical practice. He'll no longer be your business partner."

She tilts her head. "Of course. Whatever you want."

I'm not naive enough to believe her. She's staked out the battleground, and I am the enemy.

CHAPTER THIRTY

I seek asylum in my room. Dawn reveals gray skies, and a scuttling wind adds its voice to the noise that rises from the streets. Autumn has turned its face toward winter. I reach into my pocket where I've placed Royce Cooper's note, but before I can read it, I hear a rap on my door, and Mrs. Grey calls my name. I slide the note back into my pocket.

"Come in," I say as I open the door, but she remains at the threshold.

"Stephen is sleeping peacefully," she says, "but the worst is yet ahead. No addiction lets loose easily." She pulls in a deep breath. "But on to more immediate things, China. Would you be willing to visit the Reverend Doctor Dix at Trinity Church?"

"Why?"

"I hope he'll agree to make regular visits while Stephen fights through the symptoms of withdrawal."

"Stephen isn't a believer."

"You think that's an adequate reason to withhold whatever strength he might garner from spiritual sources?"

For once I agree with her. "I'll go."

She looks at my face and shakes her head. "I can see you're distraught. You truly love my son, don't you?"

"I love the man I thought he was."

She lifts her hand toward my face, but I step away. "Ah, poor child," she says. "Don't worry. We'll keep you safe. After all, you belong to us."

"I belong to myself."

She smiles grimly. "No woman belongs to herself." She hands me a thick envelope secured with a wax seal. "You'll deliver this to the Reverend Doctor. The fact that it comes from your hands may influence him toward mercy."

She leaves, and I lock the door. I take Royce Cooper's paper from my pocket. His note is not what I expect. He begins with an unseemly salutation, *My dear China*, which immediately puts me on guard. Then he writes, *I'm sure you feel a sense of betrayal. I should have told you that Stephen was addicted to opium and that I work for the Grey family. My loyalty is to Stephen, not his mother. Our friendship spans many years, and much of what I am I owe to him and his father who generously funded my education.*

My job allows me to pay for the board and schooling of my two sisters. I cannot send them into the world dependent on others.

My plans for the Destrehans are only the beginning of a greater machination that will allow you and Mrs. Settle to claim the freedom you deserve. In the past, Stephen's physical recovery from periods of addiction has taken about two months, which gives us a window of opportunity. Please do all you can to postpone your marriage, and burn this letter after you read it. I ask nothing else.

Your Willing Servant,

Royce Cooper

He asks nothing else? Untrue. He asks for my trust, and, for all I know, Mrs. Grey dictated his letter.

My breakfast is tea and muffins, brought to my room on a tray. Lillico helps me into one of my more somber church gowns then dresses my hair. When she's done, I make a quick detour to Miz Settle's room and explain my visit to the minister. Miz Settle is already packing.

"When can we leave?" she asks.

"Tonight. We'll walk to the depot and buy train tickets. You have it in you to make that long walk?"

"I do. Where do we go from there?"

"Chicago first. Then maybe Canada, maybe California."

"Money came to me last night, Sheba. Three hundert dollars."

"Good. We'll need it."

She reaches into her bag and pulls out a stethoscope. "This came, too."

"How did that happen?"

"I don't know. It musta been in my wishes all these years. Better with us than in Mr. James's store still waitin' for a buyer."

How can I argue against that?

Scot drives me to the church in the Grey's carriage. We're halfway there when I remember that I didn't burn Mr. Cooper's letter. It's still the pocket of my Missouri skirt. Safe, I assure myself. Sleet has left a layer of ice on the street, and, of necessity, Scot keeps the horses to a slow walk. When we arrive at the church, he helps me down and promises to wait.

A woman, neatly dressed in a dark skirt and belted shirtwaist, greets me at the door and escorts me back to a small anteroom. The room has no windows, but a gas sconce sheds adequate light. The only furnishings are two chairs, thickly padded, and a small side table between them. I'm there less than five minutes when the door opens, and to my surprise, Dr. Broward walks in.

He sits in the other chair and stares at me intently. I return his stare, and he says, "The Reverend Doctor Dix has asked me to discuss a delicate situation with you. It will impact his decision concerning Stephen, and I must ask that you forgive my brutal honesty."

Something akin to sorrow tightens my throat. Will I ever be able to cast Stephen out of my soul?

"Miss Creed, it's feared that Dr. Grey's current problems are the result of an attempted suicide."

My stomach cramps. Suicide? Could Stephen see no way out for himself but death?

"It would mean a great deal if you could bolster the premise that his overdose was merely the result of miscalculation."

I take a moment to gather my thoughts. My voice quivers as I speak. "He often—" I clear my throat and start again. "He often expressed a desire to protect me."

"From?"

The best answer would be greed, but I suppose that Mrs. Grey hasn't told the doctor about my abilities. "From my cousins."

"A problem of inheritance?"

"More or less."

"Good. If Dr. Grey wanted to protect you, he surely wouldn't attempt suicide."

The door behind us opens, but I answer Dr. Broward's question. "No, he wouldn't."

I shift in my chair, intending to turn toward whoever entered the room, but suddenly someone grabs my bonnet and pulls my head backward.

The bonnet ties cut painfully across my throat, and the bones at the back of my neck crackle. I reach toward Dr. Broward, cry out for his help, but he jumps up and backs away. I clasp the wrists of my assailant, but a cloth descends over my face, and I choke on a sweet, pungent smell. My consciousness fades.

The last words I hear are Dr. Broward's. "Well done, Mr. Cooper. Well done."

PART V

HOPE

From Ma Mère's Song:

The eyes play the game.

CHAPTER THIRTY-ONE

When I regain consciousness, I scan my surroundings, and shock stops my breath. I lie within a small dank cell. A barred window, high behind my narrow bed, lets in light. A small eye-height glass pane pierces the heavy door. The noise of the streets—carriages, horse hooves, the cries of hawkers—is replaced by a murmur of voices cut through by shrieks. Dear God in Heaven, where am I?

I've heard horror stories of The Tombs, a prison built in the Five Points slum area of New York City. Could I be in that terrible place? My heart begins a frantic dance. I sit up, and my head swims. Fear closes my throat and strangles my thoughts, but I swing my legs over the side of the bed. My feet are clad in coarse woolen socks, and I'm wearing a shapeless cotton dress. My gloves are gone as is my beautiful opal and diamond ring. I clasp my hands at my midriff. No corset. I peer down the gaping neck of the dress. At least I still wear my own pantalets and chemise.

I slowly get to my feet and shuffle to a wall. I feel as if I move within a dream, and I flatten my hands against the rough bricks to keep my balance. The remnants of whatever they used to knock me out must still course through my veins. I make my way to the door. It's locked. Its window is clean, and I can see a corridor and a door opposite mine. A heavy hasp and lock bind that door to its jam. No doubt mine is secured in the same way. I call out to be released, but no one comes. I continue calling until my dread becomes anger, and I begin to scream.

"What idiot put me here? Who are you? Where are you? Let me out!" I pound the door until the bones of my hands ache.

Does Mrs. Grey know I'm here? If she does, what possible motive would she have for incarcerating me here? Was my behavior at the engagement party so terrible that she decided to remove me from all decent society?

Ma Mère's calm voice comes to me. *Get control of yourself, China. Think this through.*

I hobble back to the bed and sit down. My bedding consists of a yellowed sheet and a scratchy wool blanket. I wrap the blanket around my shoulders, hoping to ease the chill that is working its way into my bones.

My thoughts flit back to Trinity Church and the letter I was to deliver. Despite my resolve to leave Stephen—or perhaps because of it—I agreed to that mission of mercy. How could I be so stupid? Mrs. Grey hadn't penned the Reverend Doctor's name on her wax-sealed envelope. I doubt the minister even knows I came to his church.

Even if Mrs. Grey believes I'm no longer worthy to be Stephen's wife, she would be reluctant to lose the golden goose who can grant her great wealth. What better place to have me available for her every whim than here? My anger, my frustration, however, are more directed at my gullibility than her avarice, and, to my surprise, I find that I'm far more destressed to know Royce Cooper held the cloth over my face.

His note to me was a lie. I'm beyond broken.

Daylight fades into evening. The room grows colder. My teeth chatter. A weak glow seeps in through the door window, and I keep my eyes on that tiny square of muted light, hoping to see what manner of demons guard my cell. I call out for food, for water. No one comes. That night, my sleep is plagued by dreams of devils, and each time I summon enough courage to fight with teeth and fists and nails, my hands are suddenly chained, my ankles shackled.

I awaken when dawn brightens the high window. Distant yelps and rattling bars echo. My tongue is thick. I sit slumped on the edge of my bed, but as I shake off the remnants of my nightmares, my fear becomes anger, and my anger turns into determination. They will not defeat me.

I yank the thin mattress from the bed. As I'd hoped, a sling of rope netting is woven across the frame. I lift the head of the bed and brace it high against the wall. I climb the ropes until I'm able to see out the window. I'm no longer in the city. The grounds are well-kept, shrubbery protected against the cold with burlap wraps. A cobbled path leads away from the building in a wide curve that ends at a gated stone wall. Beyond the gate, a dirt road bisects a field of stubble.

Two people walk toward the gate—Mrs. Grey and Dr. Broward, his head bent toward her as she clasps his arm. A carriage drives into view. Scot sits upon the seat. My heart twists. Was he also one of my betrayers?

A footman opens the gate, and, when Mrs. Grey climbs into the carriage, Dr. Broward turns toward the building, his lips pursed as if he's whistling. I remember his reference to an institute, a hospital perhaps. Is that where I am?

I climb down the netted ropes and wrestle the bed back into place. I don't want my captors to discover I've devised a way to see out. I smooth the rough sheet over the mattress, but I keep the blanket for a shawl. I startle when I hear the scrape of a key in the door lock. A sturdy young man dressed in white coveralls peers in.

"You're to come with me, Missus," he says.

Again fear scrambles my thoughts. The unknown is a fierce adversary. I follow the man into a short corridor painted pale green. Thick metal doors close it off at each end. My escort leads me toward the door on the left. Removing a small silver bell from his pocket, he shakes it into an irritating ring. A lock springs, and the door swings open. We step into another corridor, which has a similar door at the far end. Two cells also open onto this hallway, and their occupants are far from silent. I shiver at the cacophony of anger, anguish, and lunacy.

"This is an asylum," I say.

"Eyup, what'd you think it was?"

"Jail."

"And why would you be in jail, Missus?"

"Why would I be in an asylum?"

Another young man in a white coverall joins us. My keeper jerks his thumb toward me. "Missus wants to know why she's here."

They laugh.

The next door is not locked. My escort pushes me into a large room paneled in book-matched walnut. Women sit on chairs and sofas. A few of them chat as if they were paying a social visit. Some stare off into nothing. They're dressed in serviceable, clean garments, without the patches or ragged selvages that mar the gown I wear.

"You might land here, Missus, if you learn to behave yourself." A portly matron comes toward us, keys dangling from a loop of chain at her waist. She carries a sheath of papers. "I'll take her."

We traverse another hallway and ascend a curving staircase. At the top of the stairs, the matron raps sharply on a paneled door then opens it. The office is large. At the far end, Dr. Broward sits behind an ornate walnut desk.

"I've brought your patient."

"Thank you, Mrs. Godfrey."

The matron hands him the papers. "These are hers. Now, if you don't need me, Sir—"

"As a matter of fact, Mrs. Godfrey, I'd like you to stay."

He gestures toward two straight-back wooden chairs set in front of his desk. A small round table rests between them. It holds a pot of fragrant tea and a plate of frosted cookies. It takes all my willpower not to rush over and cram my mouth full. Mrs. Godfrey sets her hand at the small of my back and pushes me toward the chair on the right. As we sit down, the doctor fills the nib of his pen from an inkwell.

When the doctor finally looks up, I say, "Dr. Broward, why have you done this to me?" I pull at the sleeve of my ragged gown. "And why am I dressed like this?"

He ignores my questions and speaks to Mrs. Godfrey. "Has Miss Creed been fed yet this morning?"

"No Sir."

"Nor had anything to eat or drink since yesterday morning," I add.

"What?" He glares at the matron. "Pour her some tea, Mrs. Godfrey."

She fills a cup and hands it to me. The first sip scalds my mouth, but I swallow it and help myself to the cookies. They are hard and stale and delicious. As I drink and eat, Dr. Broward folds his hands on his desk and commences a conversation with Mrs. Godfrey.

"She suffers from hallucinations and delusions of grandeur," he states.

Mrs. Godfrey nods. "Yes."

I interrupt. "That's ridiculous."

"Then may I ask you, Miss Creed," says the doctor, "how do you know Mrs. Alberta Grey?"

"I'm engaged to marry her elder son."

He turns to Mrs. Godfrey. "Miss Creed's delusions—that she has ties to a prominent family—are not that unusual, you understand."

I lean forward and stare into his eyes. "You're saying I have no connection to the family?"

"No, I'm not. You were employed by the Greys as a seamstress and lacemaker."

"I'm Dr. Stephen Grey's fiancée."

He sighs and shakes his head.

"Her prognosis?" Mrs. Godfrey asks.

"Hopeful. Perhaps with treatment she'll reclaim mental stability. Others have."

I slap my hand on his desk. My teacup, balanced on my lap, rattles on its saucer. "Dr. Broward, I was born in a log cabin to very poor parents. After the death of my father, my mother raised me on what she could earn as a lacemaker. That doesn't sound like grandeur to me. Does it to you?"

"What were you wearing when you last left the Grey home, Miss Creed?" he asks.

"A silk dress." I splay the fingers of my left hand. "Doeskin gloves, an opal ring."

He looks at Mrs. Godfrey. "What was Miss Creed wearing when she arrived here?"

"The very dress she has on, Sir."

I hold my arms out, spreading the blanket like wings. "And I suppose I was also wearing this blanket."

"Mrs. Godfrey?"

"No, of course not. The blanket's from her bed in Ward Four."

The doctor steeples his fingers, and I decide to complicate his world. He's surely turned mine into hell.

"What did Mrs. Grey promise you, Dr. Broward? Your greatest wish?"

He frowns.

"Did they tell you I have limits?"

"See, Doctor," says the matron. "She's crazy."

"Thank you, Mrs. Godfrey, you may go. Please return for Miss Creed in fifteen minutes."

She gives him a puzzled look but leaves the room. The doctor glowers at me. "What do you want, Miss Creed?"

"Freedom."

"Obviously, I can't give you that."

"Then I want assurance that my aunt, Jesse Settle, is safe and well. I want a warm shawl. I want three meals a day and a basin of water so I can wash my hands and face."

"That's all?"

"I'm not greedy, Dr. Broward. Unfortunately for me, most people are."

CHAPTER THIRTY-TWO

D r. Broward and I meet daily, and, at the end of each meeting, I must endure a moment of hand-holding. I ask for reciprocal gifts: a more suitable dress, a pair of serviceable shoes, and my mother's Spode plate. When they bring me the plate, I cry in joy over its beautiful cracked face.

I request the opportunity to socialize with other patients, which the doctor reluctantly grants. After a breakfast alone in my cell, I'm taken out to join the other women in the dayroom, first for a homily then for what the matron calls free time. I'm supplied with a needle, an embroidery hoop, and an assortment of colored threads. They don't trust us with scissors. I must raise my hand like a schoolchild and ask the attendant to cut my thread.

I hope it appears that I've reluctantly accepted my fate. I haven't. My acquiescence is a ploy to gain enough freedom to engineer my escape.

The second week, I'm allowed to eat my midday meal in the dining hall. A large square room, its water-stained ceiling is speckled with black mold. The matron assigns me to Table Two with three other women. My first meal there is served on a metal plate that holds a small portion of mashed turnips, a pile of green peas, and a questionable pale meat cut into small squares. Servers give me a large spoon and a tin cup filled with lukewarm tea.

When I address my tablemates, they don't comment; therefore, I begin a conversation with myself.

"The rain has stopped, Miss Creed," I say. "Yes, isn't that delightful," I answer. "It's difficult to eat a meal when rain pelts down at us from the ceiling. Although, the servers don't have to fill our teacups as often." I laugh. "How like you, Miss Creed, to see something good in every circumstance."

One of the women begins to smile. "I hate it when the rain gets my slippers wet," she whispers. "They squeak like mice."

I wink at her, and she asks, "What's your name?"

"China Creed."

"I'm Isobelle."

The server points at Isobelle and then at me. "Eat-don't-talk." But several times during the remainder of our meal, Isobelle and I share a smile.

That afternoon, the matron moves me from my secure cell to a larger, more comfortable room across from Isobelle's. Although the corridor is locked at each end, our rooms are not.

I'm by far the most popular inmate at the Broward Institute. Tuesday through Friday, Mrs. Grey's dearest friends visit me. We partake of tea and pitiful sandwiches in the Receiving Room, which is dank and over-filled with mismatched sofas and chairs. My visitors shake my hand and express concern for my health, and they grow wealthier at each visit. I keep my comments light, and sometimes I tease them about the costumes they wore to my engagement ball. "Have you crossed the Delaware recently, General Washington? I see you haven't lost your head yet, Marie Antoinette. Good luck with your kite, Mr. Franklin. May lightning strike."

Although, I keep my true goal hidden, anger lurks close. My thoughts often center on the savage institution of slavery. Although Mr. Lincoln freed the slaves, I've become more cognizant of the horror that was their lives. By the third week, I've plotted a bit of revenge. When my visitors touch me, I casually mention a piece of jewelry worn by another member of their social set. Who doesn't have a moment of longing when they envision a beautiful piece of jewelry? After a few robberies, they realize I'm setting them up. Eventually, everything is returned to the rightful owners, and Mrs. Grey threatens to return me to my original cell if I don't stop my vengeful tricks.

Mondays and Saturdays are reserved for her visits alone. Each time, I inquire after Stephen and Miz Settle, and I ask for a meeting with Mr. Cooper. She always makes the same reply. Stephen is recovering well. Miz Settle will soon return to Missouri via train. Mr. Cooper is away on business. The fourth Monday of my incarceration, she pulls a folded letter from her handbag and lays it on my lap. I scan the first few lines. It's the note Mr. Cooper told me to burn.

I toss it into the hearth fire, and Mrs. Grey laughs. "Why do you want a meeting with him?" she asks. "He's the one who applied the chloroform to your face at Trinity Church."

"I need to know why."

"As I told you, China, he's my employee, and employment requires loyalty. By the way, I have news of your aunt."

A chill of fear makes me shudder. "What happened?"

Mrs. Grey pats my hand and takes another sheet of paper from her handbag. "She's fine. She sent a telegram." With fumbling fingers, I open it.

Milksnake Missouri STOP am home STOP delivered two babies yesterday STOP grateful for train fare STOP Jesse Settle FULL STOP

I know it's a lie. Miz Settle would not return to Milksnake after Del Aubright burned down her cabin, and she never would have written *delivered two babies*. She would have said *caught two babies*. I can only hope she's taken refuge at Colony House, but I don't sleep that night. Not one hour, not one minute.

CHAPTER THIRTY-THREE

The next morning, I have difficulty making myself get out of bed, and I can swallow only a few bites of my breakfast gruel.

Then, as if she were sitting beside me, I hear Ma Mère's voice in my head. *And how will this behavior help Miz Settle?* At that moment I begin to make plans, using the strongest asset available to me—my cursed gift.

I engage other inmates in conversations. I ask about their childhoods and their hopes. I note their visitors. I'm quite sure some suffer from hexes, and, in honor of Miz Settle, I do what I can, countering curses with murmured Bible verses and whatever opposites I can obtain—salt to oppose bland despair, cobwebs to recapture lost memories, a scattering of dust to calm a troubled spirit.

Regarding my schemes to escape, I begin with Isobelle. She's docile, and, for the most part, the matrons and attendants ignore her. To my surprise, I discover that she's a gifted thief. She ably steals skeins of embroidery floss, and she's adept at helping herself to a tablemate's food. During one noon meal, I see her slip her spoon into my custard.

I've been waiting for that opportunity, and I shout, "Isobelle! What are you doing?"

She jumps, and several women in the room screech.

"For heaven's sake, Miss Creed," says Mrs. Godfrey, "what is the matter?"

I stand and lean across the table, kiss Isobelle's forehead. "Nothing. Nothing. I'm sorry."

Mrs. Godfrey rolls her eyes at me and says, "You've just lost your dessert. Return to your room please."

I don't smile until I'm out of sight. I achieved my purpose—to bring Isobelle into a state of emotion. Ma Mère and I discovered that my gifts flow more abundantly when summoned within a mindset of joy, anger, fear, or startlement.

That night, after lights out, I use clothing from my storage chest to sculpt the shape of a woman asleep on my mattress. Then I crouch at the far side of the bed as the night watchman pads through the hall. He peeks into my room then continues on his way, his keys jangling as he opens the heavy door to let himself into the next corridor. When he's gone, I sneak to Isobelle's room. She's asleep.

I make a quick search, and, when I find nothing unusual, I crouch in a corner where the watchman won't see me.

The floor is cold, and I long for my own warm bed. Then something slaps down beside me. I catch the scent of ink. It's a newspaper. Isobelle wanted a newspaper? What good will that do me? Almost immediately, a possibility comes to mind. I can use it to wrap Ma Mère's Spode plate, because I will take that plate with me when I escape. I time a careful retreat and tuck the newspaper at the back of my storage chest. A small flicker of hope glows within my mind.

Four days of surreptitious touches and kindly kisses yield a promising stash. From Miss Florence—the woman who forever folds paper into hats—a nurse's cap. Although our day nurse searches the hospital in great puzzlement, I find the cap before she does. I receive a long white pinafore from an inmate who'd once been a nurse. It smells of camphor, and the fabric has yellowed, but at a distance under an unbuttoned coat, it will do. In the room of an elderly woman whose husband comes each week to visit, I find a small leather pouch full of coins. Her days are plaited with confusion, but still, she covets her husband's money.

Other gifts come to me: a heavy overcoat, a greenback dollar, boots. Soon I have all I need except one thing—the keys. When I'm with my fellow inmates, I draw attention to Mrs. Godfrey's chain of keys. I make guessing games of which key opens which door, but the keys remain securely suspended from Mrs. Godfrey's belt.

Sundays we attend a church service in the stone chapel a short distance behind the hospital building. It's constructed of brownstone cut in large square blocks mortared with narrow seams. Each pew is dark and old, and we must brace our feet against the flagstone floor to keep from sliding out of the narrow, well-polished seats. The women sit on the left and the men on the right. An attendant wielding a long pole stands at the back of the sanctuary. If one of the men looks toward the women, the attendant strides down the aisle and raps the offender on the head. It's a disruptive process, and some of the more childlike inmates moan in dread.

On my ninth Sunday at the institute, eight of us women are crammed in our pew, a tight fit, but we're the warmer for it. Mrs. Godfrey sits at the aisle edge, her keys rest upon her lap like an abundant bouquet. I'm overwhelmed by my need for those keys and can scarcely breathe as fear, discouragement, and hope roil within me. When the minister opens the service with prayer, I bow my head, but I watch the women in our pew. Two sit with their eyes fixed upon the matron's keys.

One is a gray little mouse named Claurice, an elderly woman no larger than a ten-year-old. It's well known that she's drawn like a mockingbird to anything that gleams. She's the third woman to my left, and I cannot easily touch her. My friend Isobelle, who sits beside me, is the other woman watching those keys. I've discovered that on occasion she's overtaken by fits, which cause her to writhe violently on the floor. I've overheard discussions as to whether her problem is a fault within her brain or the result of a curse, but I've been present during two fits and was unable to cast away any hex.

During the middle of the sermon, Isobelle begins to tremble, and I realize another fit has come upon her. I wrap my arms around her so she won't slip to the stone floor. Soon the pew is cleared except for the two of us.

"She's having a fit," I say, trying to remember the word Stephen used to identify seizures. It comes to me as the minister strides toward us. "Epileptic," I tell him, quite sure my diagnosis is true. "Does someone have a piece of wood I can put in her mouth?"

My request seems to baffle them, and I try again. "A length of wood or a leather strap, something to keep her from biting her tongue."

The matron unbuckles her heavy belt and hands it to me then slips the chain of keys over her wrist. Isobelle's back arches upward in a stiff curve. I take off my church gloves and slide the belt into her mouth, getting bit in the process. A few minutes later, her body relaxes. After she's regained some strength, Mrs. Godfrey and I walk her back to the hospital building.

"You did fine, Miss Creed," Mrs. Godfrey says. "You have training as a nurse?"

"A midwife, but I've tended others taken by fits."

"Doctor Broward says you're making good progress."

"I'm glad to hear it."

"Maybe, when you're released, you might return as a staff member. They pay us decent and give us living quarters." She points out a gable roof that rises above a nearby grove of trees.

I reply with a blatant lie. "I would like that."

She nods at my left hand. "I don't mean to be rude, but I've wondered about your finger."

I understand her concern. Caregivers need to be aware of any patient who practices self-mutilation. "A rattlesnake bit me last summer. Mrs. Grey's son, Stephen, saved my life, but he couldn't save the finger. You know he's a doctor?"

"So I heard."

By then we're at the front door. Mrs. Godfrey selects the proper key and lets us inside. Here, the building retains the trappings of the mansion it once was. A wide sweeping stairway with wrought iron railings bisects the foyer, and a chandelier alight with gas lamps drips crystals. The shoddy reception desk, however, breaks the spell and seems all the more tawdry in its refined setting.

"Go to your room, Miss Creed," says Mrs. Godfrey in a kind voice. "You need a nice nap."

Perhaps I do, but I can't sleep. I pace and send my thoughts toward Isobelle. *Wish for the keys. Wish for the keys.* When she receives those keys—if she receives those keys—I must escape before Mrs. Godfrey realizes they're missing.

That night in Isobelle's room, to my relief and delight, the keys arrive but with such a loud clatter that Isobelle wakes up. When she recovers from her surprise, she asks, "Where'd you get them?"

I hear the joy of possibilities in her voice. I planned to escape alone, but how can I leave her behind? "I'm an able thief. Do you want to go home?"

"More than anything."

"Lie down and turn your back to the door. When the guard makes his next round, he'll think you're asleep. Quick now. I hear him."

She pulls the covers over her shoulders, and I crouch on the other side of the bed. He shines his lantern through the door window.

Isobelle whispers, "Please God, please, please, please."

The guard walks on. After I hear the hallway door open and close, I help Isobelle dress. Then I pull off my nightgown. Underneath, I'm wearing my warmest clothing, over it all the nurse's pinafore and my coat. Besides my clothing and the bag of coins, the only thing I'm taking with me is Ma Mère's Spode plate, secured between my corset and chemise. I place the nurse's cap on my head.

"Did you steal that cap?"

"I did."

She laughs. "We make a pretty pair, you and me. You ever pick pockets?"

"No."

"I'll teach ya."

I cover my mouth to hold in my laughter. We use spare clothing to model a sleeping person in Isobelle's bed. Then I whisper, "Next, the cloakroom," which is conveniently within our corridor.

The fourth key on the chain opens the cloakroom door. We let ourselves in, close the door, and lock it. All is dark. We decide what we can use by touch alone. Isobelle finds boots, and I find a good woolen scarf. It's December. Our greatest enemy may well be the cold.

I add another coat atop mine and find one for Isobelle. I hold my breath as the watchman's light shines under the edge of the door. When he exits the hallway, we slip out.

The largest key opens the hallway door, and I start toward the day room with its access to the foyer.

"Not the front door," Isobelle whispers. "The back is better. Through the kitchen."

For me, the kitchen is unknown territory, and I'm ready to dissuade her, but she says, "I work there three afternoons a week."

We battle again with the keys, my hands shaking. Finally, Isobelle jerks them away and chooses one as bright as new copper.

"Here's what you want," she says and unlocks the door.

I worry that the maids have already begun their early morning work, but the room is empty, the large stone fireplace giving off scant heat from banked coals. Against one wall, stone steps lead down to an outside door secured by a stout wooden bar set into brackets and also a padlock. I dislodge the bar and turn toward Isobelle, who still has the keys, "Which one?" I ask.

She looks at me, a strange light in her eyes and shakes her head then shakes it again. I don't realize she's having a fit until she teeters backward and collapses onto the stone steps. The keys fall, rattling against the floor. I gasp. Now what? My first choice is to leave Isobelle where she lies, escape without her, but how can I justify such betrayal?

I sit down and pull her to my lap then unpin the nurse's cap I wear and jam it between her teeth. Her mouth foams, and her back arches. My heart races, and I'm sick with apprehension. Isobelle flails out, hitting the side of my face with a bunched fist.

"Hush, hush," I tell her. "It's me. You're safe. They haven't found us."

I'm not sure God hears a thief's prayers, but, I beg Him for mercy. A few minutes later, Isobelle opens her eyes and pulls the nurse's cap from her mouth. She coughs and gathers in breath. She sits on the steps as I try various keys in the lock. Finally, one catches and opens the padlock.

"Do you think you can stand up, Isobelle? We need to leave."

"I will if it kills me."

I help her outside and softly close the door. Snow is falling. It slides down the back of my neck, melts into chilling rivulets. Isobelle leans heavily upon me, and my heart thunders with the effort of keeping her upright. We pass the church and a carriage house. Eventually, we reach an ancient stone wall that rises about four feet high.

"I can't climb it," Isobelle says, her voice a whispered wail.

"Of course you can," I tell her, but I'm sick with worry. I run my fingers over the stones and find one near the top that sticks out far enough to offer a handhold. "Here, Isobelle, grab this." She does. "Set your left foot into my hands. Pretend the wall is a horse."

I slowly boost her to the top. Although she's small, my arms tremble under her weight. "Swing your right leg over, Isobelle. Now!"

She swings her leg then flings herself upward until she's lying belly-down on the top of the wall. For one joyous moment, I believe we have a chance, but then Isobelle moans. In the moonlight, I see her eyes roll back into her head. She opens her mouth and chomps down hard on her tongue. I cry out in frustration, but I ease her body from the wall and down to the ground. Somewhere I've lost the nurse's cap. I pull off one of my gloves and bunch it between her teeth. Eventually, the seizure subsides, but she does not regain consciousness. I hug her close to keep her warm, and my hopes for freedom fade. Disappointment batters my heart, and I fight against nausea.

Ma Mère is suddenly beside me. *Don't despair, Mon Petit Lapin,* she says. *You will have another chance.*

I close my eyes, clinging to that hope, and finally I'm able to sing one of Ma Mère's lullabies, our secret language rising beautiful into the snowy night as I drift away to kinder days.

Their discovery of us is so long delayed that, if Isobelle had regained her senses, we might yet have escaped. Strange as that night turned out to be, stranger still is what happens next, because Stephen himself is the one who finds us.

I spot him striding through the tall winter-kill grasses of the yard. The oddity of him being there paralyzes me. Like any predator Stephen seems to know where I am, and, like an animal, winded by the chase, I accept defeat with quiet stoicism.

He stops a short distance away. "How can you be here?" I ask.

"I'm here often. You are my fiancée. I want the best for you."

What I want is to spit in his face, but I summon strength enough to remain civil. "You're well?"

"Not well enough to risk touching you." He nods toward Isobelle. "What happened? Did she fall?"

"I believe she had a seizure. The second of the night. She's had them before, but she always regains consciousness soon after."

He crouches beside us and places his hand on her forehead. "No fever. That's good. He pries open her mouth. "She bit her tongue."

"I know. How badly?"

"Not terrible." He checks her pulse and, still holding her wrist, looks at me. "You destroyed my plans."

"What plans?"

"Plans to get you out of here. Royce Cooper was going to help me."

"Royce Cooper helped your mother put me here."

Someone across the field calls Stephen's name. He stands and waves his arms. Soon Dr. Broward and his men are upon us.

Stephen gives orders—a stretcher for Isobelle, water, smelling salts. He doesn't answer me when I ask about Miz Settle, nor does he protest when Dr. Broward's men drag me back to the hospital. I'm locked into my original cell where I descend into despair. I ask about Isobelle, but they won't tell me anything. I barely sample the gruel I'm given for supper. Unable to sleep, I endure the night within a fog of anguish.

CHAPTER THIRTY-FOUR

The next morning, Mrs. Godfrey brings me a silk day dress from my time with the Grey family.

"I'm being taken somewhere?" I ask.

She doesn't answer.

"How is Isobelle?"

"Not good," she says. "You're in a heap of trouble, and I can't even feel sorry for you."

"Mrs. Godfrey, please know that I intended no harm. My heart is broken for her."

She presses her lips into a tight line. "Get that dress on. Now."

She leaves, and I change into the day dress. I've lost weight. Even without my stays, I can button it around my waist. I have no petticoat or stockings to protect my lower legs from the stiff cotton organdy of the skirt's flat-lining. It will rub my shins raw, but that's an insignificant problem compared to Isobelle's health. When Mrs. Godfrey returns, she brings me a hooded cloak, also from my Grey mansion wardrobe, deep blue velvet trimmed with ermine and lined with quilted silk. I fasten it at my neck and marvel at its elegance. Those weeks at the Grey mansion seem distant enough to be a dream.

"Shoes?" I ask, lifting my skirt to show my bare feet.

"Not until we're at the door," says Mrs. Godfrey.

"May I see Isobelle before I go?"

She heaves a deep sigh but takes me to the infirmary. Isobelle lies motionless upon a cot. I squeeze her hand, and my eyes seep tears.

"Enough," says Mrs. Godfrey. "Fools the both of you."

I kiss Isobelle's hand then follow Mrs. Godfrey from the room. She takes me to the foyer and points at a pair of stylish black leather boots beside the door. I slide my bare feet into them, and she hands me a button hook.

"Where am I going?" I ask as I bend to my task.

"Best you don't know."

She opens the door and a gust of ice-flecked wind swirls around us. I tuck my hands into the cloak through its side slits, and we leave the building. Two mismatched horses pull a ragged black sledge up to the open gate. The passenger compartment is completely enclosed, its one window covered with metal mesh. A blue-clad policeman opens the sledge door, jumps out, and folds down a set of steps.

Mrs. Godfrey squints at me. "A woman like you, pretty and smart. What a waste."

"Wait," I say in a strangled voice. "This can't be right."

"Right for you, Missus," says the policeman.

"She looks harmless to me," the driver calls down from his perch.

"She just about killt somebody yesterday, and she's a thief to boot," Mrs. Godfrey says. "The Tombs is the best place for her."

When I hear that hideous name, I panic. I gather my skirts in my hands and run down the lane, but, within a few steps, the policeman is upon me. He knocks me to the ground and twists my left arm behind my back. The earth is sheathed with ice, and the ice cuts my cheek. He yanks me up, drags me to the sledge, and thrusts me inside. He clambers in and produces a pair of black metal cuffs. I try to wrestle away, but he lifts a truncheon.

"I'll use it if I have to."

He forces my hands behind me and snaps the cuffs around my wrists. He closes the door. "Now sit there and behave yourself."

The driver snaps his whip. The horses pull, and the runners of the sledge let loose of their grip on the crusted driveway. My spirit shatters. When I lost Tommy Belnap, I had my mother, and, when I lost my mother, I had Miz Settle. Now I have no one. I'm scarcely aware when the sledge finally stops, and I offer no resistance when the policeman pulls me up from the seat and yanks me out the door to Leonard Street.

Lost as I am in some limbo of the soul, I take little notice of The Tombs building and its columned portico. I entertain no wonderment that the exterior of a notorious jail should exude luxury.

"The New York Halls of Justice and House of Detention," says the officer. "Looks fancy, don't it? Like nothing bad could happen inside, but men walk to their deaths in there, and I'm guessing a woman might, too." He grips my left arm in a non-too-gentle clutch.

People loiter on the sidewalks and the wide stairs. They draw back when they see the cuffs on my wrists. One boy, dressed in rags, darts out from a gathering of his mates to slap his hand against my shoulder. I stumble and crack my shin on the sharp edge of the next step. The officer shoves him away, and the boy is welcomed back to his gang with hoots of admiration. Several women hiss at me, and men make rude comments. I'm almost relieved when we enter the building.

Papers must be filled out. I am searched for weapons and other forbidden items. They take my handkerchief and the clips in my hair. I'm allowed my gloves and cape. My shoes are exchanged for felt slippers, sloppy on my bare feet.

The matron who searches me meets my eyes. "You don't look like a murderer," she says.

"I'm not," I tell her.

"I heard you're a thief, too."

How can I deny that?

The matron takes me to a cell in the top tier of the women's prison. No larger than six feet by eight, it contains a metal pot for night soil but no privacy for those necessary moments. A hard shelf serves as both bed and divan, and a high barred window lets in minimal light through dirty glass. The top half of the entrance door is also barred but gives me a view of the walkway. The stink of urine and rot makes me gag. Little doubt I'll soon be infested with lice and fleas.

The Broward Institute has prepared me for the shouts and moans of other inmates, but their language here is as filthy as our cells. Despair shreds my hope. I am nothing. I am no one. I pray for death.

They give us two daily meals, bland and sparse. Mid-morning, they prod us into an hour of exercise, during which we women of the upper tier walk around the balcony that fronts our cells. Women who've lost their exercise privileges delight to stand at their barred doors and spit on us as we pass.

The second day, Mrs. Grey comes to see me. A matron carries in a high-back wooden chair for her, and I sit on my shelf-bed. My empty soul serves as the perfect breeding place for hate. If my eyes could kill, Mrs. Grey would be dead.

She affects a strange ebullience, chatting as if we were old friends. I say very little, but, when she assures me, once again, that Miz Settle is home safe in Missouri, I can't help but reply.

"Don't lie," I tell her. "Remember. I saw the telegram. Aunt Jesse doesn't talk like that. She would never say that she delivered two babies. The word is *caught*. She caught two babies."

Mrs. Grey frowns.

"Tell me where she is. You think they can get to me before I have a strangle hold on your throat?"

She jumps up and stands behind her chair as if its sturdy oak could stop me. She stammers, "I don't hold any ill will toward you or your aunt, China."

"Of course not," I say sarcastically.

"Fine, don't believe me, but I did buy her a train ticket to Missouri, first class, and I also gave her spending money."

I laugh.

"I did."

"And she left?"

"She packed and left, taking nothing beyond what she'd brought with her. Scot drove her to the Depot, and that's all I know."

Could Miz Settle still be in the city, waiting for me to find her? The thought gives me reason for hope.

"You believe me?" Mrs. Grey asks.

"Maybe."

She takes my answer as an invitation, removes her gloves, and leans over the chair, extending her hands toward me. "Another wish."

"You won't be happy if I get hold of your hands, Mrs. Grey."

She hisses and backs against the door, yells for the guard to let her out.

Her fear empowers me. "Don't expect anything from me, Mrs. Grey, unless you reciprocate."

When the guard arrives, Mrs. Grey sneers at me and says, "We'll do what we can, China, but you've managed to get yourself into a most difficult predicament. Especially if that woman at the Institute dies."

Part of me wants to beg for information about Isobelle, but Mrs. Grey is an artful liar. Why demean myself by begging when I can't trust what she tells me? I'm sure, if Isobelle dies, I'll know soon enough. The guard opens the door, and Mrs. Grey walks out onto the balcony. She gives my jailer a brittle smile and points at the chair. "Please allow her to keep that chair," she says as if she owns the world.

"No, Ma'am," the guard says. "She might jump off it."

Mrs. Grey looks puzzled.

"If I decide to hang myself," I tell her.

I laugh at the horror on her face. The guard drags the chair out onto the balcony and shuts the door of my cell.

Mrs. Grey shakes her head as if to collect her thoughts, and then she says, "My friends will come to visit, China, even if you must be bound and gagged."

"Warn them about the lice."

She gasps and removes a handkerchief from her sleeve, presses it to her nose. Its lavender scent wafts toward me as she hurries away from my door.

Her friends begin their visits on my second week. How desperate they must be to come to my dismal cell. They ask how they can make my life more comfortable, and I accumulate a wealth of luxuries: a cellar of salt, a pillow, a quilt, soft woolen socks, a washbasin and towel, Ma Mère's French Bible. Lillico, poor woman, comes to rid me of lice prior to Mrs. Grey's Saturday visits.

I make plans, and on Mrs. Grey's third visit, I tell her that I have a proposition.

She rearranges her skirts. "That sounds worrisome."

"Just listen."

"I'm all ears."

"Mrs. Grey, you are making your friends wealthy."

"Wealthier."

"Yes. Don't you think you deserve compensation for what you do?"

"China, the Grey accounts have swelled considerably, not only because of your gifts, but also because—" She pauses. "Because of preferences given our family when it comes to information and opportunity."

"Mrs. Grey, history remembers philanthropists. You could be touted as New York's greatest benefactor, one who inspires others to follow your example.

She almost smiles. "How do you propose that should happen?"

"A tithe."

"A what?"

"Ten percent of whatever they receive from me."

"You mean they'd donate to some godly work?"

"Yes. Hospitals, libraries, orphanages, maybe medical research, and your name and the donor's name would be on every bequest."

She strokes the fine wool of her skirt. Finally, she says, "I'll need to consult my lawyers. But if I decide to do this, may I tell my friends it was at your request?"

"If that would make it more palatable for them."

"It probably would."

She opens the rather large tapestry bag she brought with her and hands me a brown-paper wrapped book. She watches as I open the wrappings. *Great Expectations* by Charles Dickens, the 1862 edition from Chapman and Hall. It's truly a kind gift, regardless of motivating factors, and I thank her sincerely. I open the book and inhale the heady aroma of ink on paper, a far more beautiful scent than the lavender of her lace handkerchief.

The next five days, I receive no visitors but on Saturday morning, when Lillico has finished fine-combing my hair, I'm escorted from my cell to a small dank room that smells of mildew. Two chairs sit behind a narrow table. A worn rug, damp at one edge, covers most of the cement floor. My jailer that day is a large, broad-shouldered woman with a heavy-boned face and a hoarse voice. I know her only by her last name—Kreeg. She checks her pocket watch. "Visitors coming. Ten minutes."

During my incarceration, I've lived with the constant and under-lying fear of an unknown future. When she gives me no more details than that, my mouth grows dry, and my heart judders within my chest. Who will come? A judge? Members of a jury? Has Isobelle died? I know very little about the process of justice in New York City. If Isobelle is dead will I be hanged as a murderer?

Mrs. Grey is the first to arrive. She's carrying a sheaf of papers, and she greets me with a kiss. "China, we're about to do as you requested."

My arms grow limp with relief. "The tithe?"

"Yes."

She sits down, and pats the seat of the chair beside her. When I'm settled, she sets the papers on the table before us.

Within a few moments, a gentleman—one of my usual visitors—arrives, but this time he's brought his spouse. She's a plump little thing, trussed up in a dress awash with ruffles. She presses a hankie to her nose and gives her husband a look that's anything but loving. Mrs. Grey hands the husband the first paper in her stack.

"This is your contract," she says. "Please read it and affirm that my lawyers have correctly listed your legal name and choice of charity." She leans toward me and whispers, "Remove your gloves, China."

I take off my gloves and lay them in my lap.

When the gentleman finishes reading, he says, "All in order, Mrs. Grey." He signs and dates the contract then offers me his open hands.

"May I ask your choice of charity?" I say.

He raises his eyebrows at Mrs. Grey, and she shrugs. "I suppose she has the right to know."

"And if she doesn't approve?"

"You'll receive no wishes," I tell him.

The wife hisses, and Mrs. Grey laughs nervously. "China, for goodness sakes."

"The charity?" I ask again.

"Manhattan Eye, Ear, and Throat Hospital. Building maintenance."

I set my hands in his.

His wife is next, and she raises her upper lip in disgust when she notices the stump of my amputated finger, but whatever she wants must be paramount, because she takes my hands in a firm clasp. Her charity is an orphanage.

Forty people come, and every charity is admirable: libraries, orphanages, parks, hospitals, churches, and homes for fallen women.

When all forty have signed, made their wishes, and left, Mrs. Grey produces her contract, a promise to donate one hundred dollars monthly to Colony House. When she's done wishing, she looks into my eyes and says, "And that is the last time you'll see them, China."

Fear tightens my throat. "The last time? Am I to be hanged?"

She laughs. "Of course not. That woman is well recovered. Didn't anyone tell you?"

I sigh my relief. "Thank God."

"Direct your thanks to Dr. Broward," she says. "Anyway, we have far better plans for you than a death penalty."

Has she decided to keep me solely for herself? Will she go ahead with the wedding? I'm foolish enough to ask. "Stephen and I will marry?"

"What? Of course not! Do you think after what happened to my son, I'd allow you to marry him? He almost died because of you."

"He almost died because of himself, Mrs. Grey."

Her laughter is bitter. "Truth be told, China, I've found that you're as much a liability as an asset. Therefore, I've sold you to the Destrehans."

"Sold me? Slavery is illegal in this country now."

"Come, China, you're not stupid. Surely by now you've realized that people with wealth and power follow a different set of rules. The Destrehans offered three million dollars. How could we refuse? I'll return Monday for our final farewell, and then you are theirs."

She leaves, and Kreeg escorts me back to my cell. Each breath I draw seems to scald my throat. Is there nothing in this world stronger than greed?

That same evening, shortly after I've finished a supper of cabbage soup, Kreeg looks into my cell. "Ya got visitors," she says.

This late in the day?

She unlocks my door, and her smile makes me believe that my visitors won entry with a hefty bribe. I prepare myself for Julien and François, but, to my surprise, Scot steps into the cell. Has Mrs. Grey also allowed him a wish? Well, he earned it, patient as he was teaching me to ride a horse sidesaddle.

"I brung somebody with me, Miss Creed."

Philip enters the cell, and joy bubbles up within me, so sudden that I laugh.

Kreeg closes the door and locks it. "Ten minutes," she says and leaves.

"A wish for you, Scot?" I ask.

"Ach! 'Tis not the reason I'm here, but I might ask ye to conjure up something for my missus."

"Nothing alive, nothing too large," I tell him as I kiss his cheek.

Then I take off my gloves and clasp Philip's hand. "I've missed you, dear Philip. Wish well."

"I'm very good with wishes," he says.

"Only ten minutes," Scot whispers. "Be quick about it, Lad."

"Quick about what?" I ask.

"No questions, no arguments," says Philip as he steps away from me. "Take off your cloak and your dress. Remember, I can't see you."

Scot turns his back and looks out through the barred door, but I'm struck dumbfounded as Philip removes his caped overcoat and then his suit coat, pants, and shirt. "You have the dress ready for me?" he asks, standing there in his white drawers and undervest.

"What?"

"China, I told you to get undressed."

At that moment, I realize why they've come. "You can't stay in this place, Philip."

"You'd deny me my first chance at gallantry?"

"Hurry up!" Scot hisses.

I remove my bodice and help Philip get his arms into it. It's tight at his shoulders, but loose, of course, across the chest. I don his shirt then step out of my skirt and pull on his pants. His legs are a bit longer than mine, which means the pant legs will fold over my boots, a beneficial circumstance, because his feet are large. We won't be able to trade shoes. I help him step into my skirt.

"Ye decent?" Scot asks.

"Yes," I gasp, "But what about Philip's hair?"

Scot pulls a white wig from under his cloak. It's fixed into a messy bun. Philip tugs it on, and I tuck in stray strands of his hair. I tie my cloak around his neck.

"Where's your bed?" he asks.

I guide him to it. He lies down, and I pull the blanket high over his face. "How can I let you do this, Philip? You and Scot must be breaking the law."

"Likely," says Scot, "but me and my missus are off and away at the crack of dawn, and hoping your gift gets to us before we leave."

Philip laughs. "My mother won't allow her youngest son to be incarcerated for any length of time. At least I hope not."

"She has a great amount of money coming her way from my cousins," I say.

"I know about her deal with the Destrehans, but my brother asked me to do this for you, and I promised I would."

My heart squeezes tight into itself. "Stephen asked?"

"What other brother do I have?"

"He did," says Scot as he pushes Philip's bowler hat down over my head. He helps me into Philip's caped coat and turns the collar up. "There. Can't see nothing of your hair." He removes a red bandana from his pocket. "Hold that up over your nose and mouth, like the smell be terrible, which it is." He looks at his watch. "Two minutes, Philip."

I lean over Philip and kiss the side of his face. "Remember you're blind," he says.

I lose my breath at that thought. "Where's your cane?"

"They wouldn't let me bring it in. They promised to give it back when we left, but don't reach for it. Let Scot fetch it. You're blind, China. Tell yourself that at every step."

I pat Philip's shoulder. "No matter what happens, I'll love you always, Little Brother."

I hear footsteps on the walkway. Scot hisses at me, and I take his arm, holding the bandanna over my face and lowering my head. Philip begins a gentle weeping, very much like a woman might sound.

Scot huffs and says to Kreeg, "A right ninny she be, getting herself into this mess." We leave the cell. Kreeg locks it and follows us. The unlighted cells are sinking into the darkness of dusk.

You're blind, I tell myself, fixing my eyes straight ahead. To my surprise, Scot punches my shoulder. I nearly squawk at the blow.

"Your mother ever finds out you're sweet on that woman, Master Philip, ye'll have hell to pay, and I will, too, for bringin' ye here."

I nod my head.

"Stairs," Scot says as he pulls me to a halt. "Starting right here." He counts aloud and stops at fourteen.

I manage the steps and the long walk to the outside doors. I feel Scot reach toward something, but I don't look.

"Cane," he says and hands it to me.

I hold the bandanna over my face with my left hand and take the cane in my right. I move it side to side as Philip does, occasionally tapping the tip against the floor. We exit the building.

"Steps," Scot bellows again. He takes my arm and counts.

Then we're on the sidewalk. "Our sleigh is a block away," he whispers. "No mincing steps now. You're a man, walk like it."

Snow clouds bulk heavy in the darkening sky, and despite the hour, the sidewalks are crowded. I sidestep a boy who dashes past us. "No," Scot hisses. "Let me pull ye out of the way."

It's hard to trust another to be your eyes, especially when you can see what's coming, but we avoid all collisions and finally arrive at the sleigh. Scot helps me up to the driver's seat where we sit side by side. I realize I've been holding my breath since I left the cell. I breathe in, which makes me cough.

"Knees apart," Scot whispers as he flicks the whip over the horses' backs.

I blush, but I set Philip's cane between my feet. Hope batters against my heart, but I can't give it entry. I've been betrayed too many times.

"Can you tell me where we're going?" I ask.

"Grand Central Depot. Ye got train tickets to Missouri."

"I'm still trying to find Miz Settle, you know."

"Miz Settle? Your aunt?"

"Yes."

"She's back in Missouri. I drove her to the Depot myself. First-class tickets. Couldn't afford to get but second class for you. Sorry."

"Second class is wonderful. Thank you for driving Miz Settle."

I'm still sure she's in New York, but why worry Scot about that? I stare straight ahead as the night presses close. The lamplighters are at work.

"It's December now?" I ask.

"December twenty-third."

I was supposed to marry Stephen on the twenty-fourth. I can't regret that cancellation, but what if he'd been the man I thought he was? "Two days before Christmas," I say, trying to keep the hurt out of my voice.

"Count this as a Christmas present from me and Philip."

A feel a pang of guilt, thinking of Philip lying in my dark, flea-ridden cell. "It's a wonderful present, and I'll always be grateful."

"Just don't get caught."

We drive the many blocks to Grand Central Depot, and, when we arrive, Scot hands me a small roll of greenbacks. He takes Philip's cane and lays it in the sleigh's footwell. He grins at me. "'Spect he'll be wanting this. Ye got your sight back now, but remember, you're still a man. Act like one. Feet solid on the ground, good long steps, shoulders back. I'll never forget you, Lassie."

"Nor I you." My debt is so very great to so many. "Wish again," I tell him. I pull off my right glove and tweak his chin.

Then he's gone, and I'm standing alone with a ticket in my hands that will take me home. I go inside the Depot, find a ticket booth, and trade my fare for cash money. I can't leave New York without finding Miz Settle, and, if Colony House was not the haven she hoped, I suspect she would go to Central Park. She knows how to coax a living from the wilderness, and Central Park is nearly that.

Outside, snow is falling, but, despite the slush on the streets, hansom cabs still seek passengers. When a driver calls to me, I nod at him and clasp the brim of my bowler.

"No luggage?" he asks.

"Nope." I keep my voice low.

"Where to?"

"Central Park."

I climb into the cab, a much easier task when wearing pants. I settle into the seat, and the horse trots us into the flow of traffic. After a while, I lift the flap that covers the front window. As I gaze out, I'm quite sure we're near the Merchants Gate of Central Park.

I call up through the roof of the cab.

The driver slows the horse. "You want out here?"

"Yeah."

He stops, and I pay him the fare. Then I shove my hands into the pockets of Philip's coat and walk into the benevolent wilderness that Mr. Olmsted and Mr. Vaux provided for the people of New York and for me.

CHAPTER
THIRTY-FIVE

The Ramble is the best place to hide, but it's too dark to venture toward that fetching wilderness. Instead, I settle in a sheltered corner under one of the park's many arches. Afraid that the cold will lull me into a death sleep, I stand every little while to stomp my feet and flex my fingers.

By morning I'm stiff and hungry, but at least the snow clouds have dissipated, allowing me an eastward view of the pale December sun. There are few park visitors, and I decide I'm safe enough to explore. I haven't walked far into the Ramble when I happen upon a series of stone steps nearly hidden by ice-crusted undergrowth. They lead down to a small cave tucked deep into the earth. Royce Cooper had never mentioned that cave, and I'm surprised to find it, but it suits me well.

I gather windfall branches for fuel and twist lower boughs from nearby cedar trees. The trees will dissipate the smoke from any campfire I coax into being, and the boughs will serve as my bed, but I won't return to the cave until night. If Mr. Cooper learns of my escape, he may tell searchers to look for me in The Ramble. I'll make myself scarce during the day.

I venture to the shores of The Lake, taking care to avoid park workers and policemen. The cold weather has already layered the water with ice thick enough to draw skaters, although only two young men are out this early. They call to me, but I pretend not to hear. I enter a portable shelter that's been set on one shore where I find a scattering of buttered popcorn on the ground. I do not waste one kernel.

When the young men head off the ice toward the shelter, I hurry away, my hands again tucked into the wide patch pockets of Philip's coat. I notice a flock of pigeons settling near a park bench. An elderly man and woman are feeding them. I wait at a distance until the couple leaves. Then I kick through the snow where the pigeons were and find a few scraps of bread, which serve as my midday meal.

At every curve in the trails, I see Royce Cooper, his bright eyes, his crooked smile. I hear the joy in his voice. How could a man who finds delight in dells and lakes so viciously betray a friend? I banish him from my mind, but Miz Settle comes in to take his place, and pieces of my heart spall off like frost-heaved shale.

For two days, I search the park until I'm sure Miz Settle is nowhere about. The third day, I decide to risk a journey to Colony House. Perhaps Harriet Hamilton considers me enough of a friend to keep my whereabouts secret from the Grey family. Perhaps she'll lend me a bed for the night. Perhaps I'll find Miz Settle.

It's a long, bitter walk. A scouring wind funnels between the buildings, assaulting me until my bones ache. Miz Settle swirls so often into my thoughts that it seems as if she treads beside me. I stop and look about to be sure she doesn't, but I am alone amidst the strangers who scurry though the slush of the sidewalks. I'm beset by dread. Has Miz Settle died? Is that why I feel her near? Suddenly my legs no longer support me, and I sink into the dirty snow of the sidewalk.

A ragged boy hovers over me. "Hey now, my good man," he says. "Are ya all right? Can I help ya up?" As he grabs my right arm, he shoves his hand into my pocket.

I push him away. "Get off me!" My voice sounds harsh, broken.

"Just tryin' to help, ya bloody bastard," he says.

He runs off with something in his hand, and I realize that he stole the crust of bread I'd taken from the pigeons that morning, both thieves, the two of us. I stand and stomp my feet, brush off my pant legs, and continue walking. By the time I see the brick façade of Colony House, I'm exhausted beyond thought. A sheltering porch at the entryway offers respite from the wind. I blow warm breath into my hands then notice the poster pinned on the door. The line drawing of my face is surprisingly accurate. Under the picture, in bold black letters, a ten thousand dollar reward is promised to the person who brings me in, unharmed, to the New York City police. Fear claws my heart, and my lungs seize. I bend double to stop the spasms.

When I'm breathing again, I cross the street, my collar raised, Philip's bowler hat smashed tight down upon my head. I find a niche on the leeward side of a fish market where I'm able to see the Colony House door. Maybe Miz Settle is there with Harriet Hamilton. Maybe some errand will bring her outside.

I wait until dusk shadows the streets. No one leaves Colony House, and only two ragged women enter. A newsboy pins up more notices about me. A shoddy-looking man studies one of the posters.

"You catch 'er, you'll be rich," says the boy, his voice rising above the wind.

It's enough to make me abandon my hiding place and start back toward the park. Darkness settles, and I silently bless the lamplighters as they illuminate the streets. Hours later, I enter the park and struggle back to my cave. I light a fire, my teeth rattling, and, when I'm adequately warm, I fall into a sleep so bottomless that no nightmare dares intrude.

Even on the most bitter and stormy days, I search out the park's natural bounty. I blanch acorn kernels and grind them into coarse-grained flour. A stout stick, its tip hardened by the coals of my fire, serves as a hoe to dig up cattail bulbs. I roast them and strip the edible starch away from the fibers with my teeth. I boil the tips of maple and birch branches to make a tea, slightly sweet, and I find a patch of ramps, their tops still green under the snow. I cut frozen honey-filled wax from the bee tree. The honey fills my belly, and the wax soothes my lips. On rare warm days, the squirrels leave their winter lairs, and I hunt them with a throwing stick.

I'm amazed by how many things people leave behind. In the Skating House, I find coins nearly every day, and to my delight, I come across a broken skate blade that serves as an adequate knife. I rescue an abandoned woolen scarf and a beautiful poetic book by Henry David Thoreau called *Walden*. His words help me maintain my sanity, for I live more often within my head than in the real world, and sometimes, mostly at night, I confuse the two.

Again, I lose track of the days. I've no idea how long I've been in the park. Years, it seems, but winter has never yet given way to spring.

Chilblains plague my feet and fingers. My nose runs constantly. My upper lip is chapped raw.

I continue to search for Miz Settle. If she is dead, it's my fault. I was the one who conjured up the ring that made Del and his cohorts burn her cabin. I was the one who fed Stephen's addiction. I stoked the greed that drove the Destrehans to pay that hellish price which will seal me into slavery.

Thrice, on sunny days, I make the trek to Colony House, where I hide in alcoves between buildings and spy out. Miz Settle never shows her face. What if I've lost her forever?

Eventually, I decide to search the byways of Five Points. If she's not at Colony House or in the park, her next choice might be to help the women in those decrepit tenements. Dressed as I am in Philip's fine woolen clothing, I'm not able to slide into the anonymity of Five Points or boldly walk the streets where ragged people tread through the foot-deep slush of snow and mud and horse manure. Instead, I keep my head down and stay close to the buildings.

Newsboys scream headlines. Girls hawk roasted chestnuts, their hands and skirts filthy with coal soot. A few braziers flame, and people cluster near to catch the heat.

Finally, nearly frozen, I enter the low door of a rum shop. A dark-bearded man stands behind the bar. He nods at me, and I dig into my pocket. "How much for ale?"

"Heated?"

"Yes."

"Two cents."

I lay two pennies on the counter, and he fetches me golden ale in a thick glass. I take a sip, and warmth flows down my arms.

The barkeep studies me from a distance but finally ventures to approach, leans over the counter, and looks into my face. "Strange clothes for a lady," he says. I jerk away as he pulls a strand of my hair from under Philip's hat. "You find yourself a dress and clean up, I might get you some customers. Don't often see hair that color or a face that pretty."

I clamp my lips tight to keep them from trembling. I'd hoped the grease and soot of winter would hide the betraying hue of my hair. "I already have a job," I tell him.

"Doing what?"

"I'm a midwife."

"We got us a midwife." He gestures toward a young woman who's wiping down a table. "Don't need another one, do we, Blue? Our midwife saved Blue's baby."

Blue smiles. "That she did, Bill."

Her name comes to me first—Colleen McCarthy. Then I recall where I met her. Colony House. Pray she doesn't recognize me.

"I seen a lady once with hair that color," Colleen says, "but she was fancy and you ain't."

I direct the conversation back to the subject of midwives. "I suppose she's a young woman—your midwife." I try to keep the hope out of my voice.

"Old and crotchety," says Blue.

She turns to wipe another table. Her baby is tucked into a sling that hangs against Blue's back. My heart leaps. That sling is without doubt *Aniyunwiya*, a handy construction that Miz Settle often shared with mothers, an easier way to tote a baby than in your arms.

"Your midwife, is she Red Injun?" I ask.

Blue squints at me. "D'ya know somebody named Sheba?"

The narrow, noisome stairs reek of human waste, boiled cabbage, and dirt. At the fifth floor, Blue walks me down a corridor so dark I don't know how she sees her way. I place my hand on her shoulder and follow as if I were Philip, blind to all around me.

She stops and unlocks a door. We step into a room dimly lit by a shaft of light that comes from somewhere above, perhaps an aperture in the roof. The room is surprisingly clean and scented by the herbs I've always associated with Miz Settle. My hope beats as steady as a strong heart.

"Last week, she walked up to that frickin' park," says Blue, "just about froze off her arse, but she was sure somebody named Sheba would be staying there. I told her, there ain't nobody allowed to live in that park." Blue stoops over a bundle of blankets spread out in a corner of the room. "Red," she whispers. "You awake? Got somebody here to see you."

"Aunt Jesse?" I say.

The blankets move. "Sheba." I hear tears in her voice. "Ya found me." She breaks into a deep croupy cough.

"For a Red Injun, you leave a pretty easy trail."

She chuckles, which brings on another coughing spell.

"I'll get her somethin' hot to drink," Blue says. "Be right back."

I sit on the floor beside Miz Settle and ease her head and upper body onto my lap.

"That helps," she whispers. "Where you been? The Greys, they wouldn't tell me one blessed thing."

"We'll have time later to share that story, Aunt Jesse. Right now let's worry about getting you well. Then we'll find a place in a far-off land, somewhere safe."

Blue brings back a cup of broth, and Miz Settle manages to swallow a few sips. I talk to her about shared memories—her good dog Bessie, Holly Barnes and Cordell Smith, who must be married by now and maybe living on Miz Settle's land. When I bring up her squabbling chickens, most of them descendants of my mother's red hen, she laughs out loud.

I fish some coins out of my pocket. "Blue, would you go buy me a few things?"

She eyes the money in my hand, and I notice the calculating look on her face. I can't let myself contemplate what will happen if she ever sees one of those reward posters. She doesn't owe me any loyalty, and money is hard to come by.

"I need to make Red a mustard plaster."

I lift my cupped hand, and Blue takes the money. "It might help her?" She glances at Miz Settle.

"It might."

"What do ya need?"

"Mustard powder, hot water, some rags, and a bit of flour, not a lot." I prefer to use the white of an egg to bind the mix, but I'm guessing that winter chickens are surely rare in Five Points. I long for the cornucopia of herbs Miz Settle and I accumulated and stored in her cabin, now burned to ashes.

Blue nods at me and leaves the room. When an hour passes, I'm quite sure she's not coming back—at least until she's had the time to spend all my money on ale or worse. Then I hear someone outside the door. The key rattles, and the door opens.

Blue walks in shaking snow from her shawl. "Had a hell of time finding dried mustard. Finally went and begged some from a doctor up a few streets from here. Got more than my share of nasty looks, I'll tell ya. Guess I'm not worthy of walking their fine streets."

She hands me a paper folded over nearly a cup of dried mustard and another paper filled with white flour. I'd expected buckwheat at best. I ease Miz Settle back to lie upon her nest of blankets.

Blue fetches a bowl from a shelf on the wall. "I'll get Bill to heat me up some water. Be right back."

I find a spoon and measure out the necessary proportions of mustard and flour. The mustard plaster is a small hope, but better than no hope at all.

Early the fifth morning, after a wakeful night of keeping the croup from drowning her, I admit to myself that Miz Settle and I will never share any far-off adventure.

Blue's baby begins a hearty wailing, and Blue moans. She sits up in her bed of rags, puts the baby to her breast, and then comes over and stares down at Miz Settle. She leaves without a word but is soon back, carrying a burning oil lamp.

"Borrowed it," she says. "Light always lifts misery." Our eyes meet, and I know what she's not saying.

Then to my surprise, Miz Settle begins to laugh, a gentle sound, little more than a sigh. She opens her eyes, and the years seem to fall away. Her face looks young. "William A. Duke," she says, "wherever did ya get that beauteous baby?"

I'm guessing William answers her, because Miz Settle pauses as if listening, and then she asks, "Girl or boy?" Tears puddle in her eyes, and she gazes at me. "I have a daughter." She rubs her sleeve across her face. "Here, Sheba, help me sit up."

Blue and I pile blankets behind her until she's sitting fairly straight. She folds her arms and croons a lullaby. I would swear she's holding that baby. I catch a few of the Cherokee words she taught me—bird, deer, wolf, and the color blue. Then she reaches up as if to return the child to other arms, and she drifts back into sleep.

Through that day and the following night, I wait at Miz Settle's side, certain that each breath will be her last, but, when dawn breaks, she's still with us. Mid-morning, her eyes yet closed, she jerks with such a sudden move that I gasp. I clasp her shoulders, sure that her soul is trying to leave her body.

Miz Settle's eyes pop open. "Sheba, let go a me," she says in a clear voice.

I choke on my own breath and lift my hands away. "I'm sorry, Miz Settle. I thought your spirit was trying to depart."

"William Duke says I got more to do here before I can join him." She doesn't sound happy about it.

I brush my fingers across her forehead. No fever. She pushes my hand aside. "Sheba," she says, "you'll be the death of me yet." A cup of cold tea sits on the floor near her bed. She drinks it down. "Weak," she says, making a face, but that's the beginning of her recovery.

Days pass, and, when she's strong enough to leave the room, we take short walks in the dark hallway. A week later, we venture to the street, my face and hair well hidden by the scarf I found in Central Park. I buy roasted chestnuts, and we share them as we discuss how and when we'll leave the city. I find a train schedule in the gutter and memorize every arrival and departure.

Each morning, Blue is up first, paid by the barkeep Bill to stoke the stove in his rum shop, but one day she returns sooner than usual, her baby wailing from its swaddling on Blue's back. "Fancy men in sleighs out front. They're lookin' for you, Sheba. They say you're a thief, that you robbed them blind. They brung the police."

Miz Settle moans.

"Don't come with me," I tell her. "You're not strong enough."

"Since when are you my boss, Sheba? I'm stronger than you think. Besides, I'm too mad to die right now. You gonna help me down them stairs, or do I have to take them one at a time on my hind end?"

I don Philip's coat and wrap a shawl around Miz Settle's shoulders. By the time we're down two flights, a mob of tenants is following us. I suppose whatever happens next will be as fine an entertainment as any rum-shop fight.

On the street, two elegant sleighs block all traffic, their drivers in fancy livery. The owners sit under warm fur robes—my cousin François in one sleigh and Julien in the other. Three uniformed police officers stand between us and the sleighs. A crowd has gathered.

"Does it take all of ya to bring down one small woman?" Miz Settle shouts. "Shame on you."

The tallest officer confronts me. "China Creed?"

"Yes."

"You're under arrest for escape from the New York House of Detention and also for eighteen counts of robbery." He clutches a set of metal cuffs.

My knees weaken, and the noises of the street roar in my ears.

The barkeep, Bill, steps in front of me. He's as tall as the police officer, but thicker through the shoulders. "You got a warrant for Miss Creed's arrest, Gordon?"

"I'm relying on the word of these gentlemen behind me."

"I seem to recall that Miss Creed's aunt here saved your wife's life last time she gave birth. How's she doing, Gordon, that pretty wife?"

The officer blinks. "Good. She's good."

"I got me a good woman, too. Blue, get yourself over here."

"Blue, no," I say, but she walks to his side.

Bill puts his arm around her. "My woman here has been with Miss Creed and her aunt night and day. She's Miss Creed's alibi, at least when it comes to robbery."

Julien stands up in his sleigh. "You think any judge will believe the story of a prostitute over the sworn word of a gentleman?"

"My woman is a lady," Bill shouts. He lifts the cudgel clutched in his right hand. "You might be smart to remember that."

The onlookers are gradually moving forward. They're mostly men and boys, but a few women have joined the group, and I see more weapons—billy clubs, knives, hammers, crowbars. The boys start slinging broken bits of paving. More policemen arrive. They link arms to form a barrier against the crowd, and they shout for the drivers to turn the sleighs and leave Five Points.

A newsboy jumps at Julien's horse. The animal rears, and the boy falls under its hooves. Screaming, a woman grabs him by one leg and yanks him away. François's mare jerks in its traces and pulls his sleigh onto the sidewalk. A brazier falls, its coals flung wide. A man's ragged coat sleeve catches fire.

Julien's horse rears again, and two Five Point men grab the animal's harness. Julien pulls a pistol from inside his coat.

"Sir, no need for that, Sir," Officer Gordon shouts at him.

One of the men leaps for the gun and catches Julien's wrist. The barrel points my way. Miz Settle dives toward me, and the gun fires. We both land in the filthy slush of the street. Miz Settle groans and rolls away from me. Blue drops to her knees beside her. I draw in a wheezing breath and sit up. Blue's hands are covered with blood. Hers or Miz Settle's? Then I see the bright welling from Miz Settle's shoulder. I press my hands over the wound to slow the bleeding. I want to scream, but I don't have enough breath to carry my voice.

Suddenly, we're overrun by men waving sticks, voicing threats. They throw clods of filth at the sleighs and their occupants. The drivers leave their seats and launch themselves into the melee. I catch sight of my cousin's bodyguard, Mr. Blisset. He's roaring curses in French, his lips drawn back from his teeth, a knife in one hand and a pistol in the other. I hover over Miz Settle, trying to protect her from the forward surge of the crowd. I lie with my forehead pressed against her forehead, my arms draped over her shoulders. Then someone grabs me around my waist and lifts me up.

"No!" I scream. I turn my head and realize it's Bill. "Red is wounded, Bill. She'll get trampled."

He lets go of me and picks up Miz Settle, turns toward the rum shop, and forces his way through the crowd. Someone drops a stick, and I snatch it up, use it to clear a path so I can follow them. When I gain the entrance of the shop, Bill is already inside with Miz Settle. He's laid her on a table and I go to her. I pray like I've not prayed since Ma Mère was dying, and it's all I can do not to cry like a child.

She looks at me and smiles. "Don't worry, Sheba. It ain't my time to go. I already told ya that."

Then Blue is beside us. "That wound needs caut'rizing," she says. "The blacksmith will have something." She reaches back to check her baby in the sling then nods at a woman hovering close. "Katie Marie, take this ever-lovin' child until I get back and don't you dare carry her outside."

I peel back Miz Settle's shawl and unbutton her shirt to get a better look at the wound. Someone grabs my shoulder, and I look up. It's Officer Gordon. He tries to pull me away from Miz Settle, and I land a punch into his belly, hard enough that it hurts my hand. He clutches his middle, and, while he's recovering from that, Blue returns. She's clutching a metal rod, its tip heated red hot.

"If you don't let Sheba here caut'rize that old woman's wound, Officer Gordon," she says, "I'll find a right fine place to use this rod on you."

He straightens and backs away. "All right, Blue." He takes in a breath. "I'll give you one hour. Then I got no choice. I gotta take your friend in."

"Not until she helps me save this old woman's life," Blue shouts. "Red has saved others, as you well know. Somebody needs to pay for shootin' her."

"I'll do my best to make that happen," Gordon says.

"'Course you will," Blue scoffs. "Just like you take care of every frickin' thing that happens here in Five Points."

The shop is surprisingly quiet as I give orders: a basin of boiled water, lye soap, Miz Settle's medical bag, and a glass of whiskey to wash the scalpels. People scurry in all directions. I kiss Miz Settle's forehead, and she opens her eyes.

"You think the shoulder's broke?" she asks.

"I'll tell you in a minute."

"Hurts like blue blazes."

Somebody brings the lye soap and basin of water. I wash my hands then pluck away a scrap of fabric that's sticking out of the wound. The bullet entered the front of her shoulder, and I finally see it bulging dark just under the skin above her elbow. The bone must have directed its course, but I feel no break.

"Not broken," I tell her.

The medical bag makes its appearance at the table, and I clean a scalpel with a healthy dose of 100-proof whiskey.

"I need to make a small cut to remove the bullet, Miz Settle."

"Do it."

"Will ya caut'rize?" Blue asks, still clutching the metal rod.

"Yes. Can you coax more heat back into that rod?"

She strides over to the rum shop's cast iron stove and lays the metal on the top, cussing as the heat backs up into her hands.

I make a short slash in Miz Settle's skin, remove the bullet and a clot of blood. Miz Settle grinds her teeth.

A customer begins to gag, and Bill shouts for him to get out. I nod at Blue, and she brings me the metal rod, hot and glowing. Bill and Blue hold Miz Settle still, and I thrust it into the shoulder wound. Human flesh, when cauterized, first smells like roasted pork. The work is done when the odor of pork gives way to that of burnt meat. Customers leave the shop as fast as they can get out.

Bill calls after them, "I expect you to bring back them rum mugs, ya bunch a thieves! Next round on me."

Despite her fortitude, Miz Settle passes out. A few minutes after I finish cauterizing, Officer Gordon walks into the rum shop. He clasps my shoulder, and Miz Settle wakes up.

"All done but the bandaging," I tell her.

The officer waits until I've finished. Then he clasps my arm and tries to pull me away.

Miz Settle looks at me with a terrible sadness. "I love you like my own child, Sheba," she says. "I always will, but I'm supposed to stay with Blue."

Tears prickle my eyes.

"Five Points is worse than anything I ever seen," Miz Settle says. "Even that miserable trek from Georgia wasn't this bad. At least we loved each other, and we helped each other. There's not enough love here. I gotta stay and even up the odds."

I'm crying so hard that I have to grip the edge of the table to remain on my feet.

"I'll take care of her, Sheba," Blue says. "I promise. My baby needs a granny to love."

My throat eases, and I'm able to say a few words. "Aunt Jesse, I love you, ever and always."

She smiles at me. "Ya think I don't know that?" She closes her eyes, and tears run down her cheeks.

I lean close and gently hug her. "Did you make any wishes?" I whisper.

"Of course, you think I'm a fool?"

"Never."

Officer pulls me away from Miz Settle. Bill tries to push himself between us, but I shake my head at him. "It's all right. Let me go. You have two ladies here who need you."

He lifts his hands and backs away. Officer Gordon and I step out into the sun-cast shadows of the street, and my heart twists into a knot so small and tight that I'm sure I'll never be able to love anyone else ever again.

The street folk hiss as the officer and I enter a waiting police sledge. "Sit," he says and holds up the iron cuffs. "You'll behave?"

"I will."

He closes the door and takes a seat facing me, sets the cuffs on his lap.

The driver cracks his whip. The sledge runners scream against iced cobbles. My despair is so great that I cannot bear to look at Officer Gordon. I cover my face with my hands, but Ma Mère drifts close, and she whispers, *Don't give up.*

When the sledge finally stops, I stay as I am until the officer shakes my shoulder.

"Come on now," he says. "I got promises to keep."

He opens the door, and I glance out, surprised that the street is wide and well-scraped. Where are we? I stumble out and look up at the elegant marble façade of the St. Nicholas Hotel. My mind is numb, and my thoughts move slowly. They must be delivering me to the Destrehans? Can life with them be worse than what I've been through the past few months?

"I assume you're making money for this."

"No," he says. "No money. Justice is enough for me."

He takes my arm and walks with me into the hotel. A young woman standing behind the admittance desk places her hands over her mouth. I still wear Philip's clothing, and everything is stained with Miz Settle's blood.

Officer Gordon directs me up an oak staircase to the second floor and then down a carpeted corridor. He raps on a door, and it's opened by my lady's maid.

"Lillico?"

The officer tips his hat and bids me goodbye. Lillico pulls me into the room.

"You're coming with me?" I ask as she locks the door.

"I'm sorry, Miss Creed, but I'm not allowed to explain. Where's Mrs. Settle?"

I shake my head and blink back tears. "She's safe, but she wants to stay where she is."

"She'll be appreciated wherever she lives."

"That's my hope."

I bathe in a porcelain tub. Lillico washes my hair and blots it as dry as possible. Then she coaxes it into damp curls that she pins at the back of my head. She helps me into a dark blue travel dress and dainty ankle-high boots. She hands me a pair of kidskin gloves. A fur-lined hooded cloak completes my outfit. She fastens it under my chin as if I were a child.

Someone knocks, and I brace myself to meet my cousins or perhaps their bodyguard, but, when Lillico opens the door, Stephen and Philip walk in. Stephen has lost weight, but his eyes are clear.

"You're beautiful, China, despite everything," he says.

Love must be tenacious, because I feel myself drawn to him, but I address Philip. "They didn't make you stay in The Tombs. I worried about that."

He laughs. "Mother decided that one night there and a bad case of lice was enough punishment."

"You're amazing, Philip. Don't ever forget that." I look at Stephen. "What's our destination? A judge? A jury?"

"Grand Central Depot."

It's the Destrehans then. Better than The Tombs.

I turn to Lillico and stroke her face. "Thank you, dear Lillico. I wish I could pay you what you're worth, but I imagine a stack of greenbacks high enough to reach the ceiling wouldn't be enough."

We ride to the Depot in the Grey's elegant sleigh. Stephen drives, and Philip sits between us. I can't help but remember how I felt on my first day in New York—afraid but exuberant, filled with trepidation yet also with hope. Now, I'm imprisoned by dread. When we arrive at the station, the Grey's salon car is waiting for us, one of many hitched to an engine that's already roiling steam and smoke. Stephen opens the door, and I step inside. I expect to see my cousins, but the only one waiting for us is Royce Cooper.

I'm suddenly afire with anger. "Mr. Cooper. Why am I surprised? I understand the Grey family sold me for three million dollars. How much did the Destrehan's pay for you?"

His face blanches.

"China." Stephen's voice is stern. "Don't condemn Mr. Cooper. He engineered the ruse that not only deceived my mother but also duped the Destrehans."

"What ruse?"

Philip steps forward. "Talk things out, you and Mr. Cooper," he says and hands me a thick leather pocketbook. "From us to you."

Stephen looks into my eyes. The sadness in his face catches at my heart. "Although I'd love to kiss you one more time, China, I won't." He takes his brother's arm as if he, not Philip, requires a guide. "Shall we go?"

"Goodbye, Miss Creed," Philip says.

I hold back my weeping, trembling with the effort. The door of our car closes behind them, and I turn to Royce Cooper. "What did Philip mean, talk things out?" My voice is shaking.

Mr. Cooper looks exhausted, dark circles under his eyes, his hair mussed, his clothes rumpled. He points at the pocketbook. "That contains enough money for you to start over anywhere in the world, Miss Creed. Wherever you'd like to go, I promise to get you there."

I'm not courageous enough to believe him. "Liar," I say. I take a seat in one of the velvet settees.

Mr. Cooper kneels in front of me, and my cheeks burn with anger.

"All I want is your safety and happiness, Miss Creed."

"You helped them abduct me at the church."

"Did you see me there?"

"No, but Dr. Broward said your name."

"Said my name? China, I was already miles away from New York when they locked you up. I wouldn't have left if I knew what they planned."

The train begins to move, and Mr. Cooper sits beside me. I look away from him and out the window. Stephen and Philip stand on the platform. Stephen waves, and then we are gone.

When we clear the station, Mr. Cooper says, "Miss Creed, I am not delivering you to the Destrehans."

"If that's true, why didn't Stephen tell me?"

"Without doubt, your cousins or their henchmen are watching. They needed to see you enter the train in despair, as you did. I don't doubt that they have spies on this train. We must remain in this car and be adept at acting out our parts, but I promise that you'll be free long before the train reaches New Orleans."

My conflicted emotions scramble my thoughts. Why should Mr. Cooper help me? For a long time I can't do anything but remind myself to breathe, but finally I do understand. Why am I disappointed? I remove my left glove and reach out to him with my snake-bitten hand.

"Shall we begin now?" I say. "Wish well."

He clasps my hand, but he doesn't remove his gloves. "Miss Creed, I'm so sorry for what you've endured. If I had the power to change the past, I would, but, of course, I can't. What I can do is make you another promise. When we've found a safe place for you to live, I will walk away with never a touch, never a kiss, your secret unspoken for the remainder of my life."

His eyes are so blue, so deep. I'm trapped by those eyes, and, with every portion of my soul, I want to trust him.

I force myself to gaze out at the passing landscape as the great city wanes toward farmland.

"China," Mr. Cooper says, his voice so soft it barely rises above the noise of the train, "if we are to escape the Destrehans, we must be honest with one another. So in honesty, I tell you this, although I doubt you're ready to hear it." His grip tightens on my hand, and again I look into his eyes. "Even with the most ardent intimacy, and I'm not asking for that, you are safe with me, because I love nothing more in the world than you, China. You are all I want."

We start from there.

EPILOGUE

When my husband arrives home, I'm working in the exquisite orchards he designed and brought to life within this sun-drenched land. The water pipes lie cleverly hidden under the earth, a tribute to the drainage system originally mapped out for Central Park.

He comes to me carrying a child. The boy's face is streaked with dried tears. When Royce makes his rare trips to the nearest city, he sometimes brings home a child like this, belly bloated by starvation, eyes opaque. We celebrate each child, but this time, Royce is solemn rather than jubilant.

I kiss his cheek. "What's wrong?"

"He wasn't born blind."

I look away from the boy before I can lose my heart. We've learned to be careful.

"His mother begged me, China."

The mothers are always the most difficult to refuse. Their love, it flays us. "How old was he when he lost his sight?"

"About two she thinks."

"Do we know the cause? Is there any hope of a cure?"

We've been speaking in French, which the child might understand. Royce changes to English. "No cure. And yes, I know the cause."

"Which is?"

"His father. The boy is the youngest of eight children. They needed a little beggar who would elicit pity. It's easier to lead a blind child than to carry one who's crippled."

At that moment, I believe I could kill the boy's father with my bare hands. I stare upward at God's exquisite sky. When I compose myself, Royce and I resume our conversation.

"Two years might not be a problem," I say. "Visual memories fade. What's his name?"

"Jean-Paul."

"Jean-Paul," I whisper.

The child smiles in my direction. "Maman?"

He leans toward me, and I make my decision. "Oui, Maman." I take him into my arms.

It's difficult to tell how old he is. He's that starved. But prior to age five, a child cannot curl his arm over his head and touch the opposite ear. A toddler's arms are too short, the head too large. When Jean-Paul is more accustomed to us, we'll turn that experiment into a silly game. Then I'll know where to place him in our nursery.

A handbell rings. It's noon. Girls and boys stream toward us from the school. They shout in their native languages and then in French, "We heard Papa's voice. He's home?"

"Papa's home," I call to them.

Royce and I wage ferocious battles to rescue the minds, souls, and malnourished bodies of these children. We teach them French, but we fight to preserve their native languages as well. There is no quicker way to destroy a people than to kill their language. Miz Settle taught me that long ago. How you speak is how you think. How you think is who you are.

The children crowd around us, and Jean-Paul tucks his head under my chin. "*Frères, soeurs,*" I whisper. Brothers, sisters, every one of them, and every one of them blind.

You see, Stephen's best gift was not money enough to fund our travels or even to build this school, but that, with Philip's help, he solved the meaning of the last line in Ma Mère's song.

> *Something you covet deep to the bone,*
> *But nothing alive with will of its own.*
> *Nothing too large, the earth stakes its claim.*
> *Nothing unseen, the eyes play the game.*

* * *

People blind from birth have no visual memories, and, therefore, I don't connect with a subconscious mental image. I cannot steal whatever it is they covet. I'm free to touch. I'm free to hold. I'm free to love.

Royce and I have found one exception. He is not blind, yet I can kiss him. I can lie within his arms. I can be a wife in every way without the complication of unintended theft. When he told me he believed we would be safe even with the most ardent intimacy, he was right. And we have learned through our love that one thing in this world is far stronger than greed.

As we walk with our children toward the dining hall, Jean-Paul suddenly emits a squeal of surprise. I look down and see a brown-speckled egg cupped in his hands.

Royce smiles. "Surely we can deal with that, China," he says and closes the boy's fingers around the egg. "*C'est pour vous*, Jean-Paul."

The boy's face lights with a look of disbelief. Then he tilts his head to the sky and laughs.

—*China Deliverance Creed Cooper*
The Year of Our Lord 1885

AUTHOR'S NOTES

If you are familiar with Taney County, Missouri, you will realize that some of the landmarks, towns, and waterways referenced in the novel are a figment of my imagination. I've done this for various literary reasons, mostly metaphorical.

In my defense, I quote our friend Forbes McDonald, who dismissed the criticism of a research decision I made in my first novel by saying, "And that's why they put it on the shelf marked fiction." It's as fine an explanation as I've heard, and I claim it as my own.

For those readers who love research as much as I do, I include the following background notes to give you additional information that may enhance your reading experience. I'm not an expert in *any* of these subjects, and, despite my diligence, there will be errors. Please let me know if you find conflicting information out there in the real world. Sometimes that's simply a matter of differing opinions, but sometimes I'm wrong, and I appreciate being corrected, kindly.

The topics are in alphabetical order for your convenience.

Central Park, New York City
Arguably one of the most beautiful greenswards in the world, Central Park's 843 acres are located in Manhattan between the Upper East and West Sides. The original designers, Frederick Law Olmsted, a landscape architect, and Calvert Vaux, an architect and landscape designer, named their proposal for the park the "Greensward Plan," and the planning committee chose it from more than thirty proposals. The park was completed in 1873 and was designated a National

Historic Landmark in 1963. At the present time, it is managed by the Central Park Conservancy, a non-profit group that raises more than eighty million dollars per year to support the park's annual budget. To donate to this very worthy cause, please check out their website, www.centralparknyc.org.

All areas of the park mentioned in *The Midwife's Touch* were in existence in 1873, including the cave (which is no longer extant), the paths, lakes, exposed bedrock, The Ramble, the gates, and the bridges, although there have been a great number of changes since then. I did my best to confirm that every tree species I mentioned in the novel grew within the park in 1873.

Many wonderful books and articles have been written about Central Park. These two are a great starting point for your research. *Central Park, The Birth, Decline, and Renewal of a National Treasure* by Eugene Kinkead is packed with information and includes rare historical photographs. The delightful children's picture book, *A Green Place to Be, The Creation of Central Park* by Ashley Benham Yazdani highlights the history of the park and includes drawings of the thirty-four bridges and archways designed by Calvert Vaux and Jacob Wrey Mould.

A minor thread within *The Midwife's Touch* is Royce Cooper's wish for Olmstead's designs of the park's underground drainage system and Cooper's eventual use of those designs [See the Epilogue]. The drainage system drawings truly were misplaced long ago, which has caused a variety of difficulties for park planners. I believe China Creed and Royce Cooper owe them an apology.

Cherokee People

Today, with more than 300,000 members, the Cherokee Nation is the largest tribe recognized by the United States Federal Government. The Cherokee language is Iroquoian and, like all Iroquoian languages, is very grammatically intricate.

Various interactions and alliances with European and North American nations strongly influenced the history of the Cherokee People as did the diseases brought by European settlers. With the decimation of the population due to those diseases and the reduction of tribal land after the Cherokee-American or Chickamauga Wars of 1776-1795, the Cherokee Nation began to shape their society more in accord with that of European settlers. Communal land ownership gave way to individually owned farmsteads with cattle and pigs as primary meat sources rather than wild game. Various government bureaus supplied Native people with spinning wheels and seeds, and, although women had been the traditional crop cultivators, men were encouraged to fence, plow, and plant their lands. At the invitation of Cherokee chiefs, Moravian and Congregationalist missionaries introduced Christianity to the people.

In 1806, a road built by the U.S. Federal Government was constructed from Savannah, Georgia, north to Knoxville, Tennessee. Much of this road ran through Cherokee land, a convenient "trail" for non-Cherokee people, which encouraged illegal settlement on Cherokee land by non-native people.

In 1821, the brilliant Se-quo-yah (aka George Gist or George Guess) introduced a written form of the Cherokee language based on the syllabary concept. (Individual syllables rather than individual sounds are assigned letters or symbols.) Within ten years, virtually the entire adult Cherokee population was literate, an amazing feat unequaled anywhere else in the world.

Unfortunately, the Cherokee people's success as farmers and plantation owners, along with the discovery of gold in Lumpkin County (North Georgia), were catalysts for plans to remove the Cherokee people along with the Creek/Muscogee, Seminole, Chickasaw, and Choctaw from their lands in Tennessee, North Carolina, Georgia, and Alabama in a forced migration to areas west of the Mississippi.

In 1830, President Andrew Jackson rammed the Indian Removal Act through Congress. The Cherokee fought against removal, not with warfare, but legally. That legal action eventually reached the U.S. Supreme Court, which ruled in favor of the Cherokee, but President Jackson went ahead with a forced removal at gunpoint.

Some sources estimate that of the 100,000 people removed 15,000 died. Others believe at least one of every four Natives died. This great tragedy of American history gives the Cherokee people every right to view themselves as victims. However, they have risen above that crippling temptation to proudly celebrate their heritage with continued success in all areas of life, as they should—as should all people.

You will find various symbols of Native origin throughout the novel. These include: Jesse Settle breaking her spinning wheel, the bowl China uses when she's hulling strawberries, Miz Settle's pothole in the creek, a creek as a trail, water as a purifying part of Miz Settle's life, the burial moccasins of Mrs. Grey's masquerade party, the concern about using "real" names, the soft *r* in Miz Settle's speech, Philip's blindness, and many of the herbs mentioned in the novel. There are others.

Native Americans traditionally tell their stories and histories as a type of theatre art, and, as such, storytellers bend their stories in ways unique unto themselves. Please keep this in mind as you read the story of the little water beetle Dâyuni'sï in Chapter Seven.

Civil War

From 1861 into 1865, the United States was torn apart by the war between the North and the South. Although there were more issues than slavery [See **Slavery** below], including states' rights, the basic split came between non-slavery and pro-slavery states.

For many years, the U.S. Government had walked a fine line, trying to keep a balance within Congress that didn't allow one side or the other to rule supreme. One of the concessions made by both sides concerned the admittance of territories into statehood. By 1860, there were 18 free states, where slavery was illegal, and 15 pro-slavery states. (West Virginia did not split away from Virginia until 1861.) Generally, for every pro-slavery state admitted to the Union, Congress tried to counter with the admittance of a free state. One of the best known political skirmishes in this regard occurred when the Sixteenth United States Congress passed the Missouri Compromise, which admitted Missouri into the Union as a pro-slavery state and admitted Maine as an anti-slavery state. Possibly the most far-reaching portion of this compromise was the legislation that set the 36.30 parallel—excluding Missouri—as the dividing line between pro- and anti-slavery states. The Missouri Compromise was signed into law by President James Monroe on March 6, 1820.

Despite being admitted as a pro-slavery state, Missouri's location as a border state between North and South resulted in families, towns, and counties being divided. During the Civil War, approximately 110,000 Missouri men fought for the Union and 40,000 for the Confederacy.

I am adamantly against any kind of slavery or ethnic hatred, yet my family was very divided by the Civil War. One of my great great-grandfathers, who fought for the Union, spent six months interred as a prisoner of war, and as a result, his health was compromised for the remainder of his life. Another great great-grandfather fought for the Confederacy. He died in a prisoner of war camp in Indiana. Such losses generate bitterness that lasts for generations. Consider further the injury done to the individuals and families, both Black and Native American, who were forced into slavery. It's amazing that our country survived.

Within Border States like Kansas and Missouri, the fighting was not only between armies but sometimes between neighbors, resulting in a great number of illegal executions (including lynchings) of both black and white people. The Bushwhackers (Confederate) and the Jayhawkers (Union) were outlaws, often deserters, who preyed on citizens on both sides of the issue. A very good window into the Civil War period in Missouri is a memoir written by a Union soldier, James W. Erwin. Although, the reader must wade through various unpalatable prejudices of that period, *The Homefront in Civil War Missouri* gives an eye-opening account of the fear and horrors endured by the citizens of Missouri during that tumultuous time.

Clothing

Although the clothing worn by middle and lower class people of the mid-1800s was practical rather than fashionable, with women on isolated farms sometimes donning men's pants to do chores, most women did own a good dress that was designed according to fashion plates in women's magazines.

By 1860, the highly impractical hoop-supported bell skirts were very popular. These skirts, which required at least three yards of fabric to complete, emphasized a woman's narrow wasp waist produced by the use of tightly laced corsets. This was, however, a very dangerous style. Both my husband and I have many-greats grandmothers who died when still relatively young because their skirts caught fire while they were working at a hearth or in a kitchen.

One of the greatest impacts on fashions was the development of aniline dyes in 1856. These synthetic chemical dyes produced brilliant colors that didn't fade like the plant dyes previously in use. As a result, for the next twenty or more years, bright colors and unusual combinations of bright colors were considered very fashionable, especially in women's clothing.

After the Civil War, women's styles gradually changed until a skirt's front panel lay quite flat from the waist to the hem. At this time, the bustle came into use. Another difficult style—Try to sit down when you're wearing a bustle!—it was, nonetheless, somewhat safer. Within the novel, I tried to portray both men's and women's clothing as they existed at that time in rural America as well as in metropolitan New York. Like today, clothing was a sign of prosperity, or lack thereof, and impacted self-esteem.

For further study, a very good reference text is *Clothing Through American History, The Civil War Through The Gilded Age, 1861-1899* by Anita Stamper and Jill Condra. For more information about textiles and weaves, I recommend *Fabric For Fashion, The Swatch Book* by Clive Hallett and Amanda Johnston, which includes more than 125 fabric samples.

Doolin Family

When Mary-Polly Preck protects China by misleading the Destrehan brothers [See Chapter Twenty Three], she sent them on a risky journey. There really was a Doolin family, although in the 1870s their fame wouldn't have spread much beyond Johnson County, Arkansas. The Doolin parents had fifteen children, and, of the boys, four eventually turned to a life of crime. Bob Doolin, the best known Doolin brother, rode with the infamous Dalton gang. The Daltons have been called the "most cold-blooded robbers in the West."

Ether

We who live in the 21st century have long been "educated" by movies and television shows to believe that a bit of ether on a rag pressed to a person's face will put them completely out for a very long time. As convenient as that premise is for script writers—and novelists—it's not true. Ether, first used as a surgical anesthetic in the United States as early as 1842, had to be carefully administered drop by drop by someone educated in its use, and the effects tended to wear off soon after administration was discontinued.

Therefore, at the end of Chapter Thirty, when China was anesthetized, she could not have been given the drug by Royce Cooper, who lacked the medical expertise to administer it. I considered adding information about ether into the storyline but decided the explanation would "pop" the reader out of the story at a time when tension was very important. Therefore, as you see, I delegated the use of ether to my Author's Notes.

Finance

It's difficult to believe that, prior to the National Currency Act of 1863, the United States had no truly national currency. By 1862, more than 7,000 different bank-notes circulated, some of them bogus. With the destruction of the South's economy during the Civil War and the reestablishment of the Union in 1865, it was apparent to many that bank-notes should be replaced with a national currency. The National Bank Act of 1865 levied a tax on state currency, discouraging its use, and established a system of national and state-chartered banks, the first in the world. Local banks were still legal, and, during the financial boom in the Northern states after the Civil War, many entrepreneurs obtained venture capital from wealthy individuals and/or local banks.

Unfortunately, many investments of this type were purely speculation, a goodly number in railroad expansion. When one of the best known and most honest speculators, Jay Cooke, went bankrupt, it was the proverbial last straw. Added atop numerous European financial problems, the mounting failures of dishonest speculators, and the devastating fires that took place in Chicago and Boston, Cooke's bankruptcy tumbled the U. S. economy. Eventually, millions of Americans lost their jobs. The economic repercussions lasted for two decades.

The Grey Mansion

I based the Grey's elegant home on a variety of 19th century New York mansions, most of which were built after the timeline of *The Midwife's Touch*. Prior to the 1870s, homes built for New York's elite were usually constructed of brownstone, but I opted to allow the Greys a bit of visionary stylishness, and they constructed their mansion of white marble.

Guns

The two primary type of guns named in *The Midwife's Touch* are the blunderbuss and the Hawkin rifle. Early European colonists brought the first blunderbusses with them to North America. A fledgling version of a shotgun, they were German-made and featured a flared muzzle and a relatively short barrel. The blunderbuss owned by Miz Settle would have been the 1808 Harpers Ferry blunderbuss, passed down in her family for several generations. The Lewis and Clark Expedition included Harpers Ferry blunderbusses among their arsenal, but, by the middle 1800s, the inaccurate blunderbuss was no longer in use by the military. However, civilians still used them for hunting.

The Hawken rifle is a long-barrel muzzle-loader. Developed by the Hawken brothers, each gun was individually made by hand and highly treasured. They are well-known for their accuracy and long-range capabilities. They were gradually replaced in favor of breech loaders.

During the Civil War, a wide variety of handguns were used, including the Starr revolver (several models), the Colt model 1860, the Colt Dragoon Revolver, the Remington 1858, and the Smith & Wesson Model 1. The handgun used by the Bushwacker in the novel's cave scene [Chapter Nine] was a .44 caliber Starr Single Action Revolver. This handgun would have been one of the 23,000 which were manufactured in 1863–1864. States supplied these guns to Union troops, and that means the Bushwacker's gun was stolen. There is a very subtle metaphor in this scene, particularly since the make of the handgun is not named, in that China is facing death from a Starr revolver as she looks up toward a "star-filled" sky.

The best-known Civil War rifle was probably the Springfield rifle, but the Smith carbine, the Lorenz rifle, the Colt revolving rifle, the Spencer repeating rifle, and the Burnside carbine, as well as the Tarpley carbine and the Whitworth rifle, were also used.

Medicines

During the period of this novel, infection was largely misunderstood, and, of course, no antibiotics were available, although honey carries many antibacterial properties, which are variable according to environmental factors. A small wound could be a death sentence, and many women died shortly after childbirth, often due to infection. Ether was first used as an anesthesia in 1846. Prior to that time, alcohol and opium were the usual options. Some promising medicines, such as Warburg's Tincture for malaria, had been developed, but many were simply patent medicines.

My great great-grandparents were medical doctors (both graduates of Drake Medical College in the late 1800s) who supplemented their income by formulating and producing patent medicines. In her later years, "Doctor Kate" developed Alzheimer's disease and refused to take any kind of medicine, telling her caregivers and family members (my father remembers this) that "all medicines are poison," a very interesting take on what she and her husband sold to the public.

The development of medical instruments such as stethoscopes and microscopes opened new fields of medical research and enhanced a doctor's ability to diagnose maladies and prolong life.

Metaphors

Metaphors are a novelist's playground. *The Midwife's Touch* in whole stands as a metaphor for a woman's need to nurture and care for others.

In these Author's Notes I've already explained some of the metaphors and symbols I used to highlight Cherokee culture. I discuss the symbolism of snakes in another segment below.

Other symbols and metaphors refer specifically to women and their place in society. They include all the aspects of midwifery, Jesse Settle's spinning wheel, milksnakes, the masquerade engagement party, the opulence of granted wishes, China's great longing for the solace of touch, China as a thief, the ring clutched in the Aubright baby's hand, the bondage of the Broward Institute, China's time in The Tombs, the cave in Central Park and in the Ozarks, the amputation of China's finger, witchcraft as a woman's aberration, lace-making, Philip Grey's blindness, China wearing Philip's clothes, and, of course, the use of the corset. There are others. Yvette's Creed's "song" is overflowing with symbolism.

Midwifery

Although some may disagree, I believe that many midwives in the 1800s were highly competent. Their type of doctoring was passed on from woman to woman, formed and tempered by experience, and that is that type of midwifery I portray in the novel. The breech delivery by Miz Settle is a variation of what is now known as the Mariceau-Smellie-Veit Maneuver, and I don't think I'm out of line by suggesting that she would be informed enough to use it when needed.

Mortuary Science

As Dr. Stephen Grey explains in the novel, the field of mortuary science began to come into its own during the Civil War. By then, the railroad system in the United States was developed enough to permit relatively rapid transportation within and between states, allowing corpses to be shipped home. Soldiers paid ahead to have their bodies embalmed and shipped home if they should die on the battlefield or from their wounds.

Near Side, Off Side

If you are familiar with horses and riding, these terms need no explanation. If not, you may have been confused by their use within the novel. A horse is always mounted from the left side, which has come to be known as the *near* side. The right side is the *off* side. In the 1800s, horses and terminology referring to horses was as common to everyday folk as cars and related terminology are to us today. Thus, it was common to refer to the left as *near* and the right as *off*. It is interesting to note how much horse terminology is still common, phrases like *out to pasture, horse power, hold your horses, horse around.* I'm sure you can think of others.

New York City

Today the home of nearly nine million people—almost nineteen million in the entire metro area—in 1873 the city's inhabitants numbered about one million. At that time approximately sixty percent of all U.S. exports were sent through New York Harbor. Department stores had introduced a new way of shopping—consumers were allowed to handle and compare goods rather than having them displayed by store clerks. Structural steel had not yet been developed, and there were no elevators, which limited most buildings to a height of six stories. Churches with their soaring steeples took pride of place as the tallest buildings in the city.

Unfortunately, during this period of new ideas and discoveries, politics had taken a serious dive into corruption. An 1870 city charter consolidated power into the hands of William Tweed and his cohorts, who eventually bilked the city out of tens of millions of dollars. However, by 1873, Tweed had fallen from the pinnacle of power due to convictions of forgery and larceny. Others more honest, such as John Kelly, stepped in to steer Tammany Hall toward a less corrupt hierarchy of power, but New York politics were still directed by a relatively small group of men, a situation which easily lends itself to graft.

Within the social hierarchy, the wealthy elite were bound by an uneasy truce between old wealth families, such as the Astors, Roosevelts, and Schermerhorns, and those who had only recently acquired great wealth, such as the Vanderbilts and Carnegies. Added to that mix were families with ties to European royalty, such as the Rothschilds. Royalty usually trumped all, but the situation was primed to erupt into very unpleasant social situations and sometimes did.

In the novel, the Destrehan family of New Orleans (an old money family) would likely occupy a social status somewhat between the old and new wealth families of New York, simply because they were from New Orleans rather than New York.

I will not bore you with a list of all the excellent books I studied about New York and New York's Gilded Age, but Esther Crain's *The Gilded Age in New York 1870-1910* serves as a fine foundation for anyone interested in studying that era. She offers the reader an easily understood division of topics, many lesser known details, and a cornucopia of old and rare photographs.

New Orleans
Having one of the most varied histories of any city in the United States, New Orleans still carries within its traditions the mark of Spanish, French, Creole, Acadian/Cajun, African, and American traditions. During the mid-1800s, more millionaires lived in the area between New Orleans and Baton Rouge than any other place in the nation. Their wealth was accumulated due to the success of huge sugar cane plantations and the use of slave labor. Some wealthy slave owners in Louisiana were free blacks.

Although in the novel the Destrehan family owns a cotton plantation, in real life this Creole family made their fortune growing indigo and later sugar cane. I loosely based the Destrehan plantation on the Frogmore Plantation located near Ferriday in Concordia Parish, although I moved it a bit closer to New Orleans. The cotton seed so valued by Henri in the novel is fictional, but in their very interesting paper, "Innovation and Productivity Growth in the Antebellum Cotton

Economy," Alan L. Olmstead and Paul W. Rhode mention an increase of cotton harvests in the 1850s, stating, "The cliometrics literature has all but ignored these claims of sustained productivity advances. There has been little appreciation of how the evolution of cotton varieties helped shape southern development." Voilà, the Le Roy cotton seed!

Yellow fever has earned itself many names, including "black vomit" and "yellow jack". Black vomit needs no explanation. The name yellow jack comes from sailors' slang for the yellow flags that were displayed outside homes under quarantine for yellow fever. The worse year for yellow fever in the history of the deep South came in 1853 when one out of every twelve people in New Orleans died of the disease.

Ozarks

The Ozark area of the middle-south extends from Eastern Oklahoma to the boot heel of Missouri and into northern Arkansas. Higher elevations in the Ozarks affect the climate, which is somewhat cooler than in contiguous portions of Missouri, Oklahoma, and Arkansas.

The culture of the people who settled in the Ozarks is fairly uniform throughout. The first settlers, of course, were Native American, but Scots-Irish families moved in, many of them having first settled in the Appalachians to the east. Thus, you'll find many similarities between the traditions and beliefs of both areas.

As I mentioned at the beginning of my Author's Notes, anyone familiar with Taney County knows there is no Milksnake Hollow or town of Milksnake. The secret cave used by China and her mother is an amalgam of several Missouri caves, which my husband and I visited.

Railroads

The first commercial railroad in the United States to open track for use was the Baltimore and Ohio in 1830. Although that track was only fourteen miles long, it was a portent of things to come. In 1869, the Central Pacific Railroad from the West was linked with the Union Pacific Railroad from the East. Imagine the impact on the people and the economy when railroads linked the far reaches of the nation. The travel time from New York State to California was reduced from months of hardship to days of only moderate discomfort. (Trains were loud and steam engines produced smoke and cinders.)

Religion and Superstition

The people of European origin who settled in the Ozarks were generally Protestant. Many converted to Baptist or Methodist beliefs during what is known as the Second Great Awakening. At that time (late 1700s into the mid-1800s) the gospel message of salvation—redemption for believers through the death of Jesus Christ on the cross rather than through good works or predestination—was spread to hundreds of small isolated communities by traveling preachers.

During the time period of the novel, the people of the Ozarks often combined traditional Protestant beliefs with various superstitions. Witches were believed to be in league with and empowered by the devil. Thus all the references to witches and witchery in the novel allude to this belief rather than to current definitions. Hexes, charms, and tricks all refer to various types of spells. Generally, tricks were cast by witches. Hexes and charms were more the venue of ordinary people or Goomer Doctors, and yes there were (and maybe still are) Goomer Doctors. They used prayers and charms to counteract "goomering" which was another name for witchcraft. Most people believed that Goomer Doctors were servants of God.

Booger dogs (or any kind of booger animal) were thought to be witches in another form. Almost every black domesticated animal was considered a possible problem (excluding most cattle, horses, and mules) and were avoided. Some people believed that only a silver bullet could kill a booger animal.

Slavery

I believe with every ounce of my being that nations or ethnic groups who condone the subjugation of human beings set themselves up for horrendous consequences. Belief in ethnic superiority hardens the heart, skews the mind, and destroys the soul.

Slavery was well established in Europe, Asia, and Africa long before Europeans established settlements in North America. (In other words, we didn't invent it.) But most historians agree that slavery reared its ugly head in the earliest American colonies, probably beginning in 1619.

During the period between 1744 and 1804, slavery was outlawed in all northern states. Unfortunately, in the South, huge plantations and even some smaller farms produced cotton, rice, sugar, indigo, and tobacco through the economically advantageous system of slave labor.

Economic systems which primarily enrich the ruling classes serve as an effective blindfold when it comes to moral principles.

Some of the more wealthy Cherokee people, particularly those who were of Cherokee/Scots heritage, owned slaves, but their traditions of adoption and intermarriage often lessened the burdens of those whom they enslaved. When the Cherokee were forcibly removed to Indian Territory, they were allowed to take their slaves with them. Today, many descendants of those slaves have been given tribal status. Intermarriage between Black and Native Americans was not unusual in the 1700s (even in New England), and today many families proudly carry that dual heritage.

Snakes

One of the more obvious symbols in *The Midwife's Touch* is the snake. The first sentence of Chapter One mentions two—the milksnake (a beneficial snake) and the cottonmouth. China's experiences with snakes also include the blue racer, the rattlesnake, and the exotic fake asp that adorns Mrs. Grey's arm at the masquerade ball.

Songs

The few hymns mentioned in the novel were composed prior to or during the timeframe of the book. "Billy Barlow," a folksong that gained popularity during the Civil War, is much older than that, and yes, there is a particularly raucous version that mentions a raw rat tail.

Spode Plate

When I decided to name China after a plate, I went on an Internet search for a plate that would be appropriate. I found and purchased a small Spode dish that is as described in the first chapter of the book and now lives quite happily (unbroken) in my office.

Telekinesis

During the 1800s, a time of invention and discovery, telekinesis became a subject of interest, especially among upper class people of the United States and Europe. Most historians believe that any demonstration of telekinesis was perpetrated by, to quote Royce Cooper, "At best . . . a gifted sleight-of-hand artist. At worst, a charlatan."

Today, scientists actually do teleport subatomic particles. Their goal is to find the means to teleport molecules. There is disagreement among scientists as to whether the "teleportation of subatomic particles" is truly an incidence of telekinesis or simply the destruction of a particle in one place and the formation of a replica in another, which did happen in 1997 at the University of Innsbruck in Austria. If you have further interest in telekinesis, you might enjoy David Darling's book, *Teleportation The Impossible Leap.*

Wishes

Like many children, my brother Bobby and I loved to play a game where we imagined receiving a wish. Our world of wishes became more enticing when our father quipped, "I wish every wish that I wish would come true."

That game planted a seed in my brain that eventually flowered into *The Midwife's Touch,* and for me, China's abilities turned out be a great exercise in contemplation and speculation.

READING GROUP QUESTIONS

1. Did you enjoy the novel? Why or why not?

2. Author Sue Harrison has written, "Metaphors are a novelist's playground." She claims The Midwife's Touch in whole stands as a metaphor for a woman's need to nurture and care for others. Do you agree? Why or why not?

3. Did you suspect what was happening when Parnell Creed found the jugs of moonshine on the porch? Discuss the possible differences in China's life if Parnell had lived through her childhood.

4. Did you like China as a child? Discuss the relationship that she had with her mother. Did the song/poem Yvette sang to China help you decipher the limits of China's wish-granting abilities?

5. When did you realize that China was granting wishes by touching people? Why do you think Yvette tried to hide China's abilities from everyone, including China herself?

6. Were you surprised when you realized that China's wish-granting was really thievery? Do you think China's mother adequately addressed this moral issue in China's life?

7. The Destrehans of the novel are based on various real families that lived in Louisiana during the 1800s. Why did the Destrehans reject Angèle as a daughter-in-law? Do you think the young Yvette fully understood the ruthless capabilities of her grandfather Henri?

8. Discuss the impact of Miz Settle's influence on China as a child and later as a midwife. Did the information in the novel about childbirth, herbal medicines, and traditional Ozark hexes enhance your reading experience? Why or why not?

9. Goomer doctors were a real part of life in the Ozarks, as was the mix of superstition and conservative Christian beliefs. Did you understand the ideas of "opposites" and "likes" as used in Goomering and charms? Do you believe people still wear or believe in charms today?

10. Discuss the relationship between Tommy Belnap and China Creed. How do you think his death impacted China's life? Do you think she would have been less or more open to a courtship with Dr. Grey if she had never loved and lost Tommy Belnap?

11. In the novel, the Civil War is presented as fact without much digression into additional background information. Would you have liked a broader picture or did you appreciate the more intimate personal presentation that Harrison uses? How would you have reacted to the Jayhawkers and Bushwackers if they attacked your home?

12. Why did Yvette decide to have an affair with Mr. James? How did you feel about Mrs. James's decision to ignore her husband's infidelity and accept Yvette's baby as her own?

13. By smashing her spinning wheel during the Trail of Tears, Jesse Settle illustrated her rejection of "white" traditions, yet, contrary to Cherokee practice, she decided to become a midwife. How do you reconcile that contradiction in her choices? Discuss her mixed racial heritage and the guilt she felt about her darker skin color.

14. Did you catch the connection between Miz Settle's broken spinning wheel and the broken Spode plate in Chapter One? How does brokenness shape China's and Miz Settle's lives?

15. Discuss your feelings about Stephen Grey. When did you first suspect that he was addicted to opiates?

16. Did you like Mr. Cooper? Why do you think he was so loyal to the Grey family and Stephen in particular? Were you surprised by his declaration of love to China in Chapter Thirty Five?

17. Did you enjoy your "visit" to the New York City of the Gilded Age? Did the opulence of society families surprise you? Would you have enjoyed living during that era as part of a wealthy New York family?

18. Discuss the fear experienced by the Grey family in 1873 when the market crashed and banks became insolvent. Did you grow up with any family stories about the "Great Depression," which began in 1929?

19. How did you feel about the portrayal of slavery in the novel? Do you think slavery exists in other forms besides ownership and enforced labor?

20. During a moment of despair, China asks, "Is there nothing in this world stronger than greed?" Did the outcome revealed in the Epilogue answer China's question to your satisfaction? Do you believe love can be stronger than greed?

ACKNOWLEDGMENTS

My sincere thanks to all who read this manuscript in its many versions. Those people include my able and gifted-beyond-words editor, Maggie Crawford, whose vision is always brilliant and enlightening as she urges me toward a deeper understanding of my characters and the story. My agent, Victoria Skurnick, a gifted reader, amazing encourager, and wise adviser never veered from her opinion that *The Midwife's Touch* was a worthy read and should be offered to the world. Through their guidance, I was able to slash, rewrite, and tighten this novel into something far better than it might have been.

My sister-in-law, Annette McHaney, read one of the first—very needy—versions of the book, as did my friend, Jennifer Massongill Derksen. Their ideas gave me the courage to believe *The Midwife's Touch* might deserve a further investment of my time and effort. Jennifer's delightful *joie de vivre* always puts me into a hopeful state of mind. Annette's kindness and intellectual challenges encouraged me as I wandered in the wilderness of each new draft. Annette also read the final version. I'm indebted to her for her meticulous editing skills and her wise social comments. My gratitude also goes to our granddaughter, Taylor, daughter-in-law Tonya, and son Neil, and my brother Roger McHaney, gifted readers and encouragers all.

Thank you to Cristela Henriquez, of the Levine Greenberg Rostan Agency, who also read the novel and gave valuable suggestions.

The members of the Pickford Wednesday Readers (PWR) graciously agreed to read my novel in manuscript form—no easy task—and answered my battery of questions. PWR members own numerous areas of expertise: medicine, education, farm life, gardening, Native cultures, Scots culture, American history, and many more. They read with enthusiasm and offered wise and thought-provoking ideas.

My brother Roger McHaney and his wife Annette McHaney designed a beautiful and appealing cover for the book. Like many people, my first impression of any book comes through the cover art, and I've bought many novels because I loved the cover! (That's a guilty secret. Don't tell.)

I am grateful to the following people for their expertise:

Maggie Crawford for her knowledge of the French language and for guiding me with all manner of information about New York's Central Park and its designers. I have fallen in love with Central Park, and it's all Maggie's fault.

Although she is not a lacemaker, our granddaughter Rylee, an artisan without doubt, inspired me as I wrote the segments about China's and Yvette's lace-making abilities.

My niece, Frances Blue Maslanka, shared her collection and knowledge of Native American pottery and artifacts. (What a beautiful and inspiring gift you sent me, Frances, during a low time in my rewriting process!)

My niece and her husband, Erin and Logan Towsley, sent me the amazing video of the "water birth" of their third child. Every time I watch it, it brings me to tears. I hope I was able to convey some of that emotion and beauty in the novel's birth scenes.

The late Toby and Aubrey Bassett first opened my eyes to the mesmerizing history and unique melding of cultures in New Orleans and the surrounding area.

Wyatt R. Knapp shared his hands-on experience producing and using primitive weapons and his knowledge of Native cultures. (Check out Wyatt's book, *The New Atlatl and Dart Workbook*.)

Fabric artist Carol Lamb and her mother, the late Virgene MacDonald, helped me learn to sew and knit. I'm sure that took a great deal of patience and endurance on their part.

Rodney Galer, mortician, gave me a great deal of fascinating and useful information about embalming practices and the human brain.

DiAnn Firack shared her expertise about Scots idioms and heritage, and also the unique medical problems redheads face when they give birth.

ACKNOWLEDGMENTS

My husband and I had a very interesting conversation with Paul and Cheryl Harrison as Paul described the properties and the appearance of moonshine. (A disclaimer here. They don't advocate drinking it.)

My father, C. R. "Bob" McHaney, Jr. was again my go-to guy when I had questions about soils, cotton harvesting, husbandry, and Missouri idioms. When he was a kid chopping cotton on his grandparents' farm, I doubt he thought his labor would inspire one of his children to write a novel set in southern Missouri.

Dr. Clint Groover and his wife Barbara are always ready to answer my questions about animal disease and injury. They also introduced my husband and me to the joy of boiled coffee!

The late Muriel and Larry Hillock spent hours answering my questions about early farming practices.

Jim Rye allowed me to visit his huge and beautiful draft horses and patiently described early practices of logging and plowing using draft horses. John McDonald, Sheri Mastaw, Danielle Sawyers, and Jim Storey also shared their expertise and knowledge of horses.

My gratitude to:

Ronald Briggs—the healer's role in Native cultures.

Jackie Doran—languages. I'm grateful to call this gifted polyglot my friend!

Roy L. D. Knoops—19th century guns. His expertise comes from experience, and you can't find better

American musician and song writer Katie Chenoweth—primitive music and instruments. I always enjoy listening to her play when she comes from far afield to visit her parents, our neighbors.

Dinny Falkenburg—the enveloping joy and hard work of owning and training horses and of gardening.

John David Flores, a skilled hunter—boar behavior and hunting boars.

D. Gregory Van Dussen—early tent meetings and the amazing faith and dedication of circuit-riding preachers. Check out his book, *Circuit Rider Devotions, Reflections from the Lives of Early Methodist Preachers in North America*. It's a wonderful devotional and packed with historical information.

James Birch—Native cultures and primitive skills. His interests mirror mine, and I value his knowledge.

Piama Oleyer—Goomer doctoring. What a joy to discover that one of my Facebook friends had personal experience in this area of rare traditional medicines.

Tyler Bosley—guns. I was the "mouse in the corner" during a conversation he had with my husband, who is his former high school principal.

Sandra McCurdy, Jessica Heksem, and Connie Perkins—midwife skills.

My late father-in-law, Clifford Harrison—stooking grain, which he did as a child for fifty cents a day.

Bill McDowell, a cobbler—the repair and production of handmade shoes and boots.

My niece Megan McHaney Lindstrom, the hand model for some of our cover art, and her husband Jordan Lindstrom for his photography.

Debra Harrison, master gardener—plants and plant use. I love her artistic vision.

My brother-in-law N. Thomas Harrison. A gifted carver, his area of expertise is birds.

My brother Robert McHaney and my sister-of-the- heart Donna Liggett, you may recognize some of your chickens in *The Midwife's Touch*. Who knew chickens could have personalities?

Sincere gratitude to my great grandmother and grandfather, the late Julia Grace Sandoz McHaney and Thomas Cornelius McHaney, and my grandfather, Charles Robert "Bob" McHaney, Sr., whose beautiful southern Missouri accents gave me the "voice" for this novel. I'm also indebted to them for passing down the family traditions that sparked my interest in the Ozark area. I am so very fortunate to have had my great grandparents as a part of my life until I was eleven (Grandma Julia) and fifteen (Grandpa T.C.), and my Grandpa Bob until I was forty-four. There are distinct advantages to being the oldest child of the oldest child of the oldest child!

My gratitude to those who provided me with research articles and books: Maggie Crawford (books about Central Park); John and Carol Price (a whole library of research books and a great deal of encouragement!); my sister and her husband, Patricia and Thomas Walker and Tom's mother, Beverly Walker (rare medical books from the 1800s); John David Flores (articles about boar hunting); Dr. D. Greg Van Dussen (early Methodist camp meetings and circuit riders); Neil and Tonya Harrison and Krystal Harrison, who have given me more incredible books than I have space to list.

To those who answer my questions and take opinion polls on my "Sue Harrison Author" Facebook page, a gigantic thanks! I hope you will sense your input throughout the pages of *The Midwife's Touch*.

Although I'm sure that he's unaware how much he helped me, Professor Peter Selgin, novelist and the brilliant author of the "Your First Page" posts, which Jane Friedman often features on her amazing blogs, gave me hope at a very low point in the rewriting of *The Midwife's Touch*. When he chose to feature my first page, his criticisms were kind and wise, and his compliments lifted me back into self-confidence.

Gratitude unending to my brother Roger McHaney and his wife Annette for joining my husband Neil and me in our adventure as we create our publishing company, Shanty Cove Books. We surely would have floundered without their guidance and expertise, and the whole process wouldn't have been nearly as fun without their abilities to see the humorous side of frustrating situations! I also extend my appreciation to artist Travis Miller of Northern Front Sign and Design for designing our logo, which we love, and also to his wife Jill for her input.

Thank you Angel Portice of 2BU Photography for wonderful author photos.

Much gratitude to Mara Anastas and Jake Allgeier and all the brilliant people of Open Road Integrated Media who partnered with Shanty Cove Books to include *The Midwife's Touch* in their incredible pantheon of published books. I do not have adequate words to express my awe and thankfulness for your vision, persistence, and kindness. At OR/M I am indeed in heady company as is *The Midwife's Touch*.

I cannot close my acknowledgments without a quick thank you to my "office assistant" our mini-schnauzer, Tiffany Pearl, who never forgets to remind me when it's time for lunch.

I always worry that I will leave out someone who took time to share expertise, books, or articles. If you are that person, please forgive. I'm sure you will see your influence and guiding knowledge within the pages of *The Midwife's Touch*.

To our children, Neil and Tonya and Krystal, our grandchildren, Taylor and Rylee, and to a multitude of friends and extended family, I owe so much for your support, encouragement, and good humor. Thank you, Dorothy Davison, for your faithful prayers.

I will never find adequate words to thank my husband, Neil, for his expertise in so many areas, including the perplexing complications of technology. In addition, he is always willing to join me on research trips to far places, to listen when I'm discouraged, and to know exactly what I need to hear to gain the confidence to keep writing and creating. Thank you for our fun trips to Taney County—even for the time we got lost in those convoluted Ozark hills! We lift thanks to God for the beautiful life He has given us and for the strength to get through the tough times. We are abundantly blessed.

To all my readers, thank you for your support! I love to hear from you. Contact me at sue@sueharrison.com or visit my Facebook page, Sue Harrison Author.

Sue Harrison
Pickford, Michigan
North Fort Myers, Florida
January 2022

ABOUT THE AUTHOR

Sue Harrison grew up in Michigan's Upper Peninsula and graduated summa cum laude from Lake Superior State University with a bachelor of arts degree in English language and literature. At age twenty-seven, inspired by the forest that surrounded her home, and the outdoor survival skills she had learned from her father and her husband, Harrison began researching the people who understood best how to live in a harsh environment: the North American native peoples. She studied six Native American languages and completed extensive research on culture, geography, archaeology, and anthropology during the nine years she spent writing her first novel, *Mother Earth, Father Sky*. An international bestseller and selected by the American Library Association as one of the Best Books for Young Adults in 1991, *Mother Earth, Father Sky* is the first novel in Harrison's critically acclaimed Ivory Carver Trilogy, which includes *My Sister the Moon* and *Brother Wind*. She is the author of the Storyteller Trilogy, also set in prehistoric North America. Her novels have been translated into thirteen languages and published in more than twenty countries. Harrison lives with her family in Michigan.

SUE HARRISON

FROM OPEN ROAD MEDIA

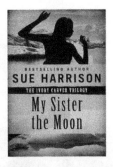

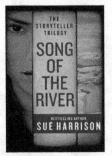

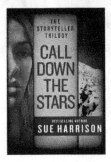

OPEN ROAD

INTEGRATED MEDIA

Find a full list of our authors and
titles at www.openroadmedia.com

FOLLOW US
@OpenRoadMedia